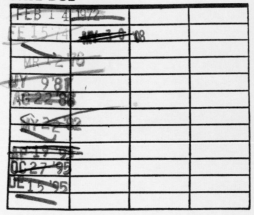

THE SHORT NOVELS OF
D. H. LAWRENCE

VOL. II

THE PHOENIX EDITION OF D. H. LAWRENCE

D. H. LAWRENCE

The Short Novels

VOL. II

HEINEMANN:LONDON

William Heinemann Ltd

LONDON   MELBOURNE   TORONTO
CAPE TOWN   AUCKLAND

First Published 1956
Reprinted 1959, 1962, 1965, 1968

434 40715 1

Printed and Bound in Great Britain by
Bookprint Limited, Crawley, Sussex

CONTENTS

ST. MAWR

ST. MAWR

LOU WITT had had her own way so long, that by the age of
twenty-five she didn't know where she was. Having one's own
way landed one completely at sea.

To be sure for a while she had failed in her grand love affair
with Rico. And then she had had something really to despair
about. But even that had worked out as she wanted. Rico had
come back to her, and was dutifully married to her. And now,
when she was twenty-five and he was three months older, they
were a charming married couple. He flirted with other women
still, to be sure. He wouldn't be the handsome Rico if he
didn't. But she had 'got' him. Oh yes! You had only to see
the uneasy backward glance at her, from his big blue eyes:
just like a horse that is edging away from its master: to know
how completely he was mastered.

She, with her odd little *museau*, not exactly pretty, but very
attractive; and her quaint air of playing at being well bred, in
a sort of charade game; and her queer familiarity with foreign
cities and foreign languages; and the lurking sense of being an
outsider everywhere, like a sort of gipsy, who is at home anywhere and nowhere: all this made up her charm and her
failure. She didn't quite belong.

Of course she was American: Louisiana family, moved
down to Texas. And she was moderately rich, with no close
relation except her mother. But she had been sent to school
in France when she was twelve, and since she had finished
school, she had drifted from Paris to Palermo, Biarritz to
Vienna and back via Munich to London, then down again to
Rome. Only fleeting trips to her America.

So what sort of American was she, after all?

And what sort of European was she either? She didn't
'belong' anywhere. Perhaps most of all in Rome, among the
artists and the Embassy people.

It was in Rome she had met Rico. He was an Australian,
son of a government official in Melbourne, who had been made
a baronet. So one day Rico would be Sir Henry, as he was
the only son. Meanwhile he floated round Europe on a very

3

small allowance—his father wasn't rich in capital—and was
being an artist.

They met in Rome when they were twenty-two, and had a
love affair in Capri. Rico was handsome, elegant, but mostly
he had spots of paint on his trousers and he ruined a neck-tie
pulling it off. He behaved in a most floridly elegant fashion,
fascinating to the Italians. But at the same time he was canny
and shrewd and sensible as any young poser could be and, on
principle, good-hearted, anxious. He was anxious for his
future, and anxious for his place in the world, he was poor,
and suddenly wasteful in spite of all his tension of economy,
and suddenly spiteful in spite of all his ingratiating efforts,
and suddenly ungrateful in spite of all his burden of grati-
tude, and suddenly rude in spite of all his good manners, and
suddenly detestable in spite of all his suave, courtier-like
amiability.

He was fascinated by Lou's quaint aplomb, her experiences,
her 'knowledge', her *gamine* knowingness, her aloneness, her
pretty clothes that were sometimes an utter failure, and her
southern 'drawl' that was sometimes so irritating. That sing-
song which was so American. Yet she used no Americanisms
at all, except when she lapsed into her odd spasms of acid
irony, when she was very American indeed!

And she was fascinated by Rico. They played to each other
like two butterflies at one flower. They pretended to be very
poor in Rome—he *was* poor: and very rich in Naples. Everybody stared their eyes out at them. And they had that love
affair in Capri.

But they reacted badly on each other's nerves. She became
ill. Her mother appeared. He couldn't stand Mrs. Witt, and
Mrs. Witt couldn't stand him. There was a terrible fortnight.
Then Lou was popped into a convent nursing-home in Umbria,
and Rico dashed off to Paris. Nothing would stop him. He
must go back to Australia.

He went to Melbourne, and while there his father died, leaving him a baronet's title and an income still very moderate.
Lou visited America once more, as the strangest of strange
lands to her. She came away disheartened, panting for Europe,
and, of course, doomed to meet Rico again.

They couldn't get away from one another, even though in
the course of their rather restrained correspondence he in-
formed her that he was 'probably' marrying a very dear girl,

friend of his childhood, only daughter of one of the oldest families in Victoria. Not saying much.

He didn't commit the probability, but reappeared in Paris, wanting to paint his head off, terribly inspired by Cézanne and by old Renoir. He dined at the Rotonde with Lou and Mrs. Witt, who, with her queer democratic New Orleans sort of conceit, looked round the drinking-hall with savage contempt, and at Rico as part of the show. "Certainly," she said, "when these people here have got any money, they fall in love on a full stomach. And when they've got no money, they fall in love with a full pocket. I never was in a more disgusting place. They take their love like some people take after-dinner pills."

She would watch with her arching, full, strong grey eyes, sitting there erect and silent in her well-bought American clothes. And then she would deliver some such charge of grape-shot. Rico always writhed.

Mrs. Witt hated Paris: "this sordid, unlucky city," she called it. "Something unlucky is bound to happen to me in this sinister, unclean town," she said. "I feel *contagion* in the air of this place. For heaven's sake, Louise, let us go to Morocco or somewhere."

"No, mother dear, I can't now. Rico has proposed to me, and I have accepted him. Let us think about a wedding, shall we?"

"There!" said Mrs. Witt. "I said it was an unlucky city!"

And the peculiar look of extreme New Orleans annoyance came round her sharp nose. But Lou and Rico were both twenty-four years old, and beyond management. And, anyhow, Lou would be Lady Carrington. But Mrs. Witt was exasperated beyond exasperation. She would almost rather have preferred Lou to elope with one of the great, evil porters at Les Halles. Mrs. Witt was at the age when the malevolent male in man, the old Adam, begins to loom above all the social tailoring. And yet—and yet—it was better to have Lady Carrington for a daughter, seeing Lou was that sort.

There was a marriage, after which Mrs. Witt departed to America, Lou and Rico leased a little old house in Westminster, and began to settle into a certain layer of English society. Rico was becoming an almost fashionable portrait-painter. At least, *he* was almost fashionable, whether his portraits were or not. And Lou, too, was almost fashionable:

almost a hit. There was some flaw somewhere. In spite of their appearances, both Rico and she would never quite go down in any society. They were the drifting artist sort. Yet neither of them was content to be of the drifting artist sort. They wanted to fit in, to make good.

Hence the little house in Westminster, the portraits, the dinners, the friends, and the visits. Mrs. Witt came and sardonically established herself in a suite in a quiet but good-class hotel not far off. Being on the spot. And her terrible grey eyes with the touch of a leer looked on at the hollow mockery of things. As if *she* knew of anything better!

Lou and Rico had a curious exhausting effect on one another: neither knew why. They were fond of one another. Some inscrutable bond held them together. But it was a strange vibration of the nerves, rather than of the blood. A nervous attachment, rather than a sexual love. A curious tension of will, rather than a spontaneous passion. Each was curiously under the domination of the other. They were a pair—they had to be together. Yet quite soon they shrank from one another. This attachment of the will and the nerves was destructive. As soon as one felt strong, the other felt ill. As soon as the ill one recovered strength, down went the one who had been well.

And soon, tacitly, the marriage became more like a friend-ship, platonic. It was a marriage, but without sex. Sex was shattering and exhausting, they shrank from it, and became like brother and sister. But still they were husband and wife. And the lack of physical relation was a secret source of un-easiness and chagrin to both of them. They would neither of them accept it. Rico looked with contemplative, anxious eyes at other women.

Mrs. Witt kept track of everything, watching, as it were, from outside the fence, like a potent well-dressed demon, full of uncanny energy and a shattering sort of sense. She said little: but her small, occasionally biting remarks revealed her attitude of contempt for the *ménage*.

Rico entertained clever and well-known people. Mrs. Witt would appear, in her New York gowns and few good jewels. She was handsome, with her vigorous grey hair. But her heavy-lidded grey eyes were the despair of any hostess. They looked too many shattering things. And it was but too obvious that these clever, well-known English people got on her nerves terribly, with their finickiness and their fine-drawn discriminations. She wanted to put her foot through all these fine-drawn distinctions. She thought continually of the house of her girlhood, the plantation, the negroes, the planters: the sardonic grimness that underlay all the big, shiftless life. And she wanted to cleave with some of this grimness of the big, dangerous America, into the safe, finicky drawing-rooms of London. So naturally she was not popular.

But being a woman of energy, she had to do *something*. During the latter part of the war she had worked in the American Red Cross in France, nursing. She loved men—real men. But, on close contact, it was difficult to define what she meant by 'real' men. She never met any.

Out of the *débâcle* of the war she had emerged with an odd piece of débris, in the shape of Gerónimo Trujillo. He was an American, son of a Mexican father and a Navajo Indian mother, from Arizona. When you knew him well, you recognised the real half-breed, though at a glance he might pass as a sunburnt citizen of any nation, particularly of France. He looked like a certain sort of Frenchman, with his curiously-set dark eyes, his straight black hair, his thin black moustache, his rather long cheeks, and his almost slouching, diffident, sardonic bearing. Only when you knew him, and looked right into his eyes, you saw that unforgettable glint of the Indian.

He had been badly shell-shocked, and was for a time a wreck. Mrs. Witt, having nursed him into convalescence, asked him where he was going next. He didn't know. His father and mother were dead, and he had nothing to take him back to Phœnix, Arizona. Having had an education in one of the Indian high schools, the unhappy fellow had now no place in life at all. Another of the many misfits.

There was something of the Paris *Apache* in his appearance: but he was all the time withheld, and nervously shut inside himself. Mrs. Witt was intrigued by him.

"Very well, Phœnix," she said, refusing to adopt his Spanish name, "I'll see what I can do."

What she did was to get him a place on a sort of manor farm, with some acquaintances of hers. He was very good with horses, and had a curious success with turkeys and geese and fowls.

Some time after Lou's marriage, Mrs. Witt reappeared in

London, from the country, with Phœnix in tow, and a couple
of horses. She had decided that she would ride in the Park in
the morning, and see the world that way. Phœnix was to be
her groom.

So, to the great misgiving of Rico, behold Mrs. Witt in
splendidly tailored habit and perfect boots, a smart black hat
on her smart grey hair, riding a grey gelding as smart as she
was, and looking down her conceited, inquisitive, scornful,
aristocratic-democratic Louisiana nose at the people in Piccadilly, as she crossed to the Row, followed by the taciturn
shadow of Phœnix, who sat on a chestnut with three white
feet as if he had grown there.

Mrs. Witt, like many other people, always expected to find
the real *beau monde* and the real *grand monde* somewhere or
other. She didn't quite give in to what she saw in the Bois de
Boulogne, or in Monte Carlo, or on the Pincio: all a bit
shoddy, and not very *beau* and not at all *grand*. There she was,
with her grey eagle eye, her splendid complexion and her
weapon-like health of a woman of fifty, dropping her eyelids
a little, very slightly nervous, but completely prepared to
despise the *monde* she was entering in Rotten Row.

In she sailed, and up and down that regatta-canal of horse-
men and horsewomen under the trees of the Park. And yes,
there were lovely girls with fair hair down their backs, on
happy ponies. And awfully well-groomed papas, and tight
mamas who looked as if they were going to pour tea between
the ears of their horses, and converse with banal skill, one eye
on the teapot, one on the visitor with whom she was talking,
and all the rest of her hostess's argus eyes upon everybody in
sight. That alert argus capability of the English matron was
startling and a bit horrifying. Mrs. Witt would at once think
of the old negro mammies, away in Louisiana. And her eyes
became dagger-like as she watched the clipped, shorn, mincing
young Englishmen. She refused to look at the prosperous
Jews.

It was still the days before motor-cars were allowed in the
Park, but Rico and Lou, sliding round Hyde Park Corner and
up Park Lane in their car, would watch the steely horsewoman and the saturnine groom with a sort of dismay. Mrs.
Witt seemed to be pointing a pistol at the bosom of every
other horseman or horsewoman and announcing: *"Your
virility or your life! Your femininity or your life!* She didn't

know herself what she really wanted them to be: but it was
something as democratic as Abraham Lincoln and as aristocratic as a Russian czar, as highbrow as Arthur Balfour, and
as taciturn and unideal as Phœnix. Everything at once.

There was nothing for it: Lou had to buy herself a horse
and ride at her mother's side, for very decency's sake. Mrs.
Witt was *so* like a smooth, levelled, gunmetal pistol, Lou had
to be a sort of sheath. And she really looked pretty, with her
clusters of dark, curly, New Orleans hair, like grapes, and
her quaint brown eyes that didn't quite match, and that
looked a bit sleepy and vague, and at the same time quick as
a squirrel's. She was slight and elegant, and a tiny bit rakish,
and somebody suggested she might be on the movies.

Nevertheless, they were in the society columns next morning—*two new and striking figures in the Row this morning
were Lady Henry Carrington and her mother, Mrs. Witt*, etc.
And Mrs. Witt liked it, let her say what she might. So did
Lou. Lou liked it immensely. She simply luxuriated in the
sun of publicity.

"Rico dear, you must get a horse."

The tone was soft and southern and drawling, but the over-
tone had a decisive finality. In vain Rico squirmed—he had a
way of writhing and squirming which perhaps he had caught
at Oxford. In vain he protested that he couldn't ride, and that
he didn't care for riding. He got quite angry, and his handsome arched nose tilted and his upper lip lifted from his teeth,
like a dog that is going to bite. Yet daren't quite bite.

And that was Rico. He daren't quite bite. Not that he was
really afraid of the others. He was afraid of himself, once he
let himself go. He might rip up in an eruption of life-long
anger all this pretty-pretty picture of a charming young wife
and a delightful little home and a fascinating success as a
painter of fashionable, and at the same time 'great' portraits:
with colour, wonderful colour, and at the same time, form,
marvellous form. He had composed this little *tableau vivant*
with great effort. He didn't want to erupt like some suddenly
wicked horse—Rico was really more like a horse than a dog,
a horse that might go nasty any moment. For the time, he
was good, very good, dangerously good.

"Why, Rico dear, I thought you used to ride so much, in
Australia, when you were young? Didn't you tell me all
about it, hm?"—and as she ended on that slow, singing *hm?*,

which acted on him like an irritant and a drug, he knew he
was beaten.

Lou kept the sorrel mare in a mews just behind the house
in Westminster, and she was always slipping round to the
stables. She had a funny little nostalgia for the place: something that really surprised her. She had never had the faintest
notion that she cared for horses and stables and grooms. But
she did. She was fascinated. Perhaps it was her childhood's
Texas associations come back. Whatever it was, her life with
Rico in the elegant little house, and all her social engagements
seemed like a dream, the substantial reality of which was
those mews in Westminster, her sorrel mare, the owner of
the mews, Mr. Saintsbury, and the grooms he employed. Mr.
Saintsbury was a horsey, elderly man like an old maid, and he
loved the sound of titles.

"Lady Carrington!—well I never! You've come to us for a
bit of company again, I see. I don't know whatever we shall
do if you go away, we shall be that lonely!" and he flashed
his old-maid's smile at her. "No matter how grey the morning, your ladyship would make a beam of sunshine. Poppy is
all right, I think. . . ."

Poppy was the sorrel mare with the no white feet and
the startled eye, and she was all right. And Mr. Saintsbury
was smiling with his old-maid's mouth, and showing all his
teeth.

"Come across with me, Lady Carrington, and look at a new
horse just up from the country. I think he's worth a look, and
I believe you have a moment to spare, your Ladyship."

Her Ladyship had too many moments to spare. She followed
the sprightly, elderly, clean-shaven man across the yard to a
loose-box, and waited while he opened the door.

In the inner dark she saw a handsome bay horse with his
clean ears pricked like daggers from his naked head as he
swung handsomely round to stare at the open doorway. He
had big, black, brilliant eyes, with a sharp questioning glint,
and that air of tense, alert quietness which betrays an animal
that can be dangerous.

"Is he quiet?" Lou asked.

"Why—yes—my Lady! He's quiet, with those that know
how to handle him. *Cup! my boy! Cup, my beauty! Cup
then! St. Mawr!*"

Loquacious even with the animals, he went softly forward

and laid his hand on the horse's shoulder, soft and quiet as a
fly settling. Lou saw the brilliant skin of the horse crinkle
a little in apprehensive anticipation, like the shadow of the
descending hand on a bright red-gold liquid. But then the
animal relaxed again.

"Quiet with those that know how to handle him, and a bit
of a ruffian with those that don't. Isn't that the ticket, eh,
St. Mawr?"

"What is his name?" Lou asked.

The man repeated it, with a slight Welsh twist—"He's from
the Welsh borders, belonging to a Welsh gentleman, Mr.
Griffith Edwards. But they're wanting to sell him."

"How old is he?" asked Lou.

"About seven years—seven years and five months," said Mr.
Saintsbury, dropping his voice as if it were a secret.

"Could one ride him in the Park?"

"Well—yes! I should say a gentleman who knew how to
handle him could ride him very well and make a very handsome figure in the Park."

Lou at once decided that this handsome figure should be
Rico's. For she was already half in love with St. Mawr. He
was of such a lovely red-gold colour, and a dark, invisible fire
seemed to come out of him. But in his big black eyes there
was a lurking afterthought. Something told her that the
horse was not quite happy: that somewhere deep in his
animal consciousness lived a dangerous, half-revealed resentment, a diffused sense of hostility. She realised that he was
sensitive, in spite of his flaming, healthy strength, and nervous
with a touchy uneasiness that might make him vindictive.

"Has he got any tricks?" she asked.

"Not that I know of, my Lady: not tricks exactly. But he's
one of these temperamental creatures, as they say. Though *I*
say, every horse is temperamental, when you come down to
it. But this one, it is as if he was a trifle raw somewhere.
Touch this raw spot, and there's no answering for him."

"Where is he raw?" asked Lou, somewhat mystified. She
thought he might really have some physical sore.

"Why, that's hard to say, my Lady. If he was a human
being, you'd say something had gone wrong in his life. But
with a horse it's not that, exactly. A high-bred animal like
St. Mawr needs understanding, and I don't know as anybody
has quite got the hang of him. I confess I haven't myself. But

I do realise that he is a special animal and needs a special sort of touch, and I'm willing he should have it, did I but know exactly what it is."

She looked at the glowing bay horse that stood there with his ears back, his face averted, but attending as if he were some lightning-conductor. He was a stallion. When she realised this, she became more afraid of him.

"Why does Mr. Griffith Edwards want to sell him?" she asked.

"Well—my Lady—they raised him for stud purposes—but he didn't answer. There are horses like that: don't seem to fancy the mares for some reason. Well, anyway, they couldn't keep him for the stud. And as you see, he's a powerful, beautiful hackney, clean as a whistle, and eaten up with his own power. But there's no putting him between the shafts. He won't stand it. He's a fine saddle-horse, beautiful action, and lovely to ride. But he's got to be handled, and there you are."

Lou felt there was something behind the man's reticence.

"Has he ever made a break?" she asked, apprehensive.

"Made a break?" replied the man. "Well, if I must admit it, he's had two accidents. Mr. Griffith Edwards's son rode him a bit wild, away there in the Forest of Dean, and the young fellow had his skull smashed in against a low oak bough. Last autumn, that was. And some time back, he crushed a groom against the side of the stall—injured him fatally. But they were both accidents, my Lady. Things will happen."

The man spoke in a melancholy, fatalistic way. The horse, with his ears laid back, seemed to be listening tensely, his face averted. He looked like something finely bred and passionate that has been judged and condemned.

"May I say *how do you do*?" she said to the horse, drawing a little nearer in her white, summery dress and lifting her hand that glittered with emeralds and diamonds.

He drifted away from her, as if some wind blew him. Then he ducked his head and looked sideway at her from his black, full eye.

"I think I'm all right," she said, edging nearer, while he watched her.

She laid her hand on his side and gently stroked him. Then she stroked his shoulder, and then the hard, tense arch of his

neck. And she was startled to feel the vivid heat of his life
come through to her, through the lacquer of red-gold gloss.
So slippery with vivid, hot life!

She paused, as if thinking, while her hand rested on the
horse's sun-arched neck. Dimly, in her weary young woman's
soul, an ancient understanding seemed to flood in.

She wanted to buy St. Mawr.

"I think," she said to Saintsbury, "if I can, I will buy him."

The man looked at her long and shrewdly.

"Well, my Lady," he said at last, "there shall be nothing
kept from you. But what would your Ladyship do with him, if
I may make so bold?"

"I don't know," she replied vaguely. "I might take him to
America."

The man paused once more, then said:

"They say it's been the making of some horses, to take
them over the water, to Australia or such places. It might
repay you—you never know."

She wanted to buy St. Mawr. She wanted him to belong to
her. For some reason the sight of him, his power, his alive,
alert intensity, his unyieldingness, made her want to cry.

She never did cry: except sometimes with vexation, or to
get her own way. As far as weeping went, her heart felt as
dry as a Christmas walnut. What was the good of tears, anyhow? You had to keep on holding on in this life, never give
way, and never give in. Tears only left one weakened and
ragged.

But now, as if that mysterious fire of the horse's body had
split some rock in her, she went home and hid herself in her
room, and just cried. The wild, brilliant, alert head of St.
Mawr seemed to look at her out of another world. It was as
if she had had a vision, as if the walls of her own world had
suddenly melted away, leaving her in a great darkness, in the
midst of which the large, brilliant eyes of that horse looked
at her with demonish question, while his naked ears stood
up like daggers from the naked lines of his inhuman head,
and his great body glowed red with power.

What was it? Almost like a god looking at her terribly out
of the everlasting dark, she had felt the eyes of that horse;
great, glowing, fearsome eyes, arched with a question and
containing a white blade of light like a threat. What was his
non-human question, and his uncanny threat? She didn't

know. He was some splendid demon, and she must worship him.

She hid herself away from Rico. She could not bear the triviality and superficiality of her human relationships. Looming like some god out of the darkness was the head of that horse, with the wide, terrible, questioning eyes. And she felt that it forbade her to be her ordinary, commonplace self. It forbade her to be just Rico's wife, young Lady Carrington, and all that.

It haunted her, the horse. It had looked at her as she had never been looked at before: terrible, gleaming, questioning eyes arching out of darkness, and backed by all the fire of that great ruddy body. What did it mean, and what ban did it put upon her? She felt it put a ban on her heart: wielded some uncanny authority over her, that she dared not, could not understand.

No matter where she was, what she was doing, at the back of her consciousness loomed a great, over-aweing figure out of a dark background: St. Mawr, looking at her without really seeing her, yet gleaming a question at her, from his wide, terrible eyes, and gleaming a sort of menace, doom. Master of doom, he seemed to be!

"You are thinking about something, Lou dear!" Rico said to her that evening.

He was so quick and sensitive to detect her moods—so exciting in this respect. And his big, slightly prominent blue eyes, with the whites a little bloodshot, glanced at her quickly, with searching and anxiety, and a touch of fear, as if his conscience were always uneasy. He, too, was rather like a horse—but forever quivering with a sort of cold, dangerous mistrust, which he covered with anxious love.

At the middle of his eyes was a central powerlessness that left him anxious. It used to touch her to pity, that central look of powerlessness in him. But now, since she had seen the full, dark, passionate blaze of power and of different life in the eyes of the thwarted horse, the anxious powerlessness of the man drove her mad. Rico was so handsome, and he was so self-controlled, he had a gallant sort of kindness and a real worldly shrewdness. One had to admire him: at least *she* had to.

But after all, and after all, it was a bluff, an attitude. He kept it all working in himself deliberately. It was an attitude.

She read psychologists who said that everything was an attitude. Even the best of everything. But now she realised that,
with men and women, everything is an attitude only when
something else is lacking. Something is lacking and they are
thrown back on their own devices. That black fiery flow in
the eyes of the horse was not 'attitude'. It was something
much more terrifying, and real, the only thing that was real.
Gushing from the darkness in menace and question, and
blazing out in the splendid body of the horse.

"Was I thinking about something?" she replied in her slow,
amused, casual fashion. As if everything was so casual and
easy to her. And so it was, from the hard, polished side of
herself. But that wasn't the whole story.

"I think you were, Loulina. May we offer the penny?"

"Don't trouble," she said. "I was thinking, if I was thinking of anything, about a bay horse called St. Mawr."—Her
secret *almost* crept into her eyes.

"The name is awfully attractive," he said with a laugh.

"Not so attractive as the creature himself. I'm going to buy
him."

"Not really!" he said. "But why?"

"He *is* so attractive. I'm going to buy him for you."

"For *me? Darling?* How you do take me for granted. He
may not be in the least attractive to me. As you know, I have
hardly any feeling for horses at all.—Besides, how much does
he cost?"

"That I don't know, Rico dear. But I'm sure you'll love
him, for my sake."—She felt, now, she was merely playing
for her own ends.

"Lou dearest, *don't* spend a fortune on a horse for me,
which I *don't* want. Honestly, I prefer a car."

"Won't you ride with me in the Park, Rico?"

"Honestly, dear Lou, I don't want to."

"Why not, dear boy? You look so beautiful. I wish
you would.—And, anyhow, come with me to look at St.
Mawr."

Rico was divided. He had a certain uneasy feeling about
horses. At the same time, he *would* like to cut a handsome
figure in the Park.

They went across to the mews. A little Welsh groom was
watering the brilliant horse.

"Yes, dear, he certainly *is* beautiful: such a marvellous

colour! Almost orange! But rather large, I should say, to
ride in the Park."

"No, for you he's perfect. You are so tall."

"He'd be marvellous in a Composition. That colour!"

And all Rico could do was to gaze with the artist's eye at
the horse, with a glance at the groom.

"Don't you think the man is rather fascinating too?" he
said, nursing his chin artistically and penetratingly.

The groom, Lewis, was a little, quick, rather bow-legged,
loosely-built fellow of indeterminate age, with a mop of black
hair and a little black beard. He was grooming the brilliant
St. Mawr out in the open. The horse was really glorious: like
a marigold, with a pure golden sheen, a shimmer of green-
gold lacquer upon a burning red-orange. There on the
shoulder you saw the yellow lacquer glisten. Lewis, a little
scrub of a fellow, worked absorbedly, unheedingly at the
horse, with an absorption that was almost ritualistic. He
seemed the attendant shadow of the ruddy animal.

"He goes with the horse," said Lou. "If we buy St. Mawr
we get the man thrown in."

"They'd be *so* amusing to paint; such an extraordinary
contrast! But darling, I *hope* you won't insist on buying the
horse. It's so frightfully expensive."

"Mother will help me.—You'd look so well on him, Rico."

"If ever I dared take the liberty of getting on his
back——!"

"Why not?" She went quickly across the cobbled yard.

"Good morning, Lewis. How is St. Mawr?"

Lewis straightened himself and looked at her from under
the falling mop of his black hair.

"All right," he said.

He peered straight at her from under his overhanging black
hair. He had pale grey eyes, that looked phosphorescent, and
suggested the eyes of a wild cat peering intent from under the
darkness of some bush where it lies unseen. Lou, with her
brown, unmatched, oddly perplexed eyes, felt herself found
out.—"He's a common little fellow," she thought to herself.
"But he knows a woman and a horse at sight."—Aloud she
said, in her Southern drawl:

"How do you think he'd be with Sir Henry?"

Lewis turned his remote, coldly watchful eyes on the young
baronet. Rico was tall and handsome and balanced on his

hips. His face was long and well-defined, and with the hair
taken straight back from the brow. It seemed as well-made as
his clothing, and as perpetually presentable. You could not
imagine his face dirty, or scrubby and unshaven, or bearded,
or even moustached. It was perfectly prepared for social
purposes. If his head had been cut off, like John the Baptist's,
it would have been a thing complete in itself, would not have
missed the body in the least. The body was perfectly tailored.
The head was one of the famous 'talking heads' of modern
youth, with eyebrows a trifle Mephistophelian, large blue
eyes a trifle bold, and curved mouth thrilling to death to
kiss.

Lewis, the groom, staring from between his bush of hair
and his beard, watched like an animal from the underbrush.
And Rico was still sufficiently a colonial to be uneasily aware
of the underbrush, uneasy under the watchfulness of the pale
grey eyes, and uneasy in that man-to-man exposure which is
characteristic of the democratic colonies and of America. He
knew he must ultimately be judged on his merits as a man,
alone without a background: an ungarnished colonial.

This lack of background, this defenceless man-to-man business which left him at the mercy of every servant, was bad
for his nerves. For he was *also* an artist. He bore up against
it in a kind of desperation, and was easily moved to rancorous
resentment. At the same time he was free of the Englishman's
water-tight *suffisance*. He really was aware that he would
have to hold his own all alone, thrown alone on his own
defences in the universe. The extreme democracy of the
Colonies had taught him this.

And this, the little aboriginal Lewis recognised in him. He
recognised also Rico's curious hollow misgiving, fear of some
deficiency in himself, beneath all his handsome, young-hero
appearance.

"He'd be all right with anybody as would meet him half-
way," said Lewis, in the quick Welsh manner of speech,
impersonal.

"You hear, Rico!" said Lou in her sing-song, turning to her
husband.

"Perfectly, darling!"

"Would you be willing to meet St. Mawr half-way, hm?"

"All the way, darling! Mahomet would go *all* the way to
that mountain. Who would dare do otherwise?"

He spoke with a laughing, yet piqued sarcasm.

"Why, I think St. Mawr would understand perfectly," she said in the soft voice of a woman haunted by love. And she went and laid her hand on the slippery, life-smooth shoulder of the horse. He, with his strange equine head lowered, its exquisite fine lines reaching a little snake-like forward, and his ears a little back, was watching her sideways from the corner of his eye. He was in a state of absolute mistrust, like a cat crouching to spring.

"St. Mawr!" she said. "St. Mawr! What is the matter? Surely you and I are all right!"

And she spoke softly, dreamily stroked the animal's neck. She could feel a response gradually coming from him. But he would not lift up his head. And when Rico suddenly moved nearer, he sprang with a sudden jerk backwards, as if lightning exploded in his four hoofs.

The groom spoke a few low words in Welsh. Lou, frightened, stood with lifted hands arrested. She had been going to stroke him.

"Why did he do that?" she said.

"They gave him a beating once or twice," said the groom in a neutral voice, "and he doesn't forget."

She could hear a neutral sort of judgment in Lewis's voice. And she thought of the 'raw spot'.

Not any raw spot at all. A battle between two worlds. She realised that St. Mawr drew his hot breaths in another world from Rico's, from our world. Perhaps the old Greek horses had lived in St. Mawr's world. And the old Greek heroes, even Hippolytus, had known it.

With their strangely naked equine heads, and something of a snake in their way of looking round, and lifting their sensitive, dangerous muzzles, they moved in a prehistoric twilight where all things loomed phantasmagoric, all on one plane, sudden presences suddenly jutting out of the matrix. It was another world, an older, heavily potent world. And in this world the horse was swift and fierce and supreme, undominated and unsurpassed.—"Meet him half-way," Lewis said. But half-way across from our human world to that terrific equine twilight was not a small step. It was a step, she knew, that Rico could never take. She knew it. But she was prepared to sacrifice Rico.

St. Mawr was bought, and Lewis was hired along with him.

At first, Lewis rode him behind Lou, in the Row, to get him going. He behaved perfectly.

Phœnix, the half Indian, was very jealous when he saw the black-bearded Welsh groom on St. Mawr.

"What horse you got there?" he asked, looking at the other man with the curious unseeing stare in his hard, Navajo eyes, in which the Indian glint moved like a spark upon a dark chaos. In Phœnix's high-boned face there was all the race misery of the dispossessed Indian, with an added blankness left by shell-shock. But at the same time, there was that unyielding, save to death, which is characteristic of his tribe; his mother's tribe. Difficult to say what subtle thread bound him to the Navajo, and made his destiny a Red Man's destiny still.

They were a curious pair of grooms, following the correct, and yet extraordinary, pair of American mistresses. Mrs. Witt and Phœnix both rode with long stirrups and straight leg, sitting close to the saddle, without posting. Phœnix looked as if he and the horse were all one piece, he never seemed to rise in the saddle at all, neither trotting nor galloping, but sat like a man riding bareback. And all the time he stared around at the riders in the Row, at the people grouped outside the rail, chatting, at the children walking with their nurses, as if he were looking at a mirage, in whose actuality he never believed for a moment. London was all a sort of dark mirage to him. His wide, nervous-looking brown eyes with a smallish brown pupil, that showed the white all round, seemed to be focused on the far distance, as if he could not see things too near. He was watching the pale deserts of Arizona shimmer with moving light, the long mirage of a shallow lake ripple, the great pallid concave of earth and sky expanding with interchanged light. And a horse-shape loom large and portentous in the mirage, like some prehistoric beast.

That was real to him: the phantasm of Arizona. But this London was something his eye passed over as a false mirage.

He looked too smart in his well-tailored groom's clothes, so smart, he might have been one of the satirised new rich. Perhaps it was a sort of half-breed physical assertion that came through his clothing, the savage's physical assertion of himself. Anyhow, he looked 'common', rather horsey and loud.

Except his face. In the golden suavity of his high-boned

Indian face, that was hairless, with hardly any eyebrows, there was a blank, lost look that was almost touching. The same startled blank look was in his eyes. But in the smallish dark pupils the dagger-point of light still gleamed unbroken.

He was a good groom, watchful, quick, and on the spot in an instant if anything went wrong. He had a curious quiet power over the horses, unemotional, unsympathetic, but silently potent. In the same way, watching the traffic of Piccadilly with his blank, glinting eye, he would calculate everything instinctively, as if it were an enemy, and pilot Mrs. Witt by the strength of his silent will. He threw around her the tense watchfulness of her own America, and made her feel at home.

"Phœnix," she said, turning abruptly in her saddle as they walked the horses past the sheltering policeman at Hyde Park Corner, "I can't tell you how glad I am to have something a hundred per cent American at the back of me when I go through these gates."

She looked at him from dangerous grey eyes as if she meant it indeed, in vindictive earnest. A ghost of a smile went up to his high cheek-bones, but he did not answer.

"Why, mother?" said Lou, sing-song. "It feels to me so friendly——!"

"Yes, Louise, it does. *So* friendly! That's why I mistrust it so entirely——"

And she set off at a canter up the Row, under the green trees, her face like the face of Medusa at fifty, a weapon in itself. She stared at everything and everybody, with that stare of cold dynamite waiting to explode them all. Lou posted trotting at her side, graceful and elegant, and faintly amused. Behind came Phœnix, like a shadow, with his yellowish, high-boned face still looking sick. And at his side, on the big brilliant bay horse, the smallish, black-bearded Welshman.

Between Phœnix and Lewis there was a latent, but unspoken and wary sympathy. Phœnix was terribly impressed by St. Mawr, he could not leave off staring at him. And Lewis rode the brilliant, handsome-moving stallion so very quietly, like an insinuation.

Of the two men, Lewis looked the darker, with his black beard coming up to his thick black eyebrows. He was swarthy, with a rather short nose, and the uncanny pale-grey eyes that watched everything and cared about nothing.

He cared about nothing in the world, except, at the present, St. Mawr. People did not matter to him. He rode his horse and watched the world from the vantage ground of St. Mawr, with a final indifference.

"You have been with that horse long?" asked Phœnix.

"Since he was born."

Phœnix watched the action of St. Mawr as they went. The bay moved proud and springy, but with perfect good sense, among the stream of riders. It was a beautiful June morning, the leaves overhead were thick and green; there came the first whiff of lime tree scent. To Phœnix, however, the city was a sort of nightmare mirage, and to Lewis, it was a sort of prison. The presence of people he felt as a prison around him.

Mrs. Witt and Lou were turning at the end of the Row, bowing to some acquaintances. The grooms pulled aside Mrs. Witt looked at Lewis with a cold eye.

"It seems an extraordinary thing to me, Louise," she said, "to see a groom with a beard."

"It isn't usual, mother," said Lou. "Do you mind?"

"Not at all. At least, I think I don't. I get very tired of modern, bare-faced young men, *very*! The clean, pure boy, don't you know! Doesn't it make you tired?—No, I think a groom with a beard is quite attractive."

She gazed into the crowd defiantly, perching her finely-shod toe with war-like firmness on the stirrup-iron. Then suddenly she reined in, and turned her horse towards the grooms.

"Lewis!" she said, "I want to ask you a question. Supposing, now, that Lady Carrington wanted you to shave off that beard, what should you say?"

Lewis instinctively put up his hand to the said beard.

"They've wanted me to shave it off, Mam," he said. "But I've never done it."

"But why? Tell me why?"

"It's part of me, Mam."

Mrs. Witt pulled on again.

"Isn't that extraordinary, Louise?" she said. "Don't you like the way he says *Mam*? It sounds so impossible to me. Could any woman think of herself as Mam? Never!—Since Queen Victoria. But, do you know it hadn't occurred to me that a man's beard was really part of him. It always seemed to me that men wore their beards, like they wear their neckties, for show. I shall always remember Lewis for saying his beard was part of him. Isn't it curious, the way he rides? He seems to sink himself in the horse. When I speak to him, I'm not sure whether I'm speaking to a man or to a horse."

A few days later, Rico himself appeared on St. Mawr for the morning ride. He rode self-consciously, as he did everything, and he was just a little nervous. But his mother-in-law was benevolent. She made him ride between her and Lou, like three ships slowly sailing abreast.

And that very day, who should come driving in an open carriage through the Park but the Queen Mother! Dear old Queen Alexandra, there was a flutter everywhere. And she bowed expressly to Rico, mistaking him, no doubt, for somebody else.

"Do you know," said Rico as they sat at lunch, he and Lou and Mrs. Witt, in Mrs. Witt's sitting-room in the dark, quiet hotel in Mayfair, "I really like riding St. Mawr *so* much. He really is a noble animal.—If ever I am made a lord—which heaven forbid!—I shall be Lord St. Mawr."

"You mean," said Mrs. Witt, "his real lordship would be the horse?"

"Very possible, I admit," said Rico, with a curl of his long upper lip.

"Don't you think, mother," said Lou, "there *is* something quite noble about St. Mawr? He strikes me as the first noble thing I have ever seen."

"Certainly I've not seen any *man* that could compare with him. Because these English noblemen—well! I'd rather look at a negro Pullman-boy, if I was looking for what *I* call nobility."

Poor Rico was getting crosser and crosser. There was a devil in Mrs. Witt. She had a hard, bright devil inside her that she seemed to be able to let loose at will.

She let it loose the next day, when Rico and Lou joined her in the Row. She was silent but deadly with the horses, balking them in every way. She suddenly crowded over against the rail in front of St. Mawr, so that the stallion had to rear to pull himself up. Then, having a clear track, she suddenly set off at a gallop, like an explosion, and the stallion, all on edge, set off after her.

It seemed as if the whole Park, that morning, were in a state of nervous tension. Perhaps there was thunder in the air. But St. Mawr kept on dancing and pulling at the bit and wheeling sideways up against the railing, to the terror of the children and the onlookers, who squealed and jumped back suddenly, sending the nerves of the stallion into a rush like rockets. He reared and fought as Rico pulled him round.

Then he went on: dancing, pulling, springily progressing sideways, possessed with all the demons of perversity. Poor Rico's face grew longer and angrier. A fury rose in him, which he could hardly control. He hated his horse, and viciously tried to force him to a quiet, straight trot. Up went St. Mawr on his hind legs, to the terror of the Row. He got the bit in his teeth and began to fight.

But Phœnix, cleverly, was in front of him.

"You get off, Rico!" called Mrs. Witt's voice, with all the calm of her wicked exultance.

And almost before he knew what he was doing, Rico had sprung lightly to the ground, and was hanging on to the bridle of the rearing stallion.

Phœnix also lightly jumped down, and ran to St. Mawr, handing his bridle to Rico. Then began a dancing and a splashing, a rearing and a plunging. St. Mawr was being wicked. But Phœnix, the indifference of conflict in his face, sat tight and immovable, without any emotion, only the heaviness of his impersonal will settling down like a weight, all the time, on the horse. There was, perhaps, a curious barbaric exultance in bare, dark will devoid of emotion or personal feeling.

So they had a little display in the Row for almost five minutes, the brilliant horse rearing and fighting. Rico, with a stiff, long face, scrambled on to Phœnix's horse and withdrew to a safe distance. Policemen came, and an officious mounted policeman rode up to save the situation. But it was obvious that Phœnix, detached and apparently unconcerned, but barbarically potent in his will, would bring the horse to order.

Which he did, and rode the creature home. Rico was requested not to ride St. Mawr in the Row any more, as the stallion was dangerous to public safety. The authorities knew all about him.

Where ended the first fiasco of St. Mawr.

"We didn't get on very well with his lordship this morning," said Mrs. Witt triumphantly.

"No, he didn't like his company *at all!*" Rico snarled back.

He wanted Lou to sell the horse again.

"I doubt if anyone would buy him, dear," she said. "He's a known character."

"Then make a gift of him—to your mother," said Rico with venom.

"Why to mother?" asked Lou innocently.

"She might be able to cope with him—or he with her!" The last phrase was deadly. Having delivered it, Rico departed.

Lou remained at a loss. She felt almost always a little bit dazed, as if she could not see clear nor feel clear. A curious deadness upon her, like the first touch of death. And through this cloud of numbness, or deadness, came all her muted experiences.

Why was it? She did not know. But she felt that in some way it came from a battle of wills. Her mother, Rico, herself, it was always an unspoken, unconscious battle of wills, which was gradually numbing and paralysing her. She knew Rico meant nothing but kindness by her. She knew her mother only wanted to watch over her. Yet always there was this tension of will, that was no numbing. As if at the depths of him, Rico were always angry, though he seemed so 'happy' on top. And Mrs. Witt was organically angry. So they were like a couple of bombs, timed to explode some day, but ticking on like two ordinary timepieces, in the meanwhile.

She had come definitely to realise this: that Rico's anger was wound up tight at the bottom of him, like a steel spring that kept his works going, while he himself was 'charming', like a bomb-clock with Sèvres paintings or Dresden figures on the outside. But his very charm was a sort of anger, and his love was a destruction in itself. He just couldn't help it.

And she? Perhaps she was a good deal the same herself. Wound up tight inside, and enjoying herself being 'lovely'. But wound up tight on some tension that, she realised now with wonder, was really a sort of anger. This, the mainspring that drove her on the round of 'joys'.

She used really to enjoy the tension, and the *élan* it gave her. While she knew nothing about it. So long as she felt it really was life and happiness, this *élan*, this tension and excitement of 'enjoying oneself'.

Now suddenly she doubted the whole show. She attributed to it the curious numbness that was overcoming her, as if she couldn't feel any more.

She wanted to come unwound. She wanted to escape this battle of wills.

Only St. Mawr gave her some hint of the possibility. He was so powerful, and so dangerous. But in his dark eye, that looked, with its cloudy brown pupil, a cloud within a dark fire, like a world beyond our world, there was a dark vitality glowing, and within the fire another sort of wisdom. She felt sure of it: even when he put his ears back, and bared his teeth, and his great eyes came bolting out of his naked horse's head, and she saw demons upon demons in the chaos of his horrid eyes.

Why did he seem to her like some living background, into which she wanted to retreat? When he reared his head and neighed from his deep chest, like deep wind-bells resounding, she seemed to hear the echoes of another darker, more spacious, more dangerous, more splendid world than ours, that was beyond her. And there she wanted to go.

She kept it utterly a secret to herself. Because Rico would just have lifted his long upper lip, in his bare face, in a condescending sort of 'understanding'. And her mother would, as usual, have suspected her of side-stepping. People, all the people she knew, seemed so entirely contained within their cardboard let's-be-happy world. Their wills were fixed like machines on happiness, or fun, or the-best-ever. This ghastly cheery-o! touch, that made all her blood go numb.

Since she had really seen St. Mawr looming fiery and terrible in an outer darkness, she could not believe the world she lived in. She could not believe it was actually happening, when she was dancing in the afternoon at Claridge's, or in the evening at the Carlton, sliding about with some suave young man who wasn't like a man at all to her. Or down in Sussex for the week-end with the Enderleys: the talk, the eating and drinking, the flirtation, the endless dancing: it all seemed far more bodiless and, in a strange way, wraith-like, than any fairy story. She seemed to be eating Barmecide food, that had been conjured up out of thin air, by the power of words. She seemed to be talking to handsome, young, bare-faced unrealities, not men at all: as she slid about with them, in the perpetual dance, they too seemed to have been conjured up out of air, merely for this soaring, slithering dance business. And she could not believe that, when the lights went out, they wouldn't melt back into thin air again and complete non-

entity. The strange nonentity of it all! Everything just conjured up, and nothing real. *'Isn't this the best ever!'* they
would beamingly assert, like wraiths of enjoyment, without
any genuine substance. And she would beam back: *'Lots of
fun!'*

She was thankful the season was over, and everybody was
leaving London. She and Rico were due to go to Scotland,
but not till August. In the meantime they would go to her
mother.

Mrs. Witt had taken a cottage in Shropshire, on the Welsh
border, and had moved down there with Phœnix and her
horses. The open, heather-and-bilberry-covered hills were
splendid for riding.

Rico consented to spend the month in Shropshire, because
for near neighbours Mrs. Witt had the Manbys, at Corrabach
Hall. The Manbys were rich Australians returned to the
old country and set up as squires, all in full blow. Rico had
known them in Victoria: they were of good family: and the
girls made a great fuss of him.

So down went Lou and Rico, Lewis, Poppy and St. Mawr,
to Shrewsbury, then out into the country. Mrs. Witt's 'cottage'
was a tall red-brick Georgian house looking straight on to the
churchyard, and the dark, looming big church.

"I never knew what a comfort it would be," said Mrs. Witt,
"to have grave-stones under my drawing-room windows, and
funerals for lunch."

She really did take a strange pleasure in sitting in her
panelled room, that was painted grey, and watching the Dean
or one of the curates officiating at the graveside, among a
group of black country mourners with black-bordered hand-
kerchiefs luxuriantly in use.

"Mother!" said Lou. "I think it's gruesome!"

She had a room at the back, looking over the walled garden
and the stables. Nevertheless, there was the *boom! boom!* of
the passing-bell, and the chiming and pealing on Sundays.
The shadow of the church, indeed! A very audible shadow,
making itself heard insistently.

The Dean was a big, burly, fat man with a pleasant manner.
He was a gentleman, and a man of learning in his own line.
But he let Mrs. Witt know that he looked down on her just a
trifle—as a parvenu American, a Yankee—though she never
was a Yankee: and at the same time he had a sincere respect

for her, as a rich woman. Yes, a sincere respect for her, as a rich woman.

Lou knew that every Englishman, especially of the upper classes, has a wholesome respect for riches. But then, who hasn't?

The Dean was more *impressed* by Mrs. Witt than by little Lou. But to Lady Carrington he was charming: she was *almost* 'one of us', you know. And he was very gracious to Rico: 'your father's splendid colonial service.'

Mrs. Witt had now a new pantomime to amuse her: the Georgian house, her own pew in church—it went with the old house: a village of thatched cottages—some of them with corrugated iron over the thatch: the cottage people, farm labourers and their families, with a few, very few, out-siders: the wicked little group of cottagers down at Mile End, famous for ill-living. The Mile-Enders were all Allisons and Jephsons, and in-bred, the Dean said: result of working through the centuries at the Quarry, and living isolated there at Mile End.

Isolated! Imagine it! A mile and a half from the railway station, ten miles from Shrewsbury. Mrs. Witt thought of Texas, and said:

"Yes, they are *very* isolated, away down there!"

And the Dean never for a moment suspected sarcasm.

But there she had the whole thing staged complete for her: English village life. Even miners breaking in to shatter the rather stuffy, unwholesome harmony.—All the men touched their caps to her, all the women did a bit of reverence, the children stood aside for her, if she appeared in the street.

They were all poor again: the labourers could no longer afford even a glass of beer in the evenings, since the Glorious War.

"Now I think that *is* terrible," said Mrs. Witt. "Not to be able to get away from those stuffy, squalid, picturesque cottages for an hour in the evening, to drink a glass of beer."

"It's a pity, I do agree with you, Mrs. Witt. But Mr. Watson has organised a men's reading-room, where the men can smoke and play dominoes, and read if they wish."

"But that," said Mrs. Witt, "is not the same as that cosy parlour in the 'Moon and Stars'."

"I quite agree," said the Dean. "It isn't."

Mrs. Witt marched to the landlord of the 'Moon and Stars' and asked for a glass of cider.

"I want," she said, in her American accent, "these poor labourers to have their glass of beer in the evenings."

"They want it themselves," said Harvey.

"Then they must have it——"

The upshot was, she decided to supply one large barrel of beer per week and the landlord was to sell it to the labourers at a penny a glass.

"My own country has gone dry," she asserted. "But not because we can't *afford* it."

By the time Lou and Rico appeared, she was deep in. She actually interfered very little: the barrel of beer was her one public act. But she *did* know everybody by sight, already, and she *did* know everybody's circumstances. And she had attended one prayer-meeting, one mothers' meeting, one sewing-bee, one 'social', one Sunday School meeting, one Band of Hope meeting, and one Sunday School treat. She ignored the poky little Wesleyan and Baptist chapels, and was true-blue Episcopalian.

"How strange these picturesque old villages are, Louise!" she said, with a duskiness around her sharp, well-bred nose. "How *easy* it all seems, all on a definite pattern. And how false! And underneath, *how corrupt!*"

She gave that queer, triumphant leer from her grey eyes, and queer demonish wrinkles seemed to twitter on her face.

Lou shrank away. She was beginning to be afraid of her mother's insatiable curiosity, that always looked for the snake under the flowers. Or rather, for the maggots.

Always this same morbid interest in other people and their doings, their privacies, their dirty linen. Always this air of alertness for personal happenings, personalities, personalities, personalities. Always this subtle criticism and appraisal of other people, this analysis of other people's motives. If anatomy presupposes a corpse, then psychology presupposes a world of corpses. Personalities, which means personal criticism and analysis, presuppose a whole world laboratory of human psyches waiting to be vivisected. If you cut a thing up, of course it will smell. Hence, nothing raises such an infernal stink, at last, as human psychology.

Mrs. Witt was a pure psychologist, a fiendish psychologist.

And Rico, in his way, was a psychologist too. But he had a formula. "Let's *know* the worst, dear! But let's look on the bright side, and believe the best."

"Isn't the Dean a priceless old darling!" said Rico at breakfast.

And it had begun. Work had started in the psychic vivi-section laboratory.

"Isn't he wonderful!" said Lou vaguely.

"So delightfully worldly!—*Some of us are not born to make money, dear boy. Luckily for us, we can marry it.*"— Rico made a priceless face.

"Is Mrs. Vyner so rich?" asked Lou.

"She is quite a wealthy woman—in coal," replied Mrs. Witt. "But the Dean is surely worth his weight even in gold. And he's a massive figure. I can imagine there would be great satisfaction in having him for a husband."

"Why, mother?" asked Lou.

"Oh, such a presence! One of these old Englishmen that nobody can put in their pocket. You can't imagine his wife asking him to thread her needle. Something after all so *robust!* So different from *young* Englishmen, who all seem to me like ladies, perfect ladies."

"*Somebody* has to keep up the tradition of the perfect lady," said Rico.

"I know it," said Mrs. Witt. "And if the women won't do it, the young gentlemen take on the burden. They bear it very well."

It was in full swing, the cut and thrust. And poor Lou, who had reached the point of stupefaction in the game, felt she did not know what to do with herself.

Rico and Mrs. Witt were deadly enemies, yet neither could keep clear of the other. It might have been they who were married to one another, their duel and their duet were so relentless.

But Rico immediately started the social round: first the Manbys: then motor twenty miles to luncheon at Lady Tewkesbury's: then young Mr. Burns came flying down in his aeroplane from Chester: then they must motor to the sea to Sir Edward Edwards's place, where there was a moonlight bathing party. Everything intensely thrilling, and so innerly wearisome, Lou felt.

But back of it all was St. Mawr, looming like a bonfire in

the dark. He really was a tiresome horse to own. He worried
the mares, if they were in the same paddock with him, always
driving them round. And with any other horse he just fought
with definite intent to kill. So he had to stay alone.

"That St. Mawr, he's a bad horse," said Phœnix.

"Maybe!" said Lewis.

"You don't like quiet horses?" said Phœnix.

"Most horses *is* quiet," said Lewis. "St. Mawr, he's different."

"Why don't he never get any foals?"

"Doesn't want to, I should think. Same as me."

"What good is a horse like that? Better shoot him, before
he kill somebody."

"What good'll they get, shooting St. Mawr?" said Lewis.

"If he kills somebody!" said Phœnix.

But there was no answer.

The two grooms both lived over the stables, and Lou, from
her window, saw a good deal of them. They were two quiet
men, yet she was very much aware of their presence, aware
of Phœnix's rather high square shoulders and his fine, straight,
vigorous black hair that tended to stand up assertively on his
head, as he went quietly drifting about his various jobs. He
was not lazy, but he did everything with a sort of diffidence,
as if from a distance, and handled his horses carefully,
cautiously, and cleverly, but without sympathy. He seemed
to be holding something back all the time, unconsciously, as
if in his very being there was some secret. But it was a secret
of *will*. His quiet, reluctant movements, as if he never really
wanted to do anything; his long, flat-stepping stride; the
permanent challenge in his high cheek-bones, the Indian glint
in his eyes, and his peculiar stare, watchful and yet unseeing,
made him unpopular with the women servants.

Nevertheless, women had a certain fascination for him: he
would stare at the pretty young maids with an intent blank
stare when they were not looking. Yet he was rather over-
bearing, domineering with them, and they resented him. It
was evident to Lou that he looked upon himself as belonging
to the master, not to the servant class. When he flirted with
the maids, as he very often did, for he had a certain crude
ostentatiousness, he seemed to let them feel that he despised
them as inferiors, servants, while he admired their pretty
charms, as fresh, country maids.

"I'm fair nervous of that Phœnix," said Fanny, the fair-haired girl. "He makes you feel what he'd do to you if he could."

"He'd better not try with me," said Mabel. "I'd scratch his cheeky eyes out. Cheek!—for it's nothing else! He's nobody —common as they're made!"

"He makes you feel you was there for him to trample on," said Fanny.

"Mercy, you *are* soft! If anybody's that it's him. Oh, my, Fanny, you've no right to let a fellow make you feel like *that!* Make *them* feel that *they're* dirt, for you to trample on: which they are!"

Fanny, however, being a shy little blonde thing, wasn't good at assuming the trampling role. She was definitely nervous of Phœnix. And he enjoyed it. An invisible smile seemed to creep up his cheek-bones, and the glint moved in his eyes as he teased her. He tormented her by his very presence, as he knew.

He would come silently up when she was busy, and stand behind her perfectly still, so that she was unaware of his presence. Then, silently, he would *make* her aware. Till she glanced nervously round, and with a scream saw him.

One day Lou watched the little play. Fanny had been picking over a bowl of blackcurrants, sitting on the bench under the maple tree in a corner of the yard. She didn't look round till she had picked up her bowl to go to the kitchen. Then there was a scream and a crash.

When Lou came out, Phœnix was crouching down silently gathering up the currants, which the little maid, scarlet and trembling, was collecting into another bowl. Phœnix seemed to be smiling down his back.

"Phœnix!" said Lou. "I wish you wouldn't startle Fanny!"

He looked up and she saw the glint of ridicule in his eyes.

"Who, me?" he said.

"Yes, you. You go up behind Fanny to startle her. You're not to do it."

He slowly stood erect and lapsed into his peculiar invisible silence. Only for a second his eyes glanced at Lou's, and then she saw the cold anger, the gleam of malevolence and contempt. He could not bear being commanded, or reprimanded, by a woman.

Yet it was even worse with a man.

"What's that, Lou?" said Rico, appearing all handsome and in the picture, in white flannels with an apricot silk shirt.

"I'm telling Phœnix he's not to torment Fanny!"

"Oh!"—and Rico's voice immediately became his father's, the important government official's. "Certainly *not!* Most certainly *not!*" He looked at the scattered currants and the broken bowl. Fanny melted into tears. "This, I suppose, is some of the results! Now look here, Phœnix, you're to leave the maids strictly alone. I shall ask them to report to me whenever, or *if* ever, you interfere with them. But I hope you *won't* interfere with them—in any way. You understand?"

As Rico became more and more Sir Harry and the government official, Lou's bones melted more and more into discomfort. Phœnix stood in his peculiar silence, the invisible smile on his cheek-bones.

"You understand what I'm saying to you?" Rico demanded, in intensified acid tones.

But Phœnix only stood there, as it were behind a cover of his own will, and looked back at Rico with a faint smile on his face and the glint moving in his eyes.

"Do you intend to answer?" Rico's upper lip lifted nastily.

"Mrs. Witt is my boss," came from Phœnix.

The scarlet flew up Rico's throat and flushed his face, his eyes went glaucous. Then quickly his face turned yellow.

Lou looked at the two men: her husband, whose rages, over-controlled, were organically terrible: the half-breed, whose dark-coloured lips were widened in a faint smile of derision, but in whose eyes caution and hate were playing against one another. She realised that Phœnix would accept *her* reprimand, or her mother's, because he could despise the two of them as mere women. But Rico's business aroused murder pure and simple.

She took her husband's arm.

"Come, dear!" she said in her half-plaintive way. "I'm sure Phœnix understands. We all understand. Go to the kitchen, Fanny, never mind the currants. There are plenty more in the garden."

Rico was always thankful to be drawn quickly, submissively away from his own rage. He was afraid of it. He was afraid lest he should fly at the groom in some horrible fashion. The very thought horrified him. But in actuality he came very near to it.

He walked stiffly, feeling paralysed by his own fury. And those words, *Mrs. Witt is my boss*, were like hot acid in his brain. An insult!

"By the way, Belle-Mère!" he said when they joined Mrs. Witt—she hated being called Belle-Mère, and once said: "If I'm the bell-mare, are you one of the colts?"—She also hated his voice of smothered fury—"I had to speak to Phœnix about persecuting the maids. He took the liberty of informing me that you were his boss, so perhaps you had better speak to him."

"I certainly will. I believe they're my maids, and nobody else's, so it's my duty to look after them. Who was he persecuting?"

"I'm the responsible one, mother," said Lou.

Rico disappeared in a moment. He must get out: get away from the house. How? Something was wrong with the car. Yet he must get away, away. He would go over to Corrabach. He would ride St. Mawr. He had been talking about the horse, and Flora Manby was dying to see him. She had said: "Oh, I can't *wait* to see that marvellous horse of yours."

He would ride him over. It was only seven miles. He found Lou's maid Elena, and sent her to tell Lewis. Meanwhile, to soothe himself, he dressed himself most carefully in white riding-breeches and a shirt of purple silk crêpe, with a flowing black tie spotted red like a ladybird, and black riding-boots. Then he took a *chic* little white hat with a black band.

St. Mawr was saddled and waiting, and Lewis had saddled a second horse.

"Thanks, Lewis, I'm going alone!" said Rico.

This was the first time he had ridden St. Mawr in the country, and he was nervous. But he was also in the hell of a smothered fury. All his careful dressing had not really soothed him. So his fury consumed his nervousness.

He mounted with a swing, blind and rough. St. Mawr reared.

"Stop that!" snarled Rico, and put him to the gate.

Once out in the village street, the horse went dancing sideways. He insisted on dancing at the sidewalk, to the exaggerated terror of the children. Rico, exasperated, pulled him across. But no, he wouldn't go down the centre of the village street. He began dancing and edging on to the other sidewalk, so the foot-passengers fled into the shops in terror.

The devil was in him. He would turn down every turning where he was not meant to go. He reared with panic at a furniture van. He *insisted* on going down the wrong side of the road. Rico was riding him with a martingale, and he could see the rolling, bloodshot eye.

"Damn you, *go*!" said Rico, giving him a dig with the spurs.

And away they went, down the high-road, in a thunder-bolt. It was a hot day, with thunder threatening, so Rico was soon in a flame of heat. He held on tight, with fixed eyes, trying all the time to rein in the horse. What he really was afraid of was that the brute would shy suddenly as he galloped. Watching for this, he didn't care when they sailed past the turning to Corrabach.

St. Mawr flew on, in a sort of *élan*. Marvellous the power and life in the creature. There was really a great joy in the motion. If only he wouldn't take the corners at a gallop, nearly swerving Rico off! Luckily the road was clear. To ride, to ride at this terrific gallop, on into eternity!

After several miles, the horse slowed down, and Rico managed to pull him into a lane that might lead to Corra-bach. When all was said and done, it was a wonderful ride. St. Mawr could go like the wind, but with that luxurious heavy ripple of life which is like nothing else on earth. It seemed to carry one at once into another world, away from the life of the nerves.

So Rico arrived, after all, something of a conqueror at Corrabach. To be sure, he was perspiring, and so was his horse. But he was a hero from another, heroic world.

"Oh, such a hot ride!" he said, as he walked on to the lawn at Corrabach Hall. "Between the sun and the horse, really!— between two fires!"

"Don't you trouble, you're looking dandy, a bit hot and flushed like," said Flora Manby. "Let's go and see your horse."

And he exclamation was: "Oh, he's *lovely*! He's fine! I'd love to try him once——"

Rico decided to accept the invitation to stay overnight at Corrabach. Usually he was very careful, and refused to stay, unless Lou was with him. But they telephoned to the post office at Chomesbury, would Mr. Jones please send a message to Lady Carrington that Sir Henry was staying the night at Corrabach Hall, but would be home next day. Mr. Jones received the request with unction, and said he would go over himself to give the message to Lady Carrington.

Lady Carrington was in the walled garden. The peculiarity of Mrs. Witt's house was that, for grounds proper, it had the churchyard.

"I never thought, Louise, that one day I should have an old English churchyard for my lawns and shrubbery and park, and funeral mourners for my herds of deer. It's curious. For the first time in my life a funeral has become a real thing to me. I feel I could write a book on them."

But Louise only felt intimidated.

At the back of the house was a flagged courtyard, with stables and a maple tree in a corner, and big doors opening on to the village street. But at the side was a walled garden, with fruit trees and currant bushes and a great bed of rhubarb, and some tufts of flowers, peonies, pink roses, sweet williams. Phœnix, who had a certain taste for gardening, would be out there thinning the carrots or tying up the lettuce. He was not lazy. Only he would not take work seriously, as a job. He would be quite amused tying up lettuces, and would tie up head after head, quite prettily. Then, becoming bored, he would abandon his task, light a cigarette, and go and stand on the threshold of the big doors, in full view of the street, watching, and yet completely indifferent.

After Rico's departure on St. Mawr, Lou went into the garden. And there she saw Phœnix working in the onion-bed. He was bending over, in his own silence, busy with nimble, amused fingers among the grassy young onions. She thought he had not seen her, so she went down another path to where a swing bed hung under the apple tree. There she sat with a book and a bundle of magazines. But she did not read.

She was musing vaguely. Vaguely, she was glad that Rico was away for a while. Vaguely, she felt a sense of bitterness, of complete futility: the complete futility of her living. This left her drifting in a sea of utter chagrin. And Rico seemed to her the symbol of the futility. Vaguely, she was aware that something else existed, but she didn't know where it was or what it was.

In the distance she could see Phœnix's dark, rather tall-built head, with its black, fine, intensely-living hair tending to stand on end, like a brush with long, very fine black bristles.

His hair, she thought, betrayed him as an animal of a different species. He was growing a little bored by weeding onions: that also she could tell. Soon he would want some other amusement.

Presently Lewis appeared. He was small, energetic, a little bit bow-legged, and he walked with a slight strut. He wore khaki riding-breeches, leather gaiters, and a blue shirt. And, like Phœnix, he rarely had any cap or hat on his head. His thick black hair was parted at the side and brushed over heavily sideways, dropping on his forehead at the right. It was very long, a real mop, under which his eyebrows were dark and steady.

"Seen Lady Carrrington?" he asked of Phœnix.

"Yes, she's sitting on that swing over there—she's been there quite a while."

The wretch—he had seen her from the very first!

Lewis came striding over, looking towards her with his pale-grey eyes, from under his mop of hair.

"Mr. Jones from the post office wants to see you, my Lady, with a message from Sir Henry."

Instantly alarm took possession of Lou's soul.

"Oh!—Does he want to see me personally?—What message? Is anything wrong?"—And her voice trailed out over the last word, with a sort of anxious nonchalance.

"I don't think it's anything amiss," said Lewis reassuringly.

"Oh! You don't," the relief came into her voice. Then she looked at Lewis with a slight, winning smile in her unmatched eyes. "I'm so afraid of St. Mawr, you know." Her voice was soft and cajoling. Phœnix was listening in the distance.

"St. Mawr's all right, if you don't do nothing to him," Lewis replied.

"I'm sure he is!—But how is one to know when one is doing something to him?—Tell Mr. Jones to come here, please," she concluded, on a changed tone.

Mr. Jones, a man of forty-five, thick-set, with a fresh complexion and rather foolish brown eyes, and a big brown moustache, came prancing down the path, smiling rather fatuously, and doffing his straw hat with a gorgeous bow the moment he saw Lou sitting in her slim white frock on the coloured swing bed under the trees with their hard green apples.

"Good-morning, Mr. Jones!"

"Good-morning, Lady Carrington.—If I may say so, what a picture you make—a beautiful picture——"

He beamed under his big brown moustache like the greatest lady-killer.

"Do I!—Did Sir Henry say he was all right?"

"He didn't *say* exactly, but I should expect he is all right——" and Mr. Jones delivered his message, in the mayonnaise of his own unction.

"Thank you so much, Mr. Jones. It's awfully good of you to come and tell me. Now I shan't worry about Sir Henry *at all.*"

"It's a great pleasure to come and deliver a satisfactory message to Lady Carrington. But it won't be kind to Sir Henry if you don't worry about him *at all* in his absence. We all enjoy being worried about by those we love—so long as there is nothing to worry about, of course!"

"Quite!" said Lou. "Now won't you take a glass of port and a biscuit, or a whisky and soda? And thank you ever so much."

"Thank *you*, my Lady. I might drink a whisky and soda, since you are so good."

And he beamed fatuously.

"Let Mr. Jones mix himself a whisky and soda, Lewis," said Lou.

"Heavens!" she thought, as the postmaster retreated a little uncomfortably down the garden path, his bald spot passing in and out of the sun, under the trees: "How ridiculous everything is, how ridiculous, ridiculous!" Yet she didn't really dislike Mr. Jones and his interlude.

Phœnix was melting away out of the garden. He had to follow the fun.

"Phœnix!" Lou called. "Bring me a glass of water, will you? Or send somebody with it."

He stood in the path looking round at her.

"All right!" he said

And he turned away again.

She did not like being alone in the garden. She liked to have the men working somewhere near. Curious how pleasant it was to sit there in the garden when Phœnix was about, or Lewis. It made her feel she could never be lonely or jumpy. But when Rico was there, she was all aching nerve.

Phœnix came back with a glass of water, lemon juice, sugar, and a small bottle of brandy. He knew Lou liked a spoonful of brandy in her iced lemonade.

"How thoughtful of you, Phœnix!" she said. "Did Mr. Jones get his whisky?"

"He was just getting it."

"That's right.—By the way, Phœnix, I wish you wouldn't get mad if Sir Henry speaks to you. He is *really* so kind."

She looked up at the man. He stood there watching her in silence, the invisible smile on his face, and the inscrutable Indian glint moving in his eyes. What was he thinking? There was something passive and almost submissive about him, but underneath this, an unyielding resistance and cruelty: yes, even cruelty. She felt that, on top, he was submissive and attentive, bringing her her lemonade as she liked it, without being told: thinking for her quite subtly. But underneath there was an unchanging hatred. He submitted circumstantially, he worked for a wage. And even circumstantially, he *liked* his mistress—*la patrona*—and her daughter. But much deeper than any circumstance or any circumstantial liking, was the categorical hatred upon which he was founded, and with which he was powerless. His liking for Lou and for Mrs. Witt, his serving them and working for a wage, was all side-tracking his own nature, which was grounded on hatred of their very existence. But what was he to do? He had to live. Therefore he had to serve, to work for a wage, and even to be faithful.

And yet *their* existence made his own existence negative. If he was to exist, positively, they would have to cease to exist. At the same time, a fatal sort of tolerance made him serve these women, and go on serving.

"Sir Henry is *so* kind to everybody," Lou insisted.

The half-breed met her eyes, and smiled uncomfortably.

"Yes, he's a kind man," he replied, as if sincerely.

"Then why do you mind if he speaks to you?"

"I don't mind," said Phœnix glibly.

"But you do. Or else you wouldn't make him so angry."

"Was he angry? I don't know," said Phœnix.

"He was very angry. And you *do* know."

"No, I don't know if he's angry. I don't know," the fellow persisted. And there was a glib sort of satisfaction in his tone.

"That's awfully unkind of you, Phœnix," she said, growing offended in her turn.

"No, I don't know if he's angry. I don't want to make him angry. I don't know——"

He had taken on a tone of naïve ignorance, which at once gratified her pride as a woman, and deceived her.

"Well, you believe me when I tell you you *did* make him angry, don't you?"

"Yes, I believe when you tell me."

"And you promise me, won't you, not to do it again? It's *so* bad for him—so bad for his nerves, and for his eyes. It makes them inflamed, and injures his eyesight. And you know, as an artist, it's terrible if anything happens to his eyesight——"

Phœnix was watching her closely, to take it in. He still was not good at understanding continuous, logical statement. Logical connection in speech seemed to stupefy him, make him stupid. He understood in disconnected assertions of fact. But he had gathered what she said. "He gets mad at you. When he gets mad, it hurts his eyes. His eyes hurt him. He can't see, because his eyes hurt him. He wants to paint a picture, he can't. He can't paint a picture, he can't see clear——"

Yes, he had understood. She saw he had understood. The bright glint of satisfaction moved in his eyes.

"So now promise me, won't you, you won't make him mad again: you won't make him angry?"

"No, I won't make him angry. I don't do anything to make him angry," Phœnix answered, rather glibly.

"And you do understand, don't you? You do know how kind he is: how he'd do a good turn to anybody?"

"Yes, he's a kind man," said Phœnix.

"I'm so glad you realise. There, that's luncheon! How nice it is to sit here in the garden, when everybody is nice to you! No, I can carry the tray, don't you bother."

But he took the tray from her hand and followed her to the house. And as he walked behind her, he watched the slim white nape of her neck, beneath the clustering of her bobbed hair, something as a stoat watches a rabbit he is following.

In the afternoon Lou retreated once more to her place in the garden. There she lay, sitting with a bunch of pillows behind her, neither reading nor working, just musing. She had

learned the new joy: to do absolutely nothing, but to lie and
let the sunshine filter through the leaves, to see the bunch of
red-hot-poker flowers pierce scarlet into the afternoon, beside
the comparative neutrality of some foxgloves. The mere
colour of hard red, like the big Oriental poppies that had
fallen, and these poker flowers, lingered in her consciousness
like a communication.

Into this peaceful indolence, when even the big, dark-grey
tower of the church beyond the wall and the yew trees was
keeping its bells in silence, advanced Mrs. Witt, in a broad
Panama hat and a white dress.

"Don't you want to ride, or do something, Louise?" she
asked ominously.

"Don't you want to be peaceful, mother?" retorted Louise.

"Yes—an *active* peace.—I can't *believe* that my daughter
can be content to lie on a hammock and do nothing, not
even read or improve her mind, the greater part of the
day."

"Well, your daughter *is* content to do that. It's her greatest
pleasure."

"I know it. I can see it. And it surprises me *very* much.
When I was your age, I was never still. I had so much
go——"

> "Those maids, thank God,
> Are 'neath the sod,
> And all the generation."

"No, but, mother, I only take life differently. Perhaps you
used up that sort of *go*. I'm the harem type, mother: only I
never want the men inside the lattice."

"Are you really my daughter?—Well! A woman never
knows what will happen to her. I'm an *American* woman,
and I suppose I've got to remain one, no matter where I am.—
What did you want, Lewis?"

The groom had approached down the path.

"If I am to saddle Poppy?" said Lewis.

"No, apparently *not*!" replied Mrs. Witt. "Your mistress
prefers the hammock to the saddle."

"Thank you, Lewis. What mother says is true this afternoon, at least." And she gave him a peculiar little cross-eyed
smile.

"Who," said Mrs. Witt to the man, "has been cutting at your hair?"

There was a moment of silent resentment.

"I did it myself, Mam! Sir Henry said it was too long."

"He certainly spoke the truth. But I believe there's a barber in the village on Saturdays—or you could ride over to Shrewsbury. Just turn round, and let me look at the back. Is it the money?"

"No, Mam. I don't like these fellows touching my head."

He spoke coldly, with a certain hostile reserve that at once piqued Mrs. Witt.

"Don't you really!" she said. "But it's quite *impossible* for you to go about as you are. It gives you a half-witted appearance. Go now into the yard and get a chair and a dust-sheet. I'll cut your hair."

The man hesitated, hostile.

"Don't be afraid, I know how it's done. I've cut the hair of many a poor wounded boy in hospital: and shaved them too. *You've got such a touch, nurse!* Poor fellow, he was dying, though none of us knew it.—Those are the compliments I value, Louise.—Get that chair now, and a dust-sheet. I'll borrow your hair-scissors from Elena, Louise."

Mrs. Witt, happily on the war-path, was herself again. She didn't care for work, actual work. But she loved trimming. She loved arranging unnatural and pretty salads, devising new and piquant-looking ice-creams, having a turkey stuffed exactly as she knew a stuffed turkey in Louisiana, with chestnuts and butter and stuff, or showing a servant how to turn waffles on a waffle-iron, or to bake a ham with brown sugar and cloves and a moistening of rum. She liked pruning rose trees, or beginning to cut a yew hedge into shape. She liked ordering her own and Louise's shoes, with an exactitude and a knowledge of shoe-making that sent the salesmen crazy. She was a demon in shoes. Reappearing from America, she would pounce on her daughter. "Louise, throw those shoes away. Give them to one of the maids."—"But, mother, they are some of the best French shoes. I like them."—"Throw them away. A shoe has only two excuses for existing: perfect comfort or perfect appearance. Those have neither. I have brought you some shoes."—Yes, she had brought ten pairs of shoes from New York. She knew her daughter's foot as she knew her own.

So now she was in her element, looming behind Lewis as he sat in the middle of the yard swathed in a dust-sheet. She had on an overall and a pair of wash-leather gloves, and she poised a pair of long scissors like one of the Fates. In her big hat she looked curiously young, but with the youth of a by-gone generation. Her heavy-lidded, laconic grey eyes were alert, studying the groom's black mop of hair. Her eyebrows made thin, uptilting black arches on her brow. Her fresh skin was slightly powdered, and she was really handsome in a bold, bygone, eighteenth-century style. Some of the curious, adventurous stoicism of the eighteenth century: and then a certain blatant American efficiency.

Lou, who had strayed into the yard to see, looked so much younger and so many thousand of years older than her mother, as she stood in her wisp-like diffidence, the clusters of grape-like bobbed hair hanging beside her face, with its fresh colouring and its ancient weariness, her slightly squint-ing eyes, that were so disillusioned they were becoming faun-like.

"Not too short, mother, not too short!" she remonstrated, as Mrs. Witt, with a terrific flourish of efficiency, darted at the man's black hair, and the thick flakes fell like black snow.

"Now, Louise, I'm right in this job, please don't interfere. Two things I hate to see: a man with his wool in his neck and ears: and a bare-faced young man who looks as if he'd bought his face as well as his hair from a men's beauty-specialist."

And efficiently she bent down, clip—clip—clipping! while Lewis sat utterly immobile, with sunken head, in a sort of despair.

Phœnix stood against the stable door, with his restless, eternal cigarette. And in the kitchen doorway the maids appeared and fled, appeared and fled in delight. The old gardener, a fixture who went with the house, creaked in and stood with his legs apart, silent in intense condemnation.

"First time I ever see such a thing!" he muttered to him-self, as he creaked on into the garden. He was a bad-tempered old soul, who thoroughly disapproved of the household, and would have given notice, but that he knew which side his bread was buttered: and there was butter unstinted on his bread in Mrs. Witt's kitchen.

Mrs. Witt stood back to survey her handiwork, holding

those terrifying shears with their beak erect. Lewis lifted his head and looked stealthily round, like a creature in a trap.

"Keep still!" she said. "I haven't finished."

And she went for his front hair, with vigour, lifting up long layers and snipping off the ends artistically: till at last he sat with a black aureole upon the floor, and his ears standing out with curious new alertness from the sides of his clean-clipped head.

"Stand up," she said, "and let me look."

He stood up, looking absurdly young, with the hair all cut away from his neck and ears, left thick only on top. She surveyed her work with satisfaction.

"You look so much younger," she said, "you would be surprised. Sit down again."

She clipped the back of his neck with the shears, and then, with a very slight hesitation, she said:

"Now about the beard!"

But the man rose suddenly from the chair, pulling the dust-cloth from his neck with desperation.

"No, I'll do that myself," he said, looking her in the eyes with a cold light in his pale-grey, uncanny eyes.

She hesitated in a kind of wonder at his queer male rebellion.

"Now, listen, I shall do it much better than you—and be-sides," she added hurriedly, snatching at the dust-cloth he was flinging on the chair—"I haven't quite finished round the ears."

"I think I shall do," he said, again looking her in the eyes, with a cold, white gleam of finality. "Thank you for what you've done."

And he walked away to the stable.

"You'd better sweep up here," Mrs. Witt called.

"Yes, Mam," he replied, looking round at her again with an odd resentment, but continuing to walk away.

"However!" said Mrs. Witt, "I suppose he'll do."

And she divested herself of gloves and overall and walked indoors to wash and to change. Lou went indoors too.

"It is extraordinary what hair that man has!" said Mrs. Witt. "Did I tell you when I was in Paris, I saw a woman's face in the hotel that I thought I knew? I couldn't place her, till she was coming towards me. 'Aren't you Rachel Fannière?' she said. 'Aren't you Janette Leroy?' We hadn't seen each other since we were girls of twelve and thirteen, at school in New Orleans. 'Oh!' she said to me. 'Is every illusion doomed to perish? You had such wonderful golden curls! All my life I've said, Oh, if only I had such lovely hair as Rachel Fannière! I've seen those beautiful golden curls of yours all my life. And now I meet you, you're grey!' Wasn't that terrible, Louise? Well, that man's hair made me think of it—so thick and curious. It's strange what a difference there is in hair; I suppose it's because he's just an animal —no mind! There's nothing I admire in a man like a good *mind*. Your father was a very clever man, and all the men I've admired have been clever. But isn't it curious now, I've never cared much to touch their hair. How strange life is! If it gives one thing, it takes away another.—And even those poor boys in hospital: I have shaved them, or cut their hair, like a mother, never thinking anything of it. Lovely, intelligent, clean boys, most of them were. Yet it never did anything to me. I never knew before that something could happen to one from a person's *hair*! Like to Janette Leroy from my curls when I was a child. And now I'm grey, as she says.—I wonder how old a man Lewis is, Louise! Didn't he look absurdly young with his ears pricking up?"

"I think Rico said he was forty or forty-one."

"And never been married?"

"No—not as far as I know."

"Isn't that curious now!—just an animal! No mind! A man with no mind! I've always thought that the *most* despicable thing. Yet such wonderful hair to touch. Your Henry has quite a good mind, yet I would simply shrink from touching his hair. I suppose one likes stroking a cat's fur, just the same. Just the animal in man. Curious that I never seem to have met it, Louise. Now I come to think of it, he has the eyes of a human cat: a human tom-cat. Would you call him stupid? Yes, he's very stupid."

"No, mother, he's not stupid. He only doesn't care about most things."

"Like an animal! But what a strange look he has in his eyes! A strange sort of intelligence! and a confidence in himself. Isn't that curious, Louise, in a man with as little mind as he has? Do you know, I should say he could see through a woman pretty well."

"Why, mother!" said Lou impatiently. "I think one gets

so tired of your men with mind, as you call it. There are so many of that sort of clever men. And there are lots of men who aren't very clever, but are rather nice: and lots are stupid. It seems to me there's something else besides mind and cleverness, or niceness or cleanness. Perhaps it is the animal. Just think of St. Mawr! I've thought so much about him. We call him an animal, but we never know what it means. He seems a far greater mystery to me than a clever man. He's a horse. Why can't one say in the same way of a man: 'He's a man?' There seems no mystery in being a man. But there's a terrible mystery in St. Mawr."

Mrs. Witt watched her daughter quizzically.

"Louise," she said, "you won't tell me that the mere animal is all that counts in a man. I will never believe it. Man is wonderful because he is able to *think*."

"But is he?" cried Lou, with sudden exasperation. "Their thinking seems to me all so childish: like stringing the same beads over and over again. Ah, men! They and their thinking are all so *paltry*. How can you be impressed?"

Mrs. Witt raised her eyebrows sardonically.

"Perhaps I'm not—any more," she said with a grim smile.

"But," she added, "I still can't see that I am to be impressed by the mere animal in man. The animals are the same as we are. It seems to me they have the same feelings and wants as we do in a commonplace way. The only difference is that they have no minds: no human minds, at least. And no matter what you say, Louise, lack of minds makes the common-place."

Lou knitted her brows nervously.

"I suppose it does, mother.—But men's minds *are* so commonplace: look at Dean Vyner and his mind! Or look at Arthur Balfour, as a shining example. Isn't *that* common-place, that cleverness? I would hate St. Mawr to be spoilt by such a mind."

"Yes, Louise, so would I. Because the men you mention are really old women, knitting the same pattern over and over again. Nevertheless, I shall never alter my belief that real mind is all that matters in a man, and it's *that* that we women love."

"Yes, mother!—But what *is* real mind? The old woman who knits the most complicated pattern? Oh, I can hear all their needles clicking, the clever men! As a matter of fact, mother, I believe Lewis has far more real mind than Dean Vyner or any of the clever ones. He has a good intuitive mind, he knows things without thinking them."

"That may be, Louise! But he is a servant. He is *under*. A real man should never be under. And then you could never be intimate with a man like Lewis."

"I don't want intimacy, mother. I'm too tired of it all. I love St. Mawr because he isn't intimate. He stands where one can't get at him. And he burns with life. And where does his life come from, to him? That's the mystery. That great burning life in him, which never is dead. Most men have a deadness in them, that frightens me so, because of my own deadness. Why can't men get their life straight, like St. Mawr, and then think? Why can't they think quick, mother: quick as a woman: only farther than we do? Why isn't men's thinking quick like fire, mother? Why is it so slow, so dead, so deadly dull?"

"I can't tell you, Louise. My own opinion of the men of to-day has grown very small. But I can live in spite of it."

"No, mother. We seemed to be living off old fuel, like the camel when he lives off his hump. Life doesn't rush into us, as it does even into St. Mawr, and he's a dependent animal. I can't live, mother. I just can't."

"I don't see why not! *I'm* full of life."

"I know you are, mother. But I'm not, and I'm your daughter.—And don't misunderstand me, mother! I don't want to be an animal like a horse or a cat or a lioness, though they all fascinate me, the way they get their life *straight*, not from a lot of old tanks, as we do. I don't admire the cave-man, and that sort of thing. But think, mother, if we could get our lives straight from the source, as the animals do, and still be ourselves. You don't like men yourself. But you've no idea how men just tire me out: even the very thought of them. You say they are too animal. But they're not, mother. It's the animal in them has gone perverse, or cringing, or humble, or domesticated, like dogs. I don't know one single man who is a proud living animal. I know they've left off really thinking. But then men always do leave off really thinking when the last bit of wild animal dies in them."

"Because we have minds——"

"We have no minds once we are tame, mother. Men are all women, knitting and crocheting words together."

"I can't altogether agree, you know, Louise."

"I know you don't.—You like clever men. But clever men are mostly such unpleasant *animals*. As animals, so very unpleasant. And in men like Rico, the animal has gone queer and wrong. And in those nice clean boys you liked so much in the war, there is no wild animal left in them. They're all tame dogs, even when they're brave and well-bred. They're all tame dogs, mother, with human masters. There's no mystery in them."

"What do you want, Louise? You *do* want the cave man, who'll knock you on the head with a club."

"Don't be silly, mother. That's much more your sub-conscious line, you admirer of Mind—I don't consider the cave man is a real human animal at all. He's a brute, a degenerate. A pure animal man would be as lovely as a deer or a leopard, burning like a flame fed straight from underneath. And he'd be part of the unseen, like a mouse is, even. And he'd never cease to wonder, he'd breathe silence and unseen wonder, as the partridges do, running in the stubble. He'd be all the animals in turn, instead of one, fixed, automatic thing, which he is now, grinding on the nerves.—Ah, no, mother, I want the wonder back again, or I shall die. I don't want to be like you, just criticising and annihilating these dreary people, and enjoying it."

"My dear daughter, whatever else the human animal might be, he'd be a dangerous commodity."

"I wish he would, mother. I'm dying of these empty danger-less men, who are only sentimental and spiteful."

"Nonsense, you're not dying."

"I am, mother. And I should be dead if there weren't St. Mawr and Phœnix and Lewis in the world."

"St. Mawr and Phœnix and Lewis! I thought you said they were servants."

"That's the worst of it. If only they were masters! If only there were some men with as much natural life as they have, and their brave, quick minds that commanded instead of serving!"

"There are no such men," said Mrs. Witt, with a certain grim satisfaction.

"I know it. But I'm young, and I've got to live. And the thing that is offered me as life just starves me, starves me to death, mother. What am I to do? You enjoy shattering people like Dean Vyner. But I am young, I can't live that way!"

"That may be."

It had long ago struck Lou how much more her mother
realised and understood than ever Rico did. Rico was afraid,
always afraid of realising. Rico, with his good manners and
his habitual kindness, and that peculiar imprisoned sneer of
his.

He arrived home next morning on St. Mawr, rather flushed
and gaudy, and over-kind, with an *empressé* anxiety about
Lou's welfare which spoke too many volumes. Especially as
he was accompanied by Flora Manby, and by Flora's sister
Elsie, and Elsie's husband, Frederick Edwards. They all came
on horseback.

"Such awful ages since I saw you!" said Flora to Lou.
"Sorry if we burst in on you. We're only just saying 'How do
you do!' and going on to the inn. They've got rooms all ready
for us there. We thought we'd stay just one night over here,
and ride to-morrow to the Devil's Chair. Won't you come?
Lots of fun! Isn't Mrs. Witt at home?"

Mrs. Witt was out for the moment. When she returned she
had on her curious stiff face, yet she greeted the newcomers
with a certain cordiality: she felt it would be diplomatic, no
doubt.

"There *are* two rooms here," she said, "and if you care to
poke into them, why, we shall be *delighted* to have you. But
I'll show them to you first, because they are poor, incon-
venient rooms, with no running water and *miles* from the
baths."

Flora and Elsie declared that they were "perfectly darling
sweet rooms—not overcrowded."

"Well," said Mrs. Witt, "the conveniences certainly don't
fill up much space. But if you like to take them for what
they are——"

"Why, we feel absolutely overwhelmed, don't we, Elsie?—
But we've no clothes——!"

Suddenly the silence had turned into a house-party. The
Manby girls appeared to lunch in fine muslin dresses, bought
in Paris, fresh as daisies. Women's clothing takes up so little
space, especially in summer! Fred Edwards was one of those
blond Englishmen with a little brush moustache and those
strong blue eyes which were always attempting the sentimental, but which Lou, in her prejudice, considered cruel:

upon what grounds she never analysed. However, he took a gallant tone with her at once, and she had to seem to simper. Rico, watching her, was so relieved when he saw the simper coming.

It had begun again, the whole clockwork of 'lots of fun'!

"Isn't Fred flirting perfectly outrageously with Lady Carrington!—She looks so *sweet!*" cried Flora, over her coffee-cup. "Don't you mind, Harry!"

They called Rico 'Harry'! His boy-name.

"Only a very little," said Harry. *"L'uomo è cacciatore."*

"Oh, now, what does that mean?" cried Flora, who always thrilled to Rico's bits of affectation.

"It means," said Mrs. Witt, leaning forward and speaking in her most suave voice, "that man is a hunter."

Even Flora shrank under the smooth acid of the irony.

"Oh, well now!" she cried. "If he is, then what is woman?"

"The hunted," said Mrs. Witt, in a still smoother acid.

"At least," said Rico, "she is always *game!*"

"Ah, is she though!" came Fred's manly, well-bred tones. "I'm not so sure."

Mrs. Witt looked from one man to the other, as if she were dropping them down the bottomless pit.

Lou escaped to look at St. Mawr. He was still moist where the saddle had been. And he seemed a little bit extinguished, as if virtue had gone out of him.

But when he lifted his lovely naked head, like a bunch of flames, to see who it was had entered, she saw he was still himself. Forever sensitive and alert, his head lifted like the summit of a fountain. And within him the clean bones striking to the earth, his hoofs intervening between him and the ground like lesser jewels.

He knew her and did not resent her. But he took no notice of her. He would never 'respond'. At first she had resented it. Now she was glad. He would never be intimate, thank heaven.

She hid herself away till tea-time, but she could not hide from the sound of voices. Dinner was early, at seven. Dean Vyner came—Mrs. Vyner was an invalid—and also an artist who had a studio in the village and did etchings. He was a man of about thirty-eight, and poor, just beginning to accept himself as a failure, as far as making money goes. But he worked at his etchings and studied esoteric matters like

astrology and alchemy. Rico patronised him, and was a little
afraid of him. Lou could not quite make him out. After
knocking about Paris and London and Munich, he was trying
to become staid, and to persuade himself that English village
life, with squire and dean in the background, humble artist in
the middle, and labourer in the common foreground, was a
genuine life. His self-persuasion was only moderately successful. This was betrayed by the curious arrest in his body: he
seemed to have to force himself into movements: and by
the curious duplicity in his yellow-grey, twinkling eyes, that
twinkled and expanded like a goat's, with mockery, irony,
and frustration.

"Your face is curiously like Pan's," said Lou to him at
dinner.

It was true, in a commonplace sense. He had the tilted eyebrows, the twinkling goaty look, and the pointed ears of a
goat-Pan.

"People have said so," he replied. "But I'm afraid it's not
the face of the Great God Pan. Isn't it rather the Great Goat
Pan!"

"I say, that's good!" cried Rico. "The Great Goat Pan!"

"I have always found it difficult," said the Dean, "to see the
Great God Pan in that goat-legged old father of satyrs. He
may have a good deal of influence—the world will always be
full of goaty old satyrs. But we find them somewhat vulgar.
The goaty old satyrs are too comprehensible to me to be
venerable, and I fail to see a Great God in the father of
them all."

"Your ears should be getting red," said Lou to Cartwright.
She, too, had an odd squinting smile that suggested nymphs,
so irresponsible and unbelieving.

"Oh no, nothing personal!" cried the Dean.

"I am not sure," said Cartwright, with a small smile.
"But don't you imagine Pan once *was* a great god before the
anthropomorphic Greeks turned him into half a man?"

"Ah!—maybe. This is very possible. But—I have noticed
the limitation in myself—my mind has no grasp whatsoever
of Europe before the Greeks arose. Mr. Wells's Outline does
not help me there, either," the Dean added with a smile.

"But what was Pan before he was a man with goat legs?"
asked Lou.

"Before he looked like me!" said Cartwright, with a faint

grin. "I should say he was the god that is hidden in everything. In those days you saw the thing, you never saw the god in it: I mean in the tree or the fountain or the animal. If you ever saw the God instead of the thing, you died. If you saw it with the naked eye, that is. But in the night you might see the God. And you knew it was there."

"The modern pantheist not only sees the God in everything, he takes photographs of it," said the Dean.

"Oh, and the divine pictures he paints!" cried Rico.

"Quite!" said Cartwright.

"But if they never *saw* the God in the thing, the old ones, how did they know he was there? How did they have any Pan at all?" said Lou.

"Pan was the hidden mystery—the hidden cause. That's how it was a Great God. Pan wasn't *he* at all: not even a great God. He was Pan. All: what you see when you see in full. In the day-time you see the thing. But if your third eye is open, which sees only the things that can't be seen, you may see Pan within the thing, hidden: you may see with your third eye, which is darkness."

"Do you think I might see Pan in a horse, for example?"

"Easily. In St. Mawr!"—Cartwright gave her a knowing look.

"But," said Mrs. Witt, "it would be difficult, I should say, to open the third eye and see Pan in a man."

"Probably," said Cartwright, smiling. "In man he is over-visible: the old satyr: the fallen Pan."

"Exactly!" said Mrs. Witt. And she fell into a muse. "The fallen Pan!" she re-echoed. "Wouldn't a man be wonderful in whom Pan hadn't fallen!"

Over the coffee in the grey drawing-room she suddenly asked:

"Supposing, Mr. Cartwright, one *did* open the third eye and see Pan in an actual man—I wonder what it would be like?"

She half lowered her eyelids and tilted her face in a strange way, as if she were tasting something, and not quite sure.

"I wonder!" he said, smiling his enigmatic smile. But she could see he did not understand.

"Louise!" said Mrs. Witt at bed-time. "Come into my room for a moment, I want to ask you something."

"What is it, mother?"

"You, you *get* something from what Mr. Cartwright said about seeing Pan with the third eye? Seeing Pan in something?"

Mrs. Witt came rather close and tilted her face with strange insinuating question at her daughter.

"I think I do, mother."

"In what?"—The question came as a pistol-shot.

"I think, mother," said Lou reluctantly, "in St. Mawr."

"In a horse!"—Mrs. Witt contracted her eyes slightly. "Yes, I can see that. I know what you mean. It *is* in St. Mawr. It *is*! But in St. Mawr it makes me *afraid*——" she dragged out the word. Then she came a step closer. "But, Louise, did you ever see it in a man?"

"What, mother?"

"Pan. Did you ever see Pan in a man, as you see Pan in St. Mawr?"

Louise hesitated.

"No, mother, I don't think I did. When I look at men with my third eye, as you call it—I think I see—mostly—a sort of—pancake." She uttered the last word with a despairing grin, not knowing quite what to say.

"Oh, Louise, isn't that it! Doesn't one always see a pancake! Now listen, Louise. Have you ever been in love?"

"Yes, as far as I understand it."

"Listen, now. Did you ever see Pan in the man you loved? Tell me if you did."

"As I see Pan in St. Mawr?—no, mother!" And suddenly her lips began to tremble and the tears came to her eyes.

"Listen, Louise. I've been in love innumerable times—and *really* in love twice. Twice!—yet for fifteen years I've left off wanting to have anything to do with a man, really. For fifteen years! And why? Do you know? Because I couldn't see that peculiar hidden Pan in any of them. And I became that I needed to. I needed it. But it wasn't there. Not in any man. Even when I was in love with a man, it was for other things: because I *understood* him so well, or he understood me, or we had such sympathy. Never the hidden Pan. Do you understand what I mean? Unfallen Pan!"

"More or less, mother."

"But now my third eye is coming open, I believe. I am tired of all these men like breakfast cakes, with a teaspoonful of mind or a teaspoonful of spirit in them, for baking-powder. Isn't it extraordinary: that young man Cartwright talks about Pan, but he knows nothing of it all. He knows nothing of the unfallen Pan: only the fallen Pan with goat legs and a leer—and that sort of power, don't you know."

"But what do you know of the unfallen Pan, mother?"

"Don't ask me, Louise! I feel all of a tremble, as if I was just on the verge."

She flashed a little look of incipient triumph, and said good-night.

An excursion on horseback had been arranged for the next day, to two old groups of rocks, called the Angel's Chair and the Devil's Chair, which crowned the moor-like hills looking into Wales, ten miles away. Everybody was going—they were to start early in the morning, and Lewis would be the guide, since no one exactly knew the way.

Lou got up soon after sunrise. There was a summer scent in the trees of early morning, and monkshood flowers stood up dark and tall, with shadows. She dressed in the green linen riding-skirt her maid had put ready for her, with a close bluish smock.

"Are you going out already, dear?" called Rico from his room.

"Just to smell the roses before we start, Rico."

He appeared in the doorway in his yellow silk pyjamas. His large blue eyes had that rolling, irritable look and the slightly bloodshot whites which made her want to escape.

"Booted and spurred!—the *energy*!" he cried.

"It's a lovely day to ride," she said.

"A lovely day to do anything *except* ride!" he said. "Why spoil the day riding?"—A curious bitter acid escaped into his tone. It was evident he hated the excursion.

"Why, we needn't go if you don't want to, Rico."

"Oh, I'm sure I shall love it, once I get started. It's all this business of *starting*, with horses and paraphernalia——"

Lou went into the yard. The horses were drinking at the trough under the pump, their colours strong and rich in the shadow of the tree.

"You're not coming with us, Phœnix?" she said.

"Lewis, he's riding my horse."

She could tell Phœnix did not like being left behind.

By half-past seven everybody was ready. The sun was in the yard, the horses were saddled. They came swishing their tails. Lewis brought out St. Mawr from his separate box, speaking to him very quietly in Welsh: a murmuring, soothing little speech. Lou, alert, could see that he was uneasy.

"How is St. Mawr this morning?" she asked.

"He's all right. He doesn't like so many people. He'll be all right once he's started."

The strangers were in the saddle: they moved out to the deep shade of the village road outside. Rico came to his horse to mount. St. Mawr jumped away as if he had seen the devil.

"Steady, fool!" cried Rico.

The bay stood with his four feet spread, his neck arched, his big dark eye glancing sideways with that watchful, frightening look.

"You shouldn't be irritable with him, Rico!" said Lou. "Steady then, St. Mawr! Be steady."

But a certain anger rose also in her. The creature was so big, so brilliant, and so stupid, standing there with his hind legs spread, ready to jump aside or to rear terrifically, and his great eye glancing with a sort of suspicious frenzy. What was there to be suspicious of, after all?—Rico would do him no harm.

"No one will harm you, St. Mawr," she reasoned, a bit exasperated.

The groom was talking quietly, murmuringly, in Welsh. Rico was slowly advancing again to put his foot in the stirrup. The stallion was watching from the corner of his eye, a strange glare of suspicious frenzy burning stupidly. Any moment his immense physical force might be let loose in a frenzy of panic —or malice. He was really very irritating.

"Probably he doesn't like that apricot shirt," said Mrs. Witt, "although it tones into him wonderfully well."

She pronounced it *ap*—ricot, and it irritated Rico terribly.

"Ought we to have *asked* him before we put it on?" he flashed, his upper lip lifting venomously.

"I should say you should," replied Mrs. Witt coolly.

Rico turned with a sudden rush to the horse. Back went the great animal, with a sudden splashing crash of hoofs on the cobble-stones, and Lewis hanging on like a shadow. Up went the forefeet, showing the belly.

"The thing is accursed," said Rico, who had dropped the reins in sudden shock, and stood marooned. His rage overwhelmed him like a black flood.

"Nothing in the world is so irritating as a horse that is acting up," thought Lou.

"Say, Harry!" called Flora from the road. "Come out here into the road to mount him."

Lewis looked at Rico and nodded. Then soothing the big, quivering animal, he led him springily out to the road under the trees, where the three friends were waiting. Lou and her mother got quickly into the saddle to follow. And in another moment Rico was mounted and bouncing down the road in the wrong direction, Lewis following on the chestnut. It was some time before Rico could get St. Mawr round. Watching him from behind, those waiting could judge how the young baronet hated it.

But at last they set off—Rico ahead, unevenly but quietly, with the two Manby girls, Lou following with the fair young man who had been in a cavalry regiment and who kept looking round for Mrs. Witt.

"Don't look round for me," she called. "I'm riding behind, out of the dust."

Just behind Mrs. Witt came Lewis. It was a whole cavalcade trotting in the morning sun past the cottages and the cottage gardens, round the field that was the recreation-ground, into the deep hedges of the lane.

"Why is St. Mawr so bad at starting? Can't you get him into better shape?" she asked over her shoulder.

"Beg your pardon, Mam!"

Lewis trotted a little nearer. She glanced over her shoulder at him, at his dark, unmoved face, his cool little figure.

"I think *Mam* is so ugly. Why not leave it out!" she said. Then she repeated her question.

"St. Mawr doesn't trust anybody," Lewis replied.

"Not you?"

"Yes, he trusts me—mostly."

"Then why not other people?"

"They're different."

"All of them?"

"About all of them."

"How are they different?"

He looked at her with his remote, uncanny grey eyes.

"Different," he said, not knowing how else to put it.

They rode on slowly, up the steep rise of the wood, then down into a glade where ran a little railway built for hauling some mysterious mineral out of the hill in war-time, and now already abandoned. Even on this countryside the dead hand of the war lay like a corpse decomposing.

They rode up again, past the foxgloves under the trees. Ahead the brilliant St. Mawr and the sorrel and grey horses were swimming like butterflies through the sea of bracken, glittering from sun to shade, shade to sun. Then once more they were on a crest, and through the thinning trees could see the slopes of the moors beyond the next dip.

Soon they were in the open, rolling hills, golden in the morning and empty save for a couple of distant bilberry-pickers, whitish figures pick—pick—picking with curious, rather disgusting assiduity. The horses were on an old trail which climbed through the pinky tips of heather and ling, across patches of green bilberry. Here and there were tufts of harebells blue as bubbles.

They were out, high on the hills. And there to west lay Wales, folded in crumpled folds, goldish in the morning light, with its moor-like slopes and patches of corn uncannily distinct. Between was a hollow, wide valley of summer haze, showing white farms among trees, and grey slate roofs.

"Ride beside me," she said to Lewis. "Nothing makes me want to go back to America like the old look of these little villages.—You have never been to America?"

"No, Mam."

"Don't you ever want to go?"

"I wouldn't mind going."

"But you're not just crazy to go?"

"No, Mam."

"Quite content as you are?"

He looked at her, and his pale, remote eyes met hers.

"I don't fret myself," he replied.

"Not about anything at all—ever?"

His eyes glanced ahead, at the other riders.

"No, Mam!" he replied, without looking at her.

She rode a few moments in silence.

"What is that over there?" she asked, pointing across the valley. "What is it called?"

"Yon's Montgomery."

"Montgomery! And is that *Wales*——?" she trailed the ending curiously.

"Yes, Mam."

"Where you come from?"

"No, Mam! I come from Merioneth."

"Not from Wales? I thought you were Welsh?"

"Yes, Mam. Merioneth *is* Wales."

"And you are Welsh?"

"Yes, Mam."

"I had a Welsh grandmother. But I come from Louisiana, and when I go back home, the negroes still call me Miss Rachel. 'Oh, my, it's little Miss Rachel come back home! Why, ain't I mighty glad to see you—u, Miss Rachel!' That gives me such a strange feeling, you know."

The man glanced at her curiously, especially when she imitated the negroes.

"Do you feel strange when you go home?" she asked.

"I was brought up by an aunt and uncle," he said. "I never want to see them."

"And you don't have any home?"

"No, Mam."

"No wife nor anything?"

"No, Mam."

"But what do you do with your life?"

"I keep to myself."

"And care about nothing?"

"I mind St. Mawr."

"But you've not always had St. Mawr—and you won't always have him.—Were you in the war?"

"Yes, Mam."

"At the front?"

"Yes, Mam—but I was a groom."

"And you came out all right?"

"I lost my little finger from a bullet."

He held up his small, dark left hand, from which the little finger was missing.

"And did you like the war—or didn't you?"

"I didn't like it."

Again his pale grey eyes met hers, and they looked so non-human and uncommunicative, so without connection, and inaccessible, she was troubled.

"Tell me," she said. "Did you never want a wife and a home and children, like other men?"

"No, Mam. I never wanted a home of my own."

"Nor a wife of your own?"

C

"No, Mam."

"Nor children of your own?"

"No, Mam."

She reined in her horse.

"Now wait a minute," she said. "Now tell me why."

His horse came to standstill, and the two riders faced one another.

"Tell me why—I must know why you never wanted a wife and children and a home. I must know why you're not like other men."

"I never felt like it," he said. "I made my life with horses."

"Did you hate people very much? Did you have a very unhappy time as a child?"

"My aunt and uncle didn't like me, and I didn't like them."

"So you've never liked anybody?"

"Maybe not," he said. "Not to get as far as marrying them."

She touched her horse and moved on.

"Isn't that curious!" she said. "I've loved people, at various times. But I don't believe *I've* ever liked anybody, except a few of our negroes. I don't like Louise, though she's my daughter and I love her. But I don't really *like* her.—I think you're the first person I've ever liked since I was on our plantation, and we had some *very fine* negroes.—And I think that's very curious.—Now I want to know if you like *me*."

She looked at him searchingly, but he did not answer.

"Tell me," she said. "I don't mind if you say no. But tell me if you like me. I feel I must know."

The flicker of a smile went over his face—a very rare thing with him.

"Maybe I do," he said. He was thinking that she put him on a level with a negro slave on a plantation: in his idea, negroes were still slaves. But he did not care where she put him.

"Well, I'm glad—I'm glad if you like me. Because you *don't* like most people, I know that."

They had passed the hollow where the old Aldecar Chapel hid in damp isolation, beside the ruined mill, over the stream that came down from the moors. Climbing the sharp slope, they saw the folded hills like great shut fingers, with steep, deep clefts between. On the near skyline was a bunch of rocks: and away to the right another bunch.

"Yon's the Angel's Chair," said Lewis, pointing to the

nearer rocks. "And yon's the Devil's Chair, where we're going."

"Oh!" said Mrs. Witt. "And aren't we going to the Angel's Chair?"

"No, mam."

"Why not?"

"There's nothing to see there. The other's higher, and bigger, and that's where folks mostly go."

"Is that so!—They give the Devil the higher seat in this country, do they? I think they're right." And as she got no answer, she added: "You believe in the Devil, don't you?"

"I never met him," he answered evasively.

Ahead, they could see the other horses twinkling in a cavalcade up the slope, the black, the bay, the two greys and the sorrel, sometimes bunching, sometimes straggling. At a gate all waited for Mrs. Witt. The fair young man fell in beside her, and talked hunting at her. He had hunted the fox over these hills, and was vigorously excited locating the spot where the hounds first gave cry, etc.

"Really!" said Mrs. Witt. "*Really!* Is that so!"

If irony could have been condensed to prussic acid, the fair young man would have ended his life's history with his reminiscences.

They came at last, trotting in file along a narrow track between heather, along the saddle of a hill, to where the knot of pale granite suddenly cropped out. It was one of those places where the spirit of aboriginal England still lingers, the old savage England, whose last blood flows still in a few Englishmen, Welshmen, Cornishmen. The rocks, whitish with weather of all the ages, jutted against the blue August sky, heavy with age-moulded roundness.

Lewis stayed below with the horses, the party scrambled rather awkwardly, in their riding-boots, up the foot-worn boulders. At length they stood in the place called the Chair, looking west, west towards Wales, that rolled in golden folds upwards. It was neither impressive nor a very picturesque landscape: the hollow valley with farms, and then the rather bare upheaval of hills, slopes with corn and moor and pasture, rising like a barricade, seemingly high, slantingly. Yet it had a strange effect on the imagination.

"Oh, mother," said Lou, "doesn't it make you feel old, old, older than anything ever was?"

"It certainly does seem aged," said Mrs. Witt.

"It makes me want to die," said Lou. "I feel we've lasted almost too long."

"Don't say that, Lady Carrington. Why, you're a spring chicken yet: or shall I say an unopened rose-bud," remarked the fair young man.

"No," said Lou. "All these millions of ancestors have used all the life up. We're not really alive, in the sense that they were alive."

"But who?" said Rico. "Who are *they*?"

"The people who lived on these hills in the days gone by."

"But the same people still live on the hills, darling. It's just the same stock."

"No, Rico. That old fighting stock that worshipped devils among these stones—I'm sure they did——"

"But look here, do you mean they were any better than we are?" asked the fair young man.

Lou looked at him quizzically.

"We don't exist," she said, squinting at him oddly.

"I jolly well know I do," said the fair young man.

"I consider these days are the best ever, especially for girls," said Flora Manby. "And, anyhow, they're our own days, so I don't jolly well see the use of crying them down."

They were all silent, with the last echoes of emphatic *joie de vivre* trumpeting on the air, across the hills of Wales.

"Spoken like a brick, Flora," said Rico. "Say it again, we may not have the Devil's Chair for a pulpit next time."

"I do," reiterated Flora. "I think this is the best age there ever was for a girl to have a good time in. I read all through H. G. Wells's History, and I shut it up and thanked my stars I live in nineteen-twenty odd, not in some other beastly date when a woman had to cringe before mouldy, domineering men."

After this they turned to scramble to another part of the rocks, to the famous Needle's Eye.

"Thank you so much, I am really better without help," said Mrs. Witt to the fair young man, as she slid downwards till a piece of grey silk stocking showed above her tall boot. But she got her toe in a safe place, and in a moment stood beside him, while he caught her arm protectively. He might as well have caught the paw of a mountain lion protectively.

"I should like *so* much to know," she said suavely, looking into his eyes with a demonish straight look, "what makes you so certain that you exist?"

He looked back at her, and his jaunty blue eyes went baffled. Then a slow, hot, salmon-coloured flush stole over his face, and he turned abruptly round.

The Needle's Eye was a hole in the ancient grey rock, like a window, looking to England; England at the moment in shadow. A stream wound and glinted in the flat shadow, and beyond that the flat, insignificant hills heaped in mounds of shade. Cloud was coming—the English side was in shadow. Wales was still in the sun, but the shadow was spreading. The day was going to disappoint them. Lou was a tiny bit chilled already.

Luncheon was still several miles away. The party hastened down to the horses. Lou picked a few sprigs of ling, and some harebells, and some straggling yellow flowers: not because she wanted them, but to distract herself. The atmosphere of 'enjoying ourselves' was becoming cruel to her: it sapped all the life out of her. "Oh, if only I needn't enjoy myself," she moaned inwardly. But the Manby girls were enjoying themselves so much. "I think it's frantically lovely up here," said the other one—not Flora—Elsie.

"It *is* beautiful, isn't it! I'm *so* glad you like it," replied Rico. And he was really relieved and gratified, because the other one said she was enjoying it so frightfully. He dared not say to Lou, as he wanted to: "I'm afraid, Lou, darling, you don't love it as much as we do."—He was afraid of her answer: "No, dear, I don't love it at all! I want to be away from these people."

Slightly piqued, he rode on with the Manby group, and Lou came behind with her mother. Cloud was covering the sky with grey. There was a cold wind. Everybody was anxious to get to the farm for luncheon, and be safely home before rain came.

They were riding along one of the narrow little foot-tracks, mere grooves of grass between heather and bright green bilberry. The blond young man was ahead, then his wife, then Flora, then Rico. Lou, from a little distance, watched the glossy, powerful haunches of St. Mawr swaying with life, always too much life, like a menace. The fair young man was whistling a new dance tune.

"That's an awfully attractive tune," Rico called. "Do whistle it again, Fred, I should like to memorise it."

Fred began to whistle it again.

At that moment St. Mawr exploded again, shied sideways as if a bomb had gone off, and kept backing through the heather.

"Fool!" cried Rico, thoroughly unnerved: he had been terribly sideways in the saddle, Lou had feared he was going to fall. But he got his seat, and pulled the reins viciously, to bring the horse to order, and put him on the track again. St. Mawr began to rear: his favourite trick. Rico got him forward a few yards, when up he went again.

"Fool!" yelled Rico, hanging in the air.

He pulled the horse over backwards on top of him.

Lou gave a loud, unnatural, horrible scream: she heard it herself, at the same time as she heard the crash of the falling horse. Then she saw a pale gold belly, and hoofs that worked and flashed in the air, and St. Mawr writhing, straining his head terrifically upwards, his great eyes starting from the naked lines of his nose. With a great neck arching cruelly from the ground, he was pulling frantically at the reins, which Rico still held tight.—Yes, Rico, lying strangely sideways, his eyes also starting from his yellow-white face, among the heather, still clutched the reins.

Young Edwards was rushing forward, and circling round the writhing, immense horse, whose pale-gold, inverted bulk seemed to fill the universe.

"Let him get up, Carrington! Let him get up!" he was yelling, darting warily near to get the reins.—Another spasmodic convulsion of the horse.

Horror! The young man reeled backwards with his face in his hands. He had got a kick in the face. Red blood running down his chin!

Lewis was there, on the ground, getting the reins out of Rico's hands. St. Mawr gave a great curve like a fish, spread his forefeet on the earth and reared his head, looking round in a ghastly fashion. His eyes were arched, his nostrils wide, his face ghastly in a sort of panic. He rested thus, seated with his forefeet planted and his face in panic, almost like some terrible lizard, for several moments. Then he heaved sickeningly to his feet, and stood convulsed, trembling.

There lay Rico, crumpled and rather sideways, staring at

the heavens from a yellow, dead-looking face. Lewis, glancing round in a sort of horror, looked in dread at St. Mawr again. Flora had been hovering.—She now rushed screeching to the prostrate Rico:

"Harry! Harry! you're not dead! Oh, Harry! Harry! Harry!"

Lou had dismounted.—She didn't know when. She stood a little way off, as if spellbound, while Flora cried: *Harry! Harry! Harry!*

Suddenly Rico sat up.

"Where is the horse?" he said.

At the same time an added whiteness came on his face, and he bit his lip with pain, and he fell prostrate again in a faint. Flora rushed to put her arm round him.

Where was the horse? He had backed slowly away, in an agony of suspicion, while Lewis murmured to him in vain. His head was raised again, the eyes still starting from their sockets, and a terrible guilty, ghost-like look on his face. When Lewis drew a little nearer he twitched and shrank like a shaken steel spring, away—not to be touched. He seemed to be seeing legions of ghosts, down the dark avenues of all the centuries that have lapsed since the horse became subject to man.

And the other young man? He was still standing, at a little distance, with his face in his hands, motionless, the blood falling on his white shirt, and his wife at his side, pleading, distracted.

Mrs. Witt, too, was there, as if cast in steel, watching. She made no sound and did not move, only from a fixed, impassive face, watched each thing.

"Do tell me what you think is the matter," Lou pleaded, distracted, to Flora, who was supporting Rico and weeping torrents of unknown tears.

Then Mrs. Witt came forward and began in a very practical manner to unclose the shirt-neck and feel the young man's heart. Rico opened his eyes again, said *"Really!"* and closed his eyes once more.

"It's fainting!" said Mrs. Witt. "We have no brandy."

Lou, too weary to be able to feel anything, said:

"I'll go and get some."

She went to her alarmed horse, who stood among the others with her head down, in suspense. Almost unconsciously

Lou mounted, set her face ahead, and was riding away.

Then Poppy shied too, with a sudden start, and Lou pulled up. "Why?" she said to her horse. "Why did you do that?"

She looked round, and saw in the heather a glimpse of yellow and black.

"A snake!" she said wonderingly.

And she looked closer.

It was a dead adder that had been drinking at a reedy pool in a little depression just off the road, and had been killed with stones. There it lay, also crumpled, its head crushed, its gold-and-yellow back still glittering dully, and a bit of pale-blue showing, killed that morning.

Lou rode on, her face set towards the farm. An unspeakable weariness had overcome her. She could not even suffer. Weariness of spirit left her in a sort of apathy.

And she had a vision, a vision of evil. Or not strictly a vision. She became aware of evil, evil, evil, rolling in great waves over the earth. Always she had thought there was no such thing—only a mere negation of good. Now, like an ocean to whose surface she had risen, she saw the dark-grey waves of evil rearing in a great tide.

And it had swept mankind away without mankind's knowing. It had caught up the nations as the rising ocean might lift the fishes, and was sweeping them on in a great tide of evil. They did not know. The people did not know. They did not even wish it. They wanted to be good and to have everything joyful and enjoyable. Everything joyful and enjoyable: for everybody. This was what they wanted, if you asked them.

But at the same time, they had fallen under the spell of evil. It was a soft, subtle thing, soft as water, and its motion was soft and imperceptible, as the running of a tide is invisible to one who is out on the ocean. And they were all out on the ocean, being borne along in the current of the mysterious evil, creatures of the evil principle, as fishes are creatures of the sea.

There was no relief. The whole world was enveloped in one great flood. All the nations, the white, the brown, the black, the yellow, all were immersed in the strange tide of evil that was subtly, irresistibly rising. No one, perhaps, deliberately wished it. Nearly every individual wanted peace and a good time all round: everybody to have a good time.

But some strange thing had happened, and the vast mysterious force of positive evil was let loose. She felt that from the core of Asia the evil welled up, as from some strange pole, and slowly was drowning earth.

It was something horrifying, something you could not escape from. It had come to her as in a vision, when she saw the pale gold belly of the stallion upturned, the hoofs working wildly, the wicked curved hams of the horse, and then the evil straining of that arched, fish-like neck, with the dilated eyes of the head. Thrown backwards, and working its hoofs in the air. Reversed, and purely evil.

She saw the same in people. They were thrown backwards, and writhing with evil. And the rider, crushed, was still reining them down.

What did it mean? Evil, evil, and a rapid return to the sordid chaos. Which was wrong, the horse or the rider? Or both?

She thought with horror of St. Mawr, and of the look on his face. But she thought with horror, a colder horror, of Rico's face as he snarled *Fool!* His fear, his impotence as a master, as a rider, his presumption. And she thought with horror of those other people, so glib, so glibly evil.

What did they want to do, those Manby girls? Undermine, undermine, undermine. They wanted to undermine Rico, just as that fair young man would have liked to undermine her. Believe in nothing, care about nothing: but keep the surface easy, and have a good time. *Let us undermine one another. There is nothing to believe in, so let us undermine everything. But look out! No scenes, no spoiling the game. Stick to the rules of the game. Be sporting, and don't do anything that would make a commotion. Keep the game going smooth and jolly, and bear your bit like a sport. Never, by any chance, injure your fellow-man openly. But always injure him secretly. Make a fool of him, and undermine his nature. Break him up by undermining him, if you can. It's good sport.*

The evil! The mysterious potency of evil. She could see it all the time, in individuals, in society, in the press. There it was in socialism and bolshevism: the same evil. But bolshevism made a mess of the outside of life, so turn it down. Try fascism. Fascism would keep the surface of life intact, and carry on the undermining business all the better. All the better sport. Never draw blood. Keep the hæmorrhage internal, invisible.

And as soon as fascism makes a break—which it is bound to, because all evil works up to a break—then turn it down. With gusto, turn it down.

Mankind, like a horse, ridden by a stranger, smooth-faced, evil rider. Evil himself, smooth-faced and pseudo-handsome, riding mankind past the dead snake, to the last break.

Mankind no longer its own master. Ridden by this pseudo-handsome ghoul of outward loyalty, inward treachery, in a game of betrayal, betrayal, betrayal. The last of the gods of our era, Judas supreme!

People performing outward acts of loyalty, piety, self-sacrifice. But inwardly bent on undermining, betraying. Directing all their subtle evil will against any positive living thing. Masquerading as the ideal, in order to poison the real.

Creation destroys as it goes, throws down one tree for the rise of another. But ideal mankind would abolish death, multiply itself million upon million, rear up city upon city, save every parasite alive, until the accumulation of mere existence is swollen to a horror. But go on saving life, the ghastly salvation army of ideal mankind. At the same time secretly, viciously, potently undermine the natural creation, betray it with kiss after kiss, destroy it from the inside, till you have the swollen rottenness of our teeming existences.— But keep the game going. Nobody's going to make another bad break, such as Germany and Russia made.

Two bad breaks the secret evil has made: in Germany and in Russia. Watch it! Let evil keep a policeman's eye on evil! The surface of life must remain unruptured. Production must be heaped upon production. And the natural creation must be betrayed by many more kisses, yet. Judas is the last God, and, by heaven, the most potent.

But even Judas made a break: hanged himself, and his bowels gushed out. Not long after his triumph.

Man must destroy as he goes, as trees fall for trees to rise. The accumulation of life and things means rottenness. Life must destroy life, in the unfolding of creation. We save up life at the expense of the unfolding, till all is full of rotten-ness. Then at last we make a break.

What's to be done? Generally speaking, nothing. The dead

will have to bury their dead, while the earth stinks of corpses. The individual can but depart from the mass, and try to cleanse himself. Try to hold fast to the living thing, which destroys as it goes, but remains sweet. And in his soul fight, fight, fight to preserve that which is life in him from the ghastly kisses and poison-bites of the myriad evil ones. Retreat to the desert, and fight. But in his soul adhere to that which is life itself, creatively destroying as it goes: destroying the stiff old thing to let the new bud come through. The one passionate principle of creative being, which recognises the natural good, and has a sword for the swarms of evil. Fights, fights, fights to protect itself. But with itself, is strong and at peace.

Lou came to the farm, and got brandy, and asked the men to come out to carry in the injured.

It turned out that the kick in the face had knocked a couple of young Edwards's teeth out, and would disfigure him a little. "To go through the war, and then get this!" he mumbled, with a vindictive glance at St. Mawr.

And it turned out that Rico had two broken ribs and a crushed ankle. Poor Rico, he would limp for life.

"I want St. Mawr *shot!*" was almost his first word when he was in bed at the farm and Lou was sitting beside him.

"What good would that do, dear?" she said.

"The brute is evil. I want him *shot!*"

Rico could make the last word sound like the spitting of a bullet.

"Do you want to shoot him yourself?"

"No. But I want to have him shot. I shall never be easy till I know he has a bullet through him. He's got a wicked character. I don't feel you are safe with him down there. I shall get one of the Manbys' gamekeepers to shoot him. You might tell Flora—or I'll tell her myself, when she comes."

"Don't talk about it now, dear. You've got a temperature."

Was it true St. Mawr was evil? She would never forget him writhing and lunging on the ground, nor his awful face when he reared up. But then that noble look of his: surely he was not mean? Whereas all evil had an inner meanness, mean! Was he mean? Was he meanly treacherous? Did he know he could kill, and meanly wait his opportunity?

She was afraid. And if this were true, then he *should* be shot. Perhaps he ought to be shot.

This thought haunted her. Was there something mean and treacherous in St. Mawr's spirit, the vulgar evil? If so, then have him shot. At moments, an anger would rise in her, as she thought of his frenzied rearing, and his mad, hideous writhing on the ground, and in the heat of her anger she would want to hurry down to her mother's house and have the creature shot at once. It would be a satisfaction, and a vindication of human rights. Because after all, Rico was so considerate of the brutal horse. But not a spark of consideration did the stallion have for Rico. No, it was the slavish malevolence of a domesticated creature that kept cropping up in St. Mawr. The slave, taking his slavish vengeance, then dropping back into subservience.

All the slaves of this world, accumulating their preparations for slavish vengeance, and then, when they have taken it, ready to drop back into servility. Freedom! Most slaves can't be freed, no matter how you let them loose. Like domestic animals, they are, in the long run, more afraid of freedom than of masters: and freed by some generous master, they will at last crawl back to some mean boss, who will have no scruples about kicking them. Because, for them, far better kicks and servility than the hard, lonely responsibility of real freedom.

The wild animal is at every moment intensely self-disciplined, poised in the tension of self-defence, self-preservation and self-assertion. The moments of relaxation are rare and most carefully chosen. Even sleep is watchful, guarded, unrelaxing, the wild courage pitched one degree higher than the wild fear. Courage, the wild thing's courage to maintain itself alone and living in the midst of a diverse universe.

Did St. Mawr have this courage?

And did Rico?

Ah, Rico! He was one of mankind's myriad conspirators, who conspire to live in absolute physical safety, whilst willing the minor disintegration of all positive living.

But St. Mawr? Was it the natural wild thing in him which caused these disasters? Or was it the slave, asserting himself for vengeance?

If the latter, let him be shot. It would be a great satisfaction to see him dead.

But if the former——

When she could leave Rico with the nurse, she motored

down to her mother for a couple of days. Rico lay in bed at the farm.

Everything seemed curiously changed. There was a new silence about the place, a new coolness. Summer had passed with several thunderstorms, and the blue, cool touch of autumn was about the house. Dahlias and perennial yellow sunflowers were out, the yellow of ending summer, the red coals of early autumn. First mauve tips of Michaelmas daisies were showing. Something suddenly carried her away to the great bare spaces of Texas, the blue sky, the flat, burnt earth, the miles of sunflowers. Another sky, another silence, towards the setting sun.

And suddenly she craved again for the more absolute silence of America. English stillness was so soft, like an inaudible murmur of voices, of presences. But the silence in the empty spaces of America was still unutterable, almost cruel.

St. Mawr was in a small field by himself: she could not bear that he should be always in stable. Slowly she went through the gate towards him. And he stood there looking at her, the bright bay creature.

She could tell he was feeling somewhat subdued, after his late escapade. He was aware of the general human condemnation: the human damning. But something obstinate and uncanny in him made him not relent.

"Hello! St. Mawr!" she said, as she drew near, and he stood watching her, his ears pricked, his big eyes glancing sideways at her.

But he moved away when she wanted to touch him.

"Don't trouble," she said. "I don't want to catch you or do anything to you."

He stood still, listening to the sound of her voice, and giving quick, small glances at her. His underlip trembled. But he did not blink. His eyes remained wide and unrelenting. There was a curious malicious obstinacy in him which roused her anger.

"I don't want to touch you," she said. "I only want to look at you, and even you can't prevent that."

She stood gazing hard at him, wanting to know, to settle the question of his meanness or his spirit. A thing with a brave spirit is not mean.

He was uneasy as she watched him. He pretended to hear something, the mares two fields away, and he lifted his head

and neighed. She knew the powerful, splendid sound so well:
like bells made of living membrane. And he looked so noble
again, with his head tilted up, listening, and his male eyes
looking proudly over the distance, eagerly.

But it was all a bluff.

He knew, and became silent again. And as he stood there a
few yards away from her, his head lifted and wary, his body
full of power and tension, his face slightly averted from her,
she felt a great animal sadness come from him. A strange
animal atmosphere of sadness, that was vague and dis-
seminated through the air, and made her feel as though she
breathed grief. She breathed it into her breast, as if it were a
great sigh down the ages, that passed into her breast. And she
felt a great woe: the woe of human unworthiness. The race
of men judged in the consciousness of the animals they have
subdued, and there found unworthy, ignoble.

Ignoble men, unworthy of the animals they have sub-
jugated, bred the woe in the spirit of their creatures. St. Mawr,
that bright horse, one of the kings of creation in the order
below man, it had been a fulfilment for him to serve the
brave, reckless, perhaps cruel men of the past, who had a
flickering, rising flame of nobility in them. To serve that
flame of mysterious further nobility. Nothing matters, but
that strange flame, of inborn nobility that obliges men to be
brave, and onward plunging. And the horse will bear him on.

But now where is the flame of dangerous, forward-pressing
nobility in men? Dead, dead, guttering out in a stink of
self-sacrifice whose feeble light is a light of exhaustion and
laissez-faire.

And the horse, is he to go on carrying man forward into
this?—this gutter?

No! Man wisely invents motor-cars and other machines,
automobile and locomotive. The horse is superannuated for
man.

But alas, man is even more superannuated for the horse.

Dimly in a woman's muse, Lou realised this, as she breathed
the horse's sadness, his accumulated vague woe from the
generations of latter-day ignobility. And a grief and a sympathy flooded her, for the horse. She realised now how his sadness recoiled into these frenzies of obstinacy and malevolence.
Underneath it all was grief, an unconscious, vague, pervading
animal grief, which perhaps only Lewis understood, because

he felt the same. The grief of the generous creature which sees all ends turning to the morass of ignoble living.

She did not want to say any more to the horse: she did not want to look at him any more. The grief flooded her soul, that made her want to be alone. She knew now what it all amounted to. She knew that the horse, born to serve nobly, had waited in vain for someone noble to serve. His spirit knew that nobility had gone out of men. And this left him high and dry, in a sort of despair.

As she walked away from him, towards the gate, slowly he began to walk after her.

Phœnix came striding through the gate towards her.

"You not afraid of that horse?" he asked sardonically, in his quiet, subtle voice.

"Not at the present moment," she replied, even more quietly, looking direct at him. She was not in any mood to be jeered at.

And instantly the sardonic grimace left his face, followed by the sudden blankness, and the look of race misery in the keen eyes.

"Do you want me to be afraid?" she said, continuing to the gate.

"No, I don't want it," he replied, dejected.

"Are you afraid of him yourself?" she said, glancing round. St. Mawr had stopped, seeing Phœnix, and had turned away again.

"I'm not afraid of no horses," said Phœnix.

Lou went on quietly. At the gate, she asked him:

"Don't you like St. Mawr, Phœnix?"

"I like him. He's a very good horse."

"Even after what he's done to Sir Henry?"

"That don't make no difference to him being a good horse."

"But suppose he'd done it to you?"

"I don't care. I say it my own fault."

"Don't you think he is wicked?"

"I don't think so. He don't kick anybody. He don't bite anybody. He don't pitch, he don't buck, he don't do nothing."

"He rears," said Lou.

"Well, what is rearing?" said the man, with a slow, contemptuous smile.

"A good deal, when a horse falls back on you."

"That horse don't want to fall back on you, if you don't

make him. If you know how to ride him. That horse wants
his own way some time. If you don't let him, you got to fight
him. Then look out!"

"Look out he doesn't kill you, you mean!"

"Look out you don't let him," said Phœnix, with his slow,
grim, sardonic smile.

Lou watched the smooth, golden face with its thin line of
moustache and its sad eyes with the glint in them. Cruel—
there was something cruel in him, right down in the abyss of
him. But at the same time, there was an aloneness, and a grim
little satisfaction in a fight, and the peculiar courage of an
inherited despair. People who inherit despair may at last turn
it into greater heroism. It was almost so with Phœnix. Three-
quarters of his blood was probably Indian and the remaining
quarter, that came through the Mexican father, had the
Spanish–American despair to add to the Indian. It was almost
complete enough to leave him free to be heroic.

"What are we going to do with him, though?" she asked.

"Why don't you and Mrs. Witt go back to America—you
never been West. You go West."

"Where, to California?"

"No. To Arizona or New Mexico or Colorado or Wyoming,
anywhere. Not to California."

Phœnix looked at her keenly, and she saw the desire dark
in him. He wanted to go back. But he was afraid to go back
alone, empty-handed, as it were. He had suffered too much,
and in that country his sufferings would overcome him, unless
he had some other background. He had been too much in
contact with the white world, and his own world was too
dejected, in a sense, too hopeless for his own hopelessness.
He needed an alien contact to give him relief.

But he wanted to go back. His necessity to go back was
becoming too strong for him.

"What is it like in Arizona?" she asked. "Isn't it all pale-
coloured sand and alkali, and a few cactuses, and terribly
hot and deathly?"

"No!" he cried. "I don't take you there. I take you to the
mountains—trees——" he lifted up his hand and looked at
the sky—"big trees—pine! *Pino-real* and *pinovetes*, smell
good. And then you come down, *piñon*, not very tall, and
cedro, cedar, smell good in the fire. And then you see the
desert, away below, go miles and miles, and where the

canyon go, the crack where it look red! I know, I been there, working a cattle ranch."

He looked at her with a haunted glow in his dark eyes. The poor fellow was suffering from nostalgia. And as he glowed at her in that queer, mystical way, she too seemed to see that country, with its dark, heavy mountains holding in their lap the great stretches of pale, creased, silent desert that still is virgin of idea, its word unspoken.

Phœnix was watching her closely and subtly. He wanted something of her. He wanted it intensely, heavily, and he watched her as if he could force her to give it him. He wanted her to take him back to America, because, rudderless, he was afraid to go back alone. He wanted her to take him back: avidly he wanted it. She was to be the means to his end.

Why shouldn't he go back by himself? Why should he crave for her to go too? Why should he want her there?

There was no answer, except that he did.

"Why, Phœnix," she said, "I might possibly go back to America. But you know, Sir Henry would never go there. He doesn't like America, though he's never been. But I'm sure he'd never go there to live."

"Let him stay here," said Phœnix abruptly, the sardonic look on his face as he watched her face. "You come, and let him stay here."

"Ah, that's a whole story!" she said, and moved away.

As she went, he looked after her, standing silent and arrested and watching as an Indian watches. It was not love. Personal love counts so little when the greater griefs, the greater hopes, the great despairs and the great resolutions come upon us.

She found Mrs. Witt rather more silent, more firmly closed within herself, than usual. Her mouth was shut tight, her brows were arched rather more imperiously than ever, she was revolving some inward problem about which Lou was far too wise to inquire.

In the afternoon Dean Vyner and Mrs. Vyner came to call on Lady Carrington.

"What bad luck this is, Lady Carrington!" said the Dean. "Knocks Scotland on the head for you this year, I'm afraid. How did you leave your husband?"

"He seems to be doing as well as he could do!" said Lou.

"But how *very* unfortunate!" murmured the invalid Mrs.

Vyner. "Such a handsome young man, in the bloom of youth!
Does he suffer much pain?"

"Chiefly his foot," said Lou.

"Oh, I *do* so hope they'll be able to restore the ankle. Oh,
how dreadful, to be lamed at his age!"

"The doctor doesn't know. There *may* be a limp," said Lou.

"That horse has certainly left his mark on two good-looking
young fellows," said the Dean. "If you don't mind my saying
so, Lady Carrington, I think he's a bad egg."

"Who, St. Mawr?" said Lou, in her American sing-song.

"Yes, Lady Carrington," murmured Mrs. Vyner, in her
invalid's low tone. "Don't you think he ought to be put
away? He seems to me the incarnation of cruelty. His neigh.
It goes through me like knives. Cruel! Cruel! Oh, I think
he should be put away."

"How put away?" murmured Lou, taking on an invalid's
low tone herself.

"Shot, I suppose," said the Dean.

"It is quite painless. He'll know nothing," murmured Mrs.
Vyner hastily. "And think of the harm he has done already!
Horrible! Horrible!" she shuddered. "Poor Sir Henry lame
for life, and Freddy Edwards disfigured. Besides all that has
gone before. Ah, no, such a creature ought not to live!"

"To live, and have a groom to look after him and feed him,"
said the Dean. "It's a bit thick, while he's smashing up the
very people that give him bread—or oats, since he's a horse.
But I suppose you'll be wanting to get rid of him?"

"Rico does," murmured Lou.

"Very naturally. So should I. A vicious horse is worse than
a vicious man—except that you are free to put him six feet
underground, and end his vice finally, by your own act."

"Do you think St. Mawr is vicious?" said Lou.

"Well, of course—if we're driven to definitions!—I *know*
he's dangerous."

"And do you think we ought to shoot everything that is
dangerous?" asked Lou, her colour rising.

"But, Lady Carrington, have you consulted your husband?
Surely his wish should be law, in a matter of this sort? And
on such an occasion! For *you*, who are a woman, it is enough
that the horse is cruel, cruel, evil! I felt it long before anything happened. That evil male cruelty! Ah!" and she clasped
her hands convulsively.

"I suppose," said Lou slowly, "that St. Mawr is really Rico's horse: I gave him to him, I suppose. But I don't believe I could let him shoot him, for all that."

"Ah, Lady Carrington," said the Dean breezily, "you can shift the responsibility. The horse is a public menace, put it at that. We can get an order to have him done away with, at the public expense. And among ourselves we can find some suitable compensation for you, as a mark of sympathy. Which, believe me, is very sincere! One hates to have to destroy a fine-looking animal. But I would sacrifice a dozen rather than have our Rico limping."

"Yes, indeed," murmured Mrs. Vyner.

"Will you excuse me one moment, while I see about tea," said Lou, rising and leaving the room. Her colour was high, and there was a glint in her eyes. These people almost roused her to hatred. Oh, these awful, house-bred, house-inbred human beings, how repulsive they were!

She hurried to her mother's dressing-room. Mrs. Witt was very carefully putting a touch of red on her lips.

"Mother, they want to shoot St. Mawr," she said.

"I know," said Mrs. Witt, as calmly as if Lou had said tea was ready.

"Well——" stammered Lou, rather put out. "Don't you think it cheek?"

"It depends, I suppose, on the point of view," said Mrs. Witt dispassionately, looking closely at her lips. "I don't think the English climate agrees with me. I need something to stand up against, no matter whether it's great heat or great cold. This climate, like the food and the people, is most always luke-warm or tepid, one or the other. And the tepid and the lukewarm are not really my line." She spoke with a slow drawl.

"But they're in the drawing-room, mother, trying to force me to have St. Mawr killed."

"What about tea?" said Mrs. Witt.

"I don't care," said Lou.

Mrs. Witt worked the bell-handle.

"I suppose, Louise," she said, in her most beaming eighteenth-century manner, "that these are your guests, so you will preside over the ceremony of pouring out."

"No, mother, you do it. I can't smile to-day."

"I can," said Mrs. Witt.

And she bowed her head slowly, with a faint, cere-
moniously-effusive smile, as if handing a cup of tea.

Lou's face flickered to a smile.

"Then you pour out for them. You can stand them better
than I can."

"Yes," said Mrs. Witt. "I saw Mrs. Vyner's hat coming
across the churchyard. It looks so like a crumpled cup and
saucer, that I have been saying to myself ever since: 'Dear
Mrs. Vyner, can't I fill your cup!'—and then pouring tea into
that hat. And I hear the Dean responding: 'My head is covered
with cream, my cup runneth over.'—That is the way they
make *me* feel."

They marched downstairs, and Mrs. Witt poured tea with
that devastating correctness which made Mrs. Vyner, who was
utterly impervious to sarcasm, pronounce her 'indecipherably
vulgar'.

But the Dean was the old bull-dog, and he had set his teeth
in a subject.

"I was talking to Lady Carrington about that stallion, Mrs.
Witt."

"Did you say stallion?" asked Mrs. Witt, with perfect
neutrality.

"Why, yes, I presume that's what he is."

"I presume so," said Mrs. Witt colourlessly.

"I'm afraid Lady Carrington is a little sensitive on the wrong
score," said the Dean.

"I beg your pardon," said Mrs. Witt, leaning forward in
her most colourless polite manner. "You mean the stallion's
score?"

"Yes," said the Dean testily. "The horse St. Mawr."

"The stallion St. Mawr," echoed Mrs. Witt, with utmost
mild vagueness. She completely ignored Mrs. Vyner, who felt
plunged like a specimen into methylated spirit. There was a
moment's full-stop.

"Yes?" said Mrs. Witt naïvely.

"You agree that we can't have any more of these accidents
to your young men?" said the Dean rather hastily.

"I certainly do!" Mrs. Witt spoke very slowly, and the
Dean's lady began to look up. She might find a loop-hole
through which to wriggle into the contest. "You know,
Dean, that my son-in-law calls me, for preference, *belle-mère!*
It sounds so awfully English when he says it: I always see

myself as an old grey mare with a bell round her neck, leading
a bunch of horses." She smiled a prim little smile, very con-
versationally. "Well!" and she pulled herself up from the
aside. "Now as the bell-mare of the bunch of horses, I shall
see to it that my son-in-law doesn't go too near that stallion
again. That stallion won't stand mischief."

She spoke so earnestly that the Dean looked at her with
round, wide eyes, completely taken aback.

"We all know, Mrs. Witt, that the author of the mischief is
St. Mawr himself," he said, in a loud tone.

"Really! you think *that*?" Her voice went up in American
surprise. "Why, how *strange*——!" and she lingered over the
last word.

"Strange, eh?—After what's just happened?" said the Dean,
with a deadly little smile.

"Why, yes! Most strange! I saw with my own eyes my
son-in-law pull that stallion over backwards, and hold him
down with the reins as tight as he could hold them; pull St.
Mawr's head backwards on to the ground, till the groom
had to crawl up and force the reins out of my son-in-law's
hands. Don't you think that was mischievous on Sir Henry's
part?"

The Dean was growing purple. He made an apoplectic
movement with his hand. Mrs. Vyner was turned to a seated
pillar of salt, strangely dressed up.

"Mrs. Witt, you are playing on words."

"No, Dean Vyner, I am not. My son-in-law pulled that horse
over backwards and pinned him down with the reins."

"I am sorry for the horse," said the Dean, with heavy
sarcasm.

"I am *very*," said Mrs. Witt, "sorry for that stallion: *very!*"

Here Mrs. Vyner rose as if a chair-spring had suddenly pro-
pelled her to her feet. She was streaky pink in the face.

"Mrs. Witt," she panted, "you misdirect your sympathies.
That poor young man—in the beauty of youth."

"Isn't he *beautiful*——" murmured Mrs. Witt, extravagantly
in sympathy. "He's my daughter's husband!" And she looked
at the petrified Lou.

"Certainly!" panted the Dean's wife. "And you can defend
that—that——"

"That stallion," said Mrs. Witt. "But you see, Mrs. Vyner,"
she added, leaning forward female and confidential, "if the old

grey mare doesn't defend the stallion, who will? All the
blooming young ladies will defend my beautiful son-in-law.
You feel so *warmly* for him yourself! I'm an American
woman, and I always have to stand up for the accused. And
I stand up for that stallion. I say it is not right. He was pulled
over backwards and then pinned down by my son-in-law—
who may have meant to do it, or may not. And now people
abuse him.—Just tell everybody, Mrs. Vyner and Dean Vyner"
—she looked round at the Dean—"that the *belle-mère's* sympathies are with the stallion."

She looked from one to the other with a faint and gracious
little bow, her black eyebrows arching in her eighteenth-
century face like black rainbows, and her full, bold, grey eyes
absolutely incomprehensible.

"Well, it's a peculiar message to have to hand round, Mrs.
Witt," the Dean began to boom, when she interrupted him by
laying her hand on his arm and leaning forward, looking up
into his face like a clinging, pleading female:

"Oh, but *do* hand it, Dean, *do* hand it," she pleaded, gazing
intently into his face.

He backed uncomfortably from that gaze.

"Since you wish it," he said, in a chest voice.

"I most certainly *do*——" she said, as if she were wishing
the sweetest wish on earth. Then turning to Mrs. Vyner:

"Good-bye, Mrs. Vyner. We *do* appreciate your coming, my
daughter and I."

"I came out of kindness——" said Mrs. Vyner.

"Oh, I know it, I know it," said Mrs. Witt. "Thank you *so*
much. Good-bye! Good-bye, Dean! Who is taking the morning service on Sunday? I hope it is you, because I want to
come."

"It *is* me," said the Dean. "Good-bye! Well, good-bye,
Lady Carrington. I shall be going over to see our young
man to-morrow, and will gladly take you or anything you
have to send."

"Perhaps mother would like to go," said Lou softly,
plaintively.

"Well, we shall see," said the Dean. "Good-bye for the
present!"

Mother and daughter stood at the window watching the two
cross the churchyard. Dean and wife knew it, but daren't look
round, and daren't admit the fact to one another.

Lou was grinning with a complete grin that gave her an odd, dryad or faun look, intensified.

"It was almost as good as pouring tea into her hat," said Mrs. Witt serenely. "People like that tire me out. I shall take a glass of sherry."

"So will I, mother.—It was even better than pouring tea in her hat.—You meant, didn't you, if you poured tea in her hat, to put cream and sugar in first?"

"I did," said Mrs. Witt.

But after the excitement of the encounter had passed away, Lou felt as if her life had passed away too. She went to bed, feeling she could stand no more.

In the morning she found her mother sitting at a window watching a funeral. It was raining heavily, so that some of the mourners even wore mackintosh coats. The funeral was in the poorer corner of the churchyard, where another new grave was covered with wreaths of sodden, shrivelling flowers. The yellowish coffin stood on wet earth in the rain: the curate held his hat, in a sort of permanent salute, above his head, like a little umbrella, as he hastened on with the service. The people seemed too wet to weep more wet.

It was a long coffin.

"Mother, do you really *like* watching?" asked Lou irritably, as Mrs. Witt sat in complete absorption.

"I do, Louise, I really enjoy it."

"Enjoy, mother!"—Lou was almost disgusted.

"I'll tell you why. I imagine I'm the one in the coffin—this is a girl of eighteen, who died of consumption—and those are my relatives, and I'm watching them put me away. And, you know, Louise, I've come to the conclusion that hardly anybody in the world really lives, and so hardly anybody really dies. They may well say: 'Oh, Death, where is thy sting-a-ling-a-ling?' Even Death can't sting those that have never really lived.—I always used to want that—to die without death stinging me.—And I'm sure the girl in the coffin is saying to herself: 'Fancy Aunt Emma putting on a drab slicker, and wearing it while they bury me. Doesn't show much respect. But then my mother's family always were common!' I feel there should be a solemn burial of a roll of newspapers containing the account of the death and funeral next week. It would be just as serious: the grave of all the world's remarks——"

"I don't want to think about it, mother. One ought to be able to laugh at it. I want to laugh at it."

"Well, Louise, I think it's just as great a mistake to laugh at everything as to cry at everything. Laughter's not the one panacea, either. I should *really* like, before I do come to be buried in a box, to know where I am. That young girl in that coffin never was anywhere—any more than the newspaper remarks on her death and burial. And I begin to wonder if I've ever been anywhere. I seem to have been a daily sequence of newspaper remarks myself. I'm sure I never really conceived you and gave you birth. It all happened in newspaper notices. It's a newspaper fact that you are my child, and that's about all there is to it."

Lou smiled as she listened.

"I always knew you were philosophic, mother. But I never dreamed it would come to elegies in a country churchyard, written to your motherhood."

"Exactly, Louise! Here I sit and sing the elegy to my own motherhood. I never had any motherhood, except in newspaper fact. I never was a wife, except in newspaper notices. I never was a young girl, except in newspaper remarks. Bury everything I ever said or that was said about me, and you've buried *me*. But since Kind Words Can Never Die, I can't be buried, and death has no sting-a-ling-a-ling for *me!*—Now listen to me, Louise: I want death to be real to me—not as it was to that young girl. I *want* it to hurt me, Louise. If it hurts me enough, I shall know I was alive."

She set her face and gazed under half-dropped lids at the funeral, stoic, fate-like, and yet, for the first time, with a certain pure wistfulness of a young, virgin girl. This frightened Lou very much. She was so used to the matchless Amazon in her mother, that when she saw her sit there, still, wistful, virginal, tender as a girl who has never taken armour, wistful at the window that only looked on graves, a serious terror took hold of the young woman. The terror of *too late!*

Lou felt years, centuries older than her mother at that moment, with the tiresome responsibility of youth to protect and guide their elders.

"What can we do about it, mother?" she asked protectively.

"Do nothing, Louise. I'm not going to have anybody wisely steering my canoe, now I feel the rapids are near. I shall go with the river. Don't you pretend to do anything for me. I've done enough mischief myself, that way. I'm going down the stream at last."

There was a pause.

"But in actuality, what?" asked Lou, a little ironically.

"I don't quite know. Wait a while."

"Go back to America?"

"That is possible."

"I may come too."

"I've always waited for you to go back of your own will."

Lou went away, wandering round the house. She was so un-utterably tired of everything—weary of the house, the grave-yard, weary of the thought of Rico. She would have to go back to him to-morrow, to nurse him. Poor old Rico, going on like an amiable machine from day to day. It wasn't his fault. But his life was a rattling nullity, and her life rattled in null correspondence. She had hardly strength enough to stop rattling and be still. Perhaps she had not strength enough.

She did not know. She felt so weak that unless something carried her away she would go on rattling her bit in the great machine of human life till she collapsed and her rattle rattled itself out, and there was a sort of barren silence where the sound of her had been.

She wandered out in the rain to the coach-house, where Lewis and Phœnix were sitting facing one another, one on a bin, the other on the inner doorstep.

"Well," she said, smiling oddly. "What's to be done?"

The two men stood up. Outside the rain fell steadily on the flagstones of the yard, past the leaves of trees. Lou sat down on the little iron step of the dog-cart.

"That's cold," said Phœnix. "You sit here." And he threw a yellow horse-blanket on the box where he had been sitting.

"I don't want to take your seat," she said.

"All right, you take it."

He moved across and sat gingerly on the shaft of the dog-cart. Lou seated herself and loosened her soft tartan shawl. Her face was pink and fresh, and her dark hair curled almost merrily in the damp. But under her eyes were the finger-prints of deadly weariness.

She looked up at the two men, again smiling in her odd fashion.

"What are we going to do?" she asked.

They looked at her closely, seeking her meaning.

"What about?" said Phœnix, a faint smile reflecting on his face, merely because she smiled.

"Oh, everything," she said, hugging her shawl again. "You know what they want? They want to shoot St. Mawr."

The two men exchanged glances.

"Who want it?" said Phœnix.

"Why—all our *friends!*" She made a little *moue*. "Dean Vyner does."

Again the men exchanged glances. There was a pause. Then Phœnix said, looking aside:

"The boss is selling him."

"Who?"

"Sir Henry."—The half-breed always spoke the title with difficulty, and with a sort of sneer. "He sell him to Miss Manby."

"How do you know?"

"The man from Corrabach told me last night. Flora, she say it."

Lou's eyes met the sardonic, empty-seeing eyes of Phœnix direct. There was too much sarcastic understanding. She looked aside.

"What else did he say?" she asked.

"I don't know," said Phœnix evasively. "He say they cut him—else shoot him. Think they cut him—and if he die, he die."

Lou understood. He meant they would geld St. Mawr—at his age.

She looked at Lewis. He sat with his head down, so she could not see his face.

"Do you think it is true?" she asked. "Lewis? Do you think they would try to geld St. Mawr—to make him a gelding?"

Lewis looked up at her. There was a faint deadly glimmer of contempt on his face.

"Very likely, Mam," he said.

She was afraid of his cold, uncanny pale eyes, with their uneasy grey dawn of contempt. These two men, with their silent, deadly inner purpose, were not like other men. They seemed like two silent enemies of all the other men she knew. Enemies in the great white camp, disguised as servants, waiting the incalculable opportunity. What the opportunity might be, none knew.

"Sir Henry hasn't mentioned anything to me about selling St. Mawr to Miss Manby," she said.

The derisive flicker of a smile came on Phœnix's face.

"He sell him first, and tell you then," he said, with his deadly impassive manner.

"But do you really think so?" she asked.

It was extraordinary how much corrosive contempt Phœnix could convey, saying nothing. She felt it almost as an insult. Yet it was a relief to her.

"You know, I can't believe it. I can't believe Sir Henry would want to have St. Mawr mutilated. I believe he'd rather shoot him."

"You think so?" said Phœnix, with a faint grin.

Lou turned to Lewis.

"Lewis, will you tell me what you truly think?"

Lewis looked at her with a hard, straight, fearless British stare.

"That man Philips was in the 'Moon and Stars' last night. He said Miss Manby told him she was buying St. Mawr, and she asked him if he thought it would be safe to cut him and make a horse of him. He said it would be better, take some of the nonsense out of him. He's no good for a sire, anyhow——"

Lewis dropped his head again, and tapped a tattoo with the toe of his rather small foot.

"And what do you think?" said Lou. It occurred to her how sensible and practical Miss Manby was, so much more so than the Dean.

Lewis looked up at her with his pale eyes.

"It won't have anything to do with me," he said. "I shan't go to Corrabach Hall."

"What will you do, then?"

Lewis did not answer. He looked at Phœnix.

"Maybe him and me go to America," said Phœnix, looking at the void.

"Can he get in?" said Lou.

"Yes, he can. I know how," said Phœnix.

"And the money?" she said.

"We got money."

There was a silence, after which she asked of Lewis:

"You'd leave St. Mawr to his fate?"

"I can't help his fate," said Lewis. "There's too many people in the world for me to help anything."

"Poor St. Mawr!"

She went indoors again and up to her room: then higher, to the top rooms of the tall Georgian house. From one window she could see the fields in the rain. She could see St. Mawr himself, alone as usual, standing with his head up, looking across the fences. He was streaked dark with rain. Beautiful, with his poised head and massive neck and his supple hind-quarters. He was neighing to Poppy. Clear on the wet wind came the sound of his bell-like, stallion's calling, that Mrs. Vyner called cruel. It was a strange noise, with a splendour that belonged to another world age. The mean cruelty of Mrs. Vyner's humanitarianism, the barren cruelty of Flora Manby, the eunuch cruelty of Rico. Our whole eunuch civilisation, nasty-minded as eunuchs are, with their kind of sneaking, sterilising cruelty.

Yet even she herself, seeing St. Mawr's conceited march along the fence, could not help addressing him:

"Yes, my boy! If you knew what Miss Flora Manby was preparing for you! *She'll* sharpen a knife that will settle you."

And Lou called her mother.

The two American women stood high at the window, over-looking the wet, close, hedged-and-fenced English landscape. Everything enclosed, enclosed, to stifling. The very apples on the trees looked so shut in, it was impossible to imagine any speck of 'Knowledge' lurking inside them. Good to eat, good to cook, good even for show. But the wild sap of untame-able and inexhaustible knowledge—no! Bred out of them. Geldings, even the apples.

Mrs. Witt listened to Lou's half-humorous statements.

"You must admit, mother, Flora is a sensible girl," she said.

"I admit it, Louise."

"She goes straight to the root of the matter."

"And eradicates the root. Wise girl! And what is your answer?"

"I don't know, mother. What would you say?"

"I know what *I* should say."

"Tell me."

"I should say: 'Miss Manby, you may have my husband, but not my horse. My husband won't need emasculating, and my horse I won't have you meddle with. I'll preserve one last male thing in the museum of this world, if I can.'"

Lou listened, smiling faintly.

"That's what I will say," she replied at length. "The funny thing is, mother, they think all their men with their bare faces or their little quotation-mark moustaches *are* so tremendously male. That fox-hunting one!"

"I know it. Like little male motor-cars. Give him a little gas, and start him on the low gear, and away he goes: all his male gear rattling, like a cheap motor-car."

"I'm afraid I dislike men altogether, mother."

"You may, Louise. Think of Flora Manby, and how you love the fair sex."

"After all, St. Mawr is better. And I'm glad if he gives them a kick in the face."

"Ah, Louise!" Mrs. Witt suddenly clasped her hands with wicked passion. "*Ay, qué gozo!* as our Juan used to say, on your father's ranch in Texas." She gazed in a sort of wicked ecstasy out of the window.

They heard Lou's maid softly calling Lady Carrington from below. Lou went to the stairs.

"What is it?"

"Lewis want to speak to you, my Lady."

"Send him into the sitting-room."

The two women went down.

"What is it, Lewis?" asked Lou.

"Am I to bring in St. Mawr, in case they send for him from Corrabach?"

"No," said Lou swiftly.

"Wait a minute," put in Mrs. Witt. "What makes you think they will send for St. Mawr from Corrabach, Lewis?" she asked, suave as a grey leopard cat.

"Miss Manby went up to Flints Farm with Dean Vyner this morning, and they've just come back. They stopped the car, and Miss Manby got out at the field gate to look at St. Mawr. I'm thinking, if she made the bargain with Sir Henry, she'll be sending a man over this afternoon, and if I'd better brush St. Mawr down a bit, in case."

The man stood strangely still, and the words came like shadows of his real meaning. It was a challenge.

"I see," said Mrs. Witt slowly.

Lou's face darkened. She, too, saw.

"So that is her game," she said. "That is why they got me down here."

"Never mind, Louise," said Mrs. Witt. Then to Lewis: "Yes, please bring in St. Mawr. You wish it, don't you, Louise?"

"Yes," hesitated Lou. She saw by Mrs. Witt's closed face that a counter-move was prepared.

"And Lewis," said Mrs. Witt, "my daughter may wish you to ride St. Mawr this afternoon—not to Corrabach Hall."

"Very good, Mam."

Mrs. Witt sat silent for some time, after Lewis had gone, gathering inspiration from the wet, grisly grave-stones.

"Don't you think it's time we made a move, daughter?" she asked.

"Any move," said Lou desperately.

"Very well then. My dearest friends, and my *only* friends, in this country, are in Oxfordshire. I will set off to *ride* to Merriton this afternoon, and Lewis will ride with me on St. Mawr."

"But you can't ride to Merriton in an afternoon," said Lou.

"I know it. I shall ride across country. I shall *enjoy* it, Louise.—Yes.—I shall consider I am on my way back to America. I am most deadly tired of this country. From Merriton I shall make my arrangements to go to America, and take Lewis and Phœnix and St. Mawr along with me. I think they want to go.—You will decide for yourself."

"Yes, I'll come too," said Lou casually.

"Very well. I'll start immediately after lunch, for I can't *breathe* in this place any longer. Where are Henry's automobile maps?"

Afternoon saw Mrs. Witt, in a large waterproof cape, mounted on her horse, Lewis, in another cape, mounted on St. Mawr, trotting through the rain, splashing in the puddles, moving slowly southwards. They took the open country, and would pass quite close to Flints Farm. But Mrs. Witt did not care. With great difficulty she had managed to fasten a small waterproof roll behind her, containing her night things. She seemed to breathe the first breath of freedom.

And sure enough, an hour or so after Mrs. Witt's departure, arrived Flora Manby in a splashed-up motor-car, accompanied by her sister, and bringing a groom and a saddle.

"Do you know, Harry sold me St. Mawr," she said. "I'm just wild to get that horse in hand."

"How?" said Lou.

"Oh, I don't know. There are ways. Do you mind if Philips rides him over now to Corrabach?—Oh, I forgot, Harry sent you a note:

"*Dearest Loulina: Have you been gone from here two days or two years? It seems the latter. You are terribly missed. Flora wanted so much to buy St. Mawr, to save us further trouble, that I have sold him to her. She is giving me what we paid: rather, what you paid, so of course the money is yours. I am thankful we are rid of the animal, and that he falls into competent hands—I asked her please to remove him from your charge to-day. And I can't tell how much easier I am in my mind, to think of him gone. You are coming back to me to-morrow, aren't you? I shall think of nothing but you, till I see you. Arrivederci, darling dear! R.*"

"I'm so sorry," said Lou. "Mother went on horseback to see some friends, and Lewis went with her on St. Mawr. He knows the road."

"She'll be back this evening?" said Flora.

"I don't know. Mother is so uncertain. She may be away a day or two."

"Well, here's the cheque for St. Mawr."

"No, I won't take it now—no, thank you—not till mother comes back with the goods."

Flora was chagrined. The two women knew they hated one another. The visit was a brief one.

Mrs. Witt rode on in the rain, which abated as the afternoon wore down, and the evening came without rain, and with a suffusion of pale yellow light. All the time she had trotted in silence, with Lewis just behind her. And she scarcely saw the heather-covered hills with the deep clefts between them, nor the oak woods, nor the lingering foxgloves, nor the earth at all. Inside herself she felt a profound repugnance for the English country: she preferred even the crudeness of Central Park in New York.

And she felt an almost savage desire to get away from Europe, from everything European. Now she was really *en route*, she cared not a straw for St. Mawr or for Lewis or anything. Something just writhed inside her, all the time, against Europe. That closeness, that sense of cohesion, that sense of being fused into a lump with all the rest—no matter how much distance you kept—this drove her mad. In America the cohesion was a matter of choice and will. But in Europe it was organic, like the helpless particles of one sprawling body. And the great body in a state of incipient decay.

She was a woman of fifty-one: and she seemed hardly to have lived a day. She looked behind her—the thin trees and swamps of Louisiana, the sultry, sub-tropical excitement of decaying New Orleans, the vast bare dryness of Texas, with mobs of cattle in an illumined dust! The half-European thrills of New York! The false stability of Boston! A clever husband, who was a brilliant lawyer, but who was far more thrilled by his cattle ranch than by his law: and who drank heavily and died. The years of first widowhood in Boston, consoled by a self-satisfied sort of intellectual courtship from clever men.—For curiously enough, while she wanted it, she had always been able to compel men to pay court to her. All kinds of men.—Then a rather dashing time in New York— when she was in her early forties. Then the long *visual* philandering in Europe. She left off 'loving', save through the eye, when she came to Europe. And when she made her trips to America, she found it was finished there also, her 'loving'.

What was the matter? Examining herself, she had long ago decided that her nature was a destructive force. But then, she justified herself, she had only destroyed that which was destructible. If she could have found something indestructible, especially in men, though she would have fought against it, she would have been glad at last to be defeated by it.

That was the point. She really wanted to be defeated, in her own eyes. And nobody had ever defeated her. Men were never really her match. A woman of terrible strong health, she felt even that in her strong limbs there was far more electric power than in the limbs of any man she had met. That curious fluid electric force, that could make any man kiss her hand, if she so willed it. A queen, as far as she wished. And not having been very clever at school, she always had the greatest respect for the mental powers. Her own were not mental powers. Rather electric, as of some strange physical dynamo within her. So she had been ready to bow before Mind.

But alas! After a brief time, she had found Mind, at least the man who was supposed to have the mind, bowing before her. Her own peculiar dynamic force was stronger than the force of Mind. She could make Mind kiss her hand.

And not by any sensual tricks. She did not really care about sensualities, especially as a younger woman. Sex was a mere adjunct. She cared about the mysterious, intense, dynamic sympathy that could flow between her and some 'live' man—a man who was highly conscious, a real live wire. That she cared about.

But she had never rested until she had made the man she admired—and admiration was the roots of her attraction to any man—made him kiss her hand. In both cases, actual and metaphorical. Physical and metaphysical. Conquered his country.

She had always succeeded. And she believed that, if she cared, she always *would* succeed. In the world of living men. Because of the power that was in her, in her arms, in her strong, shapely, but terrible hands, in all the great dynamo of her body.

For this reason she had been so terribly contemptuous of Rico, and of Lou's infatuation. Ye gods! what was Rico in the scale of men!

Perhaps she despised the younger generation too easily. Because she did not see its sources of power, she concluded it was powerless. Whereas perhaps the power of accommodating oneself to any circumstance and committing oneself to no circumstance is the last triumph of mankind.

Her generation had had its day. She had had her day. The world of her men had sunk into a sort of insignificance. And with a great contempt she despised the world that had come into place instead: the world of Rico and Flora Manby, the world represented, to her, by the Prince of Wales.

In such a world there was nothing even to conquer. It gave everything and gave nothing to everybody and anybody all the time. *Dio benedetto!* as Rico would say. A great complicated tangle of nonentities ravelled in nothingness. So it seemed to her.

Great God! This was the generation she had helped to bring into the world.

She had had her day. And, as far as the mysterious battle of life went, she had won all the way. Just as Cleopatra, in the mysterious business of a woman's life, won all the way.

Though that bald, tough Cæsar had drawn his iron from the fire without losing much of its temper. And he had gone his way. And Antony surely was splendid to die with.

In her life there had been no tough Cæsar to go his way in
cold blood, away from her. Her men had gone from her like
dogs on three legs, into the crowd. And certainly there was
no gorgeous Antony to die for and with.

Almost she was tempted in her heart to cry: "Conquer me,
oh God, before I die!"—But then she had a terrible contempt
for the God that was supposed to rule this universe. She felt
she could make *Him* kiss her hand. Here she was a woman of
fifty-one, past the change of life. And her great dread was to
die an empty, barren death. Oh, if only Death might open dark
wings of mystery and consolation. To die an easy, barren
death. To pass out as she had passed in, without mystery
or the rustling of darkness! That was her last, final, ashy
dread.

"Old!" she said to herself. "I am not *old!* I have lived many
years, that is all. But I am as timeless as an hour-glass that
turns morning and night, and spills the hours of sleep one way,
the hours of consciousness the other way, without itself being
affected. Nothing in all my life has ever truly affected me.—I
believe Cleopatra only tried the asp, as she tried her pearls in
wine, to see if it would really, really have any effect on her.
Nothing had ever really had any effect on her, neither Cæsar
nor Antony nor any of them. Never once had she really been
lost, lost to herself. Then try death, see if that trick would
work. If she would lose herself to herself that way.—Ah,
death——!"

But Mrs. Witt mistrusted death too. She felt she might pass
out as a bed of asters passes out in autumn, to mere nothingness.—And something in her longed to die, at least, *positively*:
to be folded then at last into throbbing wings of mystery, like
a hawk that goes to sleep. Not like a thing made into a parcel
and put into the last rubbish-heap.

So she rode trotting across the hills, mile after mile, in
silence. Avoiding the roads, avoiding everything, avoiding
everybody, just trotting forwards, towards night.

And by nightfall they had travelled twenty-five miles. She
had motored around this country, and knew the little towns
and the inns. She knew where she would sleep.

The morning came beautiful and sunny. A woman so strong
in health, why should she ride with the fact of death before
her eyes? But she did.

Yet in sunny morning she must do something about it.

"Lewis!" she said. "Come here and tell me something, please! Tell me," she said, "do you believe in God?"

"In God!" he said, wondering. "I never think about it."

"But do you say your prayers?"

"No, Mam!"

"Why don't you?"

He thought about it for some minutes.

"I don't like religion. My aunt and uncle were religious."

"You don't like religion," she repeated. "And you don't believe in God.—Well, then——"

"Nay!" he hesitated. "I never said I didn't believe in God.—Only I'm sure I'm not a Methodist. And I feel a fool in a proper church.—And I feel a fool saying my prayers.—And I feel a fool when ministers and parsons come getting at me.—I never think about God, if folks don't try to make me." He had a small, sly smile, almost gay.

"And you don't like feeling a fool?" She smiled rather patronisingly.

"No, Mam."

"Do I make you feel a fool?" she asked dryly.

He looked at her without answering.

"Why don't you answer?" she said, pressing.

"I think you'd like to make a fool of me sometimes," he said.

"Now?" she pressed.

He looked at her with that slow, distant look.

"Maybe!" he said, rather unconcernedly.

Curiously, she couldn't touch him. He always seemed to be watching her from a distance, as if from another country. Even if she made a fool of him, something in him would all the time be far away from her, not implicated.

She caught herself up in the personal game and returned to her own isolated question. A vicious habit made her start the personal tricks. She didn't want to, really.

There was something about this little man—sometimes, to herself, she called him *Little Jack Horner, sat in a corner*—that irritated her and made her want to taunt him. His peculiar little inaccessibility, that was so tight and easy.

Then again, there was something, his way of looking at her as if he looked from out of another country, a country of which he was an inhabitant, and where she had never been: this touched her strangely. Perhaps behind this little man was the mystery. In spite of the fact that in actual life, in her

world, he was only a groom, almost *chétif*, with his legs a
little bit horsy and bowed; and of no education, saying 'Yes,
Mam!' and 'No, Mam!' and accomplishing nothing, simply
nothing at all on the face of the earth. Strictly a nonentity.

And yet, what made him perhaps the only real entity to her,
his seeming to inhabit another world than hers. A world dark
and still, where language never ruffled the growing leaves and
seared their edges like a bad wind.

Was it an illusion, however? Sometimes she thought it was.
Just bunkum, which she had faked up, in order to have something to mystify about.

But then, when she saw Phœnix and Lewis silently together,
she knew there *was* another communion, silent, excluding her.
And sometimes when Lewis was alone with St. Mawr: and
once when she saw him pick up a bird that had stunned itself
against a wire: she had realised another world, silent, where
each creature is alone in its own aura of silence, the mystery
of power: as Lewis had power with St. Mawr, and even with
Phœnix.

The visible world and the invisible. Or rather, the audible
and the inaudible. She had lived so long, and so completely,
in the visible, audible world. She would not easily admit that
other, inaudible. She always wanted to jeer as she approached
the brink of it.

Even now she wanted to jeer at the little fellow, because of
his holding himself inaccessible within the inaudible, silent
world. And she knew he knew it.

"Did you never want to be rich, and be a gentleman, like
Sir Henry?" she asked.

"I would many times have liked to be rich. But I never
exactly wanted to be a gentleman," he said.

"Why not?"

"I can't exactly say. I should be uncomfortable if I was like
they are."

"And are you comfortable now?"

"When I'm let alone."

"And do they let you alone? Does the world let you alone?"

"No, they don't."

"Well then——!"

"I keep to myself all I can."

"And are you comfortable, as you call it, when you keep to
yourself?"

"Yes, I am."

"But when you keep to yourself, what do you keep to? What precious treasure have you to keep to?"

He looked, and saw she was jeering.

"None," he said. "I've got nothing of that sort."

She rode impatiently on ahead.

And the moment she had done so, she regretted it. She might put the little fellow, with contempt, out of her reckoning. But no, she would not do it.

She had put so much out of her reckoning: soon she would be left in an empty circle, with her empty self at the centre.

She reined in again.

"Lewis!" she said. "I don't want you to take offence at anything I say."

"No, Mam."

"I don't want you to say just 'No, Mam!' all the time!" she cried impulsively. "Promise me."

"Yes, Mam!"

"But really! Promise me you won't be offended at whatever I say."

"Yes, Mam!"

She looked at him searchingly. To her surprise, she was almost in tears. A woman of her years! And with a servant!

But his face was blank and stony, with a stony, distant look of pride that made him inaccessible to her emotions. He met her eyes again: with that cold distant look, looking straight into her hot, confused, pained self. So cold and as if merely refuting her. He didn't believe her, nor trust her, nor like her even. She was an attacking enemy to him. Only he stayed really far away from her, looking down at her from a sort of distant hill where her weapons could not reach: not quite.

And at the same time, it hurt him in a dumb, living way, that she made these attacks on him. She could see the cloud of hurt in his eyes, no matter how distantly he looked at her.

They bought food in a village shop, and sat under a tree near a field where men were already cutting oats, in a warm valley. Lewis had stabled the horses for a couple of hours to feed and rest. But he came to join her under the tree, to eat.— He sat a little distance from her, with the bread and cheese in his small brown hands, eating silently, and watching the harvesters. She was cross with him, and therefore she was stingy, would give him nothing to eat but dry bread and cheese. Herself, she was not hungry.—So all the time he kept his face a little averted from her. As a matter of fact, he kept his whole being averted from her, away from her. He did not want to touch her, nor to be touched by her. He kept his spirit there, alert, on its guard, but out of contact. It was as if he had unconsciously accepted the battle, the old battle. He was her target, the old object of her deadly weapons. But he refused to shoot back. It was as if he caught all her missiles in full flight before they touched him, and silently threw them on the ground behind him. And in some essential part of himself he ignored her, staying in another world.

That other world! Mere male armour of artificial imperviousness! It angered her.

Yet she knew, by the way he watched the harvesters, and the grasshoppers popping into notice, that it was another world. And when a girl went by, carrying food to the field, it was at him she glanced. And he gave that quick, animal little smile that came from him unawares. Another world.

Yet also there was a sort of meanness about him: a *suffisance!* A keep-yourself-for-yourself, and don't give yourself away.

Well!—she rose impatiently.

It was hot in the afternoon, and she was rather tired. She went to the inn and slept, and did not start again till tea-time. Then they had to ride rather late. The sun sank, among a smell of cornfields, clear and yellow-red behind motionless dark trees. Pale smoke rose from cottage chimneys. Not a cloud was in the sky, which held the upward-floating light like a bowl inverted on purpose. A new moon sparkled and was gone. It was beginning of night.

Away in the distance, they saw a curious pinkish glare of fire, probably furnaces. And Mrs. Witt thought she could detect the scent of furnace smoke, or factory smoke. But then she always said that of the English air: it was never quite free of the smell of smoke, coal smoke.

They were riding slowly on a path through fields, down a long slope. Away below was a puther of lights. All the darkness seemed full of half-spent crossing lights, a curious uneasiness. High in the sky a star seemed to be walking. It was an aeroplane with a light. Its buzz rattled above. Not a space, not a speck of this country that wasn't humanised, occupied by the human claim. Not even the sky.

They descended slowly through a dark wood, which they had entered through a gate. Lewis was all the time dismounting and opening gates, letting her pass, shutting the gate and mounting again.

So, in a while she came to the edge of the wood's darkness, and saw the open pale concave of the world beyond. The darkness was never dark. It shook with the concussion of many invisible lights, lights of towns, villages, mines, factories, furnaces, squatting in the valleys and behind all the hills.

Yet, as Rachel Witt drew rein at the gate emerging from the wood, a very big, soft star fell in heaven, cleaving the hubbub of this human night with a gleam from the greater world.

"See! a star falling!" said Lewis, as he opened the gate.

"I saw it," said Mrs. Witt, walking her horse past him.

There was a curious excitement of wonder, or magic, in the little man's voice. Even in this night something strange had stirred awake in him.

"You ask me about God," he said to her, walking his horse alongside in the shadow of the wood's edge, the darkness of the old Pan, that kept our artificially-lit world at bay. "I don't know about God. But when I see a star fall like that out of long-distance places in the sky: and the moon sinking saying Good-bye! Good-bye! Good-bye! and nobody listening: I think I hear something, though I wouldn't call it God."

"What then?" said Rachel Witt.

"And you smell the smell of oak leaves now," he said, "now the air is cold. They smell to me more alive than people. The trees hold their bodies hard and still, but they watch and listen with their leaves. And I think they say to me: 'Is that you passing there, Morgan Lewis? All right, you pass quickly, we shan't do anything to you. You are like a holly bush.'"

"Yes," said Rachel Witt dryly. "Why?"

"All the time the trees grow and listen. And if you cut a tree down without asking pardon, trees will hurt you sometime in your life, in the night-time."

"I suppose," said Rachel Witt, "that's an old superstition."

"They say that ash trees don't like people. When the other people were most in the country—I mean like what they call fairies, that have all gone now—they liked ash trees best. And you know the little green things with little small nuts in them, that come flying from ash trees—*pigeons*, we call them— they're the seeds—the other people used to catch them and eat them before they fell to the ground. And that made the people so they could hear trees living and feeling things.—But when all these people that there are now came to England, they liked the oak trees best, because their pigs ate the acorns. So now you can tell the ash trees are mad, they want to kill all these people. But the oak trees are many more than the ash trees "

"And do you eat the ash tree seeds?" she asked.

"I always ate them when I was little. Then I wasn't frightened of ash trees, like most of the others. And I wasn't frightened of the moon. If you didn't go near the fire all day, and if you didn't eat any cooked food nor anything that had been in the sun, but only things like turnips or radishes or pig-nuts, and then went without any clothes on, in the full moon, then you could see the people in the moon, and go with them. They never have fire, and they never speak, and their bodies are clear almost like jelly. They die in a minute if there's a bit of fire near them. But they know more than we. Because unless fire touches them, they never die. They see people live and they see people perish, and they say, people are only like twigs on a tree, you break them off the tree, and kindle fire with them. You made a fire of them, and they are gone, the fire is gone, everything is gone. But the people of the moon don't die, and fire is nothing to them. They look at it from the distance of the sky, and see it burning things up, people all appearing and disappearing like twigs that come in spring and you cut them in autumn and make a fire of them and they are gone. And they say: What do people matter? If you want to matter, you must become a moon-boy. Then all your life, fire can't blind you and people can't hurt you. Because at full moon you can join the moon people, and go through the air and pass any cool places, pass through rocks and through the trunks of trees, and when you come to people lying warm in bed, you punish them."

"How?"

"You sit on the pillow where they breathe, and you put a web across their mouth, so they can't breathe the fresh air that comes from the moon. So they go on breathing the same air again and again, and that makes them more and more stupefied. The sun gives out heat, but the moon gives out fresh air. That's what the moon people do: they wash the air clean with moonlight."

He was talking with a strange, eager *naïveté* that amused
Rachel Witt, and made her a little uncomfortable in her skin.
Was he after all no more than a sort of imbecile?

"Who told you all this stuff?" she asked abruptly.

And, as abruptly, he pulled himself up.

"We used to say it when we were children."

"But you don't believe it? It *is* only childishness, after all."

He paused a moment or two.

"No," he said, in his ironical little day voice. "I know I
shan't make anything but a fool of myself, with that talk.
But all sorts of things go through our heads, and some seem
to linger, and some don't. But you asking me about God put
it into my mind, I suppose. I don't know what sort of things
I believe in: only I know it's not what the chapel folks believe
in. We none of us believe in them when it comes to earning a
living, or, with you people, when it comes to spending your
fortune. Then we know that bread costs money, and even
your sleep you have to pay for.—That's work. Or, with you
people, it's just owning property and seeing you get your value
for your money.—But a man's mind is always full of things.
And some people's minds, like my aunt and uncle, are full of
religion and hell for everybody except themselves. And some
people's minds are all money, money, money, and how to get
hold of something they haven't got hold of yet. And some
people, like you, are always curious about what everybody
else in the world is after. And some people are all for enjoying themselves and being thought much of, and some, like
Lady Carrington, don't know what to do with themselves.
Myself, I don't want to have in my mind the things other
people have in their minds. I'm one that likes my own things
best. And if, when I see a bright star fall, like to-night, I think
to myself: 'There's movement in the sky. The world is going
to change again. They're throwing something to us from the
distance, and we've got to have it, whether we want it or not.
To-morrow there will be a difference for everybody, thrown
out of the sky upon us, whether we want it or not: then that's
how I want to think, so let me please myself.' "

"You know what a shooting star actually is, I suppose?—
and that there are always many in August, because we pass
through a region of them?"

"Yes, Mam, I've been told. But stones don't come at us from
the sky for nothing. Either it's like when a man tosses an

apple to you out of his orchard, as you go by. Or it's like
when somebody shies a stone at you to cut your head open.
You'll never make me believe the sky is like an empty house
with a slate falling from the roof. The world has its own life,
the sky has a life of its own, and never is it like stones rolling
down a rubbish-heap and falling into a pond. Many things
twitch and twitter within the sky, and many things happen
beyond us. My own way of thinking is my own way."

"I never knew you talk so much."

"No, Mam. It's your asking me that about God. Or else it's
the night-time. I don't believe in God and being good and
going to heaven. Neither do I worship idols, so I'm not a
heathen as my aunt called me. Never from a boy did I want to
believe the things they kept grinding in their guts at home,
and at Sunday school, and at school. A man's mind has to be
full of something, so I keep to what we used to think as lads.
It's childish nonsense, I know it. But it suits me. Better than
other people's stuff. Your man Phœnix is about the same,
when he lets on.—Anyhow, it's my own stuff that we believed
as lads, and I like it better than other people's stuff.—You asking about God made me let on. But I would never belong to
any club, or trades union, and God's the same to my mind."

With this he gave a little kick to his horse, and St. Mawr
went dancing excitedly along the highway they now entered,
leaving Mrs. Witt to trot after as rapidly as she could.

When she came to the hotel, to which she had telegraphed
for rooms, Lewis disappeared, and she was left thinking hard.

It was not till they were twenty miles from Merriton, riding
through a slow morning mist, and she had a rather far-away,
wistful look on her face, unusual for her, that she turned to
him in the saddle and said:

"Now don't be surprised, Lewis, at what I am going to say.
I am going to ask you, now, supposing I wanted to marry you,
what should you say?"

He looked at her quickly, and was at once on his guard.

"That you didn't mean it," he replied hastily.

"Yes"—she hesitated, and her face looked wistful and tired.
—"Supposing I *did* mean it. Supposing I did *really*, from my
heart, want to marry you and be a wife to you"—she looked
away across the fields—"then what should you say?"

Her voice sounded sad, a little broken.

"Why, Mam!" he replied, knitting his brow and shaking his

head a little. "I should say you didn't mean it, you know. Something would have come over you."

"But supposing I *wanted* something to come over me?"

He shook his head.

"It would never do, Mam! Some people's flesh and blood is kneaded like bread: and that's me. And some are rolled like fine pastry, like Lady Carrington. And some are mixed with gunpowder. They're like a cartridge you put in a gun, Mam."

She listened impatiently.

"Don't talk," she said, "about bread and cakes and pastry, it all means nothing. You used to answer short enough 'Yes, Mam! No, Mam!' That will do now. Do you mean 'Yes!' or 'No!?'"

His eyes met hers. She was again hectoring.

"No, Mam!" he said, quite neutral.

"Why?"

As she waited for his answer, she saw the foundations of his loquacity dry up, his face go distant and mute again, as it always used to be, till these last two days, when it had had a funny touch of inconsequential merriness.

He looked steadily into her eyes, and his look was neutral, sombre, and hurt. He looked at her as if infinite seas, infinite spaces divided him and her. And his eyes seemed to put her away beyond some sort of fence. An anger congealed cold like lava, set impassive against her and all her sort.

"No, Mam. I couldn't give my body to any woman who didn't respect it."

"But I do respect it, I do!"—she flushed hot like a girl.

"No, Mam. Not as *I* mean it," he replied.

There was a touch of anger against her in his voice, and a distance of distaste.

"And how do *you* mean it?" she replied, the full sarcasm coming back into her tones. She could see that, as a woman to touch and fondle he saw her as repellent: only repellent.

"I have to be a servant to women now," he said, "even to earn my wage. I could never touch with my body a woman whose servant I was."

"You're not my servant: my daughter pays your wages.—And all that is beside the point, between a man and a woman."

"No woman who I touched with my body should ever speak to me as you speak to me, or think of me as you think of me," he said.

"But!——" she stammered. "I think of you—with love. And can you be so unkind as to notice the way I speak? You know it's only my way."

"You, as a woman," he said, "you have no respect for a man."

"Respect! Respect!" she cried. "I'm likely to lose what respect I have left. I know I can *love* a man. But whether a man can love a woman——"

"No," said Lewis. "I never could, and I think I never shall. Because I don't want to. The thought of it makes me feel shame."

"What do you mean" she cried.

"Nothing in the world," he said, "would make me feel such shame as to have a woman shouting at me, or mocking at me, as I see women mocking and despising the men they marry. No woman shall touch my body and mock me or despise me. No woman."

"But men must be mocked, or despised even, sometimes."

"No. Not this man. Not by the woman I touch with my body."

"Are you perfect?"

"I don't know. But if I touch a woman with my body, it must put a lock on her, to respect what I will never have despised: never!"

"What will you never have despised?"

"My body! And my touch upon the woman."

"Why insist so on your body?"—And she looked at him with a touch of contemptuous mockery, raillery.

He looked her in the eyes steadily, and coldly, putting her away from him, and himself far away from her.

"Do you expect that any woman still stay your humble slave to-day?" she asked cuttingly.

But he only watched her coldly, distant, refusing any connection.

"Between men and women, it's a question of give and take. A man can't expect *always* to be humbly adored."

He watched her still, cold, rather pale, putting her far from him. Then he turned his horse and set off rapidly along the road, leaving her to follow.

She walked her horse and let him go, thinking to herself:

"There's a little bantam cock. And a groom! Imagine it! Thinking he can dictate to a woman!"

She was in love with him. And he, in an odd way, was in love with her. She had known it by the odd, uncanny merriment in him, and his unexpected loquacity. But he would not have her come physically near him. Unapproachable there as a cactus, guarding his 'body' from her contact. As if contact with her would be mortal insult and fatal injury to his marvellous 'body'.

What a little cock-sparrow!

Let him ride ahead. He would have to wait for her somewhere.

She found him at the entrance to the next village. His face was pallid and set. She could tell he felt he had been insulted, so he had congealed into stiff insentience.

"At the bottom of all men is the same," she said to herself: "an empty, male conceit of themselves."

She, too, rode up with a face like a mask, and straight on to the hotel.

"Can you serve dinner to myself and my servant?" she asked at the inn: which, fortunately for her, accommodated motorists, otherwise they would have said 'No!'

"I think," said Lewis as they came in sight of Merriton, "I'd better give Lady Carrington a week's notice."

A complete little stranger! And an impudent one.

"Exactly as you please," she said.

She found several letters from her daughter at Marshal Place.

"Dear Mother: No sooner had you gone off than Flora appeared, not at all in the bud, but rather in full blow. She demanded her victim; Shylock demanding the pound of flesh: and wanted to hand over the shekels.

"Joyfully I refused them. She said 'Harry' was much better, and invited him and me to stay at Corrabach Hall till he was quite well: it would be less strain on your household, while he was still in bed and helpless. So the plan is, that he shall be brought down on Friday, if he is really fit for the journey, and we drive straight to Corrabach. I am packing his bags and mine, clearing up our traces: his trunks to go to Corrabach, mine to stay here and make up their minds.—I am going to Flints Farm again to-morrow, dutifully, though I am no flower for the bedside.—I do so want to know if Rico has already called her Fiorita: or perhaps Florecita. It reminds me of old William's joke: 'Now yuh tell me, little Missy: which is the best posey that grow?' And the hushed whisper in which he said the answer: 'The Collyposy!' Oh dear, I am so tired of feeling spiteful, but how else is one to feel?

"You looked most prosaically romantic, setting off in a rubber cape, followed by Lewis. Hope the roads were not very slippery, and that you had a good time, à la Mademoiselle de Maupin. Do remember, dear, not to devour little Lewis before you have got half-way——"

"Dear Mother: I half expected word from you before I left, but nothing came. Forrester drove me up here just before lunch. Rico seems much better, almost himself, and a little more than that. He broached our staying at Corrabach very tactfully. I told him Flora had asked me, and it seemed a good plan. Then I told him about St. Mawr. He was a little piqued, and there was a pause of very disapproving silence. Then he said: 'Very well, darling. If you wish to keep the animal, do so by all means. I make a present of him again.' Me: 'That's so good of you, Rico. Because I know revenge is sweet.' Rico: 'Revenge, Loulina! I don't think I was selling him for vengeance! Merely to get rid of him to Flora, who can keep better hold over him.' Me: 'But you know, dear, she was going to geld him!' Rico: 'I don't think anybody knew it. We only wondered if it were possible, to make him more amenable. Did she tell you?' Me: 'No—Phœnix did. He had it from a groom.' Rico: 'Dear me! A concatenation of grooms! So your mother rode off with Lewis, and carried St. Mawr out of danger! I understand! Let us hope worse won't befall.' Me: 'Whom?' Rico: 'Never mind, dear! It's so lovely to see you. You are looking rested. I thought those Countess of Wilton roses the most marvellous things in the world, till you came, now they're quite in the background.' He had some very lovely roses in a crystal bowl: the room smelled of roses. Me: 'Where did they come from?' Rico: 'Oh, Flora brought them!' Me: 'Bowl and all?' Rico: 'Bowl and all! Wasn't it dear of her?' Me: 'Why, yes! But then she's the goddess of flowers, isn't she?' Poor darling, he was offended that I should twit him while he is ill, so I relented. He has had a couple of marvellous invalid's bed-jackets sent from London: one a pinkish yellow, with rose-arabesque facings: this one in fine cloth. But unfortunately he has already dropped soup on it. The other is a lovely silvery and blue and green, soft brocade. He had that one on to receive me, and I at once complimented him on it. He has got a new ring too: sent by

Aspasia Weingartner, a rather lovely intaglio of Priapus under an apple bough, at least, so he says it is. He made a naughty face, and said: 'The Priapus stage is rather advanced for poor me.' I asked what the Priapus stage was, but he said: 'Oh, nothing!' Then nurse said: 'There's a big classical dictionary that Miss Manby brought up, if you wish to see it.' So I have been studying the Classical Gods. The world always was a queer place. It's a very queer one when Rico is the god Priapus. He would go round the orchard painting life-like apples on the trees, and inviting nymphs to come and eat them. And the nymphs would pretend they were real: 'Why, Sir Prippy, what stunningly naughty apples!' There's nothing so artificial as sinning nowadays. I suppose it once was real.

"I'm bored here: wish I had my horse."

"Dear Mother: I'm so glad you are enjoying your ride. I'm sure it is like riding into history, like the Yankee at the Court of King Arthur, in those old by-lanes and Roman roads. They still fascinate me: at least, more before I get there than when I am actually there. I begin to feel real American and to resent the past. Why doesn't the past decently bury itself instead of waiting to be admired by the present?

"Phœnix brought Poppy. I am so fond of her: rode for five hours yesterday. I was glad to get away from this farm. The doctor came, and said Rico would be able to go down to Corrabach to-morrow. Flora came to hear the bulletin, and sailed back full of zest. Apparently Rico is going to do a portrait of her, sitting up in bed. What a mercy the bed-clothes won't be mine when Priapus wields his palette from the pillow.

"Phœnix thinks you intend to go to America with St. Mawr, and that I am coming too, leaving Rico this side.—I wonder. I feel so unreal, nowadays, as if I too were nothing more than a painting by Rico on a millboard. I feel almost too unreal even to make up my mind to anything. It is terrible when the life-flow dies out of one, and everything is like cardboard, and oneself is like cardboard. I'm sure it is worse than being dead. I realised it yesterday when Phœnix and I had a picnic lunch by a stream. You see, I must imitate you in all things. He found me some watercresses, and they tasted so damp and *alive*, I knew how deadened I was. Phœnix wants us to go and have a ranch in Arizona, and raise horses, with St. Mawr, if willing, for Father Abraham. I wonder if it matters what one does: if it isn't all the same thing over again? Only Phœnix, his funny blank face, makes my heart melt and go sad. But I believe he'd be cruel too. I saw it in his face when he didn't know I was looking. Anything, though, rather than this deadness and this paint-Priapus business. *Au revoir*, mother dear! Keep on having a good time——"

"Dear Mother: I had your letter from Merriton: am so glad you arrived safe and sound in body and temper. There was such a funny letter from Lewis, too: I enclose it. What makes him take this extraordinary line? But I'm writing to tell him to take St. Mawr to London, and wait for me there. I have telegraphed Mrs. Squire to get the house ready for me. I shall go straight there.

"Things developed here, as they were bound to. I just couldn't bear it. No sooner was Rico put in the automobile than a self-conscious importance came over him, like when the wounded hero is carried into the middle of the stage. 'Why so solemn, Rico dear?' I asked him, trying to laugh him out of it. 'Not solemn, dear, only feeling a little transient.' I don't think he knew himself what he meant. Flora was on the steps as the car drew up, dressed in severe white. She only needed an apron to become a nurse: or a veil to become a bride. Between the two, she had an unbearable air of a woman in seduced circumstances, as *The Times* said. She ordered two menservants about in subdued, you would have said hushed, but competent tones. And then I saw there was a touch of the priestess about her as well: Cassandra preparing for her violation: Iphigenia, with Rico for Orestes, on a stretcher: he looking like Adonis, fully prepared to be an unconscionable time in dying. They had given him a lovely room downstairs, with doors opening on to a little garden all of its own. I believe it was Flora's boudoir. I left nurse and the men to put him to bed. Flora was hovering anxiously in the passage outside. 'Oh, what a marvellous room! Oh, how colourful, how beautiful!' came Rico's tones, the hero behind the scenes. I must say, it was like a harvest festival, with roses and gaillardias in the shadow, and cornflowers in the light, and a bowl of grapes, and nectarines among leaves. 'I'm so anxious that he should be happy,' Flora said to me in the passage. 'You know him best. Is there anything else I could do for him?' Me: 'Why, if you went to the piano and sang, I'm sure he'd love it. Couldn't you sing: Oh, my love is like a rred, rred rrose!'—You know how Rico imitates Scotch!

"Thank goodness I have a bedroom upstairs: nurse sleeps in a little ante-chamber to Rico's room. The Edwards are still here, the blond young man with some very futuristic plaster on his face. 'Awfully good of you to come!' he said to me, looking at me out of one eye, and holding my hand fervently. How's that for cheek: 'It's awfully good of Miss Manby to let me come,' said I. He: 'Ah, but Flora is always a sport, a topping good sport!'

"I don't know what's the matter, but it just all put me into a fiendish temper. I felt I couldn't sit there at luncheon with that bright, youthful company, and hear about their tennis and their polo and their hunting and have their flirtatiousness making me sick. So I asked for a tray in my room. Do as I might, I couldn't help being horrid.

"Oh, and Rico! He really is too awful. Lying there in bed with every ear open, like Adonis waiting to be persuaded not to die. Seizing a hushed moment to take Flora's hand and press it to his lips, murmuring: 'How awfully good you are to me, dear Flora!' And Flora: 'I'd be better if I knew how, Harry!' So cheerful with it all! No, it's too much. My sense of humour is leaving me: which means, I'm getting into too bad a temper to be able to ridicule it all. I suppose I feel in the minority. It's an awful thought, to think that most all the young people in the world are like this: so bright and cheerful, and *sporting*, and so brimming with libido. How awful!

"I said to Rico: 'You're very comfortable here, aren't you?' He: 'Comfortable! It's comparative heaven.' Me: 'Would you mind if I went away?' A deadly pause. He is deadly afraid of being left alone with Flora. He feels safe so long as I am about, and he can take refuge in his marriage ties. He: 'Where do you want to go, dear?' Me: 'To mother. To London. Mother is planning to go to America, and she wants me to go.' Rico: 'But you don't want to go t—he—e—re—e!' You know, mother, how Rico can put a venomous emphasis on a word, till it suggests pure poison. It nettled me. 'I'm not sure,' I said. Rico: 'Oh, but you can't stand that awful America.' Me: 'I want to try again.' Rico: 'But Lou dear, it will be winter before you get there. And this is absolutely the wrong moment for me to go over there. I am only just making headway over here. When I am absolutely sure of a position in England, then we nip across the Atlantic and scoop in a few dollars, if you like. Just now, even when I am well, would be fatal. I've only just sketched in the outline of my success in London, and one ought to arrive in New York ready-made as a famous and important Artist.' Me: 'But mother and I didn't think of going to New York. We thought we'd sail straight to New Orleans—if we could: or to Havana. And then go west to Arizona.' The poor boy looked at me in such distress. 'But Loulina darling, do you mean you want to leave me in the lurch for the winter season? You can't mean it. We're just getting on so splendidly, really!'—I was surprised at the depth of feeling in his voice: how tremendously his career as an artist—a popular artist—matters to him. I can never believe it.—You know, mother, you and I feel alike about daubing paint on canvas: every possible daub that can be daubed has already been done, so people ought to leave off. Rico is so shrewd. I always think he's got his tongue in his cheek, and I'm always staggered once more to find that he takes it absolutely seriously. His career! The Modern British Society of Painters: perhaps even the Royal Academy! Those people we see in London, and those portraits Rico does! He may even be a second Laszlo, or a thirteenth Orpen, and die happy! Oh! mother! How can it really matter to anybody!

"But I was really rather upset when I realised how his heart was fixed on his career, and that I might be spoiling everything for him. So I went away to think about it. And then I realised how unpopular you are, and how unpopular I shall be myself, in a little while. A sort of hatred for people has come over me. I hate their ways and their bunk, and I feel like kicking them in the face, as St. Mawr did that young man. Not that I should ever do it. And I don't think I should ever have made my final announcement to Rico, if he hadn't been such a beautiful pig in clover, here at Corrabach Hall. He has known the Manbys all his life; they and he are sections of one engine. He would be far happier with Flora: or I won't say happier, because there is something in him which rebels: but he would on the whole fit much better. I myself am at the end of my limit, and beyond it. I can't 'mix' any more, and I refuse to. I feel like a bit of egg-shell in the mayonnaise: the only thing is to take it out, you can't beat it in. I *know* I shall cause a fiasco, even in Rico's career, if I stay. I shall go on

being rude and hateful to people as I am at Corrabach, and
Rico will lose all his nerve.

"So I have told him. I said this evening, when no one was
about: 'Rico dear, listen to me seriously. I can't stand these
people. If you ask me to endure another week of them, I shall
either become ill, or insult them, as mother does. And I don't
want to do either.' Rico: 'But darling, isn't everybody perfect
to you?' Me: 'I tell you, I shall just make a break, like St.
Mawr, if I don't get out. I simply can't stand people.'—The
poor darling, his face goes so blank and anxious. He knows
what I mean, because, except that they tickle his vanity all
the time, he hates them as much as I do. But his vanity is the
chief thing to him. He: 'Lou darling, can't you wait till I get
up, and we can go away to the Tyrol or somewhere for a
spell?' Me: 'Won't you come with me to America, to the
South-West? I believe it's marvellous country.'—I saw his
face switch into hostility; quite vicious. He: 'Are you so
keen on spoiling everything for me? Is that what I married
you for? Do you do it deliberately?' Me: 'Everything is
already spoilt for me. I tell you I can't stand people, your
Floras and your Aspasias, and your forthcoming young
Englishmen. After all, I am an American, like mother, and
I've got to go back.' He: 'Really! And am I to come along
as part of the luggage? Labelled cabin!' Me: 'You do as you
wish, Rico.' He: 'I wish to God you did as you wished, Lou
dear. I'm afraid you do as Mrs. Witt wishes. I always heard
that the holiest thing in the world was a mother.' Me: 'No,
dear, it's just that I can't stand people.' He (with a snarl):
'And I suppose I'm lumped in as PEOPLE!' And when he'd said
it, it was true. We neither of us said anything for a time. Then
he said, calculating: 'Very well, dear! You take a trip to the
land of stars and stripes, and I'll stay here and go on with my
work. And when you've seen enough of their stars and tasted
enough of their stripes, you can come back and take your
place again with me.'—We left it at that.

"You and I are supposed to have important business connected with our estates in Texas—it sounds so well—so we
are making a hurried trip to the States, as they call them. I
shall leave for London early next week——"

Mrs. Witt read this long letter with satisfaction. She herself
had one strange craving: to get back to America. It was not
that she idealised her native country: she was a tartar of rest-

lessness there, quite as much as in Europe. It was not that
she expected to arrive at any blessed abiding place. No, in
America she would go on fuming and chafing the same. But
at least she would be in America, in her own country. And
that was what she wanted.

She picked up the sheet of poor paper that had been folded
in Lou's letter. It was the letter from Lewis, quite nicely
written. "Lady Carrington, I write to tell you and Sir Henry
that I think I had better quit your service, as it would be more
comfortable all round. If you will write and tell me what you
want me to do with St. Mawr, I will do whatever you tell
me. With kind regards to Lady Carrington and Sir Henry, I
remain, Your obedient servant, Morgan Lewis."

Mrs. Witt put the letter aside, and sat looking out of the
window. She felt, strangely, as if already her soul had gone
away from her actual surroundings. She was there, in Oxfordshire, in the body, but her spirit had departed elsewhere. A
listlessness was upon her. It was with an effort she roused
herself, to write to her lawyer in London, to get her release
from her English obligations. Then she wrote to the London
hotel.

For the first time in her life she wished she had a maid to
do little things for her. All her life she had had too much
energy to endure anyone hanging round her, personally. Now
she gave up. Her wrists seemed numb, as if the power in her
were switched off.

When she went down they said Lewis had asked to speak
to her. She had hardly seen him since they arrived at Merriton.

"I've had a letter from Lady Carrington, Mam. She says will
I take St. Mawr to London and wait for her there. But she says
I am to come to you, Mam, for definite orders."

"Very well, Lewis. I shall be going to London in a few days'
time. You arrange for St. Mawr to go up one day this week,
and you will take him to the Mews. Come to me for anything
you want. And don't talk of leaving my daughter. We want
you to go with St. Mawr to America, with us and Phœnix."

"And your horse, Mam?"

"I shall leave him here at Merriton. I shall give him to Miss
Atherton."

"Very good, Mam!"

"Dear Daughter: I shall be in my old quarters in Mayfair
next Saturday, calling the same day at your house to see if

everything is ready for you. Lewis has fixed up with the railway: he goes to town to-morrow. The reason of his letter was
that I had asked him if he would care to marry me, and he
turned me down with emphasis. But I will tell you about it.
You and I are the scribe and the Pharisee; I never could write
a letter, and you could never leave off——"

"Dearest Mother: I smelt something rash, but I know it's no
use saying: How *could* you? I only wonder, though, that you
should think of marriage. You know, dear, I ache in every
fibre to be left alone, from all that sort of thing. I feel all
bruises, like one who has been assassinated. I do so understand why Jesus said: '*Noli me tangere.*' Touch me not, I am
not yet ascended unto the Father. Everything had hurt him
so much, wearied him so beyond endurance, he felt he could
not bear one little human touch on his body. I am like that.
I can hardly bear even Elena to hand me a dress. As for a
man—and marriage—ah, no! *Noli me tangere, homine!* I am
not yet ascended unto the Father. Oh, leave me alone, leave
me alone! That is all my cry to all the world.

"Curiously, I feel that Phœnix understands what I feel. He
leaves me so understandingly alone, he almost gives me my
sheath of aloneness: or at least, he protects me in my sheath.
I am grateful for him.

"Whereas Rico feels my aloneness as a sort of shame to
himself. He wants at least a blinding *pretence* of intimacy.
Ah, intimacy! The thought of it fills me with aches, and the
pretence of it exhausts me beyond myself.

"Yes, I long to go away to the West, to be away from the
world like one dead and in another life, in a valley that life
has not yet entered.

"Rico asked me: What are you doing with St. Mawr?
When I said we were taking him with us, he said: 'Oh, the
corpus delicti!' Whether that means anything, I don't know.
But he has grown sarcastic beyond my depth.

"I shall see you to-morrow——"

Lou arrived in town, at the dead end of August, with her
maid and Phœnix. How wonderful it seemed to have London
empty of all her set: her own little house to herself, with just
the housekeeper and her own maid. The fact of being alone in
those surroundings was so wonderful. It made the surroundings themselves seem all the more ghastly. Everything that
had been actual to her was turning ghostly: even her little

drawing-room was the ghost of a room, belonging to the dead
people who had known it, or to all the dead generations that
had brought such a room into being, evolved it out of their
quaint domestic desires. And now, in herself, those desires
were suddenly spent: gone out like a lamp that suddenly dies.
And then she saw her pale, delicate room with its little green
agate bowl and its two little porcelain birds and its soft,
roundish chairs, turned into something ghostly, like a room
set out in a museum. She felt like fastening little labels on the
furniture: 'Lady Louise Carrington Lounge Chair, Last used
August, 1923.' Not for the benefit of posterity: but to remove
her own self into another world, another realm of existence.

"My house, my house, my house, how can I ever have taken
so much pains about it?" she kept saying to herself. It was like
one of her old hats, suddenly discovered neatly put away in an
old hat-box. And what a horror: an old 'fashionable' hat.

Lewis came to see her, and he sat there in one of her delicate
mauve chairs, with his feet on a delicate old carpet from
Turkestan, and she just wondered. He wore his leather gaiters
and khaki breeches as usual, and a faded blue shirt. But his
beard and hair were trimmed, he was tidy. There was a certain
fineness of contour about him, a certain subtle gleam, which
made him seem, apart from his rough boots, not at all gross,
or coarse, in that setting of rather silky, Oriental furnishings.
Rather he made the Asiatic, sensuous exquisiteness of her old
rugs and her old white Chinese figures seem a weariness.
Beauty! What was beauty? she asked herself. The Oriental
exquisiteness seemed to her all like dead flowers whose hour
had come to be thrown away.

Lou could understand her mother's wanting, for a moment,
to marry him. His detachedness and his acceptance of something in destiny which people cannot accept. Right in the
middle of him he accepted something from destiny that gave
him a quality of eternity. He did not care about persons,
people, even events. In his own odd way he was an aristocrat,
inaccessible in his aristocracy. But it was the aristocracy of
the invisible powers, the greater influences, nothing to do with
human society.

"You don't really want to leave St. Mawr, do you?" Lou
asked him. "You don't really want to quit, as you said?"

He looked at her steadily from his pale grey eyes, without
answering, not knowing what to say.

"Mother told me what she said to you.—But she doesn't mind, she says you are entirely within your rights. She has a real regard for you. But we mustn't let our regards run us into actions which are beyond our scope, must we? That makes everything unreal. But you will come with us to America with St. Mawr, won't you? We depend on you."

"I don't want to be uncomfortable," he said.

"Don't be," she smiled. "I myself hate unreal situations—I feel I can't stand them any more. And most marriages are unreal situations. But apart from anything exaggerated, you like being with mother and me, don't you?"

"Yes, I do. I like Mrs. Witt as well. But not——"

"I know. There won't be any more of that——"

"You see, Lady Carrington," he said, with a little heat, "I'm not by nature a marrying man. And I'd feel I was selling myself."

"Quite!—Why do you think you are not a marrying man, though?"

"Me! I don't feel myself after I've been with women." He spoke in a low tone, looking down at his hands. "I feel messed up. I'm better to keep to myself.—Because——" and here he looked up with a flare in his eyes: "women—they only want to make you give in to them, so that they feel almighty, and you feel small."

"Don't you like feeling small?" Lou smiled. "And don't you want to make them give in to you?"

"Not me," he said. "I don't want nothing. Nothing, I want."

"Poor mother!" said Lou. "She thinks if she feels moved by a man, it must result in marriage—or that kind of thing. Surely she makes a mistake. I think you and Phœnix and mother and I might live somewhere in a far-away wild place, and make a good life: so long as we didn't begin to mix up marriage, or love or that sort of thing into it. It seems to me men and women have really hurt one another so much nowadays that they had better stay apart till they have learned to be gentle with one another again. Not all this forced passion and destructive philandering. Men and women should stay apart till their hearts grow gentle towards one another again. Now, it's only each one fighting for his own—or her own—underneath the cover of tenderness."

"Dear!—darling!—Yes, my love!" mocked Lewis, with a faint smile of amused contempt.

"Exactly. People always say *dearest!* when they hate each other most."

Lewis nodded, looking at her with a sudden sombre gloom in his eyes. A queer bitterness showed on his mouth. But even then he was so still and remote.

The housekeeper came and announced The Honourable Laura Ridley. This was like a blow in the face to Lou. She rose hurriedly—and Lewis rose, moving to the door.

"Don't go, please, Lewis," said Lou—and then Laura Ridley appeared in the doorway. She was a woman a few years older than Lou, but she looked younger. She might have been a shy girl of twenty-two, with her fresh complexion, her hesitant manner, her round, startled brown eyes, her bobbed hair.

"Hello!" said the newcomer. "Imagine your being back! I saw you in Paddington."

Those sharp eyes would see everything.

"I thought everyone was out of town," said Lou. "This is Mr. Lewis."

Laura gave him a little nod, then sat on the edge of her chair.

"No," she said. "I did go to Ireland to my people, but I came back. I prefer London when I can be more or less alone in it. I thought I'd just run in for a moment before you're gone again.—Scotland, isn't it?"

"No, mother and I are going to America."

"America! Oh, I thought it was Scotland."

"It was. But we have suddenly to go to America."

"I see!—And what about Rico?"

"He is staying on in Shropshire. Didn't you hear of his accident?"

Lou told about it briefly.

"But how awful!" said Laura. "But there! I knew it! I had a premonition when I saw that horse. We had a horse that killed a man. Then my father got rid of it. But ours was a mare, that one. Yours is a boy."

"A full-grown man, I'm afraid."

"Yes, of course, I remember.—But how awful! I suppose you won't ride in the Row. The awful people that ride there nowadays, anyhow! Oh, aren't they awful! Aren't people monstrous, really! My word, when I see the horses crossing Hyde Park Corner on a wet day and coming down smash to

those slippery stones, giving their riders a fractured skull!—
No joke!"

She inquired details of Rico.

"Oh, I suppose I shall see him when he gets back," she said.
"But I'm sorry you are going. I shall miss you, I'm afraid.
Though you won't be staying long in America. No one stays
there longer than they can help."

"I think the winter through, at least," said Lou.

"Oh, all the winter! So long? I'm sorry to hear *that*. You're
one of the few, very few people one can talk *really* simply
with. Extraordinary, isn't it, how few really simple people
there are! And they get fewer and fewer. I stayed a fortnight
with my people, and a week of that I was in bed. It was really
horrible. They really try to take the life out of me, *really*!
Just because one won't be as they are, and play their game. I
simply refused, and came away."

"But you can't cut yourself off altogether," said Lou.

"No, I suppose not. One has to see somebody. Luckily one
has a few artists for friends. They're the only real people,
anyhow——" She glanced round inquisitively at Lewis, and
said with a slight, impertinent, elvish smile on her virgin
face:

"Are you an artist?"

"No, Mam!" he said. "I'm a groom."

"Oh, I see!" She looked him up and down.

"Lewis is St. Mawr's master," said Lou.

"Oh, the horse! the terrible horse!" She paused a moment.
Then again she turned to Lewis with that faint smile, slightly
condescending, slightly impertinent, slightly flirtatious.

"Aren't you afraid of him?" she asked.

"No, Mam."

"Aren't you, *really!*—And can you always master him?"

"Mostly. He knows me."

"Yes! I suppose that's it."—She looked him up and down
again, then turned away to Lou.

"What have you been painting lately?" said Lou. Laura
was not a bad painter.

"Oh, hardly anything. I haven't been able to get on at all.
This is one of my bad intervals."

Here Lewis rose and looked at Lou.

"All right," she said. "Come in after lunch, and we'll finish
those arrangements."

Laura gazed after the man, as he dived out of the room, as if her eyes were gimlets that could bore into his secret.

In the course of the conversation she said:

"What a curious little man that was!"

"Which?"

"The groom who was here just now. *Very* curious! Such peculiar eyes. I shouldn't wonder if he had psychic powers."

"What sort of psychic powers?" said Lou.

"Could *see* things.—And hypnotic, too. He might have hypnotic powers."

"What makes you think so?"

"He gives me that sort of feeling. Very curious! Probably he hypnotises the horse.—Are you leaving the horse here, by the way, in stable?"

"No, taking him to America."

"Taking him to America! How extraordinary!"

"It's mother's idea. She thinks he might be valuable as a stock horse on a ranch. You know we still have interest in a ranch in Texas."

"Oh, I see! Yes, probably he'd be very valuable to improve the breed of the horses over there.—My father has some very lovely hunters. Isn't it disgraceful, he would never let me ride!"

"Why?"

"Because we girls weren't important, in his opinion.— So you're taking the horse to America! With the little man?"

"Yes, St. Mawr will hardly behave without him."

"I see—I see—ee—ee! Just you and Mrs. Witt and the little man. I'm sure you'll find he has psychic powers."

"I'm afraid I'm not so good at finding things out," said Lou.

"Aren't you? No, I suppose not. I am. I have a flair. I sort of *smell* things.—Then the horse is already here, is he? When do you think you'll sail?"

"Mother is finding a merchant boat that will go to Galveston, Texas, and take us along with the horse. She knows people who will find the right thing. But it takes time."

"What a much nicer way to travel than on one of those great liners! Oh, how awful they are! So vulgar! Floating palaces they call them! My word, the people inside the palaces!—Yes, I should say that would be a much pleasanter way of travelling: on a cargo boat."

Laura wanted to go down to the Mews to see St. Mawr. The two women went together.

St. Mawr stood in his box, bright and tense as usual.

"Yes!" said Laura Ridley, with a slight hiss. "Yes! Isn't he beautiful. Such very perfect legs!"—She eyed him round with those gimlet, sharp eyes of hers. "Almost a pity to let him go out of England. We need some of his perfect *bone*, I feel.— But his eye. Hasn't he got a look in it, my word!"

"I can never see that he looks wicked," said Lou.

"Can't you!"—Laura had a slight hiss in her speech, a sort of aristocratic decision in her enunciation, that got on Lou's nerves.—"He looks wicked to me!"

"He's not *mean*," said Lou. "He'd never do anything mean to you."

"Oh, mean! I dare say not. No! I'll grant him that, he gives fair warning. His eye says *Beware!*—But isn't he a beauty, *isn't* he!" Lou could feel the peculiar reverence for St. Mawr's breeding, his show qualities. Herself, all she cared about was the horse himself, his real nature. "Isn't it extraordinary," Laura continued, "that you never get a *really* perfectly satisfactory animal! There's always something wrong. And in men too. Isn't it curious? there's always something— something wrong—or something missing. Why is it?"

"I don't know," said Lou. She felt unable to cope with any more. And she was glad when Laura left her.

The days passed slowly, quietly, London almost empty of Lou's acquaintances. Mrs. Witt was busy getting all sorts of papers and permits: such a fuss! The battle light was still in her eye. But about her nose was a dusky, pinched look that made Lou wonder.

Both women wanted to be gone: they felt they had already flown in spirit, and it was weary, having the body left behind.

At last all was ready: they only awaited the telegram to say when their cargo-boat would sail. Trunks stood there packed, like great stones locked for ever. The Westminster house seemed already a shell. Rico wrote and telegraphed tenderly, but there was a sense of relentless effort in it all, rather than of any tenderness. He had taken his position.

Then the telegram came, the boat was ready to sail.

"There, now!" said Mrs. Witt, as if it had been a sentence of death.

"Why do you look like that, mother?"

"I feel I haven't an ounce of energy left in my body."

"But how queer, for you, mother. Do you think you are ill?"

"No, Louise. I just feel that way: as if I hadn't an ounce of energy left in my body."

"You'll feel yourself again, once you are away."

"Maybe I shall."

After all, it was only a matter of telephoning. The hotel and the railway porters and taxi-men would do the rest.

It was a grey, cloudy day, cold even. Mother and daughter sat in a cold first-class carriage and watched the little Hampshire country-side go past: little, old, unreal it seemed to them both, and passing away like a dream whose edges only are in consciousness. Autumn! Was this autumn? Were these trees, fields, villages? It seemed but the dim, dissolved edges of a dream, without inward substance.

At Southampton it was raining: and just a chaos, till they stepped on to a clean boat, and were received by a clean young captain, quite sympathetic, and quite a gentleman. Mrs. Witt, however, hardly looked at him, but went down to her cabin and lay down in her bunk.

There, lying concealed, she felt the engines start, she knew the voyage had begun. But she lay still. She saw the clouds and the rain, and refused to be disturbed.

Lou had lunch with the young captain, and she felt she ought to be flirty. The young man was so polite and attentive. And she wished so much she were alone.

Afterwards, she sat on deck and saw the Isle of Wight pass shadowy, in a misty rain. She didn't know it was the Isle of Wight. To her, it was just the lowest bit of the British Isles. She saw it fading away: and with it, her life, going like a clot of shadow in a mist of nothingness. She had no feelings about it, none: neither about Rico, nor her London house, nor anything. All passing in a grey curtain of rainy drizzle, like a death, and she, with not a feeling left.

They entered the Channel, and felt the slow heave of the sea. And soon the clouds broke in a little wind. The sky began to clear. By mid-afternoon it was blue summer, on the blue, running waters of the Channel. And soon, the ship steering for Santander, there was the coast of France, the rocks twinkling like some magic world.

The magic world! And back of it, that post-war Paris,

which Lou knew only too well, and which depressed her so
thoroughly. Or that post-war Monte Carlo, the Riviera still
more depressing even than Paris. No, no one must land, even
on magic coasts. Else you found yourself in a railway station
and a 'centre of civilisation' in five minutes.

Mrs. Witt hated the sea, and stayed, as a rule, practically
the whole time of the crossing in her bunk. There she was
now, silent, shut up like a steel trap, as in her tomb. She did
not even read. Just lay and stared at the passing sky. And the
only thing to do was to leave her alone.

Lewis and Phœnix hung on the rail and watched everything. Or they went down to see St. Mawr. Or they stood
talking in the doorway of the wireless operator's cabin. Lou
begged the captain to give them jobs to do.

The queer, transitory, unreal feeling, as the ship crossed the
great, heavy Atlantic. It was rather bad weather. And Lou
felt, as she had felt before, that this grey, wolf-like, cold-
blooded ocean hated men and their ships and their smoky
passage. Heavy grey waves, a low-sagging sky: rain: yellow,
weird evenings with snatches of sun: so it went on. Till they
got way south, into the westward-running stream. Then they
began to get blue weather and blue water.

To go south! Always to go south, away from the Arctic
horror as far as possible! That was Lou's instinct. To go out
of the clutch of greyness and low skies, of sweeping rain, and
of slow, blanketing snow. Never again to see the mud and
rain and snow of a northern winter, nor to feel the idealistic,
Christianised tension of the now irreligious North.

As they neared Havana, and the water sparkled at night
with phosphorus, and the flying-fishes came like drops of
bright water, sailing out of the massive-slippery waves, Mrs.
Witt emerged once more. She still had that shut-up, deathly
look on her face. But she prowled round the deck, and mani-
fested at least a little interest in affairs not her own. Here at
sea she hardly remembered the existence of St. Mawr or Lewis
or Phœnix. She was not very deeply aware even of Lou's
existence.—But, of course, it would all come back, once they
were on land.

They sailed in hot sunshine out of a blue, blue sea, past the
castle into the harbour of Havana. There was a lot of ship-
ping: and this was already America. Mrs. Witt had herself
and Lou put ashore immediately. They took a motor-car and

drove at once to the great boulevard that is the centre of Havana. Here they saw a long rank of motor-cars, all drawn up ready to take a couple of hundred American tourists for one more tour. There were the tourists, all with badges in their coats, lest they should get lost.

"They get so drunk by night," said the driver in Spanish, "that the policemen find them lying in the road—turn them over, see the badge—and, hup!—carry them to their hotel." He grinned sardonically.

Lou and her mother lunched at the Hôtel d'Angleterre, and Mrs. Witt watched transfixed while a couple of her countrymen, a stout successful man and his wife, lunched abroad. They had cocktails—then lobster—and a bottle of hock—then a bottle of champagne—then a half-bottle of port.—And Mrs. Witt rose in haste as the liqueurs came. For that successful man and his wife had gone on imbibing with a sort of fixed and deliberate will, apparently tasting nothing, but saying to themselves: Now we're drinking Rhine wine! Now we're drinking 1912 champagne. Yah, Prohibition! Thou canst not put it over me.—Their complexions became more and more lurid. Mrs. Witt fled, fearing a Havana *débâcle*. But she said nothing.

In the afternoon, they motored into the country to see the great brewery gardens, the new villa suburb, and through the lanes past the old, decaying plantations with palm trees. In one lane they met the fifty motor-cars with the two hundred tourists all with badges on their chests and self-satisfaction on their faces. Mrs. Witt watched in grim silence.

"*Plus ça change, plus c'est la même chose,*" said Lou, with a wicked little smile. "*On n'est pas mieux ici,* mother."

"I know it," said Mrs. Witt.

The hotels by the sea were all shut up: it was not yet the 'season'. Not till November. And then!—Why, then Havana would be an American city, in full leaf of green dollar bills. The green leaf of American prosperity shedding itself recklessly, from every roaming sprig of a tourist, over this city of sunshine and alcohol. Green leaves unfolded in Pittsburg and Chicago, showering in winter downfall in Havana.

Mother and daughter drank tea in a corner of the Hôtel d'Angleterre once more, and returned to the ferry.

The Gulf of Mexico was blue and rippling, with the phantom of islands on the south. Great porpoises rolled and leaped, running in front of the ship in the clear water, diving, travelling in perfect motion, straight, with the tip of the ship touching the tip of their tails, then rolling over, corkscrewing, and showing their bellies as they went. Marvellous! The marvellous beauty and fascination of natural wild things! The horror of man's unnatural life, his heaped-up civilisation!

The flying fishes burst out of the sea in clouds of silvery, transparent motion. Blue above and below, the Gulf seemed a silent, empty, timeless place where man did not really reach. And Lou was again fascinated by the glamour of the universe.

But bump! She and her mother were in a first-class hotel again, calling down the telephone for the bell-boy and iced water. And soon they were in a Pullman, off towards San Antonio.

It was America, it was Texas. They were at their ranch, on the great level of yellow autumn, with the vast sky above. And after all, from the hot, wide sky, and the hot, wide, red earth, there *did* come something new, something not used up. Lou *did* feel exhilarated.

The Texans were there, tall, blond people, ingenuously cheerful, ingenuously, childishly intimate, as if the fact that you had never seen them before was as nothing compared to the fact that you'd all been living in one room together all your lives, so that nothing was hidden from either of you. The one room being the mere shanty of the world in which we all live. Strange, uninspired cheerfulness, filling, as it were, the blank of complete incomprehension.

And off they set in their motor-cars, chiefly high-legged Fords, rattling away down the red trails between yellow sunflowers or sere grass or dry cotton, away, away into great distances, cheerfully raising the dust of haste. It left Lou in a sort of blank amazement. But it left her amused, not depressed. The old screws of emotion and intimacy that had been screwed down so tightly upon her fell out of their holes here. The Texan intimacy weighed no more on her than a postage stamp, even if, for the moment, it stuck as close. And there was a certain underneath recklessness, even a stoicism in all the apparently childish people, which left one free. They might appear childish: but they stoically depended on themselves alone, in reality. Not as in England, where every man waited to pour the burden of himself upon you.

St. Mawr arrived safely, a bit bewildered. The Texans eyed

him closely, struck silent, as ever, by anything pure-bred and beautiful. He was somehow too beautiful, too perfected, in this great open country. The long-legged Texan horses, with their elaborate saddles, seemed somehow more natural.

Even St. Mawr felt himself strange, as it were naked and singled out, in this rough place. Like a jewel among stones, a pearl before swine, maybe. But the swine were no fools. They knew a pearl from a grain of maize, and a grain of maize from a pearl. And they knew what they wanted. When it was pearls, it was pearls; though chiefly, it was maize. Which shows good sense. They could see St. Mawr's points. Only he needn't draw the point too fine or it would just not pierce the tough skin of this country.

The ranch-man mounted him—just threw a soft skin over his back, jumped on, and away down the red trail, raising the dust among the tall, wild, yellow of sunflowers, in the hot, wild sun. Then back again in a fume, and the man slipped off.

"He's got the stuff in him, he sure has," said the man.

And the horse seemed pleased with this rough handling. Lewis looked on in wonder, and a little envy.

Lou and her mother stayed a fortnight on the ranch. It was all so queer: so crude, so rough, so easy, so artificially civilised, and so meaningless. Lou could not get over the feeling that it all meant nothing. There were no roots of reality at all. No consciousness below the surface, no meaning in anything save the obvious, the blatantly obvious. It was like life enacted in a mirror. Visually, it was wildly vital. But there was nothing behind it. Or like a cinematograph: flat shapes, exactly like men, but without any substance of reality, rapidly rattling away with talk, emotions, activity, all in the flat, nothing behind it. No deeper consciousness at all. So it seemed to her.

One moved from dream to dream, from phantasm to phantasm.

But at least, this Texan life, if it had no bowels, no vitals, at least it could not prey on one's own vitals. It was this much better than Europe.

Lewis was silent, and rather piqued. St. Mawr had already made advances to the boss's long-legged, arched-necked glossy-maned Texan mare. And the boss was pleased.

What a world!

Mrs. Witt eyed it all shrewdly. But she failed to participate. Lou was a bit scared at the emptiness of it all, and the queer, phantasmal self-consciousness. Cowboys just as self-conscious as Rico, far more sentimental, inwardly vague and unreal. Cowboys that went after their cows in black Ford motor-cars: and who self-consciously saw Lady Carrington falling to them, as elegant young ladies from the East fall to the noble cowboy of the films, or in Zane Grey. It was all film-psychology.

And at the same time, these boys led a hard, hard life, often dangerous and gruesome. Nevertheless, inwardly they were self-conscious film heroes. The boss himself, a man over forty, long and lean and with a great deal of stringy energy, showed off before her in a strong silent manner, existing for the time being purely in his imagination of the sort of picture he made to her, the sort of impression he made on her.

So they all were, coloured up like a Zane Grey book-jacket, all of them living in the mirror. The kind of picture they made to somebody else.

And at the same time, with energy, courage, and a stoical grit getting their work done, and putting through what they had to put through.

It left Lou blank with wonder. And in the face of this strange, cheerful living in the mirror—a rather cheap mirror at that—England began to seem real to her again.

Then she had to remember herself back in England. And no, oh God, England was not real either, except poisonously.

What was real? What under heaven was real?

Her mother had gone dumb and, as it were, out of range. Phœnix was a bit assured and bouncy, back more or less in his own conditions. Lewis was a bit impressed by the empti-ness of everything, the *lack* of concentration. And St. Mawr followed at the heels of the boss's long-legged black Texan mare, almost slavishly.

What, in heaven's name, was one to make of it all?

Soon, she could not stand this sort of living in a film-setting, with the mechanical energy of 'making good', that is, making money, to keep the show going. The mystic duty to 'make good', meaning to make the ranch pay a laudable interest on the 'owners'' investment. Lou herself being one of the owners. And the interest that came to her, from her father's will, being the money she spent to buy St. Mawr and to fit up that house

in Westminster. Then also the mystic duty to 'feel good'.
Everybody had to *feel good, fine!* "How are you this morning,
Mr. Latham?"—"*Fine!* Eh! Don't you feel good out here, eh?
Lady Carrington?"—"*Fine!*"—Lou pronounced it with the
same ringing conviction. It was Coué all the time!

"Shall we stay here long, mother?" she asked.

"Not a day longer than you want to, Louise. I stay entirely
for your sake."

"Then let us go, mother."

They left St. Mawr and Lewis. But Phœnix wanted to come
along. So they motored to San Antonio, got into the Pullman,
and travelled as far as El Paso. Then they changed to go
North. Santa Fé would be at least 'easy'. And Mrs. Witt had
acquaintances there.

They found the fiesta over in Santa Fé: Indians, Mexicans,
artists had finished their great effort to amuse and attract the
tourists. "Welcome, Mr. Tourist" said a great board on one
side of the high-road. And on the other side, a little nearer to
town: "Thank You, Mr. Tourist."

"*Plus ça change*——" Lou began.

"*Ça ne change jamais*—except for the worse!" said Mrs.
Witt, like a pistol going off. And Lou held her peace, after she
had sighed to herself, and said in her own mind: 'Welcome
Also, Mrs. and Miss Tourist!'

There was no getting a word out of Mrs. Witt these days.
Whereas Phœnix was becoming almost loquacious.

They stayed a while in Santa Fé, in the clean, comfortable,
'homely' hotel, where 'every room had its bath': a spotless
white bath, with very hot water night and day. The tourists
and commercial travellers sat in the big hall down below,
everybody living in the mirror! And of course, they knew
Lady Carrington down to her shoe-soles. And they all expected
her to know them down to their shoe-soles. For the only
object of the mirror is to reflect images.

For two days mother and daughter ate in the mayonnaise
intimacy of the dining-room. Then Mrs. Witt struck, and
telephoned down every meal-time for her meal in her room.
She got to staying in bed later and later, as on the ship. Lou
became uneasy. This was worse than Europe.

Phœnix was still there, as a sort of half-friend, half-servant
retainer. He was perfectly happy, roving round among the
Mexicans and Indians, talking Spanish all day, and telling

about England and his two mistresses, rolling the ball of his own importance.

"I'm afraid we've got Phœnix for life," said Lou.

"Not unless we wish," said Mrs. Witt indifferently. And she picked up a novel which she didn't want to read, but which she was going to read.

"What shall we do next, mother?" Lou asked.

"As far as I am concerned, there is no next," said Mrs. Witt.

"Come, mother! Let's go back to Italy or somewhere, if it's as bad as that."

"Never again, Louise, shall I cross that water. I have come home to die."

"I don't see much home about it—the Gonsalez Hotel in Santa Fé."

"Indeed not! But as good as anywhere else to die in."

"Oh, mother, don't be silly! Shall we look for somewhere where we can be by ourselves?"

"I leave it to you, Louise. I have made my last decision."

"What is that, mother?"

"Never, never to make another decision!"

"Not even to decide to die?"

"No, not even that."

"Or *not* to die?"

"Not that either."

Mrs. Witt shut up like a trap. She refused to rise from her bed that day.

Lou went to consult Phœnix. The result was, the two set out to look at a little ranch that was for sale.

It was autumn, and the loveliest time in the south-west, where there is no spring, snow blowing into the hot lap of summer; and no real summer, hail falling in thick ice from the thunderstorms: and even no very definite winter, hot sun melting the snow and giving an impression of spring at any time. But autumn there is, when the winds of the desert are almost still, and the mountains fume no clouds. But morning comes cold and delicate, upon the wild sunflowers and the puffing, yellow-flowered greasewood. For the desert blooms in autumn. In spring it is grey ash all the time, and only the strong breath of the summer sun, and the heavy splashing of thunder rain succeeds at last, by September, in blowing it into soft puffy yellow fire.

It was such a delicate morning when Lou drove out with

Phœnix towards the mountains, to look at this ranch that a
Mexican wanted to sell. For the brief moment the high mountains had lost their snow: it would be back again in a fortnight: and stood dim and delicate with autumn haze. The
desert stretched away pale, as pale as the sky, but silvery and
sere, with hummock-mounds of shadow, and long wings of
shadow, like the reflection of some great bird. The same eagle
shadows came like rude paintings of the outstretched bird,
upon the mountains, where the aspens were turning yellow.
For the moment, the brief moment, the great desert-and-
mountain landscape had lost its certain cruelty, and looked
tender, dreamy. And many, many birds were flickering around.

Lou and Phœnix bumped and hesitated over a long trail:
then wound down into a deep canyon: and then the car began
to climb, climb, climb, in steep rushes, and in long, heart-
breaking, uneven pulls. The road was bad, and driving was
no joke. But it was the sort of road Phœnix was used to. He
sat impassive and watchful, and kept on, till his engine boiled.
He was *himself* in this country: impassive, detached, self-
satisfied, and silently assertive. Guarding himself at every
moment, but, on his guard, sure of himself. Seeing no difference at all between Lou or Mrs. Witt and himself, except
that they had money and he had none, while he had a native
importance which they lacked. He depended on them for
money, they on him for the power to live out here in the
West. Intimately, he was as good as they. Money was their
only advantage.

As Lou sat beside him in the front seat of the car, where
it bumped less than behind, she felt this. She felt a peculiar,
tough-necked arrogance in him, as if he were asserting himself to put something over her. He wanted her to allow him to
make advances to her, to allow him to suggest that he should
be her lover. And then, finally, she would marry him, and he
would be on the same footing as she and her mother.

In return, he would look after her, and give her his support
and countenance, as a man, and stand between her and the
world. In this sense, he would be faithful to her, and loyal.
But as far as other women went, Mexican women or Indian
women: why, that was none of her business. His marrying
her would be a pact between two aliens, on behalf of one
another, and he would keep his part of it all right. But himself, as a private man and a predative alien-blooded male, this

had nothing to do with her. It didn't enter into her scope and count. She was one of these nervous white women with lots of money. She was very nice, too. But as a squaw—as a real woman in a shawl whom a man went after for the pleasure of the night—why, she hardly counted. One of these white women who talk clever and know things like a man. She could hardly expect a half-savage male to acknowledge her as his female counterpart.—No! She had the bucks! And she had all the paraphernalia of the white man's civilisation, which a savage can play with and so escape his own hollow boredom. But his own real female counterpart?—Phœnix would just have shrugged his shoulders, and thought the question not worth answering. How could there be any answer in *her*, to the phallic male in him? Couldn't! Yet it would flatter his vanity and his self-esteem immensely, to possess her. That would be possessing the very clue to the white man's over-whelming world. And if she would let him possess her, he would be absolutely loyal to her, as far as affairs and appear-ances went. Only, the aboriginal phallic male in him simply couldn't recognise her as a woman at all. In this respect, she didn't exist. It needed the shawled Indian or Mexican women, with their squeaky, plaintive voices, their shuffling, watery humility, and the dark glances of their big, knowing eyes. When an Indian woman looked at him from under her black fringe, with dark, half-secretive suggestion in her big eyes: and when she stood before him hugged in her shawl, in such apparently complete quiescent humility: and when she spoke to him in her mousey squeak of a high, plaintive voice, as if it were difficult for her female bashfulness even to emit so much sound: and when she shuffled away with her legs wide apart, because of her wide-topped, white, high buckskin boots with tiny white feet, and her dark-knotted hair so full of hard, yet subtle lure: and when he remembered the almost watery softness of the Indian woman's dark, warm flesh: then he was a male, an old, secretive, rat-like male. But before Lou's straightforwardness and utter sexual incompetence, he just stood in contempt. And to him, even a French cocotte was utterly devoid of the right sort of sex. She couldn't really move him. She couldn't satisfy the furtiveness in him. He needed this plaintive, squeaky, dark-fringed Indian quality, something furtive and soft and rat-like, really to rouse him.

Nevertheless, he was ready to trade his sex, which, in his

opinion, every white woman was secretly pining for, for the
white woman's money and social privileges. In the day-time,
all the thrill and excitement of the white man's motor-cars and
moving pictures and ice-cream sodas, and so forth. In the
night, the soft, watery-soft warmth of an Indian or half-
Indian woman. This was Phœnix's idea of life for himself.

Meanwhile, if a white woman gave him the privileges of
the white man's world, he would do his duty by her as far
as all that went.

Lou, sitting very, very still beside him as he drove the car—
he was not a very good driver, not quick and marvellous as
some white men are, particularly some French chauffeurs she
had known, but usually a little behindhand in his movements—she knew more or less all that he felt. More or less
she divined as a woman does. Even from a certain rather
assured stupidity of his shoulders, and a certain rather stupid
assertiveness of his knees, she knew him.

But she did not judge him too harshly. Somewhere deep,
deep in herself she knew she too was at fault. And this made
her sometimes inclined to humble herself, as a woman, before
the furtive assertiveness of this underground, 'knowing' savage.
He was so different from Rico.

Yet, after all, *was* he? In his rootlessness, his drifting, his
real meaninglessness, was he different from Rico? And his
childish, spellbound absorption in the motor-car, or in the
moving pictures, or in an ice-cream soda—was it very different
from Rico? Anyhow, was it really any better? Pleasanter,
perhaps, to a woman, because of the childishness of it.

The same with his opinion of himself as a sexual male! So
childish, really, it was almost thrilling to a woman. But then,
so stupid also, with that furtive lurking in holes and imagin-
ing it could not be detected He imagined he kept himself dark, in his sexual rat-holes. He imagined he was not
detected.

No, no, Lou was not such a fool as she looked, in his eyes,
anyhow. She knew what she wanted. She wanted relief from
the nervous tension and irritation of her life, she wanted to
escape from the friction which is the whole stimulus in
modern social life. She wanted to be still: only that, to be
very, very still, and recover her own soul.

When Phœnix presumed she was looking for some secretly
sexual male such as himself, he was ridiculously mistaken.

Even the illusion of the beautiful St. Mawr was gone. And
Phœnix, roaming round like a sexual rat in promiscuous back
yards!—*Merci, mon cher!* For that was all he was: a sexual
rat in the great barn-yard of man's habitat, looking for female
rats!

Merci, mon cher! You are had.

Nevertheless, in his very mistakenness, he was a relief to
her. His mistake was amusing rather than impressive. And
the fact that one half of his intelligence was a complete dark
blank, that too was a relief.

Strictly, and perhaps in the best sense, he was a servant.
His very unconsciousness and his very limitation served as a
shelter, as one shelters within the limitations of four walls.
The very decided limits to his intelligence were a shelter to
her. They made her feel safe.

But that feeling of safety did not deceive her. It was the
feeling one derived from having a *true* servant attached to
one, a man whose psychic limitations left him incapable of
anything but service, and whose strong flow of natural life,
at the same time, made him need to serve.

And Lou, sitting there so very still and frail, yet self-
contained, had not lived for nothing. She no longer wanted
to fool herself. She had no desire at all to fool herself into
thinking that a Phœnix might be a husband and a mate. No
desire that way at all. His obtuseness was a servant's obtuseness. She was grateful to him for serving, and she paid him
a wage. Moreover, she provided him with something to do, to
occupy his life. In a sense, she gave him his life, and rescued
him from his own boredom. It was a balance.

He did not know what she was thinking. There was a certain
physical sympathy between them. His obtuseness made him
think it was also a sexual sympathy.

"It's a nice trip, you and me," he said suddenly, turning and
looking her in the eyes with an excited look, and ending on a
foolish little laugh.

She realised that she should have sat in the back seat.

"But it's a bad road," she said. "Hadn't you better stop and
put the sides of the hood up? Your engine is boiling."

He looked away with a quick switch of interest to the red
thermometer in front of his machine.

"She's boiling," he said, stopping, and getting out with a
quick alacrity to go to look at the engine.

Lou got out also, and went to the back seat, shutting the door decisively.

"I think I'll ride at the back," she said, "it gets so frightfully hot in front when the engine heats up.—Do you think she needs some water? Have you got some in the canteen?"

"She's full," he said, peering into the steaming valve.

"You can run a bit out, if you think there's any need. I wonder if it's much farther!"

"*Quién sabe!*" said he, slightly impertinent.

She relapsed into her own stillness. She realised how careful, how very careful she must be of relaxing into sympathy, and reposing, as it were, on Phœnix. He would read it as a sexual appeal. Perhaps he couldn't help it. She had only herself to blame. He was obtuse, as a man and a savage. He had only one interpretation, sex, for any woman's approach to him.

And she knew, with the last clear knowledge of weary disillusion, that she did not want to be mixed up in Phœnix's sexual promiscuities. The very thought was an insult to her. The crude, clumsy servant-male: no, no, not that. He was a good fellow, a very good fellow, as far as he went. But he fell far short of physical intimacy.

"No, no," she said to herself, "I was wrong to ride in the front seat with him. I must sit alone, just alone. Because sex, mere sex, is repellent to me. I will never prostitute myself again. Unless something touches my very spirit, the very quick of me, I will stay alone, just alone. Alone, and give myself only to the unseen presences, serve only the other, unseen presences."

She understood now the meaning of the Vestal Virgins, the Virgins of the holy fire in the old temples. They were symbolic of herself, of woman weary of the embrace of incompetent men, weary, weary, weary of all that, turning to the unseen gods, the unseen spirits, the hidden fire, and devoting herself to that, and that alone. Receiving thence her pacification and her fulfilment.

Not these little, incompetent, childish self-opinionated men! Not these to touch her. She watched Phœnix's rather stupid shoulders as he drove the car on between the piñon trees and the cedars of the narrow mesa ridge, to the mountain foot. He was a good fellow. But let him run among women of his own sort. Something was beyond him. And this something must remain beyond him, never allow itself to come within his reach. Otherwise he would paw it and mess it up, and be as miserable as a child that has broken its father's watch.

No, no! She had loved an American, and lived with him for a fortnight. She had had a long, intimate friendship with an Italian. Perhaps it was love on his part. And she had yielded to him. Then her love and marriage to Rico.

And what of it all? Nothing. It was almost nothing. It was as if only the outside of herself, her top layers, were human. This inveigled her into intimacies. As soon as the intimacy penetrated, or attempted to penetrate, inside her, it was a disaster. Just a humiliation and a breaking down.

Within these outer layers of herself lay the successive inner sanctuaries of herself. And these were inviolable. She accepted it.

"I am not a marrying woman," she said to herself. "I'm not a lover nor a mistress nor a wife. It is no good. Love can't really come into me from the outside, and I can never, never mate with any man, since the mystic new man will never come to me. No, no, let me know myself and my role. I am one of the eternal Virgins, serving the eternal fire. My dealings with men have only broken my stillness and messed up my doorways. It has been my own fault. I ought to stay virgin, and still, very, very still, and serve the most perfect service. I want my temple and my loneliness and my Apollo mystery of the inner fire. And with men, only the delicate, subtler, more remote relations. No coming near. A coming near only breaks the delicate veils, and broken veils, like broken flowers, only lead to rottenness."

She felt a great peace inside herself as she made this realisation. And a thankfulness. Because, after all, it seemed to her that the hidden fire was alive and burning in this sky, over the desert, in the mountains. She felt a certain latent holiness in the very atmosphere, a young, spring-fire of latent holiness, such as she had never felt in Europe or in the East. "For me," she said, as she looked away at the mountains in shadow and the pale, warm desert beneath, with wings of shadow upon it: "For me, this place is sacred. It is blessed."

But as she watched Phœnix: as she remembered the motor-cars and tourists, and the rather dreary Mexicans of Santa Fé, and the lurking, invidious Indians, with something of a rat-like secretiveness and defeatedness in their bearing, she realised that the latent fire of the vast landscape struggled under a great weight of dirt-like inertia. She had to mind the dirt, most carefully and vividly avoid it and keep it away from her, here in this place that at last seemed sacred to her.

The motor-car climbed up, past the tall pine trees, to the foot of the mountains, and came at last to a wire gate, where nothing was to be expected. Phœnix opened the gate, and they drove on, through more trees, into a clearing where dried-up bean plants were yellow.

"This man got no water for his beans," said Phœnix. "Not got much beans this year."

They climbed slowly up the incline, through more pine trees, and out into another clearing, where a couple of horses were grazing. And there they saw the ranch itself, little low cabins with patched roofs, under a few pine trees, and facing the long twelve-acre clearing, or field, where the Michaelmas daisies were purple mist, and spangled with clumps of yellow flowers.

"Not got no alfalfa here neither!" said Phœnix, as the car waded past the flowers. "Must be a dry place up here. Got no water, sure they haven't."

Yet it was the place Lou wanted. In an instant, her heart sprang to it. The instant the car stopped, and she saw the two cabins inside the rickety fence, the rather broken corral beyond, and behind all, tall, blue balsam pines, the round hills, the solid up-rise of the mountain flank: and getting down, she looked across the purple and gold of the clearing, downwards at the ring of pine trees standing so still, so crude and untameable, the motionless desert beyond the bristles of the pine crests, a thousand feet below: and beyond the desert, blue mountains, and far, far-off blue mountains in Arizona: "This is the place," she said to herself.

This little tumbledown ranch, only a homestead of a hundred and sixty acres, was, as it were, man's last effort towards the wild heart of the Rockies, at this point. Sixty years before, a restless schoolmaster had wandered out from the East, looking for gold among the mountains. He found a very little, then no more. But the mountains had got hold of him, he could not go back.

There was a little trickling spring of pure water, a thread of treasure perhaps better than gold. So the schoolmaster took up a homestead on the lot where this little spring arose. He struggled, and got himself his log cabin erected, his fence put up, sloping at the mountain-side through the pine trees and dropping into the hollows where the ghost-white mariposa lilies stood leafless and naked in flower, in spring, on tall, invisible stems. He made the long clearing for alfalfa.

And fell so into debt that he had to trade his homestead away, to clear his debt. Then he made a tiny living teaching the children of the few American prospectors who had squatted in the valleys, beside the Mexicans.

The trader who got the ranch tackled it with a will. He built another log cabin and a big corral, and brought water from the canyon two miles and more across the mountain slope, in a little runnel ditch, and more water, piped a mile or more down the little canyon immediately above the cabins. He got a flow of water for his houses: for being a true American, he felt he could not *really* say he had conquered his environment till he had got running water, taps, and wash-hand basins inside his house.

Taps, running water and wash-hand basins he accomplished. And, undaunted through the years, he prepared the basin for a fountain in the little fenced-in enclosure, and he built a little bath-house. After a number of years, he sent up the enamelled bath-tub to be put in the little log bath-house on the little wild ranch hung right against the savage Rockies, above the desert.

But here the mountains finished him. He was a trader down below, in the Mexican village. This little ranch was, as it were, his hobby, his ideal. He and his New England wife spent their summers there: and turned on the taps in the cabins and turned them off again, and felt really that civilisation had conquered.

All this plumbing from the savage ravines of the canyons—one of them nameless to this day—cost, however, money. In fact, the ranch cost a great deal of money. But it was all to be got back. The big clearing was to be irrigated for alfalfa, the little clearing for beans, and the third clearing, under the corral, for potatoes. All these things the trader could trade to the Mexicans, very advantageously.

And, moreover, since somebody had started a praise of the famous goats' cheese made by Mexican peasants in New Mexico, goats there should be.

Goats there were: five hundred of them, eventually. And they fed chiefly in the wild mountain hollows, the no-man's-land. The Mexicans call them fire-mouths, because everything they nibble dies. Not because of their flaming mouths, really, but because they nibble a live plant down, down to the quick, till it can put forth no more.

So, the energetic trader, in the course of five or six years, had got the ranch ready. The long three-roomed cabin was for him and his New England wife. In the two-roomed cabin lived the Mexican family who really had charge of the ranch. For the trader was mostly fixed to his store, seventeen miles away, down in the Mexican village.

The ranch lay over eight thousand feet up, the snows of winter came deep and the white goats, looking dirty yellow, swam in snow with their poor curved horns poking out like dead sticks. But the corral had a long, cosy, shut-in goat-shed all down one side, and into this crowded the five hundred, their acrid goat smell rising like hot acid over the snow. And the thin, pock-marked Mexican threw them alfalfa out of the log barn. Until the hot sun sank the snow again, and froze the surface, when patter-patter went the two thousand little goat-hoofs, over the silver-frozen snow, up at the mountain. Nibble, nibble, nibble, the fire-mouths, at every tender twig. And the goat-bell climbed, and the baa-ing came from among the dense and shaggy pine trees. And sometimes, in a soft drift under the trees, a goat, or several goats, went through, into the white depths, and some were lost thus, to reappear dead and frozen at the thaw.

By evening, they were driven down again, like a dirty yellowish-white stream carrying dark sticks on its yeasty surface, tripping and bleating over the frozen snow, past the bustling dark green pine trees, down to the trampled mess of the corral. And everywhere, everywhere over the snow, yellow stains and dark pills of goat-droppings melting into the surface crystal. On still, glittering nights, when the frost was hard, the smell of goats came up like some uncanny acid fire, and great stars sitting on the mountain's edge seemed to be watching like the eyes of a mountain lion, brought by the scent. Then the coyotes in the near canyon howled and sobbed, and ran like shadows over the snow. But the goat corral had been built tight.

In the course of years the goat-herd had grown from fifty to five hundred, and surely that was increase. The goat-milk cheeses sat drying on their little racks. In spring, there was a great flowing and skipping of kids. In summer and early autumn, there was a pest of flies, rising from all that goat smell and that cast-out whey of goats' milk, after the cheese-making. The rats came, and the pack-rats, swarming.

And after all, it was difficult to sell or trade the cheeses, and little profit to be made. And in dry summers, no water came down in the narrow ditch-channel, that straddled in wooden runnels over the deep clefts in the mountain-side. No water meant no alfalfa. In winter the goats scarcely drank at all. In summer they could be watered at the little spring. But the thirsty land was not so easy to accommodate.

Five hundred fine white Angora goats, with their massive handsome padres! They were beautiful enough. And the trader made all he could of them. Come summer, they were run down into the narrow tank filled with the fiery dipping fluid. Then their lovely white wool was clipped. It was beautiful, and valuable, but comparatively little of it.

And it all cost, cost, cost. And a man was always let down. At one time no water. At another a poison weed. Then a sick-ness. Always some mysterious malevolence fighting, fighting against the will of man. A strange invisible influence coming out of the livid rock fastnesses in the bowels of those un-created Rocky Mountains, preying upon the will of man, and slowly wearing down his resistance, his onward-pushing spirit. The curious, subtle thing, like a mountain fever, got into the blood, so that the men at the ranch, and the animals with them, had bursts of queer, violent, half-frenzied energy, in which, however, they were wont to lose their wariness. And then, damage of some sort. The horses ripped and cut them-selves, or they were struck by lightning, the men had great hurts or sickness. A curious disintegration working all the time, a sort of malevolent breath, like a stupefying, irritant gas coming out of the unfathomed mountains.

The pack-rats with their bushy tails and big ears came down out of the hills, and were jumping and bouncing about: symbols of the curious debasing malevolence that was in the spirit of the place. The Mexicans in charge, good honest men, worked all they could. But they were like most of the Mexicans in the south-west, as if they had been pithed, to use one of Kipling's words. As if the invidious malevolence of the country itself had slowly taken all the pith of manhood from them, leaving a hopeless sort of corpus of a man.

And the same happened to the white men, exposed to the

open country. Slowly, they were pithed. The energy went out of them. And more than that, the interest. An inertia of indifference invading the soul, leaving the body healthy and active, but wasting the soul, the living interest, quite away.

It was the New England wife of the trader who put most energy into the ranch. She looked on it as her home. She had a little white fence put all round the two cabins: the bright brass water-taps she kept shining in the two kitchens: outside the kitchen door she had a little kitchen garden and nasturtiums, after a great fight with invading animals, that nibbled everything away. And she got so far as the preparation of the round concrete basin which was to be a little pool, under the few enclosed pine trees between the two cabins, a pool with a tiny fountain jet.

But this, with the bath-tub, was her limit, as the five hundred goats were her man's limit. Out of the mountains came two breaths of influence: the breath of the curious, frenzied energy, that took away one's intelligence as alcohol or any other stimulus does: and then the most strange indiviousness that ate away the soul. The woman loved her ranch, almost with passion. It was she who felt the stimulus more than the men. It seemed to enter her like a sort of sex passion, intensifying her ego, making her full of violence and of blind female energy. The energy and the blindness of it! A strange blind frenzy, like an intoxication while it lasted. And the sense of beauty that thrilled her New England woman's soul.

Her cabin faced the slow down-slope of the clearing, the alfalfa field: her long, low cabin, crouching under the great pine tree that threw up its trunk sheer in front of the house, in the yard. That pine tree was the guardian of the place. But a bristling, almost demonish guardian, from the far-off crude ages of the world. Its great pillar of pale, flakey-ribbed copper rose there in strange, callous indifference, and the grim permanence, which is in pine trees. A passionless, non-phallic column, rising in the shadows of the pre-sexual world, before the hot-blooded ithyphallic column ever erected itself. A cold, blossomless, resinous sap surging and oozing gum, from that pallid brownish bark. And the wind hissing in the needles, like a vast nest of serpents. And the pine cones falling plumb as the hail hit them. Then lying all over the yard, open in the sun like wooden roses, but hard, sexless, rigid with a blind will.

Past the column of that pine tree, the alfalfa field sloped gently down, to the circling guard of pine trees, from which silent, living barrier isolated pines rose to ragged heights at intervals, in blind assertiveness. Strange, those pine trees! In some lights all their needles glistened like polished steel, all subtly glittering with a whitish glitter among darkness, like real needles. Then again, at evening, the trunks would flare up orange red, and the tufts would be dark, alert tufts like a wolf's tail touching the air. Again, in the morning sunlight they would be soft and still, hardly noticeable. But all the same, present and watchful. Never sympathetic, always watchfully on their guard, and resistant, they hedged one in with the aroma and the power and the slight horror of the pre-sexual primeval world. The world where each creature was crudely limited to its own ego, crude and bristling and cold, and then crowding in packs like pine trees and wolves.

But beyond the pine trees, ah, there beyond, there was beauty for the spirit to soar in. The circle of pines, with the loose trees rising high and ragged at intervals, this was the barrier, the fence to the foreground. Beyond was only distance, the desert a thousand feet below, and beyond.

The desert swept its great fawn-coloured circle around, away beyond and below like a beach, with a long mountain-side of pure blue shadow closing in the near corner, and strange, bluish hummocks of mountains rising like wet rock from a vast strand, away in the middle distance, and beyond, in the farthest distance, pale blue crests of mountains look-ing over the horizon from the west, as if peering in from another world altogether.

Ah, that was beauty!—perhaps the most beautiful thing in the world. It was pure beauty, *absolute* beauty! There! That was it. To the little woman from New England, with her tense, fierce soul and her egoistic passion of service, this beauty was absolute, a *ne plus ultra*. From her doorway, from her porch, she could watch the vast, eagle-like wheeling of the daylight, that turned as the eagles which lived in the near rocks turned overhead in the blue, turning their luminous, dark-edged-patterned bellies and underwings upon the pure air, like winged orbs. So the daylight made the vast turn upon the desert, brushing the farthest out-watching mountains. And sometimes the vast strand of the desert would float with curious undulations and exhalations amid the blue fragility of

mountains, whose upper edges were harder than the floating
bases. And sometimes she would see the little brown adobe
houses of the village Mexicans, twenty miles away, like little
cube crystals of insect-houses dotting upon the desert, very
distinct, with a cotton-wood tree or two rising near. And
sometimes she would see the far-off rocks thirty miles away,
where the canyon made a gateway between the mountains.
Quite clear, like an open gateway out of the vast yard, she
would see the cut-out bit of the canyon passage. And on the
desert itself, curious, puckered folds of mesa-sides. And a
blackish crack which in places revealed the otherwise invisible canyon of the Rio Grande. And beyond everything, the
mountains like icebergs showing up from an outer sea. Then
later, the sun would go down blazing above the shallow
cauldron of simmering darkness, and the round mountains of
Colorado would lump up into uncanny significance, north-
wards. That was always rather frightening. But morning
came again, with the sun peeping over the mountain slopes
and lighting the desert away in the distance long, long before
it lighted on her yard. And then she would see another valley,
like magic and very lovely, with green folds and long tufts of
cotton-wood trees, and a few long-cubical adobe houses, lying
floating in shallow light below, like a vision.

Ah! it was beauty, beauty absolute, at any hour of the
day: whether the perfect clarity of morning or the mountains
beyond the simmering desert at noon, or the purple lumping
of northern mounds under a red sun at night. Or whether the
dust whirled in tall columns, travelling across the desert far
away, like pillars of cloud by day, tall, leaning pillars of dust
hastening with ghostly haste: or whether, in the early part
of the year, suddenly in the morning a whole sea of solid
white would rise rolling below, a solid mist from melted
snow, ghost-white under the mountain sun, the world below
blotted out: or whether the black rain and cloud streaked
down, far across the desert, and lightning stung down with
sharp white stings on the horizon: or the cloud travelled and
burst overhead, with rivers of fluid blue fire running out of
heaven and exploding on earth, and hail coming down like a
world of ice shattered above: or the hot sun rode in again: or
snow fell in heavy silence: or the world was blinding white
under a blue sky, and one must hurry under the pine trees for
shelter against that vast, white, back-beating light which

rushed up at one and made one almost unconscious, amid the snow.

It was always beauty, *always!* It was always great, and splendid, and, for some reason, natural. It was never grandiose or theatrical. Always, for some reason, perfect. And quite simple, in spite of it all.

So it was, when you watched the vast and living landscape. The landscape lived, and lived as the world of the gods, unsullied and unconcerned. The great circling landscape lived its own life, sumptuous and uncaring. Man did not exist for it.

And if it had been a question simply of living through the eyes, into the *distance*, then this would have been Paradise, and the little New England woman on her ranch would have found what she was always looking for, the earthly paradise of the spirit.

But even a woman cannot live only into the distance, the beyond. Willy-nilly she finds herself juxtaposed to the near things, the thing in itself. And willy-nilly she is caught up into the fight with the immediate object.

The New England woman had fought to make the nearness as perfect as the distance: for the distance was absolute beauty. She had been confident of success. She had felt quite assured, when the water came running out of her bright brass taps, the wild water of the hills caught, tricked into the narrow iron pipes, and led tamely to her kitchen, to jump out over her sink, into her wash-basin, at her service. "There!" she said. "I have tamed the waters of the mountain to my service."

So she had, for the moment.

At the same time, the invisible attack was being made upon her. While she revelled in the beauty of the luminous world that wheeled around and below her, the grey, rat-like spirit of the inner mountains was attacking her from behind. She could not keep her attention. And, curiously, she could not keep even her speech. When she was saying something, suddenly the next word would be gone out of her, as if a pack-rat had carried it off. And she sat blank, stuttering, staring in the empty cupboard of her mind, like Mother Hubbard, and seeing the cupboard bare. And this irritated her husband intensely.

Her chickens, of which she was so proud, were carried away. Or they strayed. Or they fell sick. At first she could cope with their circumstances. But after a while, she couldn't. She couldn't care. A drug-like numbness possessed her spirit, and at the very middle of her, she couldn't care what happened to her chickens.

The same when a couple of horses were struck by lightning. It frightened her. The rivers of fluid fire that suddenly fell out of the sky and exploded on the earth nearby, as if the whole earth had burst like a bomb, frightened her from the very core of her, and made her know, secretly and with cynical certainty, *that there was no merciful God in the heavens.* A very tall, elegant pine tree just above her cabin took the lightning, and stood tall and elegant as before, but with a white seam spiralling from its crest, all down its tall trunk, to earth. The perfect scar, white and long as lightning itself. And every time she looked at it, she said to herself, in spite of herself: "There is no Almighty loving God. The God there is shaggy as the pine trees, and horrible as the lightning." Outwardly, she never confessed this. Openly, she thought of her dear New England Church as usual. But in the violent undercurrent of her woman's soul, after the storms, she would look at that living, seamed tree, and the voice would say in her, almost savagely: 'What nonsense about Jesus and a God of Love, in a place like this! This is more awful and more splendid. I like it better.' The very chipmunks, in their jerky helter-skelter, the blue jays wrangling in the pine tree in the dawn, the grey squirrel undulating to the tree-trunk, then pausing to chatter at her and scold her, with a shrewd fearlessness, as if she were the alien, the outsider, the creature that should not be permitted among the trees, all destroyed the illusion she cherished, of love, universal love. There was no love on this ranch. There was life, intense, bristling life, full of energy, but also, with an undertone of savage sordidness.

The black ants in her cupboard, the pack-rats bouncing on her ceiling like hippopotami in the night, the two sick goats: there was a peculiar undercurrent of squalor, flowing under the curious *tussle* of wild life. That was it. The wild life, even the life of the trees and flowers seemed one bristling, hair-raising tussle. The very flowers came up bristly, and many of them were fang-mouthed, like the dead-nettle: and none had any real scent. But they were very fascinating, too, in their very fierceness. In May, the curious columbines of the stream-beds, columbines scarlet outside and yellow in, like the red and yellow of a herald's uniform—farther from the dove nothing could be: then the beautiful rosy-blue of the great

tufts of the flower they called bluebell, but which was really a
flower of the snap-dragon family: these grew in powerful
beauty in the little clearing of the pine trees, followed by the
flower the settlers had mysteriously called herb honeysuckle:
a tangle of long drops of pure fire-red, hanging from slim invisible stalks of smoke colour. The purest, most perfect
vermilion scarlet, cleanest fire-colour, hanging in long drops
like a shower of fire-rain that is just going to strike the earth.
A little later, more in the open, there came another sheer fire-
red flower, sparking, fierce red stars running up a bristly grey
ladder, as if the earth's fire-centre had blown out some red
sparks, white-speckled and deadly inside, puffing for a moment
in the day air.

So it was! The alfalfa field was one raging, seething conflict of plants trying to get hold. One dry year, and the bristly
wild things had got hold: the spiky, blue-leaved thistle-poppy
with its moon-white flowers, the low clumps of blue nettle-
flower, the later rush, after the sereneness of June and July,
the rush of red sparks and Michaelmas daisies, and the tough,
wild sunflowers, strangling and choking the dark, tender
green of the clover-like alfalfa! A battle, a battle, with
banners of bright scarlet and yellow.

When a really defenceless flower did issue, like the moth-
still, ghost-centred mariposa lily, with its inner moth-dust of
yellow, it came invisible. There was nothing to be seen but a
hair of greyish grass near the oak scrub. Behold, this invisible
long stalk was balancing a white, ghostly, three-petalled
flower, naked out of nothingness. A mariposa lily!

Only the pink wild roses smelled sweet, like the old world.
They were sweet-briar roses. And the dark blue harebells
among the oak scrub, like the ice-dark bubbles of the mountain flowers in the Alps, the Alpenglocken.

The roses of the desert are the cactus flowers, crystal of
translucent yellow or of rose-colour. But set among spines
the devil himself must have conceived in a moment of sheer
ecstasy.

Nay, it was a world before and after the God of Love. Even
the very humming-birds hanging about the flowering squaw-
berry bushes, when the snow had gone, in May, they were
before and after the God of Love. And the blue jays were
crested dark with challenge, and the yellow-and-dark wood-
pecker was fearless like a warrior in war-paint, as he struck

the wood. While on the fence the hawks sat motionless, like dark fists clenched under heaven, ignoring man and his ways.

Summer, it was true, unfolded the tender cotton-wood leaves, and the tender aspen. But what a tangle and a ghostly aloofness in the aspen thickets high up on the mountains, the coldness that is in the eyes and the long cornelian talons of the bear.

Summer brought the little wild strawberries, with their savage aroma, and the late summer brought the rose-jewel raspberries in the valley cleft. But how lonely, how harsh-lonely and menacing it was, to be alone in that shadowy, steep cleft of a canyon just above the cabins, picking raspberries, while the thunder gathered thick and blue-purple at the mountain-tops. The many wild raspberries hanging rose-red in the thickets. But the stream bed below all silent, waterless. And the trees all bristling in silence, and waiting like warriors at an outpost. And the berries waiting for the sharp-eyed, cold, long-snouted bear to come rambling and shaking his heavy, sharp fur. The berries grew for the bears, and the little New England woman, with her uncanny sensitiveness to under-lying influences, felt all the time she was stealing. Stealing the wild raspberries in the secret little canyon behind her home. And when she had made them into jam, she could almost taste the theft in her preserves.

She confessed nothing of this. She tried even to confess nothing of her dread. But she was afraid. Especially she was conscious of the prowling, intense aerial electricity all the summer, after June. The air was thick with wandering currents of fierce electric fluid, waiting to discharge them-selves. And almost every day there was the rage and battle of thunder. But the air was never cleared. There was no relief. However, the thunder raged, and spent itself, yet, afterwards, among the sunshine was the strange lurking and wandering of the electric currents, moving invisible, with strange menace, between the atoms of the air. She knew. Oh, she knew!

And her love for her ranch turned sometimes into a certain repulsion. The underlying rat-dirt, the everlasting bristling tussle of the wild life, with the tangle and the bones strewing. Bones of horses struck by lightning, bones of dead cattle, skulls of goats with little horns: bleached, unburied bones. Then the cruel electricity of the mountains. And then, most mysterious but worst of all, the animosity of the spirit of place: the crude, half-created spirit of place, like some serpent-bird for ever attacking man, in a hatred of man's onward struggle towards further creation.

The seething cauldron of lower life, seething on the very tissue of the higher life, seething the soul away, seething at the marrow. The vast and unrelenting will of the swarming lower life, working forever against man's attempt at a higher life, a further created being.

At last, after many years, the little woman admitted to herself that she was glad to go down from the ranch, when November came with snows. She was glad to come to a more human home, her house in the village. And as winter passed by and spring came again, she knew she did not want to go up to the ranch again. It had broken something in her. It had hurt her terribly. It had maimed her for ever in her hope, her belief in paradise on earth. Now she hid from herself her own corpse, the corpse of her New England belief in a world ultimately all for love. The belief, and herself with it, was a corpse. The gods of those inner mountains were grim and invidious and relentless, huger than man, and lower than man. Yet man could never master them.

The little woman in her flower-garden away below, by the stream-irrigated village, hid away from the thought of it all. She would not go to the ranch any more.

The Mexicans stayed in charge, looking after the goats. But the place didn't pay. It didn't pay, not quite. It had paid. It might pay. But the effort, the effort! And as the marrow is eaten out of a man's bones and the soul out of his belly, contending with the strange rapacity of savage life, the lower stage of creation, he cannot make the effort any more.

Then also, the war came, making many men give up their enterprises at civilisation.

Every new stroke of civilisation has cost the lives of countless brave men, who have fallen defeated by the 'dragon', in their efforts to win the apples of the Hesperides, or the fleece of gold. Fallen in their efforts to overcome the old, half-sordid savagery of the lower stages of creation, and win to the next stage.

For all savagery is half sordid. And man is only himself when he is fighting on and on, to overcome the sordidness.

And every civilisation, when it loses its inward vision and its cleaner energy, falls into a new sort of sordidness, more vast and more stupendous than the old savage sort. An Augean stable of metallic filth.

And all the time, man has to rouse himself afresh to cleanse the new accumulations of refuse. To win from the crude, wild nature the victory and the power to make another start, and to cleanse behind him the century-deep deposits of layer upon layer of refuse: even of tin cans.

The ranch dwindled. The flock of goats declined. The water ceased to flow. And at length the trader gave it up.

He rented the place to a Mexican, who lived on the handful of beans he raised, and who was being slowly driven out by the vermin.

And now arrived Lou, new blood to the attack. She went back to Santa Fé, saw the trader and a lawyer, and bought the ranch for twelve hundred dollars. She was so pleased with herself.

She sent upstairs to tell her mother.

"Mother, I've bought a ranch."

"It is just as well, for I can't stand the noise of automobiles outside here another week."

"It is quiet on my ranch, mother: the stillness simply speaks."

"I had rather it held its tongue. I am simply drugged with all the bad novels I have read. I feel as if the sky was a big cracked bell and a million clappers were hammering human speech out of it."

"Aren't you interested in my ranch, mother?"

"I hope I may be, by and by."

Mrs. Witt actually got up the next morning and accompanied her daughter in the hired motor-car, driven by Phœnix, to the ranch: which was called Las Chivas. She sat like a pillar of salt, her face looking what the Indians call a False Face, meaning a mask. She seemed to have crystallised into neutrality. She watched the desert with its tufts of yellow greasewood go lurching past: she saw the fallen apples on the ground in the orchards near the adobe cottages: she looked down into the deep arroyo, and at the stream they forded in the car, and at the mountains blocking up the sky ahead, all with indifference. High on the mountains was snow: lower, blue-grey livid rock: and below the livid rock the aspens were expiring their daffodil yellow, this year, and the oak scrub was dark and reddish, like gore. She saw it all with a sort of stony indifference.

"Don't you think it's lovely?" said Lou.

"I can *see* it is lovely," replied her mother.

The Michaelmas daisies in the clearing as they drove up to the ranch were sharp-rayed with purple, like a coming night.

Mrs. Witt eyed the two log cabins, one of which was dilapidated and practically abandoned. She looked at the rather rickety corral, whose long planks had silvered and warped in the fierce sun. On one of the roof-planks a pack-rat was sitting erect like an old Indian keeping watch on a pueblo roof. He showed his white belly, and folded his hands and lifted his big ears, for all the world like an old immobile Indian.

"Isn't it for all the world as if *he* were the real boss of the place, Louise?" she said cynically.

And turning to the Mexican, who was a rag of a man but a pleasant, courteous fellow, she asked him why he didn't shoot the rat.

"Not worth a shell!" said the Mexican, with a faint, hopeless smile.

Mrs. Witt paced round and saw everything: it did not take long. She gazed in silence at the water of the spring, trickling out of an iron pipe into a barrel, under the cotton-wood tree in an arroyo.

"Well, Louise," she said. "I am glad you feel competent to cope with so much hopelessness and so many rats."

"But, mother, you must admit it is beautiful."

"Yes, I suppose it is. But to use one of your Henry's phrases, beauty is a cold egg, as far as I am concerned."

"Rico never would have said that beauty was a cold egg to him."

"No, he wouldn't. He sits on it like a broody old hen on a china imitation.—Are you going to bring him here?"

"*Bring* him!—No. But he can come if he likes," stammered Lou.

"*Oh—h!* won't it be beau—ti—ful!" cried Mrs. Witt, rolling her head and lifting her shoulders in savage imitation of her son-in-law.

"Perhaps he won't come, mother," said Lou, hurt.

"He will most certainly come, Louise, to see what's doing: unless you tell him you don't want him."

"Anyhow, I needn't think about it till spring," said Lou, anxiously pushing the matter aside.

Mrs. Witt climbed the steep slope above the cabins to the mouth of the little canyon. There she sat on a fallen tree and surveyed the world beyond: a world not of men. She could not fail to be roused.

"What is your idea in coming here, daughter?" she asked.

"I love it here, mother."

"But what do you expect to achieve by it?"

"I was rather hoping, mother, to escape achievement. I'll tell you—and you mustn't get cross if it sounds silly. As far as people go, my heart is quite broken. And far as people go, I don't want any more. I can't stand any more. What heart I ever had for it—for life with people—is quite broken. I want to be alone, mother: with you here, and Phœnix perhaps to look after horses and drive a car. But I want to be by myself, really."

"With Phœnix in the background! Are you sure he won't be coming into the foreground before long?"

"No, mother, no more of that. If I've got to say it, Phœnix is a servant: he's really placed, as far as I can see. Always the same, playing about in the old back yard. I can't take those men seriously. I can't fool round with them, or fool myself about them. I can't and I won't fool myself any more, mother, especially about men. They don't count. So why should you want them to pay me out?"

For the moment, this silenced Mrs. Witt. Then she said:

"Why, *I* don't want it. Why should I? But after all, you've got to live. You've never *lived* yet: not in my opinion."

"Neither, mother, in my opinion, have you," said Lou dryly.

And this silenced Mrs. Witt altogether. She had to be silent, or angrily on the defensive. And the latter she wouldn't be. She couldn't really, in honesty.

"What do you call life?" Lou continued. "Wriggling half naked at a public show and going off in a taxi to sleep with some half-drunken fool who thinks he's a man because—Oh, mother, I don't even want to think of it. I know you have a lurking idea that *that is life*. Let it be so then. But leave me out. Men in that aspect simply nauseate me: so grovelling and ratty. Life in that aspect simply drains all my life away. I tell you, for all that sort of thing, I'm broken, absolutely broken: if I wasn't broken to start with."

"Well, Louise," said Mrs. Witt after a pause, "I'm convinced that ever since men and women were men and women, people who took things seriously, and had time for it, got their hearts broken. Haven't I had mine broken! It's as sure as having your virginity broken: and it amounts to about as much. It's a beginning rather than an end."

"So it is, mother. It's the beginning of something else, and the end of something that's done with. I *know*, and there's no altering it, that I've got to live differently. It sounds silly, but I don't know how else to put it. I've got to live for something that matters, way, way down in me. And I think sex would matter, to my very soul, if it was really sacred. But cheap sex kills me."

"You have had a fancy for rather cheap men, perhaps."

"Perhaps I have. Perhaps I should always be a fool, where people are concerned. Now I want to leave off that kind of foolery. There's something else, mother, that I want to give myself to. I know it. I know it absolutely. Why should I let myself be shouted down any more?"

Mrs. Witt sat staring at the distance, her face a cynical mask.

"What is the something bigger? And *pray*, what is it bigger than?" she asked, in that tone of honeyed suavity which was her deadliest poison. "I want to learn. I am out to know. I'm terribly intrigued by it. Something bigger! Girls in my generation occasionally entered convents for *something bigger*. I always wondered if they found it. They seemed to me inclined in the imbecile direction, but perhaps that was because I was *something less*——"

There was a definite pause between the mother and daughter, a silence that was a pure breach. Then Lou said:

"You know quite well I'm not conventy, mother, whatever else I am—even a bit of an imbecile. But that kind of religion seems to me the other half of men. Instead of running after them you run away from them, and get the thrill that way. I don't hate men *because* they're men, as nuns do. I dislike them because they're not men enough: babies, and playboys, and poor things showing off all the time, even to themselves. I don't say I'm any better. I only wish, with all my soul, that some men *were* bigger and stronger and *deeper* than I am . . ."

"How do you know they're not?——" asked Mrs. Witt.

"How *do* I know?——" said Lou mockingly.

And the pause that was a breach resumed itself. Mrs. Witt

was teasing with a little stick the bewildered black ants among the fir-needles.

"And no doubt you are right about men," she said at length. "But at your age, the only sensible thing is to try and keep up the illusion. After all, as you say, you may be no better."

"I may be no better. But keeping up the illusion means fooling myself. And I won't do it. When I see a man who is even a bit attractive to me—even as much as Phœnix—I say to myself: 'Would you care for him afterwards? Does he really mean anything to you, except just a sensation?'—And I know he doesn't. No, mother, of this I am convinced: either my taking a man shall have a meaning and a mystery that penetrates my very soul, or I will keep to myself.—And what I *know* is, that the time has come for me to keep to myself. No more messing about."

"Very well, daughter. You will probably spend your life keeping to yourself."

"Do you think I mind! There's something else for me, mother. There's something else even that loves me and wants me. I can't tell you what it is. It's a spirit. And it's here, on this ranch. It's here, in this landscape. It's something more real to me than men are, and it soothes me, and it holds me up. I don't know what it is, definitely. It's something wild, that will hurt me sometimes and will wear me down sometimes. I know it. But it's something big, bigger than men, bigger than people, bigger than religion. It's something to do with wild America. And it's something to do with me. It's a mission, if you like. I am imbecile enough for that! —But it's my mission to keep myself for the spirit that is wild, and has waited so long here: even waited for such as me. Now I've come! Now I'm here. Now I am where I want to be: with the spirit that wants me.—And that's how it is. And neither Rico nor Phœnix nor anybody else really matters to me. They are in the world's back-yard. And I am here, right deep in America, where there's a wild spirit wants me, a wild spirit more than men. And it doesn't want to save me either. It needs me. It craves for me. And to it, my sex is deep and sacred, deeper than I am, with a deep nature aware deep down of my sex. It saves me from cheapness, mother. And even you could never do that for me."

Mrs. Witt rose to her feet and stood looking far, far away at the turquoise ridge of mountains half sunk under the horizon.

"How much did you say you paid for Las Chivas?" she asked

"Twelve hundred dollars," said Lou, surprised.

"Then I call it cheap, considering all there is to it: even the name."

THE VIRGIN AND THE GIPSY

THE VIRGIN AND THE GIPSY

I

WHEN the vicar's wife went off with a young and penniless man the scandal knew no bounds. Her two little girls were only seven and nine years old respectively. And the vicar was such a good husband. True, his hair was grey. But his moustache was dark, he was handsome, and still full of furtive passion for his unrestrained and beautiful wife.

Why did she go? Why did she burst away with such an *éclat* of revulsion, like a touch of madness?

Nobody gave any answer. Only the pious said she was a bad woman. While some of the good women kept silent. They knew.

The two little girls never knew. Wounded, they decided that it was because their mother found them negligible.

The ill wind that blows nobody any good swept away the vicarage family on its blast. Then lo and behold! the vicar, who was somewhat distinguished as an essayist and a controversialist, and whose case had aroused sympathy among the bookish men, received the living of Papplewick. The Lord had tempered the wind of misfortune with a rectorate in the north country.

The rectory was a rather ugly stone house down by the River Papple, before you come into the village. Farther on, beyond where the road crosses the stream, were the big old stone cotton-mills, once driven by water. The road curved up-hill, into the bleak stone streets of the village.

The vicarage family received decided modification, upon its transference into the rectory. The vicar, now the rector, fetched up his old mother and his sister, and a brother from the city. The two little girls had a very different milieu from the old house.

The rector was now forty-seven years old; he had displayed an intense and not very dignified grief after the flight of his wife. Sympathetic ladies had stayed him from suicide. His hair was almost white, and he had a wild-eyed, tragic look.

3

You had only to look at him to know how dreadful it all was, and how he had been wronged.

Yet somewhere there was a false note. And some of the ladies, who had sympathised most profoundly with the vicar, secretly rather disliked the rector. There was a certain furtive self-righteousness about him, when all was said and done.

The little girls, of course, in the vague way of children, accepted the family verdict. Granny, who was over seventy and whose sight was failing, became the central figure in the house. Aunt Cissie, who was over forty, pale, pious, and gnawed by an inward worm, kept house. Uncle Fred, a stingy and grey-faced man of forty, who just lived dingily for himself, went into town every day. And the rector, of course, was the most important person, after Granny.

They called her the Mater. She was one of those physically vulgar, clever old bodies who had got her own way all her life by buttering the weaknesses of her men-folk. Very quickly she took her cue. The rector still 'loved' his delinquent wife, and would 'love her' till he died. Therefore hush! The rector's feeling was sacred. In his heart was enshrined the pure girl he had wedded and worshipped.

Out in the evil world, at the same time, there wandered a disreputable woman who had betrayed the rector and abandoned his little children. She was now yoked to a young and despicable man, who no doubt would bring her the degradation she deserved. Let this be clearly understood, and then hush! For in the pure loftiness of the rector's heart still bloomed the pure white snow-flower of his young bride. This white snow-flower did not wither. That other creature, who had gone off with that despicable young man, was none of his affair.

The Mater, who had been somewhat diminished and insignificant as a widow in a small house, now climbed into the chief arm-chair in the rectory, and planted her old bulk firmly again. She was not going to be dethroned. Astutely she gave a sigh of homage to the rector's fidelity to the pure white snow-flower, while she pretended to disapprove. In sly reverence for her son's great love, she spoke no word against that nettle which flourished in the evil world, and which had once been called Mrs. Arthur Saywell. Now, thank heaven, having married again, she was no more Mrs. Arthur Saywell. No woman bore the rector's name. The pure white snow-flower bloomed *in perpetuum*, without nomenclature. The family even thought of her as She-who-was-Cynthia.

All this was water on the Mater's mill. It secured her against Arthur's ever marrying again. She had him by his feeblest weakness, his skulking self-love. He had married an imperishable white snow-flower. Lucky man! He had been injured. Unhappy man! He had suffered. Ah, what a heart of love! And he had—forgiven! Yes, the white snow-flower was forgiven. He even had made provision in his will for her, when that other scoundrel—But hush! Don't even *think* too near to that horrid nettle in the rank outer world! She-who-was-Cynthia. Let the white snow-flower bloom inaccessible on the heights of the past. The present is another story.

The children were brought up in this atmosphere of cunning self-sanctification and of unmentionability. They, too, saw the snow-flower on inaccessible heights. They, too, knew that it was throned in lone splendour aloft their lives, never to be touched.

At the same time, out of the squalid world sometimes would come a rank, evil smell of selfishness and degraded lust, the smell of that awful nettle, She-who-was-Cynthia. This nettle actually contrived at intervals, to get a little note through to the girls, her children. And at this the silver-haired Mater shook inwardly with hate. For if She-who-was-Cynthia ever came back, there wouldn't be much left of the Mater. A secret gust of hate went from the old granny to the girls, children of that foul nettle of lust, that Cynthia who had had such an affectionate contempt for the Mater.

Mingled with all this was the children's perfectly distinct recollection of their real home, the vicarage in the south, and their glamorous but not very dependable mother, Cynthia. She had made a great glow, a flow of life, like a swift and dangerous sun in the home, forever coming and going. They always associated her presence with brightness, but also with danger; with glamour, but with fearful selfishness.

Now the glamour was gone, and the white snow-flower, like a porcelain wreath, froze on its grave. The danger of instability, the peculiarly *dangerous* sort of selfishness, like lions and tigers, was also gone. There was now a complete stability, in which one could perish safely.

But they were growing up. And as they grew, they became more definitely confused, more actively puzzled. The Mater,

as she grew older, grew blinder. Somebody had to lead her
about. She did not get up till towards midday. Yet blind or
bed-ridden, she held the house.

Besides, she wasn't bed-ridden. Whenever the *men* were
present, the Mater was in her throne. She was too cunning to
court neglect. Especially as she had rivals.

Her great rival was the younger girl, Yvette. Yvette had
some of the vague, careless blitheness of She-who-was-
Cynthia. But this one was more docile. Granny perhaps had
caught her in time. Perhaps!

The rector adored Yvette, and spoiled her with a doting
fondness; as much as to say: am I not a soft-hearted, indul-
gent old boy! He liked to have this opinion of himself, and
the Mater knew his weaknesses to a hair's-breadth. She knew
them, and she traded on them by turning them into decorations for him, for his character. He wanted, in his own eyes,
to have a fascinating character, as women want to have
fascinating dresses. And the Mater cunningly put beauty-
spots over his defects and deficiencies. Her mother-love gave
her the clue to his weaknesses, and she hid them for him
with decorations. Whereas She-who-was-Cynthia——! But
don't mention *her* in this connection. In her eyes, the rector
was almost hump-backed and an idiot.

The funny thing was, Granny secretly hated Lucille, the
elder girl, more than the pampered Yvette. Lucille, the
uneasy and irritable, was more conscious of being under
Granny's power than was the spoilt and vague Yvette.

On the other hand, Aunt Cissie hated Yvette. She hated her
very name. Aunt Cissie's life had been sacrificed to the Mater,
and Aunt Cissie knew it, and the Mater knew she knew it. Yet
as the years went on, it became a convention. The convention
of Aunt Cissie's sacrifice was accepted by everybody, including
the self-same Cissie. She prayed a good deal about it. Which
also showed that she had her own private feelings somewhere,
poor thing. She had ceased to be Cissie, she had lost her life
and her sex. And now she was creeping towards fifty, strange
green flares of rage would come up in her, and at such times
she was insane.

But Granny held her in her power. And Aunt Cissie's one
object in life was to look after the Mater.

Aunt Cissie's green flares of hellish hate would go up against
all young things, sometimes. Poor thing, she prayed and tried

o obtain forgiveness from heaven. But what had been done to her, *she* could not forgive, and the vitriol would spurt in her veins sometimes.

It was not as if the Mater were a warm, kindly soul. She wasn't. She only seemed it, cunningly. And the fact dawned gradually on the girls. Under her old-fashioned lace cap, under her silver hair, under the black silk of her stout, short, forward-bulging body, this old woman had a cunning heart, seeking for-ever her own female power. And through the weakness of the unfresh, stagnant men she had bred, she kept her power, as her years rolled on, from seventy to eighty, and from eighty on the new lap, towards ninety.

For in the family there was a whole tradition of 'loyalty'; loyalty to one another, and especially to the Mater. The Mater, of course, was the pivot of the family. The family was her own extended ego. Naturally she covered it with her power. And her sons and daughters, being weak and disintegrated, naturally were loyal. Outside the family, what was there for them but danger and insult and ignominy? Had not the rector experienced it in his marriage? So now, caution! Caution and loyalty, fronting the world! Let there be as much hate and friction *inside* the family as you like. To the outer world, a stubborn fence of unison.

II

But it was not until the girls finally came home from school that they felt the full weight of Granny's dead old hand on their lives. Lucille was now nearly twenty-one, and Yvette nineteen. They had been to a good girls' school, and had had a finishing year in Lausanne, and were quite the usual thing, tall young creatures with fresh, sensitive faces and bobbed hair and young-manly, deuce-take-it manners.

"What's so awfully *boring* about Papplewick," said Yvette, as they stood on the Channel boat watching the grey, grey cliffs of Dover draw near, "is that there are no *men* about. Why doesn't Daddy have some good old sports for friends? As for Uncle Fred, he's the limit!"

"Oh, you never know what will turn up," said Lucille, more philosophic.

"You jolly well know what to expect," said Yvette. "Choir on Sundays, and I hate mixed choirs. Boys' voices are *lovely* when there are no women. And Sunday School and Girls' Friendly, and socials, all the dear old souls that inquire after Granny! Not a decent young fellow for miles."

"Oh, I don't know!" said Lucille. "There's always the Framleys. And you know Gerry Somercotes *adores* you."

"Oh, but I *hate* fellows who adore me!" cried Yvette, turning up her sensitive nose. "They *bore* me. They hang on like lead."

"Well, what *do* you want, if you can't stand being adored? I think it's perfectly all right to be adored. You know you'll never marry them, so why not let them go on adoring, if it amuses them?"

"Oh, but I *want* to get married," cried Yvette.

"Well, in that case, let them go on adoring you till you find one that you can *possibly* marry."

"I never should, that way. Nothing puts me off like an adoring fellow. They *bore* me so! They make me feel beastly."

"Oh, so they do me, if they get pressing. But at a distance, I think they're rather nice."

"I should like to fall *violently* in love."

"Oh, very likely! I shouldn't! I should hate it. Probably so would you, if it actually happened. After all, we've got to settle down a bit before we know what we want."

"But don't you *hate* going back to Papplewick?" cried Yvette, turning up her young, sensitive nose.

"No, not particularly. I suppose we shall be rather bored. I wish Daddy would get a car. I suppose we shall have to drag the old bikes out. Wouldn't you like to go to Tansy Moor?"

"Oh, *love* it! Though it's an awful *strain*, shoving an old push-bike up those hills."

The ship was nearing the grey cliffs. It was summer, but a grey day. The two girls wore their coats with fur collars turned up, and little *chic* hats pulled down over their ears. Tall, slender, fresh-faced, naïve, yet confident, too confident, in their school-girlish arrogance, they were so terribly English. They seemed so free, and were, as a matter of fact, so tangled and tied up, inside themselves. They seemed so dashing and unconventional, and were really so conventional, so, as it were, shut up indoors inside themselves. They looked like bold, tall young sloops, just slipping from the harbour into the wide seas of life. And they were, as a matter of fact, two poor, young, rudderless lives, moving from one chain anchorage to another.

The rectory struck a chill into their hearts as they entered. It seemed ugly, and almost sordid, with the dank air of that middle-class, degenerate comfort which has ceased to be comfortable and has turned stuffy, unclean. The hard, stone house struck the girls as being unclean, they could not have said why. The shabby furniture seemed somehow sordid, nothing was fresh. Even the food at meals had that awful, dreary sordidness which is so repulsive to a young thing coming from abroad. Roast beef and wet cabbage, cold mutton and mashed potatoes, sour pickles, inexcusable puddings.

Granny, who 'loved a bit of pork', also had special dishes, beef-tea and rusks, or a small savoury custard. The grey-faced Aunt Cissie ate nothing at all. She would sit at table and take a single lonely and naked boiled potato on to her plate. She never ate meat. So she sat in sordid durance, while the meal went on, and Granny quickly slobbered her portion—lucky if she spilled nothing on her protuberant stomach. The food was not appetising in itself: how could it be, when Aunt Cissie hated food herself, hated the fact of eating, and never could keep a maid-servant for three months? The girls ate with repulsion, Lucille bravely bearing up, Yvette's tender nose showing her disgust. Only the rector, white-haired, wiped his long grey moustache with his serviette, and cracked jokes. He, too, was getting heavy and inert, sitting in his study all day, never taking exercise. But he cracked sarcastic little jokes all the time, sitting there under the shelter of the Mater.

The country, with its steep hills and its deep, narrow valleys, was dark and gloomy, yet had a certain powerful strength of its own. Twenty miles away was the black industrialism of the north. Yet the village of Papplewick was comparatively lonely, almost lost, the life in it stony and dour. Everything was stone, with a hardness that was almost poetic, it was so unrelenting.

It was as the girls had known: they went back into the choir, they helped in the parish. But Yvette struck absolutely against Sunday School, the Band of Hope, the Girls' Friendlies—indeed against all those functions that were conducted by determined old maids and obstinate, stupid, elderly men. She avoided church duties as much as possible, and got away from the rectory whenever she could. The Framleys, a

big, untidy, jolly family up at the Grange, were an enormous
stand-by. And if anybody asked her out to a meal, even if a
woman in one of the workmen's houses asked her to stay to
tea, she accepted at once. In fact, she was rather thrilled. She
liked talking to the working men, they had often such fine,
hard heads. But of course they were in another world.

So the months went by. Gerry Somercotes was still an
adorer. There were others, too, sons of farmers or mill-
owners. Yvette really ought to have had a good time. She
was always out to parties and dances, friends came for her
in their motor-cars, and off she went to the city, to the afternoon dance in the chief hotel, or in the gorgeous new Palais
de Danse, called the Pally.

Yet she always seemed like a creature mesmerised. She was
never free to be quite jolly. Deep inside her worked an intoler-
able irritation, which she thought she *ought* not to feel, and
which she hated feeling, thereby making it worse. She never
understood at all whence it arose.

At home, she truly was irritable, and outrageously rude to
Aunt Cissie. In fact, Yvette's awful temper became one of the
family by-words.

Lucille, always more practical, got a job in the city as private
secretary to a man who needed somebody with fluent French
and shorthand. She went back and forth every day by the
same train as Uncle Fred. But she never travelled with him,
and wet or fine, bicycled to the station, while he went on foot.

The two girls were both determined that what they wanted
was a really jolly social life. And they resented with fury that
the rectory was, for their friends, impossible. There were only
four rooms downstairs: the kitchen, where lived the two dis-
contented maid-servants: the dark dining-room: the rector's
study: and the big, 'homely', dreary living-room or drawing-
room. In the dining-room there was a gas fire. Only in the
living-room was a good hot fire kept going. Because, of course,
here Granny reigned.

In this room the family was assembled. At evening, after
dinner, Uncle Fred and the rector invariably played crossword
puzzles with Granny.

"Now, Mater, are you ready? N blank blank blank blank
W: a Siamese functionary."

"Eh? Eh? M blank blank blank blank W?"

Granny was hard of hearing.

"No, Mater. Not M! N blank blank blank blank W: a Siamese functionary."

"N blank blank blank blank W: a Chinese functionary."

"SIAMESE."

"Eh?"

"SIAMESE! SIAM!"

"A Siamese functionary! Now what can that be?" said the old lady profoundly, folding her hands on her round stomach. Her two sons proceeded to make suggestions, at which she said Ah! Ah! The rector was amazingly clever at crossword puzzles. But Fred had a certain technical vocabulary.

"This certainly is a hard nut to crack," said the old lady, when they were all stuck.

Meanwhile Lucille sat in a corner with her hands over her ears, pretending to read, and Yvette irritably made drawings, or hummed loud and exasperating tunes, to add to the family concert. Aunt Cissie continually reached for a chocolate, and her jaws worked ceaselessly. She literally lived on chocolates. Sitting in the distance, she put another into her mouth, then looked again at the parish magazine. Then she lifted her head, and saw it was time to fetch Granny's cup of Horlicks.

While she was gone, in nervous exasperation Yvette would open the window. The room was never fresh, she imagined it smelt: smelt of Granny. And Granny, who was hard of hearing, heard like a weasel when she wasn't wanted to.

"Did you open the window, Yvette? I think you might remember there are older people than yourself in the room," she said.

"It's stifling! It's unbearable! No wonder we've all of us always got colds."

"I'm sure the room is large enough, and a good fire burning." The old lady gave a little shudder. "A draught to give us all our death."

"Not a draught at all," roared Yvette. "A breath of fresh air."

The old lady shuddered again, and said: "Indeed!"

The rector, in silence, marched to the window and firmly closed it. He did not look at his daughter meanwhile. He hated thwarting her. But she must know what's what!

The crossword puzzles, invented by Satan himself, continued till Granny had had her Horlicks, and was to go to bed. Then came the ceremony of Good-night! Everybody stood up. The girls went to be kissed by the blind old woman, the rector gave his arm, and Aunt Cissie followed with a candle.

But this was already nine o'clock, although Granny was really getting old, and should have been in bed sooner. But when she was in bed, she could not sleep, till Aunt Cissie came.

"You see," said Granny, "I have *never* slept alone. For fifty-four years I never slept a night without the Pater's arm round me. And when he was gone I tried to sleep alone. But as sure as my eyes closed to sleep, my heart nearly jumped out of my body, and I lay in a palpitation. Oh, you may think what you will, but it was a fearful experience, after fifty-four years of perfect married life! I would have prayed to be taken first, but the Pater, well, no, I don't think he would have been able to bear up."

So Aunt Cissie slept with Granny. And she hated it. She said *she* could never sleep. And she grew greyer and greyer, and the food in the house got worse, and Aunt Cissie had to have an operation.

But the Mater rose as ever, towards noon, and at the mid-day meal she presided from her arm-chair, with her stomach protruding; her reddish, pendulous face, that had a sort of horrible majesty, dropping soft under the wall of her high brow, and her blue eyes peering unseeing. Her white hair was getting scanty, it was altogether a little indecent. But the rector jovially cracked his jokes to her, and she pretended to disapprove. But she was perfectly complacent, sitting in her ancient obesity, and after meals, getting the wind from her stomach, pressing her bosom with her hand as she 'rifted' in gross physical complacency.

What the girls minded most was that, when they brought their young friends to the house, Granny always was there, like some awful idol of old flesh, consuming all the attention. There was only the one room for everybody. And there sat the old lady, with Aunt Cissie keeping an acrid guard over her. Everybody must be presented first to Granny: she was ready to be genial, she liked company. She had to know who everybody was, where they came from, every circumstance of their lives. And then, when she was *au fait*, she could get hold of the conversation.

Nothing could be more exasperating to the girls. "Isn't old

Mrs. Saywell wonderful! She takes *such* an interest in life, at nearly ninety!"

"She does take an interest in people's affairs, if that's life," said Yvette.

Then she would immediately feel guilty. After all, it *was* wonderful to be nearly ninety, and have such a clear mind! And Granny never *actually* did anybody any harm. It was more that she was in the way. And perhaps it was rather awful to hate somebody because they were old and in the way.

Yvette immediately repented, and was nice. Granny blossomed forth into reminiscences of when she was a girl in the little town in Buckinghamshire. She talked and talked away, and was *so* entertaining. She really *was* rather wonderful.

Then in the afternoon Lottie and Ella and Bob Framley came, with Leo Wetherell.

"Oh, come in!"—and in they all trooped to the sitting-room, where Granny, in her white cap, sat by the fire.

"Granny, this is Mr. Wetherell."

"Mr. what-did-you-say? You must excuse me, I'm a little deaf!"

Granny gave her hand to the uncomfortable young man, and gazed silently at him, sightlessly.

"You are not from our parish?" she asked him.

"Dinnington!" he shouted.

"We want to go a picnic to-morrow, to Bonsall Head, in Leo's car. We can all squeeze in," said Ella, in a low voice.

"Did you say Bonsall Head?" asked Granny.

"Yes!"

There was a blank silence.

"Did you say you were going in a car?"

"Yes! In Mr. Wetherell's."

"I hope he's a good driver. It's a very dangerous road."

"He's a *very* good driver."

"Not a very good driver?"

"Yes! He *is* a very good driver."

"If you go to Bonsall Head, I think I must send a message to Lady Louth."

Granny always dragged in this miserable Lady Louth when there was company.

"Oh, we shan't go that way," cried Yvette.

"Which way?" said Granny. "You must go by Heanor."

The whole party sat, as Bob expressed it, like stuffed ducks, fidgeting on their chairs.

Aunt Cissie came in—and then the maid with the tea. There was the eternal and everlasting piece of bought cake. Then appeared a plate of little fresh cakes. Aunt Cissie had actually sent to the baker's.

"Tea, Mater!"

The old lady gripped the arms of her chair. Everybody rose and stood, while she waded slowly across, on Aunt Cissie's arm, to her place at table.

During tea Lucille came in from town, from her job. She was simply worn out, with black marks under her eyes. She gave a cry, seeing all the company.

As soon as the noise had subsided, and the awkwardness was resumed, Granny said:

"You have never mentioned Mr. Wetherell to me, have you, Lucille?"

"I don't remember," said Lucille.

"You can't have done. The name is strange to me."

Yvette absently grabbed another cake from the now almost empty plate. Aunt Cissie, who was driven almost crazy by Yvette's vague and inconsiderate ways, felt the green rage fuse in her heart. She picked up her own plate, on which was the one cake she allowed herself, and said with vitriolic politeness, offering it to Yvette:

"Won't you have mine?"

"Oh, thanks!" said Yvette, starting in her angry vagueness. And with an appearance of the same insouciance, she helped herself to Aunt Cissie's cake also, adding as an afterthought: "If you're sure you don't want it."

She now had two cakes on her plate. Lucille had gone white as a ghost, bending to her tea. Aunt Cissie sat with a green look of poisonous resignation. The awkwardness was an agony.

But Granny, bulkily enthroned and unaware, only said, in the centre of the cyclone:

"If you are motoring to Bonsall Head to-morrow, Lucille, I wish you would take a message from me to Lady Louth."

"Oh!" said Lucille, giving a queer look across the table at the sightless old woman. Lady Louth was the King Charles's Head of the family, invariably produced by Granny for the benefit of visitors. "Very well!"

"She was so very kind last week. She sent her chauffeur over with a Crossword Puzzle book for me."

"But you thanked her then," cried Yvette.

"I should like to send her a note."

"We can post it," cried Lucille.

"Oh no! I should like you to take it. When Lady Louth called last time . . ."

The young ones sat like a shoal of young fishes dumbly mouthing at the surface of the water, while Granny went on about Lady Louth. Aunt Cissie, the two girls knew, was still helpless, almost unconscious in a paroxysm of rage about the cake. Perhaps, poor thing, she was praying.

It was a mercy when the friends departed. But by that time the two girls were both haggard-eyed. And it was then that Yvette, looking round, suddenly saw the stony, implacable will-to-power in the old and motherly-seeming Granny. She sat there bulging backwards in her chair, impassive, her reddish, pendulous old face rather mottled, almost unconscious, but implacable, her face like a mask that hid something stony, relentless. It was the static inertia of her unsavoury power. Yet in a minute she would open her ancient mouth to find out every detail about Leo Wetherell. For the moment she was hibernating in her oldness, her agedness. But in a minute her mouth would open, her mind would flicker awake and with her insatiable greed for life, other people's life, she would start on her quest for every detail. She was like the old toad which Yvette had watched, fascinated, as it sat on the ledge of the beehive, immediately in front of the little entrance by which the bees emerged, and which, with a demonish lightning-like snap of its pursed jaws, caught every bee as it came out to launch into the air, swallowed them one after the other, as if it could consume the whole hiveful, into its aged, bulging, purse-like wrinkledness. It had been swallowing bees as they launched into the air of spring, year after year, year after year, for generations.

But the gardener, called by Yvette, was in a rage, and killed the creature with a stone.

" 'Appen tha *art* good for th' snails," he said, as he came down with the stone. "But tha 'rt none goin' ter emp'y th' bee-'ive into thy guts."

III

The next day was dull and low, and the roads were awful,
for it had been raining for weeks, yet the young ones set off
on their trip, without taking Granny's message either. They
just slipped out while she was making her slow trip upstairs
after lunch. Not for anything would they have called at Lady
Louth's house. That widow of a knighted doctor, a harmless
person indeed, had become an obnoxity in their lives.

Six young rebels, they sat very perkily in the car as they
swished through the mud. Yet they had a peaked look too.
After all, they had nothing really to rebel against, any of them.
They were left so very free in their movements. Their parents
let them do almost entirely as they liked. There wasn't really
a fetter to break, nor a prison bar to file through, nor a bolt
to shatter. The keys of their lives were in their own hands.
And there they dangled inert.

It is very much easier to shatter prison bars than to open
undiscovered doors to life. As the younger generation finds
out somewhat to its chagrin. True, there was Granny. But
poor old Granny, you couldn't actually say to her: "Lie down
and die, you old woman!" She might be an old nuisance, but
she never really *did* anything. It wasn't fair to hate her.

So the young people set off on their jaunt, trying to be very
full of beans. They could really do as they liked. And so, of
course, there was nothing to do but sit in the car and talk a
lot of criticism of other people, and silly flirty gallantry that
was really rather a bore. If there had only been a few 'strict
orders' to be disobeyed! But nothing: beyond the refusal to
carry the message to Lady Louth, of which the rector would
approve because he didn't encourage King Charles's Head
either.

They sang, rather scrappily, the latest would-be comic songs
as they went through the grim villages. In the great park the
deer were in groups near the road, roe deer and fallow, nestling
in the gloom of the afternoon under the oaks by the road, as if
for the stimulus of human company.

Yvette insisted on stopping and getting out to talk to them.
The girls, in their Russian boots, tramped through the damp
grass, while the deer watched them with big, unfrightened
eyes. The hart trotted away mildly, holding back his head,

because of the weight of the horns. But the doe, balancing her big ears, did not rise from under the tree, with her half-grown young ones, till the girls were almost in touch. Then she walked light-foot away, lifting her tail from her spotted flanks, while the young ones nimbly trotted.

"Aren't they awfully dainty and nice!" cried Yvette. "You'd wonder they could lie so cosily in this horrid wet grass."

"Well, I suppose they've got to lie down *some time*," said Lucille. "And it's *fairly* dry under the tre." She looked at the crushed grass, where the deer had lain.

Yveette went and put her hand down to feel how it felt.

"Yes!" she said doubtfully, "I believe it's a bit warm."

The deer had bunched again a few yards away, and were standing motionless in the gloom of the afternoon. Away below the slopes of grass and trees, beyond the swift river with its balustraded bridge, sat the huge ducal house, one or two chimneys smoking bluely. Behind it rose purplish woods.

The girls, pushing their fur collars up to their ears, dangling one long arm, stood watching in silence, their wide Russian boots protecting them from the wet grass. The great house squatted square and creamy-grey below. The deer, in little groups, were scattered under the old trees close by. It all seemed so still, so unpretentious, and so sad.

"I wonder where the Duke is now," said Ella.

"Not here, wherever he is," said Lucille. "I expect he's abroad where the sun shines."

The motor-horn called from the road, and they heard Leo's voice:

"Come on, boys! If we're going to get to the Head and down to Amberdale for tea, we'd better move."

They crowded into the car again, with chilled feet, and set off through the park past the silent spire of the church, out through the great gates and over the bridge, on into the wide, damp, stony village of Woodlinkin, where the river ran. And thence, for a long time, they stayed in the mud and dark and dampness of the valley, often with sheer rock above them; the water brawling on one hand, the steep rock or dark trees on the other.

Till, through the darkness of overhanging trees, they began to climb, and Leo changed the gear. Slowly the car toiled up through the whitey-grey mud, into the stony village of Bole-hill, that hung on the slope, round the old cross, with its steps,

that stood where the road branched, on past the cottages
whence came a wonderful smell of hot tea-cakes, and beyond,
still upwards, under dripping trees and past broken slopes of
bracken, always climbing. Until the cleft became shallower,
and the trees finished, and the slopes on either side were bare,
gloomy grass, with low dry-stone walls. They were emerging
on to the Head.

The party had been silent for some time. On either side the
road was grass, then a low stone fence, and the swelling curve
of the hill-summit, traced with the low, dry stone walls. Above
this, the low sky.

The car ran out, under the low, grey sky, on the naked tops.

"Shall we stay a moment?" called Leo.

"Oh yes!" cried the girls.

And they scrambled out once more, to look around. They
knew the place quite well. But still, if one came to the Head,
one got out to look.

The hills were like the knuckles of a hand, the dales were
below, between the fingers, narrow, steep, and dark. In the
deeps a train was steaming, slowly pulling north: a small
thing of the underworld. The noise of the engine re-echoed
curiously upwards. Then came the dull, familiar sound of
blasting in a quarry.

Leo, always on the go, moved quickly.

"Shall we be going?" he said. "Do we *want* to get down to
Amberdale for tea? Or shall we try somewhere nearer?"

They all voted for Amberdale, for the 'Marquis of
Grantham'.

"Well, which way shall we go back? Shall we go by Codnor
and over Crosshill, or shall we go by Ashbourne?"

There was the usual dilemma. Then they finally decided on
the Codnor top road. Off went the car gallantly.

They were on the top of the world, now, on the back of the
fist. It was naked, too, as the back of your fist, high under
heaven, and dull, heavy green. Only it was veined with a network of old stone walls, dividing the fields, and broken here
and there with ruins of old lead-mines and works. A sparse
stone farm bristled with six naked sharp trees. In the distance
was a patch of smoky grey stone, a hamlet. In some fields
grey, dark sheep fed silently, sombrely. But there was not a
sound nor a movement. It was the roof of England, stony and
arid as any roof. Beyond, below, were the shires.

" 'And see the coloured counties,' " said Yvette to herself. Here, anyhow, they were not coloured. A stream of rooks trailed out from nowhere. They had been walking, pecking, on a naked field that had been manured. The car ran on between the grass and the stone walls of the upland lane, and the young people were silent, looking out over the far network of stone fences, under the sky, looking for the curves downward that indicated a drop to one of the underneath, hidden dales.

Ahead was a light cart, driven by a man, and trudging along at the side was a woman, sturdy and elderly, with a pack on her back. The man in the cart had caught her up, and now was keeping pace.

The road was narrow. Leo sounded the horn sharply. The man on the cart looked round, but the woman on foot only trudged steadily, rapidly forward, without turning her head.

Yvette's heart gave a jump. The man on the cart was a gipsy, one of the black, loose-bodied, handsome sort. He remained seated on his cart, turning round and gazing at the occupants of the motor-car from under the brim of his cap. And his pose was loose, his gaze insolent in its indifference. He had a thin black moustache under his thin, straight nose, and a big silk handkerchief of red and yellow tied round his neck. He spoke a word to the woman. She stood a second, solid, to turn round and look at the occupants of the car, which had now drawn quite close. Leo honked the horn again imperiously. The woman, who had a grey-and-white kerchief tied round her head, turned sharply, to keep pace with the cart, whose driver also had settled back, and was lifting the reins, moving his loose, light shoulders. But still he did not pull aside.

Leo made the horn scream as he put the brakes on, and the car slowed up near the back of the cart. The gipsy turned round at the din, laughing in his dark face under his dark-green cap, and said something which they did not hear, showing white teeth under the line of black moustache, and making a gesture with his dark, loose hand.

"Get out o' the way then!" yelled Leo.

For answer the man delicately pulled the horse to a standstill as it curved to the side of the road. It was a good roan horse and a good, natty, dark-green cart.

Leo, in a rage, had to jam on the brake and pull up too.

"Don't the pretty young ladies want to hear their fortunes?"

said the gipsy on the cart, laughing except for his dark, watchful eyes, which went from face to face, and lingered on Yvette's young, tender face.

She met his dark eyes for a second, their level search, their insolence, their complete indifference to people like Bob and Leo, and something took fire in her breast. She thought: 'He is stronger than I am! He doesn't care!'

"Oh yes! Let's!" cried Lucille at once.

"Oh yes!" chorused the girls.

"I say! What about the time?" cried Leo.

"Oh, bother the old time! Somebody's always dragging in time by the forelock," cried Lucille.

"Well, if you don't mind *when* we get back, *I* don't!" said Leo heroically.

The gipsy man had been sitting loosely on the side of his cart, watching the faces. He now jumped softly down from the shaft, his knees a bit stiff. He was apparently a man something over thirty, and a beau in his way. He wore a sort of shooting-jacket, double-breasted, coming only to the hips, of dark green-and-black frieze; rather tight black trousers, black boots, and a dark-green cap; with the big yellow-and-red bandanna handkerchief round his neck. His appearance was curiously elegant, and quite expensive in its gipsy style. He was handsome, too, pressing in his chin with the old, gipsy conceit, and now apparently not heeding the strangers any more, as he led his good roan horse off the road, preparing to back his cart.

The girls saw for the first time a deep recess in the side of the road, and two caravans smoking. Yvette got quickly down. They had suddenly come upon a disused quarry, cut into the slope of the road-side, and in this sudden lair, almost like a cave, were three caravans, dismantled for the winter. There was also, deep at the back, a shelter built of boughs, as a stable for the horse. The grey, crude rock rose high above the caravans, and curved round towards the road. The floor was heaped chips of stone, with grasses growing among. It was a hidden, snug winter camp.

The elderly woman with the pack had gone into one of the caravans, leaving the door open. Two children were peeping out, showing black heads. The gipsy man gave a little call as he backed his cart into the quarry, and an elderly man came out to help him untackle.

The gipsy himself went up the steps into the newest caravan, that had its door closed. Underneath, a tied-up dog ranged
forth. It was a white hound spotted liver-coloured. It gave a
low growl as Leo and Bob approached.

At the same moment, a dark-faced gipsy woman with a pink
shawl or kerchief round her head and big gold ear-rings in her
ears, came down the steps of the newest caravan, swinging
her flounced, voluminous green skirt. She was handsome in a
bold, dark, long-faced way, just a bit wolfish. She looked like
one of the bold, loping Spanish gipsies.

"Good-morning, my ladies and gentlemen," she said, eyeing
the girls from her bold, predative eyes. She spoke with a
certain foreign stiffness.

"Good-afternoon!" said the girls.

"Which beautiful little lady like to hear her fortune? Give
me her little hand?"

She was a tall woman, with a frightening way of reaching
forward her neck like a menace. Her eyes went from face to
face, very active, heartlessly searching out what she wanted.
Meanwhile the man, apparently her husband, appeared at the
top of the caravan steps smoking a pipe, and with a small,
black-haired child in his arms. He stood on his limber legs,
casually looking down on the group, as if from a distance, his
long, black lashes lifted from his full, conceited, impudent
black eyes. There was something peculiarly transfusing in his
stare. Yvette felt it, felt it in her knees. She pretended to be
interested in the white-and-liver-coloured hound.

"How much do you want if we all have our fortunes told?"
asked Lottie Framley, as the six fresh-faced young Christians
hung back rather reluctantly from this pagan pariah woman.

"All of you? ladies and gentlemen, all?" said the woman
shrewdly.

"I don't want mine told! You go ahead!" cried Leo.

"Neither do I," said Bob. "You four girls."

"The four ladies?" said the gipsy woman, eyeing them
shrewdly, after having looked at the boys. And she fixed her
price. "Each one give me a sheeling, and a little bit more for
luck? a little bit!" She smiled in a way that was more wolfish
than cajoling, and the force of her will was felt, heavy as iron
beneath the velvet of her words.

"All right," said Leo. "Make it a shilling a head. Don't spin
it out too long."

"Oh, *you*!" cried Lucille at him. "We want to hear it *all*."

The woman took two wooden stools from under a caravan and placed them near the wheel. Then she took the tall, dark Lottie Framley by the hand and bade her sit down.

"You don't care if everybody hear?" she said, looking up curiously into Lottie's face.

Lottie blushed dark with nervousness as the gipsy woman held her hand, and stroked her palm with hard, cruel-seeming fingers.

"Oh, I don't mind," she said.

The gipsy woman peered into the palm tracing the lines of the hand with a hard, dark forefinger. But she seemed clean.

And slowly she told the fortune, while the others, standing listening, kept on crying out: "Oh, that's Jim Baggaley! Oh, I don't believe it! Oh, that's not true! A fair woman who lives beneath a tree! Why, whoever's this?" until Leo stopped them with a manly warning:

"Oh, hold on, girls! You give everything away."

Lottie retired blushing and confused, and it was Ella's turn. She was much more calm and shrewd, trying to read the oracular words. Lucille kept breaking out with: "Oh, I say!" The gipsy man at the top of the steps stood imperturbable, without any expression at all. But his bold eyes kept staring at Yvette, she could feel them on her cheek, on her neck, and she dared not look up. But Framley would sometimes look up at him, and got a level stare back from the handsome face of the male gipsy, from the dark, conceited, proud eyes. It was a peculiar look, in the eyes that belonged to the tribe of the humble: the pride of the pariah, the half-sneering challenge of the outcast, who sneered at law-abiding men, and went his own way. All the time the gipsy man stood there, holding his child in his arms, looking on without being concerned.

Lucille was having her hand read—"You have been across the sea, and there you met a man—a brown-haired man—but he was too old——"

"Oh, I *say*!" cried Lucille, looking round at Yvette.

But Yvette was abstracted, agitated, hardly heeding: in one of her mesmerised states.

"You will marry in a few years—not now, but a few years —perhaps four—and you will not be rich, but you will have plenty—enough—and you will go away, a long journey."

"With my husband, or without?" cried Lucille.

"With him——"

When it came to Yvette's turn, and the woman looked up boldly, cruelly, searching for a long time in her face, Yvette said nervously:

"I don't think I want mine told. No, I won't have mine told! No, I won't, really!"

"You are afraid of something?" said the gipsy woman cruelly.

"No, it's not that——" Yvette fidgeted.

"You have some secret? You are afraid I shall say it? Come, would you like to go in the caravan, where nobody hears?"

The woman was curiously insinuating; while Yvette was always wayward, perverse. The look of perversity was on her soft, frail young face now, giving her a queer hardness.

"Yes!" she said suddenly. "Yes! I might do that!"

"Oh, I say!" cried the others. "Be a sport!"

"I don't think you'd *better*!" cried Lucille.

"Yes!" said Yvette, with that hard little way of hers. "I'll do that. I'll go in the caravan."

The gipsy woman called something to the man on the steps. He went into the caravan for a moment or two, then reappeared, and came down the steps, setting the small child on its uncertain feet, and holding it by the hand. A dandy, in his polished black boots, tight black trousers and tight, dark-green jersey, he walked slowly across with the toddling child to where the elderly gipsy was giving the roan horse a feed of oats, in the bough shelter between pits of grey rock, with dry bracken upon the stone chip floor. He looked at Yvette as he passed, staring her full in the eyes, with his pariah's bold yet dishonest stare. Something hard inside her met his stare. But the surface of her body seemed to turn to water. Nevertheless, something hard in her registered the peculiar pure lines of his face, of his straight, pure nose, of his cheeks and temples. The curious dark, suave purity of all his body, outlined in the green jersey: a purity like a living sneer.

And as he loped slowly past her, on his flexible hips, it seemed to her still that he was stronger than she was. Of all the men she had ever seen, this one was the only one who was stronger than she was, in her own kind of strength, her own kind of understanding.

So, with curiosity, she followed the woman up the steps of the caravan, the skirts of her well-cut tan coat swinging and almost showing her knees, under the pale-green cloth dress. She had long, long-striding, fine legs, too slim rather than too thick, and she wore curiously-patterned pale-and-fawn stockings of fine wool, suggesting the legs of some delicate animal.

At the top of the steps she paused and turned, debonair, to the others, saying in her naïve, lordly way, so off-hand:

"I won't let her be long."

Her grey fur collar was open, showing her soft throat and pale green dress, her little plaited tan-coloured hat came down to her ears, round her soft, fresh face. There was something soft and yet overbearing, unscrupulous, about her. She knew the gipsy man had turned to look at her. She was aware of the pure dark nape of his neck, the black hair groomed away. He watched as she entered his house.

What the gipsy told her, no one ever knew. It was a long time to wait, the others felt. Twilight was deepening on the gloom, and it was turning raw and cold. From the chimney on the second caravan came smoke and a smell of rich food. The horse was fed, a yellow blanket strapped round him, and two gipsy men talked together in the distance in low tones. There was a peculiar feeling of silence and secrecy in that lonely, hidden quarry.

At last the caravan door opened, and Yvette emerged, bending forward and stepping with long, witch-like slim legs down the steps. There was a stooping, witch-like silence about her as she emerged on the twilight.

"Did it seem long?" she said vaguely, not looking at anybody and keeping her own counsel hard within her soft, vague waywardness. "I hope you weren't bored! Wouldn't tea be nice! Shall we go?"

"You get in!" said Bob. "I'll pay."

The gipsy woman's full, metallic skirts of jade-green alpaca came swinging down the steps. She rose to her height, a big, triumphant-looking woman with a dark wolf face. The pink cashmere kerchief stamped with red roses was slipping to one side over her black and crimped hair. She gazed at the young people in the twilight with bold arrogance.

Bob put two half-crowns in her hand.

"A little bit more for luck, for your young lady's luck," she wheedled, like a wheedling wolf. "Another bit of silver, to bring you luck."

"You've got a shilling for luck, that's enough," said Bob calmly and quietly, as they moved away to the car.

"A little bit of silver! Just a little bit, for your luck in love!"

Yvette, with the sudden long, startling gestures of her long limbs, swung round as she was entering the car, and with long arm outstretched, strode and put something into the gipsy's hand, then stepped, bending her height, into the car.

"Prosperity to the beautiful young lady, and the gipsy's blessing on her," came the suggestive, half-sneering voice of the woman.

The engine *birred!* then *birred!* again more fiercely, and started. Leo switched on the lights, and immediately the quarry with the gipsies fell back into the blackness of night.

"Good-night!" called Yvette's voice, as the car started. But hers was the only voice that piped up, chirpy and impudent in its nonchalance. The headlights glared down the stone lane.

"Yvette, you've got to tell us what she said to you," cried Lucille, in the teeth of Yvette's silent will *not* to be asked.

"Oh, nothing at *all* thrilling," said Yvette, with false warmth. "Just the usual old thing: a dark man who means good luck, and a fair one who means bad: and a death in the family, which if it means Granny, won't be so *very* awful: and I shall marry when I'm twenty-three, and have heaps of money and heaps of love, and two children. All sounds very nice, but it's a bit too much of a good thing, you know."

"Oh, but why did you give her more money?"

"Oh, well, I wanted to! You *have* to be a bit lordly with people like that——"

IV

There was a terrific rumpus down at the rectory, on account of Yvette and the Window Fund. After the war, Aunt Cissie had set her heart on a stained glass window in the church, as a memorial for the men of the parish who had fallen. But the bulk of the fallen had been nonconformists, so the memorial took the form of an ugly little monument in front of the Wesleyan chapel.

This did not vanquish Aunt Cissie. She canvassed, she had bazaars, she made the girls get up amateur theatrical shows, for her precious window. Yvette, who quite liked the acting and showing-off part of it, took charge of the farce called *Mary in the Mirror*, and gathered in the proceeds, which were to be paid to the Window Fund when accounts were settled. Each of the girls was supposed to have a money-box for the Fund.

Aunt Cissie, feeling that the united sums must now almost suffice, suddenly called in Yvette's box. It contained fifteen shillings. There was a moment of green horror.

"Where is all the rest?"

"Oh!" said Yvette casually. "I just borrowed it. It wasn't so awfully much."

"What about the three pounds thirteen for *Mary in the Mirror*?" asked Aunt Cissie, as if the jaws of Hell were yawning.

"Oh, quite! I just borrowed it. I can pay it back."

Poor Aunt Cissie! The green tumour of hate burst inside her, and there was a ghastly, abnormal scene, which left Yvette shivering with fear and nervous loathing.

Even the rector was rather severe.

"If you needed money, why didn't you tell me?" he said coldly. "Have you ever been refused anything in reason?"

"I—I thought it didn't matter," stammered Yvette.

"And what have you done with the money?"

"I suppose I've spent it," said Yvette, with wide, distraught eyes and a peaked face.

"Spent it, on what?"

"I can't remember everything: stockings and things, and I gave some of it away."

Poor Yvette! Her lordly airs and ways were already hitting back at her, on the reflex. The rector was angry: his face had a snarling, doggish look, a sort of sneer. He was afraid his daughter was developing some of the rank, tainted qualities of She-who-was-Cynthia.

"You *would* do the large with somebody else's money, wouldn't you?" he said, with a cold, mongrel sort of sneer, which showed what an utter unbeliever he was at the heart. The inferiority of a heart which has no core of warm belief in it, no pride in life. He had utterly no belief in her.

Yvette went pale and very distant. Her pride, that frail,

precious flame which everybody tried to quench, recoiled like a flame blown far away on a cold wind, as if blown out, and her face, white now and still like a snowdrop, the white snow-flower of his conceit, seemed to have no life in it, only this pure, strange abstraction.

'He has no belief in me!' she thought in her soul. 'I am really nothing to him. I am nothing, only a shameful thing. Everything is shameful, everything is shameful!'

A flame of passion or rage, while it might have over-whelmed or infuriated her, would not have degraded her as did her father's unbelief, his final attitude of a sneer against her.

He became a little afraid, in the silence of sterile thought. After all, he needed the *appearance* of love and belief and bright life, he would never dare to face the fat worm of his own unbelief, that stirred in his heart.

"What have you to say for yourself?" he asked.

She only looked at him from that senseless snowdrop face which haunted him with fear, and gave him a helpless sense of guilt. That other one, She-who-was-Cynthia, she had looked back at him with the same numb, white fear, the fear of his degrading unbelief, the worm which was his heart's core. He *knew* his heart's core was a fat, awful worm. His dread was lest anyone else should know. His anguish of hate was against anyone who knew and recoiled.

He saw Yvette recoiling, and immediately his manner changed to the worldly old good-humoured cynic which he affected.

"Ah well!" he said. "You have to pay it back, my girl, that's all. I will advance you the money out of your allow-ance. But I shall charge you four per cent a month interest. Even the devil himself must pay a percentage on his debts. Another time, if you can't trust yourself, don't handle money which isn't your own. Dishonesty isn't pretty."

Yvette remained crushed, and deflowered and humiliated. She crept about, trailing the rays of her pride. She had a re-vulsion even from herself. Oh, why had she ever touched the leprous money! Her whole flesh shrank as if it were defiled. Why was that? Why, why was that?

She admitted herself wrong in having spent the money. "Of course I shouldn't have done it. They are quite right to be angry," she said to herself.

But where did the horrible wincing of her flesh come from?
Why did she feel she had caught some physical contagion?

"Where you're so *silly*, Yvette," Lucille lectured her: poor
Lucille was in great distress—"is that you give yourself away
to them all. You might *know* they'd find out. I could have
raised the money for you, and saved all this bother. It's perfectly awful! But you never will think beforehand where
your actions are going to land you! Fancy Aunt Cissie saying all those things to you! How *awful!* Whatever would
Mamma have said if she'd heard it?"

When things went very wrong, they thought of their
mother, and despised their father and all the low brood of
the Saywells. Their mother, of course, had belonged to a
higher, if more dangerous and 'immortal', world. More selfish,
decidedly. But with a showier gesture. More unscrupulous
and more easily moved to contempt: but not so humiliating.

Yvette always considered that she got her fine, delicate flesh
from her mother. The Saywells were all a bit leathery, and
grubby somewhere inside. But then the Saywells never let you
down. Whereas the fine She-who-was-Cynthia had let the
rector down with a bang, and his little children along with
him. Her little children? They could not quite forgive her.

Only dimly, after the row, Yvette began to realise the other
sanctity of herself, the sanctity of her sensitive, clean flesh
and blood, which the Saywells with their so-called morality
succeeded in defiling. They always wanted to defile it. They
were the life unbelievers. Whereas, perhaps She-who-was-
Cynthia had only been a moral unbeliever.

Yvette went about dazed and peaked and confused. The
rector paid in the money to Aunt Cissie, much to that lady's
rage. The helpless tumour of her rage was still running. She
would have liked to announce her niece's delinquency in the
parish magazine. It was anguish to the destroyed woman that
she could not publish the news to all the world. The selfishness! The selfishness! The selfishness!

Then the rector handed his daughter a little account with
himself: her debt to him, interest thereon, the amount de-
ducted from her small allowance. But to her credit he
had placed a guinea, which was the fee he had to pay for
complicity.

"As father of the culprit," he said humorously, "I am fined
one guinea. And with that I wash the ashes out of my hair."

He was always generous about money. But somehow he seemed to think that by being free about money he could absolutely call himself a generous man. Whereas he used money, even generosity, as a hold over her.

But he let the affair drop entirely. He was by this time more amused than anything, to judge from appearances. He thought still he was safe.

Aunt Cissie, however, could not get over her convulsion. One night when Yvette had gone rather early, miserably, to bed, when Lucille was away at a party, and she was lying with soft, peaked limbs aching with a sort of numbness and defilement, the door softly opened, and there stood Aunt Cissie, pushing her grey-green face through the opening of the door. Yvette started up in terror.

"Liar! Thief! Selfish little beast!" hissed the maniacal face of Aunt Cissie. "You little hypocrite! You liar! You selfish beast! You greedy little beast!"

There was such extraordinary impersonal hatred in that grey-green mask, and those frantic words, that Yvette opened her mouth to scream with hysterics. But Aunt Cissie shut the door as suddenly as she had opened it and disappeared. Yvette leaped from her bed and turned the key. Then she crept back, half demented with fear of the squalid abnormal, half numbed with paralysis of damaged pride. And amid it all, up came a bubble of distracted laughter. It *was* so filthily ridiculous!

Aunt Cissie's behaviour did not hurt the girl so very much. It was, after all, somewhat fantastic. Yet hurt she was: in her limbs, in her body, in her sex, hurt. Hurt, numbed, and half destroyed, with only her nerves vibrating and jangled. And still so young, she could not conceive what was happening.

Only she lay and wished she were a gipsy. To live in a camp, in a caravan, and never set foot in a house, not know the existence of a parish, never look at a church. Her heart was hard with repugnance against the rectory. She loathed these houses with their indoor sanitation and their bathrooms, and their extraordinary repulsiveness. She hated the rectory and everything it implied. The whole stagnant, sewerage sort of life, where sewerage is never mentioned, but where it seems to smell from the centre to every two-legged inmate, from Granny to the servants, was foul. If gipsies had no bathrooms, at least they had no sewerage. There was fresh air.

In the rectory there was *never* fresh air. And in the souls of the people, the air was stale till it stank.

Hate kindled her heart, as she lay with numbed limbs. And she thought of the words of the gipsy woman: "There is a dark man who never lived in a house. He loves you. The other people are treading on your heart. They will tread on your heart till you think it is dead. But the dark man will blow the one spark up into fire again, good fire. You will see what good fire."

Even as the woman was saying it, Yvette felt there was some duplicity somewhere. But she didn't mind. She hated with the cold, acrid hatred of a child the rectory interior, the sort of putridity in the life. She liked that big, swarthy, wolf-like gipsy woman, with the big gold rings in her ears, the pink scarf over her wavy black hair, the tight bodice of brown velvet, the green, fan-like skirt. She liked her dusky, strong, relentless hands, that had pressed so firm, like wolf's paws, in Yvette's own soft palm. She liked her. She liked the danger and the covert fearlessness of her. She liked her covert, un-yielding sex, that was immoral, but with a hard, defiant pride of its own. Nothing would ever get that woman under. She would despise the rectory and the rectory morality utterly! She would strangle Granny with one hand. And she would have the same contempt for Daddy and for Uncle Fred, as men, as she would have for fat old slobbery Rover, the New-foundland dog. A great, sardonic female contempt, for such domesticated dogs, calling themselves men.

And the gipsy man himself! Yvette quivered suddenly, as if she had seen his big, bold eyes upon her, with the naked insinuation of desire in them. The absolutely naked insinuation of desire made her lie prone and powerless in the bed, as if a drug had cast her in a new, molten mould.

She never confessed to anybody that two of the ill-starred Window Fund pounds had gone to the gipsy woman. What if Daddy and Aunt Cissie knew *that*! Yvette stirred luxuriously in the bed. The thought of the gipsy had released the life of her limbs, and crystallised in her heart the hate of the rectory: so that now she felt potent, instead of impotent.

When, later, Yvette told Lucille about Aunt Cissie's dramatic interlude in the bedroom doorway, Lucille was indignant.

"Oh, hang it all!" cried she. "She might let it drop now. I should think we've heard enough about it by now! Good

heavens, you'd think Aunt Cissie was a perfect bird of paradise! Daddy's dropped it, and after all, it's his business if it's
anybody's. Let Aunt Cissie shut up!"

It was the very fact that the rector had dropped it, and that
he again treated the vague and inconsiderate Yvette as if she
were some specially-licensed being, that kept Aunt Cissie's bile
flowing. The fact that Yvette really was most of the time unaware of other people's feelings, and being unaware, couldn't
care about them, nearly sent Aunt Cissie mad. Why should
that young creature, with a delinquent mother, go through
life as a privileged being, even unaware of other people's
existence, though they were under her nose?

Lucille at this time was very irritable. She seemed as if she
simply went a little unbalanced, when she entered the rectory.
Poor Lucille, she was so thoughtful and responsible. She did
all the extra troubling, thought about doctors, medicines,
servants, and all that sort of thing. She slaved conscientiously
at her job all day in town, working in a room with artificial
light from ten till five. And she came home to have her nerves
rubbed almost to frenzy by Granny's horrible and persistent
inquisitiveness and parasitic agedness.

The affair of the Window Fund had apparently blown over,
but there remained a stuffy tension in the atmosphere. The
weather continued bad. Lucille stayed at home on the afternoon of her half holiday, and did herself no good by it.
The rector was in his study, she and Yvette were making a
dress for the latter young woman, Granny was resting on the
couch.

The dress was of blue silk velours, French material, and was
going to be very becoming. Lucille made Yvette try it on
again: she was nervously uneasy about the hang under the
arms.

"Oh, bother!" cried Yvette, stretching her long, tender,
childish arms, that tended to go bluish with the cold. "Don't
be so frightfully *fussy*, Lucille! It's quite all right."

"If that's all the thanks I get, slaving my half-day away
making dresses for you, I might as well do something for
myself!"

"Well, Lucille! You know I never *asked* you! You know
you can't bear it unless you *do* supervise," said Yvette, with
that irritating blandness of hers, as she raised her naked elbows
and peered over her shoulder into the long mirror.

"Oh yes! you never *asked* me!" cried Lucille. "As if I didn't know what you meant, when you started sighing and flouncing about."

"I!" said Yvette, with vague surprise. "Why, when did I start sighing and flouncing about?"

"Of course, you know you did."

"Did I? No, I didn't know! When was it?" Yvette could put a peculiar annoyance into her mild, straying questions.

"I shan't do another thing to this frock, if you don't stand still and *stop* it," said Lucille, in her rather sonorous, burning voice.

"You know you are most awfully nagging and irritable, Lucille," said Yvette, standing as if on hot bricks.

"Now, Yvette!" cried Lucille, her eyes suddenly flashing in her sister's face, with wild flashes. "Stop it at once! Why should everybody put up with your abominable and over-bearing temper?"

"Well, I don't know about *my* temper," said Yvette, writhing slowly out of the half-made frock, and slipping into her dress again.

Then, with an obstinate little look on her face, she sat down again at the table, in the gloomy afternoon, and began to sew at the blue stuff. The room was littered with blue clippings, the scissors were lying on the floor, the work-basket was spilled in chaos all over the table, and a second mirror was perched perilously on the piano.

Granny, who had been in a semi-coma, called a doze, roused herself on the big, soft couch and put her cap straight.

"I don't get much peace for my nap," she said, slowly feeling her thin white hair, to see that it was in order. She had heard vague noises.

Aunt Cissie came in, fumbling in a bag for a chocolate.

"I never saw such a mess!" she said. "You'd better clear some of that litter away, Yvette."

"All right," said Yvette. "I will in a minute."

"Which means never!" sneered Aunt Cissie, suddenly darting and picking up the scissors.

There was silence for a few moments, and Lucille slowly pushed her hands in her hair, as she read a book.

"You'd better clear away, Yvette," persisted Aunt Cissie.

"I will, before tea," replied Yvette, rising once more and pulling the blue dress over her head, flourishing her long, naked arms through the sleeveless arm-holes. Then she went between the mirrors to look at herself once more.

As she did so, she sent the second mirror, that she had perched carelessly on the piano, sliding with a rattle to the floor. Luckily it did not break. But everybody started badly.

"She's smashed the mirror!" cried Aunt Cissie.

"Smashed a mirror! Which mirror! Who's smashed it?" came Granny's sharp voice.

"I haven't smashed anything," came the calm voice of Yvette. "It's quite all right."

"You'd better not perch it up there again," said Lucille.

Yvette, with a little impatient shrug at all the fuss, tried making the mirror stand in another place. She was not successful.

"If one had a fire in one's own room," she said crossly, "one needn't have a lot of people fussing when one wants to sew."

"Which mirror are you moving about?" asked Granny.

"One of our own that came from the vicarage," said Yvette rudely.

"Don't break it in *this* house, wherever it came from," said Granny.

There was a sort of family dislike for the furniture that had belonged to She-who-was-Cynthia. It was most of it shoved into the kitchen and the servants' bedrooms.

"Oh, *I'm* not superstitious," said Yvette, "about mirrors or any of that sort of thing."

"Perhaps you're not," said Granny. "People who never take the responsibility for their own actions usually don't see what happens."

"After all," said Yvette, "I may say it's my own looking-glass, even if I did break it."

"And I say," said Granny, "that there shall be no mirrors broken in *this* house, if we can help it; no matter who they belong to, or did belong to. Cissie, have I got my cap straight?"

Aunt Cissie went over and straightened the old lady. Yvette loudly and irritatingly trilled a tuneless tune.

"And now, Yvette, will you please clear away?" said Aunt Cissie.

"Oh, bother!" cried Yvette angrily. "It's simply *awful* to

live with a lot of people who are always nagging and fussing over trifles."

"What people, may I ask?" said Aunt Cissie ominously.

Another row was imminent. Lucille looked up with a queer cast in her eyes. In the two girls, the blood of She-who-was-Cynthia was roused.

"Of course you may ask! You know quite well I mean the people in this beastly house," said the outrageous Yvette.

"At least," said Granny, "we don't come of half-depraved stock."

There was a second's electric pause. Then Lucille sprang from her low seat, with sparks flying from her.

"You shut up!" she shouted, in a blast full upon the mottled majesty of the old lady.

The old woman's breast began to heave with heaven knows what emotions. The pause this time, as after the thunderbolt, was icy.

Then Aunt Cissie, livid, sprang upon Lucille, pushing her like a fury.

"Go to your room!" she cried hoarsely. "Go to your room!"

And she proceeded to push the white but fiery-eyed Lucille from the room. Lucille let herself be pushed, while Aunt Cissie vociferated:

"Stay in your room till you've apologised for this!—till you've apologised to the Mater for this!"

"I shan't apologise!" came the clear voice of Lucille, from the passage, while Aunt Cissie shoved her.

Aunt Cissie drove her more wildly upstairs.

Yvette stood tall and bemused in the sitting-room, with the air of offended dignity, at the same time bemused, which was so odd on her. She still was bare-armed, in the half-made blue dress. And even *she* was half aghast at Lucille's attack on the majesty of age. But also, she was coldly indignant against Granny's aspersion of the maternal blood in their veins.

"Of course I meant no offence," said Granny.

"Didn't you?" said Yvette coolly.

"Of course not. I only said we're not depraved, just because we happen to be superstitious about breaking mirrors."

Yvette could hardly believe her ears. Had she heard right? Was it possible! Or was Granny, at her age, just telling a bare-faced lie?

Yvette knew that the old woman was telling a cool, bare-

'aced lie. But already, so quickly, Granny believed her own
statement.

The rector appeared, having left time for a lull.

"What's wrong?" he asked cautiously, genially.

"Oh, nothing!" drawled Yvette. "Lucille told Granny to
shut up when she was saying something. And Aunt Cissie
drove her up to her room. *Tant de bruit pour une omelette!*
Though Lucille *was* a bit over the mark, that time."

The old lady couldn't catch what Yvette said.

"Lucille really will have to learn to control her nerves," said
the old woman. "The mirror fell down, and it worried me. I
said so to Yvette, and she said something about superstitions
and the people in the beastly house. I told her the people in
the house were not depraved, if they happened to mind when
a mirror was broken. And at that Lucille flew at me and told
me to shut up. It really is disgraceful how these children give
way to their nerves. I know it's nothing but nerves."

Aunt Cissie had come in during this speech. At first even
she was dumb. Then it seemed to her, it was as Granny had
said.

"I have forbidden her to come down until she comes to
apologise to the Mater," she said.

"I doubt if she'll apologise," said the calm, queenly Yvette,
holding her bare arms.

"And I don't want any apology," said the old lady. "It is
merely nerves. I don't know what they'll come to, if they
have nerves like that, at their age! She must take Vibrofat.—
I am sure Arthur would like his tea, Cissie."

Yvette swept her sewing together, to go upstairs. And
again she trilled her tune, rather shrill and tuneless. She was
trembling inwardly.

"More glad rags!" said her father to her genially.

"More glad rags!" she reiterated sagely, as she sauntered upstairs, with her day dress over her arm. She wanted to console
Lucille, and ask her how the blue stuff hung now.

At the first landing she stood as she nearly always did, to
gaze through the window that looked to the road and the
bridge. Like the Lady of Shalott, she seemed always to
imagine that someone would come along singing *Tirra-lirra!*
or something equally intelligent, by the river.

V

It was nearly tea-time. The snowdrops were out by the short drive going to the gate from the side of the house, and the gardener was pottering at the round, damp flower-beds on the wet grass that sloped to the stream. Past the gate went the whitish, muddy road, crossing the stone bridge almost immediately, and winding in a curve up to the steep, clustering, stony, smoking northern village, that perched over the grim stone mills which Yvette could see ahead down the narrow valley, their tall chimneys long and erect.

The rectory was on one side the Papple, in the rather steep valley, the village was beyond and above, farther down, on the other side the swift stream. At the back of the rectory the hill went up steep, with a grove of dark, bare larches, through which the road disappeared. And immediately across stream from the rectory, facing the house, the river-bank rose steep and bushy, up to the sloping, dreary meadows, that sloped up again to dark hillsides of trees, with grey rock cropping out.

But from the end of the house, Yvette could only see the road curving round past the wall with its laurel hedge, down to the bridge, then up again round the shoulder to that first hard cluster of houses in Papplewick village, beyond the dry-stone walls of the steep fields.

She always expected *something* to come down the slant of the road from Papplewick, and she always lingered at the landing window. Often a cart came, or a motor-car, or a lorry with stone, or a labourer, or one of the servants. But never anybody who sang *Tirra-lirra!* by the river. The tirra-lirraing days seem to have gone by.

This day, however, round the corner on the white-grey road, between the grass and the low stone walls, a roan horse came stepping bravely and briskly down-hill, driven by a man in a cap, perched on the front of his light cart. The man swayed loosely to the swing of the cart, as the horse stepped down-hill, in the silent sombreness of the afternoon. At the back of the cart, long duster-brooms of reed and feather stuck out, nodding on their stalks of cane.

Yvette stood close to the window, and put the casement-cloth curtains behind her, clutching her bare upper arms with her hands.

At the foot of the slope the horse started into a brisk trot to the bridge. The cart rattled on the stone bridge, the brooms bobbed and flustered, the driver sat as if in a kind of dream, swinging along. It was like something seen in a sleep.

But as he crossed the end of the bridge, and was passing along the rectory wall, he looked up at the grim stone house that seemed to have backed away from the gate, under the hill. Yvette moved her hands quickly on her arms. And as quickly, from under the peak of his cap, he had seen her, his swarthy predative face was alert.

He pulled up suddenly at the white gate, still gazing upwards at the landing window; while Yvette, always clasping her cold and mottled arms, still gazed abstractedly down at him from the window.

His head gave a little, quick jerk of signal, and he led his horse well aside, on to the grass. Then, limber and alert, he turned back the tarpaulin of the cart, fetched out various articles, pulled forth two or three of the long brooms of reed or turkey-feathers, covered the cart, and turned towards the house, looking up at Yvette as he opened the white gate.

She nodded to him, and flew to the bathroom to put on her dress, hoping he had disguised her nod so that he wouldn't be sure she had nodded. Meanwhile she heard the hoarse, deep roaring of that old fool, Rover, punctuated by the yapping of that young idiot, Trixie.

She and the housemaid arrived at the same moment at the sitting-room door.

"Was it the man selling brooms?" said Yvette to the maid. "All right!" and she opened the door. "Aunt Cissie, there's a man selling brooms. Shall I go?"

"What sort of a man?" said Aunt Cissie, who was sitting at tea with the rector and the Mater: the girls having been excluded for once from the meal.

"A man with a cart," said Yvette.

"A gipsy," said the maid.

Of course Aunt Cissie rose at once. She had to look at him.

The gipsy stood at the back door, under the steep, dark bank where the larches grew. The long brooms flourished from one hand, and from the other hung various objects of

G

shining copper and brass: a saucepan, a candlestick, plates of beaten copper. The man himself was neat and dapper, almost rakish, in his dark green cap and double-breasted green check coat. But his manner was subdued, very quiet: and at the same time proud, with a touch of condescension and aloofness.

"Anything to-day, lady?" he said, looking at Aunt Cissie with dark, shrewd, searching eyes, but putting a very quiet tenderness into his voice.

Aunt Cissie saw how handsome he was, saw the flexible curve of his lips under the line of black maustache, and she was fluttered. The merest hint of roughness or aggression on the man's part would have made her shut the door contemptuously in his face. But he managed to insinuate such a subtle suggestion of submission into his male bearing, that she began to hesitate.

"The candlestick is lovely!" said Yvette. "Did you make it?"

And she looked up at the man with her naïve, childlike eyes, that were as capable of double meaning as his own.

"Yes, lady!" He looked back into her eyes for a second, with that naked suggestion of desire which acted on her like a spell, and robbed her of her will. Her tender face seemed to go into a sleep.

"It's awfully nice!" she murmured vaguely.

Aunt Cissie began to bargain for the candlestick: which was a low, thick stem of copper, rising from a double bowl. With patient aloofness the man attended to her, without ever looking at Yvette, who leaned against the doorway and watched in a muse.

"How is your wife?" she asked him suddenly, when Aunt Cissie had gone indoors to show the candlestick to the rector, and ask him if he thought it was worth it.

The man looked fully at Yvette, and a scarcely discernible smile curled his lips. His eyes did not smile: the insinuation in them only hardened to a glare.

"She's all right. When are you coming that way again?" he murmured in a low, caressive, intimate voice.

"Oh, I don't know," said Yvette vaguely.

"You come Fridays, when I'm there," he said.

Yvette gazed over his shoulder as if she had not heard him. Aunt Cissie returned, with the candlestick and the money to pay for it. Yvette turned nonchalant away, trilling one of her broken tunes, abandoning the whole affair with a certain rudeness.

Nevertheless, hiding this time at the landing window, she stood to watch the man go. What she wanted to know was whether he really had any power over her. She did not intend him to see her this time.

She saw him go down to the gate, with his brooms and pans, and out to the cart. He carefully stowed away his pans and his brooms and fixed down the tarpaulin over the cart. Then with a slow, effortless spring of his flexible loins, he was on the cart again, and touching the horse with the reins. The roan horse was away at once, the cart-wheels grinding up-hill, and soon the man was gone, without looking round. Gone like a dream which was only a dream, yet which she could not shake off.

"No, he hasn't any power over me!" she said to herself: rather disappointed really, because she wanted somebody, or something, to have power over her.

She went up to reason with the pale and overwrought Lucille, scolding her for getting into a state over nothing.

"What does it *matter*," she expostulated, "if you told Granny to shut up? Why, everybody ought to be told to shut up when they're being beastly. But she didn't mean it, you know. No, she didn't mean it. And she's quite sorry she said it. There's absolutely no reason to make a fuss. Come on, let's dress ourselves up and sail down to dinner like duchesses. Let's have our own back that way. Come on, Lucille!"

There was something strange and mazy, like having cob-webs over one's face, about Yvette's vague blitheness; her queer, misty side-stepping from an unpleasantness. It was cheering, too. But it was like walking in one of those autumn mists, when gossamer strands blow over your face. You don't quite know where you are.

She succeeded, however, in persuading Lucille, and the girls got out their best party frocks: Lucille in green and silver, Yvette in a pale lilac colour with turquoise chenille threading. A little rouge and powder, and their best slippers, and the gardens of paradise began to blossom. Yvette hummed and looked at herself, and put on her most *dégagé* airs of one of the young marchionesses. She had an odd way of slanting her eyebrows and pursing her lips, and to all appearances detach-ing herself from every earthly consideration, and floating through the cloud of her own pearl-coloured reserves. It was amusing, and not quite convincing.

"Of course I am beautiful, Lucille," she said blandly. "And you're perfectly lovely, now you look a bit reproachful. Of course you're the most aristocratic of the two of us, with your nose! And now your eyes look reproachful, that adds an appealing look, and you're perfect, perfectly lovely. But I'm more *winning*, in a way.—Don't you agree?" She turned with arch, complicated simplicity to Lucille.

She was truly simple in what she said. It was just what she thought. But it gave no hint of the very different *feeling* that also preoccupied her: the feeling that she had been looked upon, not from the outside, but from the inside, from her secret female self. She was dressing herself up and looking her most dazzling, just to counteract the effect that the gipsy had had on her, when he had looked at her, and seen none of her pretty face and her pretty ways, but just the dark, tremulous potent secret of her virginity.

The two girls started downstairs in state when the dinner-gong rang: but they waited till they heard the voices of the men. Then they sailed down and into the sitting-room, Yvette preening herself in her vague, debonair way, always a little bit absent; and Lucille shy, ready to burst into tears.

"My goodness gracious!" exclaimed Aunt Cissie, who was still wearing her dark-brown knitted sports coat. "What an apparition! Wherever do you think you're going?"

"We're dining with the family," said Yvette naïvely, "and we've put on our best gewgaws in honour of the occasion."

The rector laughed aloud, and Uncle Fred said:

"The family feels itself highly honoured."

Both the elderly men were quite gallant, which was what Yvette wanted.

"Come and let me feel your dresses, do!" said Granny. "Are they your best? It *is* a shame I can't see them."

"To-night, Mater," said Uncle Fred, "we shall have to take the young ladies in to dinner, and live up to the honour. Will you go with Cissie?"

"I certainly will," said Granny. "Youth and beauty must come first."

"Well, to-night, Mater!" said the rector, pleased.

And he offered his arm to Lucille, while Uncle Fred escorted Yvette.

But it was a draggled, dull meal, all the same. Lucille tried
to be bright and sociable, and Yvette really was most amiable,
in her vague, cobwebby way. Dimly, at the back of her mind,
she was thinking: Why are we all only like mortal pieces of
furniture? Why is nothing *important*?

That was her constant refrain to herself: Why is nothing
important? Whether she was in church, or at a party of young
people, or dancing in the hotel in the city, the same little
bubble of a question rose repeatedly on her consciousness:
Why is nothing important?

There were plenty of young men to make love to her: even
devotedly. But with impatience she had to shake them off.
Why were they so unimportant?—so irritating!

She never even thought of the gipsy. He was a perfectly
negligible incident. Yet the approach of Friday loomed
strangely significant. "What are we doing on Friday?" she
said to Lucille. To which Lucille replied that they were doing
nothing. And Yvette was vexed.

Friday came, and in spite of herself she thought all day of
the quarry off the road up high Bonsall Head. She wanted to
be there. That was all she was conscious of. She wanted to
be there. She had not even a dawning idea of going there.
Besides, it was raining again. But as she sewed the blue
dress, finishing it for the party up at Lambley Close to-
morrow, she just felt that her soul was up there, at the quarry,
among the caravans, with the gipsies. Like one lost, or whose
soul was stolen, she was not present in her body, the shell of
her body. Her intrinsic body was away at the quarry, among
the caravans.

The next day, at the party, she had no idea that she was
being sweet to Leo. She had no idea that she was snatching
him away from the tortured Ella Framley. Not until, when
she was eating her pistachio ice, he said to her:

"Why don't you and me get engaged, Yvette? I'm absolutely sure it's the right thing for us both."

Leo was a bit common, but good-natured and well off.
Yvette quite liked him. But engaged! How perfectly silly!
She felt like offering him a set of her silk underwear, to get
engaged to.

"But I thought it was Ella!" she said, in wonder.

"Well! It might ha' been, but for you. It's your doings,
you know! Ever since those gipsies told your fortune, I felt

it was me or nobody, for you, and you or nobody, for me."

"Really!" said Yvette, simply lost in amazement. "Really!"

"Didn't you feel a bit the same?" he asked.

"Really!" Yvette kept on gasping softly, like a fish.

"You felt a bit the same, didn't you?" he said.

"What? About what?" she asked, coming to.

"About me, as I feel about you."

"Why? What? Getting engaged, you mean? I? No!
Why, how *could* I? I could never have dreamed of such an
impossible thing."

She spoke with her usual heedless candour, utterly un-
occupied with his feelings.

"What was to prevent you?" he said, a bit nettled. "I
thought you did."

"Did you *really now*?" she breathed in amazement, with
that soft, virgin, heedless candour which made her her
admirers and her enemies.

She was so completely amazed, there was nothing for him
to do but twiddle his thumbs in annoyance.

The music began, and he looked at her.

"No! I won't dance any more," she said, drawing herself
up and gazing away rather loftily over the assembly, as if he
did not exist. There was a touch of puzzled wonder on her
brow, and her soft, dim, virgin face did indeed suggest the
snowdrop of her father's pathetic imagery.

"But of course *you* will dance," she said, turning to him
with young condescension. "Do ask somebody to have this
with you."

He rose, angry, and went down the room.

She remained soft and remote in her amazement. Expect
Leo to propose to her! She might as well have expected old
Rover the Newfoundland dog to propose to her. Get engaged,
to any man on earth? No, good heavens, nothing more ridiculous could be imagined!

It was then, in a fleeting side-thought, that she realised that
the gipsy existed. Instantly, she was indignant. Him, of all
things! Him! Never!

"Now why?" she asked herself, again in hushed amazement.
"Why? It's *absolutely* impossible: absolutely! So why is it?"

This was a nut to crack. She looked at the young man
dancing, elbows out, hips prominent, waists elegantly in.
They gave her no clue to her problem. Yet she did particularly

dislike the forced elegance of the waists and the prominent hips, over which the well-tailored coats hung with such effeminate discretion.

"There is something about me which they don't see and never would see," she said angrily to herself. And at the same time, she was relieved that they didn't and couldn't. It made life so very much simpler.

And again, since she was one of the people who are conscious in visual images, she saw the dark-green jersey rolled on the black trousers of the gipsy, his fine, quick hips, alert as eyes. They were elegant. The elegance of these dancers seemed so stuffed, hips merely wadded with flesh. Leo the same, thinking himself such a fine dancer! and a fine figure of a fellow!

Then she saw the gipsy's face; the straight nose, the slender mobile lips, and the level, significant stare of the black eyes, which seemed to shoot her in some vital, undiscovered place, unerring.

She drew herself up angrily. How dared he look at her like that? So she gazed glaringly at the insipid beaux on the dancing-floor. And she despised him. Just as the raggletaggle gipsy women despise men who are not gipsies, despise their dog-like walk down the streets, she found herself despising this crowd. Where among them was the subtle, lonely, insinuating challenge that could reach her?

She did not want to mate with a house-dog.

Her sensitive nose turned up, her soft brown hair fell like a soft sheath round her tender, flower-like face, as she sat musing. She seemed so virginal. At the same time, there was a touch of the tall young virgin *witch* about her, that made the house-dog men shy off. She might metamorphose into something uncanny before you knew where you were.

This made her lonely, in spite of all the courting. Perhaps the courting only made her lonelier.

Leo, who was a sort of mastiff among the house-dogs, returned after his dance, with fresh cheery-o! courage.

"You've had a little think about it, haven't you?" he said, sitting down beside her: a comfortable, well-nourished, determined sort of fellow. She did not know why it irritated her so unreasonably, when he hitched up his trousers at the knee, over his good-sized but not very distinguished legs, and lowered himself assuredly on to a chair.

"Have I?" she said vaguely. "About what?"

"You know what about," he said. "Did you make up your mind?"

"Make up my mind about what?" she asked innocently.

In her upper consciousness, she truly had forgotten.

"Oh!" said Leo, settling his trousers again. "About me and you getting engaged, you know." He was almost as off-hand as she.

"Oh, that's *absolutely* impossible," she said, with mild amiability, as if it were some stray question among the rest. "Why, I never even thought of it again. Oh, don't talk about that sort of nonsense! That sort of thing is *absolutely* impossible," she reiterated like a child.

"That sort of thing is, is it?" he said, with an odd smile at her calm, distant assertion. "Well, what sort of thing *is* possible, then? You don't want to die an old maid, do you?"

"Oh, I don't mind," she said absently.

"I do," he said.

She turned round and looked at him in wonder.

"Why?" she said. "Why should you mind if I was an old maid?"

"Every reason in the world," he said, looking up at her with a bold, meaningful smile, that wanted to make its meaning blatant, if not patent.

But instead of penetrating into some deep, secret place, and shooting her there, Leo's bold and patent smile only hit her on the outside of the body, like a tennis ball, and caused the same kind of sudden irritated reaction.

"I think this sort of thing is awfully silly," she said, with minx-like spite. "Why, you're practically engaged to—to——" she pulled herself up in time—"probably half a dozen other girls. I'm not flattered by what you've said. I should hate it if anybody knew!—Hate it!—I shan't breathe a word of it, and I hope you'll have the sense not to.—There's Ella!"

And keeping her face averted from him, she sailed away like a tall, soft flower, to join poor Ella Framley.

Leo flapped his white gloves.

"Catty little bitch!" he said to himself. But he was of the mastiff type, he rather liked the kitten to fly in his face. He began definitely to single her out.

VI

The next week it poured again with rain. And this irritated Yvette with strange anger. She had intended it should be fine. Especially she insisted it should be fine towards the week-end. Why, she did not ask herself.

Thursday, the half-holiday, came with a hard frost, and sun. Leo arrived with his car, the usual bunch. Yvette disagreeably and unaccountably refused to go.

"No, thanks, I don't feel like it," she said.

She rather enjoyed being Mary-Mary-quite-contrary.

Then she went for a walk by herself, up the frozen hills, to the Black Rocks.

The next day also came sunny and frosty. It was February, but in the north country the ground did not thaw in the sun. Yvette announced that she was going for a ride on her bicycle, and taking her lunch as she might not be back till afternoon.

She set off, not hurrying. In spite of the frost, the sun had a touch of spring. In the park, the deer were standing in the distance, in the sunlight, to be warm. One doe, white-spotted, walked slowly across the motionless landscape.

Cycling, Yvette found it difficult to keep her hands warm, even when bodily she was quite hot. Only when she had to walk up the long hill, to the top, and there was no wind.

The upland was very bare and clear, like another world. She had climbed on to another level. She cycled slowly, a little afraid of taking the wrong lane, in the vast maze of stone fences. As she passed along the lane she thought was the right one, she heard a faint tapping noise, with a slight metallic resonance.

The gipsy man was seated on the ground with his back to the cart shaft, hammering a copper bowl. He was in the sun, bare-headed, but wearing his green jersey. Three small children were moving quietly round, playing in the horse's shelter: the horse and cart were gone. An old woman, bent, with a kerchief round her head, was cooking over a fire of sticks. The only sound was the rapid, ringing tap-tap-tap of the small hammer on the dull copper.

The man looked up at once, as Yvette stepped from her bicycle, but he did not move, though he ceased hammering. A delicate, barely discernible smile of triumph was on his face.

The old woman looked round, keenly, from under her dirty grey hair. The man spoke a half-audible word to her, and she turned again to her fire. He looked up at Yvette.

"How are you all getting on?" she asked politely.

"All right, eh! You sit down a minute?" He turned as he sat, and pulled a stool from under the caravan for Yvette. Then, as she wheeled her bicycle to the side of the quarry, he started hammering again, with that bird-like, rapid light stroke.

Yvette went to the fire to warm her hands.

"Is this the dinner cooking?" she asked childishly of the old gipsy, as she spread her long tender hands, mottled red with the cold, to the embers.

"Dinner, yes!" said the old woman. "For him! And for the children."

She pointed with the long fork at the three black-eyed, staring children, who were staring at her from under their black fringes. But they were clean. Only the old woman was not clean. The quarry itself they had kept perfectly clean.

Yvette crouched in silence, warming her hands. The man rapidly hammered away with intervals of silence. The old hag slowly climbed the steps to the third, oldest caravan. The children began to play again, like little wild animals, quiet and busy.

"Are they your children?" asked Yvette, rising from the fire and turning to the man.

He looked her in the eyes and nodded.

"But where's your wife?"

"She's gone out with the basket. They've all gone out, cart and all, selling things. I don't go selling things, I make them, but I don't go selling them. Not often. I don't often."

"You make all the copper and brass things?" she said.

He nodded, and again offered her the stool. She sat down.

"You said you'd be here on Friday's," she said. "So I came this way, as it was so fine."

"Very fine day!" said the gipsy, looking at her cheek, that was still a bit blanched by the cold, and the soft hair over her reddened ear, and the long, still mottled hands on her knee.

"You get cold, riding a bicycle?" he asked.

"My hands!" she said, clasping them nervously.

"You didn't wear gloves?"

"I did, but they weren't much good."

"Cold comes through," he said.

"Yes!" she replied.

The old woman came slowly, grotesquely down the steps of the caravan, with some enamel plates.

"The dinner cooked, eh?" he called softly.

The old woman muttered something as she spread the plates near the fire. Two pots hung from a long, iron, horizontal bar over the embers of the fire. A little pan seethed on a small iron tripod. In the sunshine, heat and vapour wavered together.

He put down his tools and the pot and rose from the ground.

"You eat something along of us?" he asked Yvette, not looking at her.

"Oh, I brought my lunch," said Yvette.

"You eat some stew?" he said. And again he called quietly, secretly to the old woman, who muttered in answer, as she slid the iron pot towards the end of the bar.

"Some beans, and some mutton in it," he said.

"Oh, thanks awfully!" said Yvette. Then, suddenly taking courage, added: "Well, yes, just a very little, if I may."

She went across to untie her lunch from her bicycle, and he went up the steps to his own caravan. After a minute, he emerged, wiping his hands on a towel.

"You want to come up and wash your hands?" he said.

"No, I think not," she said. "They are clean."

He threw away his wash-water and set off down the road with a high brass jug to fetch clean water from the spring that trickled into a small pool, taking a cup to dip it with.

When he returned, he set the jug and the cup by the fire, and fetched himself a short log to sit on. The children sat on the floor by the fire, in a cluster, eating beans and bits of meat with spoon or fingers. The man on the log ate in silence, absorbedly. The woman made coffee in the black pot on the tripod, hobbling upstairs for the cups. There was silence in the camp. Yvette sat on her stool, having taken off her hat and shaken her hair in the sun.

"How many children have you?" Yvette asked suddenly.

"Say five," he replied slowly, as he looked up into her eyes.

And again the bird of her heart sank down and seemed to die. Vaguely, as in a dream, she received from him the cup of coffee. She was aware only of his silent figure, sitting like a shadow there on the log, with an enamel cup in his hand, drinking his coffee in silence. Her will had departed from her limbs, he had power over her: his shadow was on her.

And he, as he blew his hot coffee, was aware of one thing only, the mysterious fruit of her virginity, her perfect tenderness in the body.

At length he put down his coffee-cup by the fire, then looked round at her. Her hair fell across her face as she tried to sip from the hot cup. On her face was that tender look of sleep, which a nodding flower has when it is full out. Like a mysterious early flower, she was full out, like a snowdrop which spreads its three white wings in a flight into the waking sleep of its brief blossoming. The waking sleep of her full-opened virginity, entranced like a snowdrop in the sunshine, was upon her.

The gipsy, supremely aware of her, waited for her like the substance of shadow, as shadow waits and is there.

At length his voice said, without breaking the spell:

"You want to go in my caravan now and wash your hands?"

The childlike, sleep-waking eyes of her moment of perfect virginity looked into his, unseeing. She was only aware of the dark, strange effluence of him bathing her limbs, washing her at last purely will-less. She was aware of *him*, as a dark, complete power.

"I think I might," she said.

He rose silently, then turned to speak, in a low command, to the old woman. And then again he looked at Yvette, and putting his power over her, so that she had no burden of herself, or of action.

"Come!" he said.

She followed simply, followed the silent, secret, over-powering motion of his body in front of her. It cost her nothing. She was gone in his will.

He was at the top of the steps, and she at the foot, when she became aware of an intruding sound. She stood still at the foot of the steps. A motor-car was coming. He stood at the top of the steps, looking round strangely. The old woman harshly called something, as with rapidly increasing sound a car rushed near. It was passing.

Then they heard the cry of a woman's voice and the brakes on the car. It had pulled up just beyond the quarry.

The gipsy came down the steps, having closed the door of the caravan.

"You want to put your hat on," he said to her.

Obediently she went to the stool by the fire and took up her hat. He sat down by the cart-wheel, darkly, and took up his tools. The rapid tap-tap-tap of his hammer, rapid and angry now like the sound of a tiny machine-gun, broke out just as the voice of the woman was heard crying:

"May we warm our hands at the camp-fire?"

She advanced, dressed in a sleek but bulky coat of sable fur. A man followed, in a blue greatcoat; pulling off his fur gloves and pulling out a pipe.

"It looked so tempting," said the woman in the coat of many dead little animals, smiling a broad, half-condescending, half-hesitant simper around the company.

No one said a word.

She advanced to the fire, shuddering a little inside her coat with the cold. They had been driving in an open car.

She was a very small woman, with a rather large nose: probably a Jewess. Tiny almost as a child, in that sable coat she looked much more bulky than she should, and her wide, rather resentful brown eyes of a spoilt Jewess gazed oddly out of her expensive get-up.

She crouched over the low fire, spreading her little hands, on which diamonds and emeralds glittered.

"Ugh!" she shuddered. "Of course we ought not to have come in an open car! But my husband won't even let me say I'm cold!" She looked round at him with her large, childish, reproachful eyes, that had still the canny shrewdness of a bourgeois Jewess: a rich one, probably.

Apparently she was in love, in a Jewess's curious way, with the big, blond man. He looked back at her with his abstracted blue eyes, that seemed to have no lashes, and a small smile creased his smooth, curiously naked cheeks. The smile didn't mean anything at all.

He was a man one connects instantly with winter sports, ski-ing and skating. Athletic, unconnected with life, he slowly filled his pipe, pressing in the tobacco with long, powerful, reddened finger.

The Jewess looked at him to see if she got any response from him. Nothing at all, but that odd, blank smile. She turned again to the fire, tilting her eyebrows and looking at her small, white, spread hands.

He slipped off his heavily-lined coat and appeared in one of the handsome, sharp-patterned knitted jerseys, in yellow and grey and black, over well-cut trousers, rather wide. Yes, they were both expensive! And he had a magnificent figure, an athletic, prominent chest. Like an experienced camper, he began building the fire together quietly: like a soldier on campaign.

"D'you think they'd mind if we put some fir-cones on to make a blaze?" he asked of Yvette, with a silent glance at the hammering gipsy.

"Love it, I should think," said Yvette in a daze, as the spell of the gipsy slowly left her, feeling stranded and blank.

The man went to the car, and returned with a little sack of cones, from which he drew a handful.

"Mind if we make a blaze?" he called to the gipsy.

"Eh?"

"Mind if we make a blaze with a few cones?"

"You go ahead!" said the gipsy.

The man began placing the cones lightly, carefully on the red embers. And soon, one by one, they caught fire, and burned like roses of flame, with a sweet scent.

"Ah, lovely! lovely!" cried the little Jewess, looking up at her man again. He looked down at her quite kindly, like the sun on ice. "Don't you love fire? Oh, I love it!" the little Jewess cried to Yvette, across the hammering.

The hammering annoyed her. She looked round with a slight frown on her fine little brows, as if she would bid the man stop. Yvette looked round too. The gipsy was bent over his copper bowl, legs apart, head down, lithe arm lifted. Already he seemed so far from her.

The man who accompanied the little Jewess strolled over to the gipsy and stood in silence looking down on him, holding his pipe in his mouth. Now they were two men, like two strange male dogs, having to sniff one another.

"We're on our honeymoon," said the little Jewess, with an arch, resentful look at Yvette. She spoke in a rather high, defiant voice, like some bird, a jay, or a rook, calling.

"Are you really?" said Yvette.

"Yes! Before we're married! Have you heard of Simon Fawcett?"—she named a wealthy and well-known engineer of the north country. "Well, I'm Mrs. Fawcett, and he's just divorcing me!" She looked at Yvette with curious defiance and wistfulness.

"Are you really!" said Yvette.

She understood now the look of resentment and defiance in

the little Jewess's big, childlike brown eyes. She was an honest little thing, but perhaps her honesty was *too* rational. Perhaps it partly explained the notorious unscrupulousness of the well-known Simon Fawcett.

"Yes! As soon as we get the divorce, I'm going to marry Major Eastwood."

Her cards were now all on the table. She was not going to deceive anybody.

Behind her, the two men were talking briefly. She glanced round, and fixed the gipsy with her big brown eyes.

He was looking up, as if shyly, at the big fellow in the sparkling jersey, who was standing pipe in mouth, man to man, looking down.

"With the horses back of Arras," said the gipsy, in a low voice.

They were talking war. The gipsy had served with the artillery teams in the Major's own regiment.

"*Ein schöner Mensch!*" said the Jewess. "A handsome man, eh?"

For her, too, the gipsy was one of the common men, the Tommies.

"Quite handsome!" said Yvette.

"You are cycling?" asked the Jewess in a tone of surprise.

"Yes! Down to Papplewick. My father is rector of Papplewick: Mr. Saywell."

"Oh!" said the Jewess. "I know! A clever writer! Very clever! I have read him."

The fir-cones were all consumed already, the fire was a tall pile now of crumbling, shattering fire-roses. The sky was clouding over for afternoon. Perhaps towards evening it would snow.

The Major came back and slung himself into his coat.

"I thought I remembered his face!" he said. "One of our grooms, A1 man with horses."

"Look!" cried the Jewess to Yvette. "Why don't you let us motor you down to Normanton. We live in Scoresby. We can tie the bicycle on behind."

"I think I will," said Yvette.

"Come!" called the Jewess to the peeping children, as the blond man wheeled away the bicycle. "Come! Come here!" and taking out her little purse, she held out a shilling.

"Come!" she cried. "Come and take it!"

The gipsy had laid down his work and gone into his caravan. The old woman called hoarsely to the children from her enclosure. The two elder children came stealing forward. The Jewess gave them the two bits of silver, a shilling and a florin, which she had in her purse, and again the hoarse voice of the unseen old woman was heard.

The gipsy descended from his caravan and strolled to the fire. The Jewess searched his face with the peculiar bourgeois boldness of her race.

"You were in the war, in Major Eastwood's regiment?" she said.

"Yes, lady!"

"Imagine you both being here now!—It's going to snow." She looked up at the sky.

"Later on," said the man, looking at the sky.

He too had gone inaccessible. His race was very old, in its peculiar battle with established society, and had no conception of winning. Only now and then it could score.

But since the war, even the old sporting chance of scoring now and then was pretty well quenched. There was no question of yielding. The gipsy's eyes still had their bold look: but it was hardened and directed far away, the touch of insolent intimacy was gone. He had been through the war.

He looked at Yvette.

"You're going back in the motor-car?" he said.

"Yes!" she replied, with a rather mincing mannerism. "The weather is so treacherous!"

"Treacherous weather!" he repeated, looking at the sky.

She could not tell in the least what his feelings were. In truth, she wasn't very much interested. She was rather fascinated, now, by the little Jewess, mother of two children, who was taking her wealth away from the well-known engineer and transferring it to the penniless, sporting young Major Eastwood, who must be five or six years younger than she. Rather intriguing!

The blond man returned.

"A cigarette, Charles!" cried the little Jewess plaintively.

He took out his case slowly, with his slow, athletic movement. Something sensitive in him made him slow, cautious, as if he had hurt himself against people. He gave a cigarette to his wife, then one to Yvette, then offered the case, quite simply, to the gipsy. The gipsy took one.

"Thank you, sir!"

And he went quietly to the fire, and stooping, lit it at the red embers. Both women watched him.

"Well, good-bye!" said the Jewess, with her old bourgeois freemasonry. "Thank you for the warm fire."

"Fire is everybody's," said the gipsy.

The young child came toddling to him.

"Good-bye!" said Yvette. "I hope it won't snow for you."

"We don't mind a bit of snow," said the gipsy.

"Don't you?" said Yvette. "I should have thought you would!"

"No!" said the gipsy.

She flung her scarf royally over her shoulder and followed the fur coat of the Jewess, which seemed to walk on little legs of its own.

VII

Yvette was rather thrilled by the Eastwoods, as she called them. The little Jewess had only to wait three months now for the final decree. She had boldly rented a small summer cottage by the moors up at Scoresby, not far from the hills. Now it was dead winter, and she and the Major lived in comparative isolation, without any maid-servant. He had already resigned his commission in the regular army, and called himself Mr. Eastwood. In fact, they were already Mr. and Mrs. Eastwood to the common world.

The little Jewess was thirty-six, and her two children were both over twelve years of age. The husband had agreed that she should have the custody, as soon as she was married to Eastwood.

So there they were, this queer couple, the tiny, finely-formed little Jewess with her big, resentful, reproachful eyes, and her mop of carefully-barbered black, curly hair, an elegant little thing in her way; and the big, pale-eyed young man, powerful and wintry, the remnant, surely, of some old uncanny Danish stock: living together in a small modern house near the moors and the hills, and doing their own housework.

It was a funny household. The cottage was hired furnished, but the little Jewess had brought along her dearest pieces of furniture. She had an odd little taste for the rococo, strange curving cupboards inlaid with mother-of-pearl, tortoise-shell, ebony, heaven knows what; strange, tall, flamboyant chairs from Italy, with sea-green brocade: astonishing saints with wind-blown, richly-coloured carven garments and pink faces: shelves of weird old Saxe and Capo di Monte figurines: and finally, a strange assortment of astonishing pictures painted on the back of glass, done probably in the early years of the nineteenth century or in the late eighteenth.

In this crowded and extraordinary interior she received Yvette, when the latter made a stolen visit. A whole system of stoves had been installed into the cottage, every corner was warm, almost hot. And there was the tiny rococo figurine of the Jewess herself, in a perfect little frock and an apron, putting slices of ham on the dish, while the great snow-bird of a major, in a white sweater and grey trousers, cut bread, mixed mustard, prepared coffee, and did all the rest. He had even made the dish of jugged hare which followed the cold meats and caviare.

The silver and the china were really valuable, part of the bride's trousseau. The Major drank beer from a silver mug, the little Jewess and Yvette had champagne in lovely glasses, the Major brought in coffee. They talked away. The little Jewess had a burning indignation against her first husband. She was intensely moral, so moral, that she was a divorcée. The Major, too, strange wintry bird, so powerful, handsome, too, in his way, but pale round the eyes as if he had no eye-lashes, like a bird, he, too, had a curious indignation against life, because of the false morality. That powerful, athletic chest hid a strange, snowy sort of anger. And his tenderness for the little Jewess was based on his sense of outraged justice, the abstract morality of the north blowing him, like a strange wind, into isolation.

As the afternoon drew on, they went to the kitchen, the Major pushed back his sleeves, showing his powerful athletic white arms, and carefully, deftly washed the dishes, while the women wiped. It was not for nothing his muscles were trained. Then he went round attending to the stoves of the small house, which only needed a moment or two of care each day. And after this he brought out the small, closed car and drove Yvette home, in the rain, depositing her at the back gate, a little wicket among the larches, through which the earthen steps sloped downwards to the house.

She was really amazed by this couple.

"Really, Lucille!" she said. "I do meet the most extraordinary people!" And she gave a detailed description.

"I think they sound rather nice!" said Lucille. "I like the Major doing the housework, and looking so frightfully Bond Streety with it all. I should think, *when they're married*, it would be rather fun knowing them."

"Yes!" said Yvette vaguely. "Yes! Yes, it would!"

The very strangeness of the connection between the tiny Jewess and that pale-eyed, athletic young officer made her think again of her gipsy, who had been utterly absent from her consciousness, but who now returned with sudden painful force.

"What is it, Lucille," she asked, "that brings people together? People like the Eastwoods, for instance? and Daddy and Mamma, so frightfully unsuitable?—and that gipsy woman who told my fortune, like a great horse, and the gipsy man, so fine and delicately cut? What is it?"

"I suppose it's sex, whatever that is," said Lucille.

"Yes, what is it? It's not really anything *common*, like common sensuality, you know, Lucille. It really isn't."

"No, I suppose not," said Lucille. "Anyhow, I suppose it needn't be."

"Because, you see, the *common* fellows, you know, who make a girl feel *low*: nobody cares much about them. Nobody feels any connection with them. Yet they're supposed to be the sexual sort."

"I suppose," said Lucille, "there's the low sort of sex, and there's the other sort, that isn't low. It's frightfully complicated, really! I *loathe* common fellows. And I never feel anything *sexual*"—she laid a rather disgusted stress on the word —"for fellows who aren't common. Perhaps I haven't got any sex."

"That's just it!" said Yvette. "Perhaps neither of us has. Perhaps we haven't really *got* any sex, to connect us with men."

"How horrible it sounds: *connect us with men!*" cried Lucille, with revulsion. "Wouldn't you hate to be connected with men that way? Oh, I think it's an awful pity there has to *be* sex! It would be so much better if we could still be men and women, without that sort of thing."

Yvette pondered. Far in the background was the image of the gipsy as he had looked round at her, when she had said:

"The weather is so treacherous." She felt rather like Peter when the cock crew, as she denied him. Or rather, she did not deny the gipsy; she didn't care about his part in the show, anyhow. It was some hidden part of herself which she denied: that part which mysteriously and unconfessedly responded to him. And it was a strange, lustrous black cock which crew in mockery of her.

"Yes!" she said vaguely. "Yes! Sex is an awful bore, you know, Lucille. When you haven't got it, you feel you *ought* to have it, somehow. And when you've got it—or *if* you have it"—she lifted her head and wrinkled her nose disdainfully—"you hate it."

"Oh, I don't know!" cried Lucille. "I think I should *like* to be awfully in love with a man."

"You think so!" said Yvette, again wrinkling her nose. "But if you were you wouldn't."

"How do you know?" asked Lucille.

"Well, I don't really," said Yvette. "But I think so! Yes, I think so!"

"Oh, it's very likely!" said Lucille disgustedly. "And, anyhow, one would be sure to get out of love again, and it would be merely disgusting."

"Yes," said Yvette. "It's a problem." She hummed a little tune.

"Oh, hang it all, it's not a problem for us two yet. We're neither of us really in love, and we probably never shall be, so the problem is settled that way."

"I'm not so sure!" said Yvette sagely. "I'm not so sure. I believe, one day, I shall fall *awfully* in love."

"Probably you never will," said Lucille brutally. "That's what most old maids are thinking all the time."

Yvette looked at her sister from pensive but apparently insouciant eyes.

"Is it?" she said. "Do you really think so, Lucille? How perfectly awful for them, poor things! Why ever do they *care*?"

"Why do they?" said Lucille. "Perhaps they don't, really.—Probably it's all because people say: 'Poor old girl, she couldn't catch a man.'"

"I suppose it is!" said Yvette. "They get to mind the beastly things people always do say about old maids. What a shame!"

"Anyhow, we have a good time, and we do have lots of boys who make a fuss of us," said Lucille.

"Yes!" said Yvette. "Yes! But I couldn't possibly marry any of them."

"Neither could I," said Lucille. "But why shouldn't we? Why should we bother about marrying, when we have a perfectly good time with the boys, who are awfully good sorts, and you must say, Yvette, awfully sporting and *decent* to us."

"Oh, they are!" said Yvette absently.

"I think it's time to think of marrying somebody," said Lucille, "when you feel you're *not* having a good time any more. Then marry, and just settle down."

"Quite!" said Yvette.

But now, under all her bland, soft amiability, she was annoyed with Lucille. Suddenly she wanted to turn her back on Lucille.

Besides, look at the shadows under poor Lucille's eyes, and the wistfulness in the beautiful eyes themselves. Oh, if some awfully nice, kind, protective sort of man would but marry her! And if the sporting Lucille would let him!

Yvette did not tell the rector or Granny about the Eastwoods. It would only have started a lot of talk, which she detested. The rector wouldn't have minded, for himself, privately. But he, too, knew the necessity of keeping as clear as possible from that poisonous, many-headed serpent, the tongue of the people.

"But I don't *want* you to come if your father doesn't know," cried the little Jewess.

"I suppose I'll have to tell him," said Yvette. "I'm sure he doesn't mind, really. But if he knew, he'd have to, I suppose."

The young officer looked at her with an odd amusement, bird-like and unemotional, in his keen eyes. He, too, was by way of falling in love with Yvette. It was her peculiar virgin tenderness, and her straying, absent-minded detachment from things, which attracted him.

She was aware of what was happening, and she rather preened herself. Eastwood piqued her fancy. Such a smart young officer, awfully good class, so calm and amazing with a motor-car, and quite a champion swimmer, it was intriguing to see him quietly, calmly washing dishes, smoking his pipe, doing his job so alert and skilful. Or, with the same interested care with which he made his investigation into the mysterious inside of an automobile, concocting jugged hare in the cottage kitchen. Then going out in the icy weather and cleaning his car till it looked like a live thing, like a cat when she has licked herself. Then coming in to talk so unassumingly and responsively, if briefly, with the little Jewess. And apparently, never bored. Sitting at the window with his pipe in bad weather, silent for hours, abstracted, musing, yet with his athletic body alert in its stillness.

Yvette did not flirt with him. But she *did* like him.

"But what about your future?" she asked him.

"What about it?" he said, taking his pipe from his mouth, the unemotional point of a smile in his bird's eyes.

"A career! Doesn't every man have to carve out a career? —like some huge goose with gravy?" She gazed with odd *naïveté* into his eyes.

"I'm perfectly all right to-day, and I shall be all right to-morrow," he said, with a cold, decided look. "Why shouldn't my future be continuous to-days and to-morrows?"

He looked at her with unmoved searching.

"Quite!" she said. "I hate jobs, and all that side of life." But she was thinking of the Jewess's money.

To which he did not answer. His anger was of the soft, snowy sort, which comfortably muffles the soul.

They had come to the point of talking philosophically together. The little Jewess looked a bit wan. She was curiously naïve, and not possessive in her attitude to the man. Nor was she at all catty with Yvette. Only rather wan and dumb.

Yvette, on a sudden impulse, thought she had better clear herself.

"I think life's *awfully* difficult," she said.

"Life is!" cried the Jewess.

"What's so beastly, is that one is supposed to *fall in love* and get married!" said Yvette, curling up her nose.

"Don't you *want* to fall in love and get married?" cried the Jewess, with great glaring eyes of astounded reproach.

"No, not particularly!" said Yvette. "Especially as one feels there's nothing else to do. It's an awful chicken-coop one has to run into."

"But you don't know what love is?" cried the Jewess.

"No!" said Yvette. "Do you?"

"I!" bawled the tiny Jewess. "I! My goodness, don't I!"

She looked with reflective gloom at Eastwood, who was smoking his pipe, the dimples of his disconnected amusement showing on his smooth, scrupulous face. He had a very fine, smooth skin, which yet did not suffer from the weather, so that his face looked naked as a baby's. But it was not a round face: it was characteristic enough, and took queer, ironical dimples, like a mask which is comic but frozen.

"Do you mean to say you don't know what love is?" insisted the Jewess.

"No!" said Yvette, with insouciant candour. "I don't believe I do! Is it awful of me, at my age?"

"Is there never any man that makes you feel quite, quite different?" said the Jewess, with another big-eyed look at Eastwood. He smoked, utterly unimplicated.

"I don't think there is," said Yvette. "Unless—yes!—unless it is that gipsy"—she had put her hand pensively sideways.

"Which gipsy?" bawled the little Jewess.

"The one who was a Tommy and looked after horses in Major Eastwood's regiment in the war," said Yvette coolly.

The little Jewess gazed at Yvette with great eyes of stupor.

"You're not in love with that *gipsy!*" she said.

"Well!" said Yvette. "I don't know. He's the only one that makes me feel—different! He really is!"

"But how? How? Has he ever *said* anything to you?"

"No! No!"

"Then how? What has he done?"

"Oh, just looked at me!"

"How?"

"Well, you see, I don't know. But different! Yes, different! Different, quite different from the way any man ever looked at me."

"But *how* did he look at you?" insisted the Jewess.

"Why—as if he really, but *really*, *desired* me," said Yvette, her meditative face looking like the bud of a flower.

"What a vile fellow! What *right* had he to look at you like that?" cried the indignant Jewess.

"A cat may look at a king," calmly interposed the Major, and now his face had the smile of a cat's face.

"You think he oughtn't to?" asked Yvette, turning to him.

"Certainly not! A gipsy fellow, with half a dozen dirty women trailing after him! Certainly not!" cried the tiny Jewess.

"I wondered!" said Yvette. "Because it *was* rather wonderful, really! And it was something quite different in my life."

"I think," said the Major, taking his pipe from his mouth, "that desire is the most wonderful thing in life. Anybody who can really feel it is a king, and I envy nobody else!" He put back his pipe.

The Jewess looked at him stupefied.

"But, Charles!" she cried. "Every common low man in Halifax feels nothing else!"

He again took his pipe from his mouth.

"That's merely appetite," he said.

And he put back his pipe.

"You think the gipsy is the real thing?" Yvette asked him.

He lifted his shoulders.

"It's not for me to say," he replied. "If I were you, I should know, I shouldn't be asking other people."

"Yes—but——" Yvette trailed out.

"Charles! You're wrong! How *could* it be a real thing? As if she could possibly marry him and go round in a caravan!"

"I didn't say marry him," said Charles.

"Or a love affair! Why, it's monstrous! What would she think of herself!—That's not love! That's—that's prostitution!"

Charles smoked for some moments.

"That gipsy was the best man we had, with horses. Nearly died of pneumonia. I thought he *was* dead. He's a resurrected man to me. I'm a resurrected man myself, as far as that goes." He looked at Yvette. "I was buried for twenty hours under snow," he said. "And not much the worse for it, when they dug me out."

There was a frozen pause in the conversation.

"Life's awful!" said Yvette.

"They dug me out by accident," he said.

"Oh!——" Yvette trailed slowly. "It might be destiny, you know."

To which he did not answer.

VIII

The rector heard about Yvette's intimacy with the Eastwoods, and she was somewhat startled by the result. She had thought he wouldn't care. Verbally, in his would-be humorous fashion, he was so entirely unconventional, such a frightfully good sport. As he said himself, he was a conservative anarchist; which meant, he was like a great many more people, a mere unbeliever. The anarchy extended to his humorous talk, and his secret thinking. The conservatism, based on a mongrel fear of the anarchy, controlled every action. His thoughts, secretly, were something to be scared of. Therefore, in his life he was fanatically afraid of the unconventional.

When his conservatism and his abject sort of fear were uppermost, he always lifted his lip and bared his teeth a little, in a dog-like sneer.

"I hear your latest friends are the half-divorced Mrs. Fawcett and the *maquereau* Eastwood," he said to Yvette.

She didn't know what a *maquereau* was, but she felt the poison in the rector's fangs.

"I just know them," she said. "They're awfully nice, really. And they'll be married in about a month's time."

The rector looked at her insouciant face with hatred. Somewhere inside him he was cowed, he had been born cowed. And those who are born cowed are natural slaves, and deep instinct makes them fear with poisonous fear those who might suddenly snap the slave's collar round their necks.

It was for this reason the rector had so abjectly curled up, still so abjectly curled up before She-who-was-Cynthia: because of his slave's fear of her contempt, the contempt of a born-free nature for a base-born nature.

Yvette too had a free-born quality. She, too, one day, would know him, and clap the slave's collar of her contempt round his neck.

But should she? He would fight to the death, this time, first. The slave in him was cornered this time, like a cornered rat, and with the courage of a cornered rat.

"I suppose they're your sort!" he sneered.

"Well, they are, really," she said, with that blithe vagueness. "I do like them awfully. They seem so solid, you know, so honest."

"You've got a peculiar notion of honesty!" he sneered. "A young sponge going off with a woman older than himself, so that he can live on her money! The woman leaving her home and her children! I don't know where you get your idea of honesty. Not from me, I hope—And you seem to be very well acquainted with them, considering you say you just know them. Where did you meet them?"

"When I was out bicycling. They came along in their car, and we happened to talk. She told me at once who she was, so that I shouldn't make a mistake. She *is* honest."

Poor Yvette was struggling to bear up.

"And how often have you seen them since?"

"Oh, I've just been over twice."

"Over where?"

"To their cottage in Scoresby."

He looked at her in hate, as if he could kill her. And he backed away from her, against the window-curtains of his study, like a rat at bay. Somewhere in his mind he was thinking unspeakable depravities about his daughter, as he had thought them of She-who-was-Cynthia. He was powerless against the lowest insinuations of his own mind. And these depravities which he attributed to the still-uncowed but frightened girl in front of him, made him recoil, showing all his fangs in his handsome face.

"So you just know them, do you?" he said. "Lying is in your blood, I see. I don't believe you get it from me."

Yvette half averted her mute face, and thought of Granny's bare-faced prevarication. She did not answer.

"What takes you creeping round such couples?" he sneered. "Aren't there enough decent people in the world for you to know? Anyone would think you were a stray dog, having to run round indecent couples, because the decent ones wouldn't have you. Have you got something worse than lying in your blood?"

"What have I got worse than lying in my blood?" she asked. A cold deadness was coming over her. Was she abnormal, one of the semi-criminal abnormals? It made her feel cold and dead.

In his eyes, she was just brazening out the depravity that underlay her virgin, tender, bird-like face. She-who-was-Cynthia had been like this: a snow-flower. And he had had convulsions of sadistic horror, thinking what might be the *actual* depravity of She-who-was-Cynthia. Even his *own* love for her, which had been the lust-love of the born cowed, had been a depravity, in secret, to him. So what must an illegal love be?

"You know best yourself, what you have got," he sneered.

"But it is something you had best curb, and quickly, if you don't intend to finish in a criminal-lunacy asylum."

"Why?" she said, pale and muted, numbed with frozen fear. "Why criminal lunacy? What have I done?"

"That is between you and your Maker," he jeered. "I shall never ask. But certain tendencies end in criminal lunacy, unless they are curbed in time."

"Do you mean like knowing the Eastwoods?" asked Yvette, after a pause of numb fear.

"Do I mean like nosing round such people as Mrs. Fawcett, a Jewess, and ex-Major Eastwood, a man who goes off with an older woman for the sake of her money? Why, yes, I do!"

"But you *can't* say that," cried Yvette. "He's an awfully simple, straightforward man."

"He is apparently one of your sort."

"Well.—In a way, I thought he was. I thought you'd like him, too," she said simply, hardly knowing what she said.

The rector backed into the curtains, as if the girl menaced him with something fearful.

"Don't say any more," he snarled, abject. "Don't say any more. You've said too much to implicate you. I don't want to learn any more horrors."

"But what horrors?" she persisted.

The very *naïveté* of her unscrupulous innocence repelled him, cowed him still more.

"Say no more!" he said in a low, hissing voice. "But I will kill you before you shall go the way of your mother."

She looked at him as he stood there backed against the velvet curtains of his study, his face yellow, his eyes distraught like a rat's with fear and rage and hate, and a numb, frozen loneliness came over her. For her, too, the meaning had gone out of everything.

It was hard to break the frozen, sterile silence that ensued. At last, however, she looked at him. And in spite of herself, beyond her own knowledge, the contempt for him was in her young, clear, baffled eyes. It fell like the slave's collar over his neck, finally.

"Do you mean I mustn't know the Eastwoods?" she said.

"You can know them if you wish," he sneered. "But you must not expect to associate with your Granny, and your Aunt Cissie, and Lucille, if you do. I cannot have *them* contaminated. Your Granny was a faithful wife and a faithful

mother, if ever one existed. She has already had one shock
of shame and abomination to endure. She shall never be
exposed to another."

Yvette heard it dimly, half hearing.

"I can send a note and say you disapprove," she said dimly.

"You follow your own course of action. But remember,
you have to choose between clean people and reverence for
your Granny's blameless old age, and people who are unclean
in their minds and their bodies."

Again there was a silence. Then she looked at him, and her
face was more puzzled than anything. But somewhere at the
back of her perplexity was that peculiar calm, virgin contempt
of the free-born for the base-born. He, and all the Saywells,
were base-born.

"All right," she said. "I'll write and say you disapprove."

He did not answer. He was partly flattered, secretly
triumphant, but abjectly.

"I have tried to keep this from your Granny and Aunt
Cissie," he said. "It need not be public property, since you
choose to make your friendship clandestine."

There was a dreary silence.

"All right," she said. "I'll go and write."

And she crept out of the room.

She addressed her little note to Mrs. Eastwood. "Dear Mrs.
Eastwood, Daddy doesn't approve of my coming to see you.
So you will understand if we have to break it off. I'm awfully
sorry——" That was all.

Yet she felt a dreary blank when she had posted her letter.
She was now even afraid of her own thoughts. She wanted,
now, to be held against the slender, fine-shaped breast of the
gipsy. She wanted him to hold her in his arms, if only for
once, for once, and comfort and confirm her. She wanted
to be confirmed by him against her father, who had only a
repulsive fear of her.

And at the same time she cringed and winced, so that she
could hardly walk, for fear the thought was obscene, a
criminal lunacy. It seemed to wound her heels as she walked,
the fear. The fear, the great cold fear of the base-born, her
father, everything human and swarming. Like a great bog
humanity swamped her, and she sank in, weak at the knees,
filled with repulsion and fear of every person she met.

She adjusted herself, however, quite rapidly to her new con-

:eption of people. She had to live. It is useless to quarrel with
)ne's bread and butter. And to expect a great deal out of life
s puerile. So, with the rapid adaptability of the post-war
generation, she adjusted herself to the new facts. Her father
was what he was. He would always play up to appearances.
She would do the same. She, too, would play up to appearances.

So, underneath the blithe, gossamer-straying insouciance, a
certain hardness formed, like rock crystallising in her heart.
She lost her illusions in the collapse of her sympathies. Outwardly, she seemed the same. Inwardly she was hard and
detached, and, unknown to herself, revengeful.

Outwardly she remained the same. It was part of her game.
While circumstances remained as they were, she must remain,
at least in appearance, true to what was expected of her.

But the revengefulness came out in her new vision of people.
Under the rector's apparently gallant handsomeness, she saw
the weak, feeble nullity. And she despised him. Yet still, in a
way, she liked him too. Feelings are so complicated.

It was Granny whom she came to detest with all her soul.
That obese old woman, sitting there in her blindness like some
great red-blotched fungus, her neck swallowed between her
heaped-up shoulders and her rolling, ancient chins, so that she
was neckless as a double potato, her Yvette really hated, with
that pure, sheer hatred which is almost a joy. Her hate was
so clear, that while she was feeling strong, she enjoyed it.

The old woman sat with her big, reddened face pressed a
little back, her lace cap perched on her thin white hair, her
stub nose still assertive, and her old mouth shut like a trap.
This motherly old soul, her mouth gave her away. It always
had been one of the compressed sort. But in her great age, it
had gone like a toad's, lipless, the jaw pressing up like the
lower jaw of a trap. The look Yvette most hated was the look
of that lower jaw pressing relentlessly up, with an ancient
prognathous thrust, so that the snub nose in turn was forced
to press upwards, and the whole face was pressed a little back,
beneath the big, wall-like forehead. The will, the ancient, toad-
like, obscene will in the old woman, was fearful, once you saw
it: a toad-like self-will that was godless, and less than human!
It belonged to the old, enduring race of toads, or tortoises. And
it made one feel that Granny would never die. She would live
on like these higher reptiles, in a state of semi-coma, for ever.

Yvette dared not even suggest to her father that Granny was

not perfect. He would have threatened his daughter with the
lunatic asylum. That was the threat he always seemed to have
up his sleeve: the lunatic asylum. Exactly as if a distaste for
Granny and for that horrible house of relatives was in itself a
proof of lunacy, dangerous lunacy.

Yet in one of her moods of irritable depression, she did once
fling out:

"How perfectly beastly this house is! Aunt Lucy comes,
and Aunt Nell, and Aunt Alice, and they make a ring like a
ring of crows, with Granny and Aunt Cissie, all lifting their
skirts up and warming their legs at the fire, and shutting
Lucille and me out. We're nothing but outsiders in this
beastly house!"

Her father glanced at her curiously. But she managed to put
a petulance into her speech and a mere cross rudeness into her
look, so that he could laugh, as at a childish tantrum. Somewhere, though, he knew that she coldly, venomously meant
what she said, and he was wary of her.

Her life seemed now nothing but an irritable friction against
the unsavoury household of the Saywells, in which she was
immersed. She loathed the rectory with a loathing that consumed her life, a loathing so strong that she could not really
go away from the place. While it endured, she was spellbound to it, in revulsion.

She forgot the Eastwoods again. After all, what was the
revolt of the little Jewess, compared to Granny and the Saywell bunch! A husband was never more than a semi-casual
thing! But a family!—an awful, smelly family that would
never disperse, stuck half dead round the base of a fungoid
old woman! How was one to cope with that?

She did not forget the gipsy entirely. But she had no time
for him. She, who was bored almost to agony, and who had
nothing at all to do, she had not time to think even, seriously,
of anything. Time being, after all, only the current of the soul
in its flow.

She saw the gipsy twice. Once he came to the house with
things to sell. And she, watching him from the landing
window, refused to go down. He saw her, too, as he was putting his things back into his cart. But he, too, gave no sign.
Being of a race that exists only to be harrying the outskirts
of our society, forever hostile and living only by spoil, he was
too much master of himself, and too wary, to expose himself

openly to the vast and gruesome clutch of our law. He had been through the war. He had been enslaved against his will, that time.

So now, he showed himself at the rectory, and slowly, quietly busied himself at his cart outside the white gate, with that air of silent and for ever-unyielding outsideness which gave him his lonely, predative grace. He knew she saw him. And she should see him unyielding, quietly hawking his copper vessels, on an old, old war-path against such as herself.

Such as herself? Perhaps he was mistaken. Her heart, in its stroke, now rang hard as his hammer upon his copper, beating against circumstances. But he struck stealthily on the outside, and she still more secretly on the inside of the establishment. She liked him. She liked the quiet, noiseless, clean-cut presence of him. She liked that mysterious endurance in him, which endures in opposition, without any idea of victory. And she liked that peculiar added relentlessness, the disillusion in hostility, which belongs to after the war. Yes, if she belonged to any side, and to any clan, it was to his. Almost she could have found it in her heart to go with him, and be a pariah gipsy woman.

But she was born inside the pale. And she liked comfort, and a certain prestige. Even as a mere rector's daughter, one did have a certain prestige. And she liked that. Also she liked to chip against the pillars of the temple from the inside. She wanted to be safe under the temple roof. Yet she enjoyed chipping fragments off the supporting pillars. Doubtless many fragments had been whittled away from the pillars of the Philistine before Samson pulled the temple down.

"I'm not sure one shouldn't have one's fling till one is twenty-six, and then give in, and marry!"

This was Lucille's philosophy, learned from older women. Yvette was twenty-one. It meant she had five more years in which to have this precious fling. And the fling meant, at the moment, the gipsy. The marriage, at the age of twenty-six, meant Leo or Gerry.

So, a woman could eat her cake and have her bread and butter.

Yvette, pitched in gruesome, deadlocked hostility to the Saywell household, was very old and very wise: with the agedness and the wisdom of the young, which always overleaps the agedness and the wisdom of the old or the elderly.

The second time she met the gipsy by accident. It was
March, and sunny weather, after unheard-of rains. Celandines
were yellow in the hedges, and primroses among the rocks.
But still there came a smell of sulphur from far-away steel-
works, out of the steel-blue sky.

And yet it was spring!

Yvette was cycling slowly along by Codnor Gate, past the
lime quarries, when she saw the gipsy coming away from the
door of a stone cottage. His cart stood there in the road.
He was returning with his brooms and copper things to the
cart.

She got down from her bicycle. As she saw him, she loved
with curious tenderness the slim lines of his body in the green
jersey, the turn of his silent face. She felt she knew him better
than she knew anybody on earth, even Lucille, and belonged
to him, in some way, for ever.

"Have you made anything new and nice?" she asked
innocently, looking at his copper things.

"I don't think," he said, glancing back at her.

The desire was still there, still curious and naked, in his eyes.
But it was more remote, the boldness was diminished. There
was a tiny glint, as if he might dislike her. But this dissolved
again as he saw her looking among his bits of copper and brass-
work. She searched them diligently.

There was a little oval brass plate, with a queer figure like
a palm tree beaten upon it.

"I like that," she said. "How much is it?"

"What you like," he said.

This made her nervous: he seemed off-hand, almost
mocking.

"I'd rather you said," she told him, looking up at him.

"You give me what you like," he said.

"No!" she said suddenly. "If you won't tell me I won't
have it."

"All right," he said. "Two shilling."

She found half a crown, and he drew from his pocket a
handful of silver, from which he gave her sixpence.

"The old gipsy dreamed something about you," he said,
looking at her with curious, searching eyes.

"Did she!" cried Yvette, at once interested. "What was it?"

"She said: 'Be braver in your heart, or you lose your game.'
She said it this way: 'Be braver in your body, or your luck

will leave you.' And she said as well: 'Listen for the voice of water.' "

Yvette was very much impressed.

"And what does it mean?" she asked.

"I asked her," he said. "She says she don't know."

"Tell me again what it was," said Yvette.

" 'Be braver in your body, or your luck will go.' And: 'Listen for the voice of water.' "

He looked in silence at her soft, pondering face. Something almost like a perfume seemed to flow from her young bosom direct to him, in a grateful connection.

"I'm to be braver in my body, and I'm to listen for the voice of water! All right!" she said. "I don't understand, but perhaps I shall."

She looked at him with clear eyes. Man or woman is made up of many selves. With one self, she loved this gipsy man. With many selves, she ignored him or had a distaste for him.

"You're not coming up to the Head no more?" he asked.

Again she looked at him absently.

"Perhaps I will," she said, "some time. Some time."

"Spring weather!" he said, smiling faintly and glancing round at the sun. "We're going to break camp soon and go away."

"When?" she said.

"Perhaps next week."

"Where to?"

Again he made a move with his head.

"Perhaps up north," he said.

She looked at him.

"All right!" she said. "Perhaps I *will* come up before you go, and say good-bye to your wife and to the old woman who sent me the message."

IX

Yvette did not keep her promise. The few March days were lovely, and she let them slip. She had a curious reluctance, always, towards taking action, or making any real move of her own. She always wanted someone else to make a move for her, as if she did not want to play her own game of life.

She lived as usual, went out to her friends, to parties, and danced with the undiminished Leo. She wanted to go up and say good-bye to the gipsies. She wanted to. And nothing prevented her.

On the Friday afternoon especially she wanted to go. It was sunny, and the last yellow crocuses down the drive were in full blaze, wide open, the first bees rolling in them. The Papple rushed under the stone bridge, uncannily full, nearly filling the arches. There was the scent of a mezereon tree.

And she felt too lazy, too lazy, too lazy. She strayed in the garden by the river, half dreamy, expecting something. While the gleam of spring sun lasted, she would be out of doors. Indoors Granny, sitting back like some awful old prelate, in her bulk of black silk and her white lace cap, was warming her feet by the fire, and hearing everything that Aunt Nell had to say. Friday was Aunt Nell's day. She usually came for lunch, and left after an early tea. So the mother and the large, rather common daughter, who was a widow at the age of forty, sat gossiping by the fire, while Aunt Cissie prowled in and out. Friday was the rector's day for going to town: it was also the housemaid's half-day.

Yvette sat on a wooden seat in the garden, only a few feet above the bank of the swollen river, which rolled a strange, uncanny mass of water. The crocuses were passing in the ornamental beds, the grass was dark green where it was mown, the laurels looked a little brighter. Aunt Cissie appeared at the top of the porch steps, and called to ask if Yvette wanted that early cup of tea. Because of the river just below, Yvette could not hear what Aunt Cissie said, but she guessed, and shook her head. An early cup of tea, indoors, when the sun actually shone? No, thanks!

She was conscious of her gipsy, as she sat there musing in the sun. Her soul had the half painful, half easing knack of leaving her, and straying away to some place, to somebody that had caught her imagination. Some days she would be at the Framleys', even though she did not go near them. Some days she was all the time in spirit with the Eastwoods. And to-day it was the gipsies. She was up at their encampment in the quarry. She saw the man hammering his copper, lifting his head to look at the road; and the children playing in the horse-shelter: and the women, the gipsy's wife and the strong, elderly woman, coming home with their packs, along with the elderly man. For this afternoon, she felt intensely that

that was home for her: the gipsy camp, the fire, the stool, the man with the hammer, the old crone.

It was part of her nature, to get these fits of yearning for some place she knew; to be in a certain place; with somebody who meant home to her. This afternoon it was the gipsy camp. And the man in the green jersey made it home to her. Just to be where he was, that was to be at home. The caravans, the brats, the other women: everything was natural to her, her home, as if she had been born there. She wondered if the gipsy was aware of her: if he could see her sitting on the stool by the fire; if he would lift his head and see her as she rose, looking at him slowly and significantly, turning towards the steps of his caravan. Did he know? Did he know?

Vaguely she looked up the steep of dark larch trees north of the house, where unseen the road climbed, going towards the Head. There was nothing, and her glance strayed down again. At the foot of the slope the river turned, thrown back harshly, ominously, against the low rocks across stream, then pouring past the garden to the bridge. It was unnaturally full, and whitey-muddy, and ponderous. "Listen for the voice of water," she said to herself. "No need to listen for it, if the voice means the noise!"

And again she looked at the swollen river breaking angrily as it came round the bend. Above it the black-looking kitchen garden hung, and the hard-natured fruit trees. Everything was on the tilt, facing south and south-west, for the sun. Behind, above the house and the kitchen garden hung the steep little wood of withered-seeming larches. The gardener was working in the kitchen garden, high up there, by the edge of the larchwood.

She heard a call. It was Aunt Cissie and Aunt Nell. They were on the drive, waving good-bye! Yvette waved back. Then Aunt Cissie, pitching her voice against the waters, called:

"I shan't be long. Don't forget Granny is alone!"

"All right!" screamed Yvette rather ineffectually.

And she sat on her bench and watched the two undignified, long-coated women walk slowly over the bridge and begin the curving climb on the opposite slope, Aunt Nell carrying a sort of suit-case in which she brought a few goods for Granny and took back vegetables or whatever the rectory garden or cupboard was yielding. Slowly the two figures diminished on the whitish, up-curving road, labouring slowly up towards Papple-

wick village. Aunt Cissie was going as far as the village for
something.

The sun was yellowing to decline. What a pity! Oh, what
a pity the sunny day was going, and she would have to turn
indoors, to those hateful rooms, and Granny! Aunt Cissie
would be back directly: it was past five. And all the others
would be arriving from town, rather irritable and tired, soon
after six.

As she looked uneasily round, she heard, across the running
water, the sharp noise of a horse and cart rattling on the road
hidden in the larch trees. The gardener was looking up too.
Yvette turned away again, lingering, strolling by the full river
a few paces, unwilling to go in; glancing up the road to see
if Aunt Cissie were coming. If she saw her, she would go
indoors.

She heard somebody shouting, and looked round. Down the
path through the larch trees the gipsy was bounding. The
gardener, away beyond, was also running. Simultaneously
she became aware of a great roar, which, before she could
move, accumulated to a vast deafening snarl. The gipsy was
gesticulating. She looked round behind her.

And to her horror and amazement, round the bend of the
river she saw a shaggy, tawny wave-front of water advancing
like a wall of lions. The roaring sound wiped out everything.
She was powerless, too amazed and wonder-struck, she wanted
to see it.

Before she could think twice, it was near, a roaring cliff of
water. She almost fainted with horror. She heard the scream
of the gipsy, and looked up to see him bounding upon her, his
black eyes starting out of his head.

"Run!" he screamed, seizing her arm.

And in the instant the first wave was washing her feet from
under her, swirling, in the insane noise, which suddenly for
some reason, seemed like stillness, with a devouring flood over
the garden. The horrible mowing of water!

The gipsy dragged her heavily, lurching, plunging, but still
keeping foot-hold both of them, towards the house. She was
barely conscious: as if the flood was in her soul.

There was one grass-banked terrace of the garden, near the
path round the house. The gipsy clawed his way up this terrace
to the dry level of the path, dragging her after him, and sprang
with her past the windows to the porch steps. Before they got

there, a new great surge of water came mowing, mowing trees
down even, and mowed them down too.

Yvette felt herself gone in an agonising mill race of icy
water, whirled, with only the fearful grip of the gipsy's hand
on her wrist. They were both down and gone. She felt a dull
but stunning bruise somewhere.

Then he pulled her up. He was up, streaming forth water,
clinging to the stem of the great wistaria that grew against
the wall, crushed against the wall by the water. Her head was
above water, he held her arm till it seemed dislocated: but
she could not get her footing. With a ghastly sickness like
a dream, she struggled and struggled, and could not get her
feet. Only his hand was locked on her wrist.

He dragged her nearer till her one hand caught his leg. He
nearly went down again. But the wistaria held him, and he
pulled her up to him. She clawed at him, horribly; and got to
her feet, he hanging on like a man torn in two to the wistaria
trunk.

The water was above her knees. The man and she looked
into each other's ghastly, streaming faces.

"Get to the steps!" he screamed.

It was only just round the corner: four strides! She looked
at him: she could not go. His eyes glared on her like a tiger's,
and he pushed her from him. She clung to the wall, and the
water seemed to abate a little. Round the corner she staggered,
but staggering, reeled and was pitched up against the cornice
of the balustrade of the porch steps, the man after her.

They got on to the steps, when another roar was heard amid
the roar, and the wall of the house shook. Up heaved the water
round their legs again, but the gipsy had opened the hall door.
In they poured with the water, reeling to the stairs. And as
they did so, they saw the short but strange bulk of Granny
emerge in the hall, away down from the dining-room door.
She had her hands lifted and clawing, as the first water swirled
round her legs, and her coffin-like mouth was opened in a
hoarse scream.

Yvette was blind to everything but the stairs. Blind, unconscious of everything save the steps rising beyond the water,
she clambered up like a wet, shuddering cat, in a state of unconsciousness. It was not till she was on the landing, dripping
and shuddering till she could not stand erect, clinging to the
banisters, while the house shook and the water raved below,

that she was aware of the sodden gipsy, in paroxysms of coughing at the head of the stairs, his cap gone, his black hair over his eyes, peering between his washed-down hair at the sickening heave of water below in the hall. Yvette, fainting, looked, too, and saw Granny bob up, like a strange float, her face purple, her blind blue eyes bolting, spume hissing from her mouth. One old purple hand clawed at a banister-rail and held for a moment, showing the glint of a wedding ring.

The gipsy, who had coughed himself free and pushed back his hair, said to that awful float-like face below:

"Not good enough! Not good enough!"

With a low thud like thunder, the house was struck again, and shuddered, and a strange cracking, rattling, spitting noise began. Up heaved the water like a sea. The hand was gone, all sigh of anything was gone, but upheaving water.

Yvette turned in blind unconscious frenzy, staggering like a wet cat to the upper staircase, and climbing swiftly. It was not till she was at the door of her room that she stopped, paralysed by the sound of a sickening, tearing crash, while the house swayed.

"The house is coming down!" yelled the green-white face of the gipsy in her face.

He glared into her crazed face.

"Where is the chimney? the back chimney?—which room? The chimney will stand——"

He glared with strange ferocity into her face, forcing her to understand. And she nodded with a strange, crazed poise, nodded quite serenely, saying:

"In here! In here! It's all right."

They entered her room, which had a narrow fire-place. It was a back room with two windows, one on each side the great chimney-flue. The gipsy, coughing bitterly and trembling in every limb, went to the window to look out.

Below, between the house and the steep rise of the hill, was a wild mill-race of water rushing with refuse, including Rover's green dog-kennel. The gipsy coughed and coughed, and gazed down blankly. Tree after tree went down, mown by the water, which must have been ten feet deep.

Shuddering and pressing his sodden arms on his sodden breast, a look of resignation on his livid face, he turned to Yvette. A fearful tearing noise tore the house, then there was a deep, watery explosion. Something had gone down, some part of the house, the floor heaved and wavered beneath them. For some moments both were suspended, stupefied. Then he roused.

"Not good enough! Not good enough! This will stand. This here will stand. See! that chimney! like a tower. Yes! All right! All right! You take your clothes off and go to bed. You'll die of the cold."

"It's all right! It's quite all right!" she said to him, sitting on a chair and looking up into his face with her white, insane little face, round which the hair was plastered.

"No!" he cried. "No! Take your things off and I'll rub you with this towel. I rub myself. If the house falls then die warm. If it don't fall, then live, not die of pneumonia."

Coughing, shuddering violently, he pulled up his jersey hem and wrestled with all his shuddering, cold-racked might, to get off his wet, tight jersey.

"Help me!" he cried, his face muffled.

She seized the edge of the jersey, obediently, and pulled with all her might. The garment came over his head, and he stood in his braces.

"Take your things off! Rub with this towel!" he commanded ferociously, the savageness of the war on him. And like a thing obsessed, he pushed himself out of his trousers and got out of his wet, clinging shirt, emerging slim and livid, shuddering in every fibre with cold and shock.

He seized a towel, and began quickly to rub his body, his teeth chattering like plates rattling together. Yvette dimly saw it was wise. She tried to get out of her dress. He pulled the horrible, wet, death-gripping thing off her, then, resuming his rubbing, went to the door, tiptoeing on the wet floor.

There he stood, naked, towel in hand, petrified. He looked west, towards where the upper landing window had been, and was looking into the sunset, over an insane sea of waters, bristling with up-torn trees and refuse. The end corner of the house where the porch had been, and the stairs, had gone. The wall had fallen, leaving the floors sticking out. The stairs had gone.

Motionless, he watched the water. A cold wind blew in upon him. He clenched his rattling teeth with a great effort of will, and turned into the room again, closing the door.

Yvette, naked, shuddering so much that she was sick, was trying to wipe herself dry.

"All right!" he cried. "All right! The water don't rise no more! All right!"

With his towel he began to rub her, himself shaking all over, but holding her gripped by the shoulder, and slowly, numbedly rubbing her tender body, even trying to rub up into some dryness the pitiful hair of her small head.

Suddenly he left off.

"Better lie in the bed," he commanded, "I want to rub myself."

His teeth went snap-snap-snap-snap in great snaps, cutting off his words. Yvette crept shaking and semi-conscious into her bed. He, making strained efforts to hold himself still and rub himself warm, went again to the north window to look out.

The water had risen a little. The sun had gone down, and there was a reddish glow. He rubbed his hair into a black, wet tangle, then paused for breath, in a sudden access of shuddering, then looked out again, then rubbed again on his breast, and began to cough afresh, because of the water he had swallowed. His towel was red: he had hurt himself somewhere: but he felt nothing.

There was still the strange, huge noise of water, and the horrible bump of things bumping against the walls. The wind was rising with sundown, cold and hard. The house shook with explosive thuds, and weird, weird, frightening noises came up.

A terror creeping over his soul, he went again to the door. The wind, roaring with the waters, blew in as he opened it. Through the awesome gap in the house he saw the world, the waters, the chaos of horrible waters, the twilight, the perfect new moon high above the sunset, a faint thing, and clouds pushing dark into the sky, on the cold, blustery wind.

Clenching his teeth again, fear mingling with resignation, or fatalism, in his soul, he went into the room and closed the door, picking up her towel to see if it were drier than his own, and less blood-stained, again rubbing his head and going to the window.

He turned away, unable to control his spasms of shivering. Yvette had disappeared right under the bedclothes, and nothing of her was visible but a shivering mound under the white quilt. He laid his hand on this shivering mound, as if for company. It did not stop shivering.

"All right!" he said. "All right! Water's going down!"

She suddenly uncovered her head and peered out at him from a white face. She peered into his greenish, curiously calm face, semi-conscious. His teeth were chattering unheeded as he gazed down at her, his black eyes still full of the fire of life and a certain vagabond calm of fatalistic resignation.

"Warm me!" she moaned, with chattering teeth. "Warm me! I shall die of shivering."

A terrible convulsion went through her curled-up white body, enough indeed to rupture her and cause her to die.

The gipsy nodded, and took her in his arms, and held her in a clasp like a vice, to still his own shuddering. He himself was shuddering fearfully, and only semi-conscious. It was the shock.

The vice-like grip of his arms round her seemed to her the only stable point in her consciousness. It was a fearful relief to her heart, which was strained to bursting. And though his body, wrapped round her strange and lithe and powerful, like tentacles, rippled with shuddering as an electric current, still the rigid tension of the muscles that held her clenched steadied them both, and gradually the sickening violence of the shuddering, caused by shock, abated, in his body first, then in hers, and the warmth revived between them. And as it roused, their tortured semi-conscious minds became unconscious, they passed away into sleep.

X

The sun was shining in heaven before men were able to get across the Papple with ladders. The bridge was gone. But the flood had abated, and the house, that leaned forwards as if it were making a stiff bow to the stream, stood now in mud and wreckage, with a great heap of fallen masonry and debris at the south-west corner. Awful were the gaping mouths of rooms!

Inside, there was no sign of life. But across-stream the gardener had come to reconnoitre, and the cook appeared, thrilled with curiosity. She had escaped from the back door and up through the larches to the high-road, when she saw the gipsy bound past the house: thinking he was coming to murder somebody. At the little top gate she had found his cart standing. The gardener had led the horse away to the 'Red Lion' up at Darley, when night had fallen.

This the men from Papplewick learned when at last they got
across the stream with ladders, and to the back of the house.
They were nervous, fearing a collapse of the building, whose
front was all undermined and whose back was choked up.
They gazed with horror at the silent shelves of the rector's
rows of books in his torn-open study; at the big brass bedstead
of Granny's room, the bed so deep and comfortably made, but
one brass leg of the bedstead perching tentatively over the
torn void; at the wreckage of the maid's room upstairs. The
housemaid and the cook wept. Then a man climbed in
cautiously through a smashed kitchen window, into the jungle
and morass of the ground floor. He found the body of the
old woman: or at least he saw her foot, in its flat black
slipper, muddily protruding from a mud-heap of debris. And
he fled.

The gardener said he was sure that Miss Yvette was not in
the house. He had seen her and the gipsy swept away. But
the policeman insisted on a search, and the Framley boys
rushing up at last, the ladders were roped together. Then the
whole party set up a loud yell. But without result. No answer
from within.

A ladder was up, Bob Framley climbed, smashed a window,
and clambered into Aunt Cissie's room. The perfect homely
familiarity of everything terrified him like ghosts. The house
might go down any minute.

They had just got the ladder up to the top floor when men
came running from Darley, saying the old gipsy had been to
the 'Red Lion' for the horse and cart, leaving word that his
son had seen Yvette at the top of the house. But by that time
the policeman was smashing the window of Yvette's room.

Yvette, fast asleep, started from under the bedclothes with
a scream as the glass flew. She clutched the sheets round her
nakedness. The policeman uttered a startled yell, which he
converted into a cry of: "Miss Yvette! Miss Yvette!"

He turned round on the ladder and shouted to the faces
below:

"Miss Yvette's in bed!—in bed!"

And he perched there on the ladder, an unmarried man,
clutching the window in peril, not knowing what to do.

Yvette sat up in bed, her hair in a matted tangle, and stared
with wild eyes, clutching up the sheets at her naked breast.
She had been so very fast asleep, that she was still not there.

The policeman, terrified at the flabby ladder, climbed into the room, saying:

"Don't be frightened, miss! Don't you worry any more about it. You're safe now."

And Yvette, so dazed, thought he meant the gipsy. Where was the gipsy? This was the first thing in her mind. Where was her gipsy of this world's-end night?

He was gone! He was gone! And a policeman was in the room! A policeman!

She rubbed her hand over her dazed brow.

"If you'll get dressed, miss, we can get you down to safe ground. The house is likely to fall. I suppose there's nobody in the other rooms?"

He stepped gingerly into the passage and gazed in terror through the torn-out end of the house, and far off saw the rector coming down in a motor-car, on the sunlit hill.

Yvette, her face gone numb and disappointed, got up quickly, closing the bedclothes, and looked at herself a moment, then opened her drawers for clothing. She dressed herself, then looked in a mirror, and saw her matted hair with horror. Yet she did not care. The gipsy was gone, anyhow.

Her own clothes lay in a sodden heap. There was a great sodden place on the carpet where his had been, and two blood-stained filthy towels. Otherwise there was no sign of him.

She was tugging at her hair when the policeman tapped at her door. She called him to come in. He saw with relief that she was dressed and in her right senses.

"We'd better get out of the house as soon as possible, miss," he reiterated. "It might fall any minute."

"Really!" said Yvette calmly. "Is it as bad as that?"

There were great shouts. She had to go to the window. There, below, was the rector, his arms wide open, tears streaming down his face.

"I'm perfectly all right, daddy!" she said, with the calmness of her contradictory feelings. She would keep the gipsy a secret from him. At the same time, tears ran down her face.

"Don't you cry, miss, don't you cry! The rector's lost his mother, but he's thanking his stars to have his daughter. We all thought you were gone as well, we did that!"

"Is Granny drowned?" said Yvette.

"I'm afraid she is, poor lady!" said the policeman, with a grave face.

Yvette wept away into her hanky, which she had had to fetch from a drawer.

"Dare you go down that ladder, miss?" said the policeman.

Yvette looked at the sagging depth of it, and said promptly to herself: "No! Not for anything!"—But then she remembered the gipsy's saying: "Be braver in the body."

"Have you been in all the other rooms?" she said, in her weeping, turning to the policeman.

"Yes, miss! But you was the only person in the house, you know, save the old lady. Cook got away in time, and Lizzie was up at her mother's. It was only you and the poor old lady we was fretting about. Do you think you dare go down that ladder?"

"Oh yes!" said Yvette, with indifference. The gipsy was gone, anyway.

And now the rector in torment watched his tall, slender daughter slowly stepping backwards down the sagging ladder, the policeman, peering heroically from the smashed window, holding the ladder's top end.

At the foot of the ladder Yvette appropriately fainted in her father's arms, and was borne away with him, in the car, by Bob, to the Framley home. There the poor Lucille, a ghost of ghosts, wept with relief till she had hysterics, and even Aunt Cissie cried out among her tears: "Let the old be taken and the young spared! Oh, I *can't* cry for the Mater, now Yvette is spared!"

And she wept gallons.

The flood was caused by the sudden bursting of the great reservoir, up in Papple Highdale, five miles from the rectory. It was found out later that an ancient, perhaps even a Roman mine tunnel, unsuspected, undreamed of, beneath the reservoir dam, had collapsed, undermining the whole dam. That was why the Papple had been, for that last day, so uncannily full. And then the dam had burst.

The rector and the two girls stayed on at the Framleys' till a new home could be found. Yvette did not attend Granny's funeral. She stayed in bed.

Telling her tale, she only told how the gipsy had got her inside the porch, and she had crawled to the stairs out of the water. It was known that he had escaped: the old gipsy had said so, when he fetched the horse and cart from the 'Red Lion'.

Yvette could tell little. She was vague, confused, she seemed hardly to remember anything. But that was just like her.

It was Bob Framley who said:

"You know, I think that gipsy deserves a medal."

The whole family suddenly was struck.

"Oh, we *ought* to thank him!" cried Lucille.

The rector himself went with Bob in the car. But the quarry was deserted. The gipsies had lifted camp and gone, no one knew whither.

And Yvette, lying in bed, moaned in her heart: "Oh, I love him! I love him! I love him!" The grief over him kept her prostrate. Yet practically she too was acquiescent in the fact of his disappearance. Her young soul knew the wisdom of it.

But after Granny's funeral, she received a little letter, dated from some unknown place.

"Dear Miss, I see in the paper you are all right after your ducking, as is the same with me. I hope I see you again one day, maybe at Tideswell cattle fair, or maybe we come that way again. I come that day to say good-bye! and I never said it, well, the water give no time, but I live in hopes. Your obdt. servant, Joe Boswell."

And only then she realised that he had a name.

THE MAN WHO DIED

THE MAN WHO DIED

THERE was a peasant near Jerusalem who acquired a young gamecock which looked a shabby little thing, but which put on brave feathers as spring advanced, and was resplendent with arched and orange neck by the time the fig trees were letting out leaves from their end-tips.

This peasant was poor, he lived in a cottage of mud-brick, and had only a dirty little inner courtyard with a tough fig tree for all his territory. He worked hard among the vines and olives and wheat of his master, then came home to sleep in the mud-brick cottage by the path. But he was proud of his young rooster. In the shut-in yard were three shabby hens which laid small eggs, shed the few feathers they had, and made a disproportionate amount of dirt. There was also, in a corner under a straw roof, a dull donkey that often went out with the peasant to work, but sometimes stayed at home. And there was the peasant's wife, a black-browed youngish woman who did not work too hard. She threw a little grain, or the remains of the porridge mess, to the fowls, and she cut green fodder with a sickle for the ass.

The young cock grew to a certain splendour. By some freak of destiny, he was a dandy rooster, in that dirty little yard with three patchy hens. He learned to crane his neck and give shrill answers to the crowing of other cocks, beyond the walls, in a world he knew nothing of. But there was a special fiery colour to his crow, and the distant calling of the other cocks roused him to unexpected outbursts.

"How he sings," said the peasant, as he got up and pulled his day-shirt over his head.

"He is good for twenty hens," said the wife.

The peasant went out and looked with pride at his young rooster. A saucy, flamboyant bird, that has already made the final acquaintance of the three tattered hens. But the cockerel was tipping his head, listening to the challenge of far-off unseen cocks, in the unknown world. Ghost voices, crowing at

3

him mysteriously out of limbo. He answered with a ringing
defiance, never to be daunted.

"He will surely fly away one of these days," said the
peasant's wife.

So they lured him with grain, caught him, though he fought
with all his wings and feet, and they tied a cord round his
shank, fastening it against the spur; and they tied the other
end of the cord to the post that held up the donkey's straw
pent-roof.

The young cock, freed, marched with a prancing stride of
indignation away from the humans, came to the end of his
string, gave a tug and a hitch of his tied leg, fell over for a
moment, scuffled frantically on the unclean earthen floor, to
the horror of the shabby hens, then with a sickening lurch,
regained his feet, and stood to think. The peasant and the
peasant's wife laughed heartily, and the young cock heard
them. And he knew, with a gloomy, foreboding kind of knowledge that he was tied by the leg.

He no longer pranced and ruffled and forged his feathers.
He walked within the limits of his tether sombrely. Still he
gobbled up the best bits of food. Still, sometimes, he saved an
extra-best bit for his favourite hen of the moment. Still he
pranced with quivering, rocking fierceness upon such of his
harem as came nonchalantly within range, and gave off the
invisible lure. And still he crowed defiance to the cock-crows
that showered up out of limbo, in the dawn.

But there was now a grim voracity in the way he gobbled
his food, and a pinched triumph in the way he seized upon
the shabby hens. His voice, above all, had lost the full gold
of its clangour. He was tied by the leg, and he knew it. Body,
soul and spirit were tied by that string.

Underneath, however, the life in him was grimly unbroken.
It was the cord that should break. So one morning, just before
the light of dawn, rousing from his slumbers with a sudden
wave of strength, he leaped forward on his wings, and the
string snapped. He gave a wild, strange squawk, rose in one
lift to the top of the wall, and there he crowed a loud and
splitting crow. So loud, it woke the peasant.

At the same time, at the same hour before dawn, on the
same morning, a man awoke from a long sleep in which he
was tied up. He woke numb and cold, inside a carved hole in
the rock. Through all the long sleep his body had been full

of hurt, and it was still full of hurt. He did not open his eyes. Yet he knew that he was awake, and numb, and cold, and rigid, and full of hurt, and tied up. His face was banded with cold bands, his legs were bandaged together. Only his hands were loose.

He could move if he wanted: he knew that. But he had no want. Who would want to come back from the dead? A deep, deep nausea stirred in him, at the premonition of movement. He resented already the fact of the strange, incalculable moving that had already taken place in him: the moving back into consciousness. He had not wished it. He had wanted to stay outside, in the place where even memory is stone dead.

But now, something had returned to him, like a returned letter, and in that return he lay overcome with a sense of nausea. Yet suddenly his hands moved. They lifted up, cold, heavy and sore. Yet they lifted up, to drag away the cloth from his face, and push at the shoulder-bands. Then they fell again, cold, heavy, numb, and sick with having moved even so much, unspeakably unwilling to move further.

With his face cleared and his shoulders free, he lapsed again, and lay dead, resting on the cold nullity of being dead. It was the most desirable. And almost, he had it complete: the utter cold nullity of being outside.

Yet when he was most nearly gone, suddenly, driven by an ache at the wrists, his hands rose and began pushing at the bandages of his knees, his feet began to stir, even while his breast lay cold and dead still.

And at last, the eyes opened. On to the dark. The same dark! Yet perhaps there was a pale chink, of the all-disturbing light, prising open the pure dark. He could not lift his head. The eyes closed. And again it was finished.

Then suddenly he leaned up, and the great world reeled. Bandages fell away. And narrow walls of rock closed upon him, and gave the new anguish of imprisonment. There were chinks of light. With a wave of strength that came from revulsion, he leaned forward, in that narrow well of rock, and leaned frail hands on the rock near the chinks of light.

Strength came from somewhere, from revulsion; there was a crash and a wave of light, and the dead man was crouching in his lair, facing the animal onrush of light. Yet it was hardly dawn. And the strange, piercing keenness of daybreak's sharp breath was on him. It meant full awakening.

Slowly, slowly he crept down from the cell of rock with the caution of the bitterly wounded. Bandages and linen and perfume fell away, and he crouched on the ground against the wall of rock, to recover oblivion. But he saw his hurt feet touching the earth again, with unspeakable pain, the earth they had meant to touch no more, and he saw his thin legs that had died, and pain unknowable, pain like utter bodily disillusion, filled him so full that he stood up, with one torn hand on the ledge of the tomb.

To be back! To be back again, after all that! He saw the linen swathing-bands fallen round his dead feet, and stooping, he picked them up, folded them, and laid them back in the rocky cavity from which he had emerged. Then he took the perfumed linen sheet, wrapped it round him as a mantle, and turned away, to the wanness of the chill dawn.

He was alone; and having died, was even beyond loneliness.

Filled still with the sickness of unspeakable disillusion, the man stepped with wincing feet down the rocky slope, past the sleeping soldiers, who lay wrapped in their woollen mantles under the wild laurels. Silent, on naked scarred feet, wrapped in a white linen shroud, he glanced down for a moment on the inert, heap-like bodies of the soldiers. They were repulsive, a slow squalor of limbs, yet he felt a certain compassion. He passed on towards the road, lest they should wake.

Having nowhere to go, he turned from the city that stood on her hills. He slowly followed the road away from the town, past the olives, under which purple anemones were drooping in the chill of dawn, and rich-green herbage was pressing thick. The world, the same as ever, the natural world, thronging with greenness, a nightingale winsomely, wistfully, coaxingly calling from the bushes beside a runnel of water, in the world, the natural world of morning and evening, forever undying, from which he had died.

He went on, on scarred feet, neither of this world nor of the next. Neither here nor there, neither seeing nor yet sightless, he passed dimly on, away from the city and its precincts, wondering why he should be travelling, yet driven by a dim, deep nausea of disillusion, and a resolution of which he was not even aware.

Advancing in a kind of half-consciousness under the dry

stone wall of the olive orchard, he was roused by the shrill, wild crowing of a cock just near him, a sound which made him shiver as if electricity had touched him. He saw a black and orange cock on a bough above the road, then running through the olives of the upper level, a peasant in a grey woollen shirt-tunic. Leaping out of greenness, came the black and orange cock with the red comb, his tail-feathers streaming lustrous.

"O, stop him, master!" called the peasant. "My escaped cock!"

The man addressed, with a sudden flicker of smile, opened his great white wings of a shroud in front of the leaping bird. The cock fell back with a squawk and a flutter, the peasant jumped forward, there was a terrific beating of wings and whirring of feathers, then the peasant had the escaped cock safely under his arm, its wings shut down, its face crazily craning forward, its round eyes goggling from its white chops.

"It's my escaped cock!" said the peasant, soothing the bird with his left hand, as he looked perspiringly up into the face of the man wrapped in white linen.

The peasant changed countenance, and stood transfixed, as he looked into the dead-white face of the man who had died. That dead-white face, so still, with the black beard growing on it as if in death; and those wide-open, black, sombre eyes, that had died! and those washed scars on the waxy forehead! The slow-blooded man of the field let his jaw drop, in childish inability to meet the situation.

"Don't be afraid," said the man in the shroud. "I am not dead. They took me down too soon. So I have risen up. Yet if they discover me, they will do it all over again . . ."

He spoke in a voice of old disgust. Humanity! Especially humanity in authority! There was only one thing it could do. He looked with black, indifferent eyes into the quick, shifty eyes of the peasant. The peasant quailed, and was powerless under the look of deathly indifference and strange, cold resoluteness. He could only say the one thing he was afraid to say:

"Will you hide in my house, master?"

"I will rest there. But if you tell anyone, you know what will happen. You will have to go before a judge."

"Me! I shan't speak. Let us be quick!"

The peasant looked round in fear, wondering sulkily why

he had let himself in for this doom. The man with scarred feet
climbed painfully up to the level of the olive garden, and
followed the sullen, hurrying peasant across the green wheat
among the olive trees. He felt the cool silkiness of the young
wheat under his feet that had been dead, and the roughishness
of its separate life was apparent to him. At the edges of rocks,
he saw the silky, silvery-haired buds of the scarlet anemone
bending downwards. And they, too, were in another world.
In his own world he was alone, utterly alone. These things
around him were in a world that had never died. But he himself had died, or had been killed from out of it, and all that
remained now was the great void nausea of utter disillusion.

They came to a clay cottage, and the peasant waited
dejectedly for the other man to pass.

"Pass!" he said. "Pass! We have not been seen."

The man in white linen entered the earthen room, taking
with him the aroma of strange perfumes. The peasant closed
the door, and passed through the inner doorway into the yard,
where the ass stood within the high walls, safe from being
stolen. There the peasant, in great disquietude, tied up the
cock. The man with the waxen face sat down on a mat near
the hearth, for he was spent and barely conscious. Yet he heard
outside the whispering of the peasant to his wife, for the
woman had been watching from the roof.

Presently they came in, and the woman hid her face. She
poured water, and put bread and dried figs on a wooden platter.

"Eat, master!" said the peasant. "Eat! No one has seen."

But the stranger had no desire for food. Yet he moistened a
little bread in the water, and ate it, since life must be. But
desire was dead in him, even for food and drink. He had risen
without desire, without even the desire to live, empty save for
the all-overwhelming disillusion that lay like nausea where
his life had been. Yet perhaps, deeper even than disillusion,
was a desireless resoluteness, deeper even than consciousness.

The peasant and his wife stood near the door, watching.
They saw with terror the livid wounds on the thin, waxy
hands and the thin feet of the stranger, and the small lacera-
tions in the still dead forehead. They smelled with terror the
scent of rich perfumes that came from him, from his body.
And they looked at the fine, snowy, costly linen. Perhaps
really he was a dead king, from the region of terrors. And
he was still cold and remote in the region of death, with

perfumes coming from his transparent body as if from some
strange flower.

Having with difficulty swallowed some of the moistened
bread, he lifted his eyes to them. He saw them as they were:
limited, meagre in their life, without any splendour of gesture
and of courage. But they were what they were, slow, inevit-
able parts of the natural world. They had no nobility, but fear
made them compassionate.

And the stranger had compassion on them again, for he
knew that they would respond best to gentleness, giving back
a clumsy gentleness again.

"Do not be afraid," he said to them gently. "Let me stay a
little while with you. I shall not stay long. And then I shall
go away for ever. But do not be afraid. No harm will come to
you through me."

They believed him at once, yet the fear did not leave them.
And they said:

"Stay, master, while ever you will. Rest! Rest quietly!"

But they were afraid.

So he let them be, and the peasant went away with the ass.
The sun had risen bright, and in the dark house with the door
shut, the man was again as if in the tomb. So he said to the
woman: "I would lie in the yard."

And she swept the yard for him, and laid him a mat, and
he lay down under the wall in the morning sun. There he saw
the first green leaves spurting like flames from the ends of the
enclosed fig tree, out of the bareness to the sky of spring above.
But the man who had died could not look, he only lay quite
still in the sun, which was not yet too hot, and had no desire
in him, not even to move. But he lay with his thin legs in the
sun, his black, perfumed hair falling into the hollows of his
neck, and his thin, colourless arms utterly inert. As he lay
there, the hens clucked, and scratched, and the escaped cock,
caught and tied by the leg again, cowered in a corner.

The peasant woman was frightened. She came peeping, and,
seeing him never move, feared to have a dead man in the yard.
But the sun had grown stronger, he opened his eyes and looked
at her. And now she was frightened of the man who was alive,
but spoke nothing.

He opened his eyes, and saw the world again bright as glass.
It was life, in which he had no share any more. But it shone
outside him, blue sky, and a bare fig tree with little jets of

green leaf. Bright as glass, and he was not of it, for desire had failed.

Yet he was there, and not extinguished. The day passed in a kind of coma, and at evening he went into the house. The peasant man came home, but he was frightened, and had nothing to say. The stranger, too, ate of the mess of beans, a little. Then he washed his hands and turned to the wall, and was silent. The peasants were silent too. They watched their guest sleep. Sleep was so near death he could still sleep.

Yet when the sun came up, he went again to lie in the yard. The sun was the one thing that drew him and swayed him, and he still wanted to feel the cool air of the morning in his nostrils, see the pale sky overhead. He still hated to be shut up.

As he came out, the young cock crowed. It was a diminished, pinched cry, but there was that in the voice of the bird stronger than chagrin. It was the necessity to live, and even to cry out the triumph of life. The man who had died stood and watched the cock who had escaped and been caught, ruffling himself up, rising forward on his toes, throwing up his head, and parting his beak in another challenge from life to death. The brave sounds rang out, and though they were diminished by the cord round the bird's leg, they were not cut off. The man who had died looked nakedly on life, and saw a vast resoluteness everywhere flinging itself up in stormy or subtle wave-crests, foam-tips emerging out of the blue invisible, a black and orange cock or the green flame-tongues out of the extremes of the fig tree. They came forth, these things and creatures of spring, glowing with desire and with assertion. They came like crests of foam, out of the blue flood of the invisible desire, out of the vast invisible sea of strength, and they came coloured and tangible, evanescent, yet deathless in their coming. The man who had died looked on the great swing into existence of things that had not died, but he saw no longer their tremulous desire to exist and to be. He heard instead their ringing, ringing, defiant challenge to all other things existing.

The man lay still, with eyes that had died now wide open and darkly still, seeing the everlasting resoluteness of life. And the cock, with the flat, brilliant glance, glanced back at him, with a bird's half-seeing look. And always the man who had died saw not the bird alone, but the short, sharp wave of

life of which the bird was the crest. He watched the queer,
beaky motion of the creature as it gobbled into itself the
scraps of food; its glancing of the eye of life, ever alert and
watchful, over-weening and cautious, and the voice of its life,
crowing triumph and assertion, yet strangled by a cord of
circumstance. He seemed to hear the queer speech of very
life, as the cock triumphantly imitated the clucking of the
favourite hen, when she had laid an egg, a clucking which still
had, in the male bird, the hollow chagrin of the cord round
his leg. And when the man threw a bit of bread to the cock,
it called with an extraordinary cooing tenderness, tousling and
saving the morsel for the hens. The hens ran up greedily, and
carried the morsel away beyond the reach of the string.

Then, walking complacently after them, suddenly the male
bird's leg would hitch at the end of his tether, and he would
yield with a kind of collapse. His flag fell, he seemed to
diminish, he would huddle in the shade. And he was young,
his tail-feathers, glossy as they were, were not fully grown.
It was not till evening again that the tide of life in him made
him forget. Then when his favourite hen came strolling unconcernedly near him, emitting the lure, he pounced on her
with all his feathers vibrating. And the man who had died
watched the unsteady, rocking vibration of the bent bird, and
it was not the bird he saw, but one wave-tip of life overlap-
ping for a minute another, in the tide of the swaying ocean
of life. And the destiny of life seemed more fierce and com-
pulsive to him even than the destiny of death. The doom of
death was a shadow compared to the raging destiny of life,
the determined surge of life.

At twilight the peasant came home with the ass, and he
said: "Master! It is said that the body was stolen from the
garden, and the tomb is empty, and the soldiers are taken
away, accursed Romans! And the women are there to weep."

The man who had died looked at the man who had not died.

"It is well," he said. "Say nothing, and we are safe."

And the peasant was relieved. He looked rather dirty and
stupid, and even as much flaminess as that of the young cock,
which he had tied by the leg, would never glow in him. He
was without fire. But the man who had died thought to himself:

"Why, then, should he be lifted up? Clods of earth are
turned over for refreshment, they are not to be lifted up. Let

the earth remain earthy, and hold its own against the sky. I
was to seek to lift it up. I was wrong to try to interfere. The
ploughshare of devastation will be set in the soil of Judea, and
the life of this peasant will be overturned like the sods of the
field. No man can save the earth from tillage. It is tillage, not
salvation . . ."

So he saw the man, the peasant, with compassion; but the
man who had died no longer wished to interfere in the soul of
the man who had not died, and who could never die, save to
return to earth. Let him return to earth in his own good hour,
and let no one try to interfere when the earth claims her
own.

So the man with scars let the peasant go from him, for the
peasant had no rebirth in him. Yet the man who had died said
to himself: "He is my host."

And at dawn, when he was better, the man who had died
rose up, and on slow, sore feet retraced his way to the garden.
For he had been betrayed in a garden, and buried in a garden.
And as he turned round the screen of laurels, near the rock-
face, he saw a woman hovering by the tomb, a woman in
blue and yellow. She peeped again into the mouth of the hole,
that was like a deep cupboard. But still there was nothing.
And she wrung her hands and wept. And as she turned away,
she saw the man in white, standing by the laurels, and she gave
a cry, thinking it might be a spy, and she said:

"They have taken him away!"

So he said to her:

"Madeleine!"

Then she reeled as if she would fall, for she knew him. And
he said to her:

"Madeleine! Do not be afraid. I am alive. They took me
down too soon, so I came back to life. Then I was sheltered in
a house."

She did not know what to say, but fell at his feet to kiss
them.

"Don't touch me, Madeleine," he said. "Not yet! I am not
yet healed and in touch with men."

So she wept because she did not know what to do. And he
said:

"Let us go aside, among the bushes, where we can speak
unseen."

So in her blue mantle and her yellow robe, she followed him

among the trees, and he sat down under a myrtle bush. And he said:

"I am not yet quite come to. Madeleine, what is to be done next?"

"Master!" she said. "Oh, we have wept for you! And will you come back to us?"

"What is finished is finished, and for me the end is past," he said. "The stream will run till no more rains fill it, then it will dry up. For me, that life is over."

"And will you give up your triumph?" she said sadly.

"My triumph," he said, "is that I am not dead. I have out-lived my mission and know no more of it. It is my triumph. I have survived the day and the death of my interference, and am still a man. I am young still, Madeleine, not even come to middle age. I am glad all that is over. It had to be. But now I am glad it is over, and the day of my interference is done. The teacher and the saviour are dead in me; now I can go about my business, into my own single life."

She heard him, and did not fully understand. But what he said made her feel disappointed.

"But you will come back to us?" she said, insisting.

"I don't know what I shall do," he said. "When I am healed, I shall know better. But my mission is over, and my teaching is finished, and death has saved me from my own salvation. Oh, Madeleine, I want to take my single way in life, which is my portion. My public life is over, the life of my self-importance. Now I can wait on life, and say nothing, and have no one betray me. I wanted to be greater than the limits of my hands and feet, so I brought betrayal on myself. And I know I wronged Judas, my poor Judas. For I have died, and now I know my own limits. Now I can live without striving to sway others any more. For my reach ends in my finger-tips, and my stride is no longer than the ends of my toes. Yet I would embrace multitudes, I who have never truly embraced even one. But Judas and the high priests saved me from my own salvation, and soon I can turn to my destiny like a bather in the sea at dawn, who has just come down to the shore alone."

"Do you want to be alone henceforward?" she asked. "And was your mission nothing? Was it all untrue?"

"Nay!" he said. "Neither were your lovers in the past nothing. They were much to you, but you took more than you gave. Then you came to me for salvation from your own excess. And I, in my mission, I too ran to excess. I gave more than I took, and that also is woe and vanity. So Pilate and the high priests saved me from my own excessive salvation. Don't run to excess now in living, Madeleine. It only means another death."

She pondered bitterly, for the need for excessive giving was in her, and she could not bear to be denied.

"And will you not come back to us?" she said. "Have you risen for yourself alone?"

He heard the sarcasm in her voice, and looked at her beautiful face which still was dense with excessive need for salvation from the woman she had been, the female who had caught men at her will. The cloud of necessity was on her, to be saved from the old, wilful Eve, who had embraced many men and taken more than she gave. Now the other doom was on her. She wanted to give without taking. And that, too, is hard, and cruel to the warm body.

"I have not risen from the dead in order to seek death again," he said.

She glanced up at him, and saw the weariness settling again on his waxy face, and the vast disillusion in his dark eyes, and the underlying indifference. He felt her glance, and said to himself:

"Now my own followers will want to do me to death again, for having risen up different from their expectation."

"But you will come to us, to see us, us who love you?" she said.

He laughed a little and said:

"Ah, yes." Then he added: "Have you a little money? Will you give me a little money? I owe it."

She had not much, but it pleased her to give it to him.

"Do you think," he said to her, "that I might come and live with you in your house?"

She looked up at him with large blue eyes, that gleamed strangely.

"Now?" she said with peculiar triumph.

And he, who shrank now from triumph of any sort, his own or another's, said:

"Not now! Later, when I am healed, and . . . and I am in touch with the flesh."

The words faltered in him. And in his heart he knew he

would never go to live in her house. For the flicker of triumph
had gleamed in her eyes; the greed of giving. But she murmured in a humming rapture:

"Ah, you know I would give up everything to you."

"Nay!" he said. "I didn't ask that."

A revulsion from all the life he had known came over him
again, the great nausea of disillusion, and the spear-thrust
through his bowels. He crouched under the myrtle bushes,
without strength. Yet his eyes were open. And she looked at
him again, and she saw that it was not the Messiah. The
Messiah had not risen. The enthusiasm and the burning purity
were gone, and the rapt youth. His youth was dead. This man
was middle-aged and disillusioned, with a certain terrible indifference, and a resoluteness which love would never conquer.
This was not the Master she had so adored, the young, flamy,
unphysical exalter of her soul. This was nearer to the lovers
she had known of old, but with a greater indifference to the
personal issue, and a lesser susceptibility.

She was thrown out of the balance of her rapturous,
anguished adoration. This risen man was the death of her
dream.

"You should go now," he said to her. "Do not touch me, I
am in death. I shall come again here, on the third day. Come
if you will, at dawn. And we will speak again."

She went away, perturbed and shattered. Yet as she went,
her mind discarded the bitterness of the reality, and she conjured up rapture and wonder, that the Master was risen and
was not dead. He was risen, the Saviour, the exalter, the
wonder-worker! He was risen, but not as man; as pure God,
who should not be touched by flesh, and who should be rapt
away into Heaven. It was the most glorious and most ghostly
of the miracles.

Meanwhile the man who had died gathered himself together
at last, and slowly made his way to the peasant's house. He
was glad to go back to them, and away from Madeleine and
his own associates. For the peasants had the inertia of earth
and would let him rest, and as yet, would put no compulsion
on him.

The woman was on the roof, looking for him. She was
afraid that he had gone away. His presence in the house had
become like gentle wine to her. She hastened to the door, to
him.

"Where have you been?" she said. "Why did you go away?"

"I have been to walk in a garden, and I have seen a friend, who gave me a little money. It is for you."

He held out his thin hand, with the small amount of money, all that Madeleine could give him. The peasant's wife's eyes glistened, for money was scarce, and she said:

"Oh, master! And is it truly mine?"

"Take it!" he said. "It buys bread, and bread brings life."

So he lay down in the yard again, sick with relief at being alone again. For with the peasants he could be alone, but his own friends would never let him be alone. And in the safety of the yard, the young cock was dear to him, as it shouted in the helpless zest of life, and finished in the helpless humiliation of being tied by the leg. This day the ass stood swishing her tail under the shed. The man who had died lay down and turned utterly away from life, in the sickness of death in life.

But the woman brought wine and water, and sweetened cakes, and roused him, so that he ate a little, to please her. The day was hot, and as she crouched to serve him, he saw her breasts sway from her humble body, under her smock. He knew she wished he would desire her, and she was youngish, and not unpleasant. And he, who had never known a woman, would have desired her if he could. But he could not want her, though he felt gently towards her soft, crouching, humble body. But it was her thoughts, her consciousness, he could not mingle with. She was pleased with the money, and now she wanted to take more from him. She wanted the embrace of his body. But her little soul was hard, and short-sighted, and grasping, her body had its little greed, and no gentle reverence of the return gift. So he spoke a quiet, pleasant word to her and turned away. He could not touch the little, personal body, the little, personal life of this woman, nor in any other. He turned away from it without hesitation.

Risen from the dead, he had realised at last that the body, too, has its little life, and beyond that, the greater life. He was virgin, in recoil from the little, greedy life of the body. But now he knew that virginity is a form of greed; and that the body rises again to give and to take, to take and to give, ungreedily. Now he knew that he had risen for the woman, or women, who knew the greater life of the body, not greedy to give, not greedy to take, and with whom he could mingle his body. But having died, he was patient, knowing there was time, an eternity of time. And he was driven by no greedy desire, either to give himself to others, or to grasp anything for himself. For he had died.

The peasant came home from work and said:

"Master, I thank you for the money. But we did not want it. And all I have is yours."

But the man who had died was sad, because the peasant stood there in the little, personal body, and his eyes were cunning and sparkling with the hope of greater rewards in money later on. True, the peasant had taken him in free, and had risked getting no reward. But the hope was cunning in him. Yet even this was as men are made. So when the peasant would have helped him to rise, for night had fallen, the man who had died said:

"Don't touch me, brother. I am not yet risen to the Father."

The sun burned with greater splendour, and burnished the young cock brighter. But the peasant kept the string renewed, and the bird was a prisoner. Yet the flame of life burned up to a sharp point in the cock, so that it eyed askance and haughtily the man who had died. And the man smiled and held the bird dear, and he said to it:

"Surely thou art risen to the Father, among birds."

And the young cock, answering, crowed.

When at dawn on the third morning the man went to the garden, he was absorbed, thinking of the greater life of the body, beyond the little, narrow, personal life. So he came through the thick screen of laurel and myrtle bushes, near the rock, suddenly, and he saw three women near the tomb. One was Madeleine, and one was the woman who had been his mother, and the third was a woman he knew, called Joan. He looked up, and saw them all, and they saw him, and they were all afraid.

He stood arrested in the distance, knowing they were there to claim him back, bodily. But he would in no wise return to them. Pallid, in the shadow of a grey morning that was blowing to rain, he saw them, and turned away. But Madeleine hastened towards him.

"I did not bring them," she said. "They have come of themselves. See, I have brought you money! . . . Will you not speak to them?"

She offered him some gold pieces, and he took them, saying:

"May I have this money? I shall need it. I cannot speak to them, for I am not yet ascended to the Father. And I must leave you now."

"Ah! Where will you go?" she cried.

He looked at her, and saw she was clutching for the man in him who had died and was dead, the man of his youth and his mission, of his chastity and his fear, of his little life, his giving without taking.

"I must go to my Father!" he said.

"And you will leave us? There is your mother!" she cried, turning round with the old anguish, which yet was sweet to her.

"But now I must ascend to my Father," he said, and he drew back into the bushes, and so turned quickly, and went away, saying to himself:

"Now I belong to no one and have no connection, and mission or gospel is gone from me. Lo! I cannot make even my own life, and what have I to save? . . . I can learn to be alone."

So he went back to the peasants' house, to the yard where the young cock was tied by the leg with a string. And he wanted no one, for it was best to be alone; for the presence of people made him lonely. The sun and the subtle salve of spring healed his wounds, even the gaping wound of dis-illusion through his bowels was closing up. And his need of men and women, his fever to have them and to be saved by them, this too was healing in him. Whatever came of touch between himself and the race of men, henceforth, should come without trespass or compulsion. For he said to himself:

"I tried to compel them to live, so they compelled me to die. It is always so, with compulsion. The recoil kills the advance. Now is my time to be alone."

Therefore he went no more to the garden, but lay still and saw the sun, or walked at dusk across the olive slopes, among the green wheat, that rose a palm-breadth higher every sunny day. And always he thought to himself:

'How good it is to have fulfilled my mission, and to be be-yond it. Now I can be alone, and leave all things to them-selves, and the fig tree may be barren if it will, and the rich may be rich. My way is my own alone.'

So the green jets of leaves unspread on the fig tree, with the bright, translucent, green blood of the tree. And the young cock grew brighter, more lustrous with the sun's burnishing; yet always tied by the leg with a string. And the sun went down more and more in pomp, out of the gold and red-flushed air. The man who had died was aware of it all, and he thought:

'The Word is but the midge that bites at evening. Man is tormented with words like midges, and they follow him right into the tomb. But beyond the tomb they cannot go. Now I have passed the place where words can bite no more and the air is clear, and there is nothing to say, and I am alone within my own skin, which is the walls of all my domain.'

So he healed of his wounds, and enjoyed his immortality of being alive without fret. For in the tomb he had slipped that noose which we call care. For in the tomb he had left his striving self, which cares and asserts itself. Now his uncaring self healed and became whole within his skin, and he smiled to himself with pure aloneness, which is one sort of immortality.

Then he said to himself: "I will wander the earth, and say nothing. For nothing is so marvellous as to be alone in the phenomenal world, which is raging, and yet apart. And I have not seen it, I was too much blinded by my confusion within it. Now I will wander among the stirring of the phenomenal world, for it is the stirring of all things among themselves which leaves me purely alone."

So he communed with himself, and decided to be a physician. Because the power was still in him to heal any man or child who touched his compassion. Therefore he cut his hair and his beard after the right fashion, and smiled to himself. And he bought himself shoes, and the right mantle, and put the right cloth over his head, hiding all the little scars. And the peasant said:

"Master, will you go forth from us?"

"Yes, for the time is come for me to return to men."

So he gave the peasant a piece of money, and said to him:

"Give me the cock that escaped and is now tied by the leg. For he shall go forth with me."

So for a piece of money the peasant gave the cock to the man who had died, and at dawn the man who had died set out into the phenomenal world, to be fulfilled in his own loneliness in the midst of it. For previously he had been too

I

much mixed up in it. Then he had died. Now he must come back, to be alone in the midst. Yet even now he did not go quite alone, for under his arm, as he went, he carried the cock, whose tail fluttered gaily behind, and who craned his head excitedly, for he too was adventuring out for the first time into the wider phenomenal world, which is the stirring of the body of cocks also. And the peasant woman shed a few tears, but then went indoors, being a peasant, to look again at the pieces of money. And it seemed to her, a gleam came out of the pieces of money, wonderful.

The man who had died wandered on, and it was a sunny day. He looked around as he went, and stood aside as the pack-train passed by, towards the city. And he said to himself:

"Strange is the phenomenal world, dirty and clean together! And I am the same. Yet I am apart! And life bubbles variously. Why should I have wanted it to bubble all alike? What a pity I preached to them! A sermon is so much more likely to cake into mud, and to close the fountains, than is a psalm or a song. I made a mistake. I understand that they executed me for preaching to them. Yet they could not finally execute me, for now I am risen in my own aloneness, and inherit the earth, since I lay no claim on it. And I will be alone in the seethe of all things; first and foremost, for ever, I shall be alone. But I must toss this bird into the seethe of phenomena, for he must ride his wave. How hot he is with life! Soon, in some place, I shall leave him among the hens. And perhaps one evening I shall meet a woman who can lure my risen body, yet leave me my aloneness. For the body of my desire has died, and I am not in touch anywhere. Yet how do I know! All at least is life. And this cock gleams with bright aloneness, though he answers the lure of hens. And I shall hasten on to that village on the hill ahead of me; already I am tired and weak, and want to close my eyes to everything."

Hastening a little with the desire to have finished going, he overtook two men going slowly, and talking. And being soft-footed, he heard they were speaking of himself. And he remembered them, for he had known them in his life, the life of his mission. So he greeted them, but did not disclose himself in the dusk, and they did not know him. He said to them:

"What then of him who would be king, and was put to death for it?"

They answered suspiciously: "Why ask you of him?"

"I have known him, and thought much about him," he said.

So they replied: "He has risen."

"Yea! And where is he, and how does he live?"

"We know not, for it is not revealed. Yet he is risen, and in a little while will ascend unto the Father."

"Yea! And where then is his Father?"

"Know ye not? You are then of the Gentiles! The Father is in Heaven, above the cloud and the firmament."

"Truly? Then how will he ascend?"

"As Elijah the Prophet, he shall go up in a glory."

"Even into the sky."

"Into the sky."

"Then is he not risen in the flesh?"

"He is risen in the flesh."

"And will he take flesh up into the sky?"

"The Father in Heaven will take him up."

The man who had died said no more, for his say was over, and words beget words, even as gnats. But the man asked him: "Why do you carry a cock?"

"I am a healer," he said, "and the bird hath virtue."

"You are not a believer?"

"Yea! I believe the bird is full of life and virtue."

They walked on in silence after this, and he felt they disliked his answer. So he smiled to himself, for a dangerous phenomenon in the world is a man of narrow belief, who denies the right of his neighbour to be alone. And as they came to the outskirts of the village, the man who had died stood still in the gloaming and said in his old voice:

"Know ye me not?"

And they cried in fear: "Master!"

"Yea!" he said, laughing softly. And he turned suddenly away, down a side lane, and was gone under the wall before they knew.

So he came to an inn where the asses stood in the yard. And he called for fritters, and they were made for him. So he slept under a shed. But in the morning he was wakened by a loud crowing, and his cock's voice ringing in his ears. So he saw the rooster of the inn walking forth to battle, with his hens, a goodly number, behind him. Then the cock of the man who had died sprang forth, and a battle began between the birds. The man of the inn ran to save his rooster, but the man who had died said:

"If my bird wins I will give him thee. And if he lose, thou shalt eat him."

So the birds fought savagely, and the cock of the man who had died killed the common cock of the yard. Then the man who had died said to his young cock:

"Thou at least hast found thy kingdom, and the females to thy body. Thy aloneness can take on splendour, polished by the lure of thy hens."

And he left his bird there, and went on deeper into the phenomenal world, which is a vast complexity of entanglements and allurements. And he asked himself a last question:

"From what, and to what, could this infinite whirl be saved?"

So he went his way, and was alone. But the way of the world was past belief, as he saw the strange entanglement of passions and circumstance and compulsion everywhere, but always the dread insomnia of compulsion. It was fear, the ultimate fear of death, that made men mad. So always he must move on, for if he stayed, his neighbours wound the strangling of their fear and bullying round him. There was nothing he could touch, for all, in a mad assertion of the ego, wanted to put a compulsion on him, and violate his intrinsic solitude. It was the mania of cities and societies and hosts, to lay a compulsion upon a man, upon all men. For men and women alike were mad with the egoistic fear of their own nothingness. And he thought of his own mission, how he had tried to lay the compulsion of love on all men. And the old nausea came back on him. For there was no contact without a subtle attempt to inflict a compulsion. And already he had been compelled even into death. The nausea of the old wound broke out afresh, and he looked again on the world with repulsion, dreading its mean contacts.

II

The wind came cold and strong from inland, from the invisible snows of Lebanon. But the temple, facing south and west, towards Egypt, faced the splendid sun of winter as he curved down towards the sea, the warmth and radiance flooded in between the pillars of painted wood. But the sea was invisible, because of the trees, though its dashing sounded among the hum of pines. The air was turning golden to afternoon. The woman who served Isis stood in her yellow robe, and looked up at the steep slopes coming down to the sea, where the olive trees silvered under the wind like water splashing. She was alone save for the goddess. And in the winter afternoon the light stood erect and magnificent off the invisible sea, filling the hills of the coast. She went towards the sun, through the grove of Mediterranean pine trees and evergreen oaks, in the midst of which the temple stood, on a little, tree-covered tongue of land between two bays.

It was only a very little way, and then she stood among the dry trunks of the outermost pines, on the rocks under which the sea smote and sucked, facing the open where the bright sun gloried in winter. The sea was dark, almost indigo, running away from the land, and crested with white. The hand of the wind brushed it strangely with shadow, as it brushed the olives of the slopes with silver. And there was no boat out.

The three boats were drawn high up on the steep shingle of the little bay, by the small grey tower. Along the edge of the shingle ran a high wall, inside which was a garden occupying the brief flat of the bay, then rising in terraces up the steep slope of the coast. And there, some little way up, within another wall, stood the low white villa, white and alone as the coast, overlooking the sea. But higher, much higher up, where the olives had given way to pine trees again, ran the coast road, keeping to the height to be above the gullies that came down to the bays.

Upon it all poured the royal sunshine of the January afternoon. Or rather, all was part of the great sun, glow and substance and immaculate loneliness of the sea, and pure brightness.

Crouching in the rocks above the dark water, which only swung up and down, two slaves, half naked, were dressing pigeons for the evening meal. They pierced the throat of a blue, live bird, and let the drops of blood fall into the heaving sea, with curious concentration. They were performing some sacrifice, or working some incantation. The woman of the temple, yellow and white and alone like a winter narcissus, stood between the pines of the small, humped peninsula where the temple secretly hid, and watched.

A black-and-white pigeon, vividly white, like a ghost escaped over the low dark sea, sped out, caught the wind, tilted, rode, soared and swept over the pine trees, and wheeled away, a speck, inland. It had escaped. The priestess heard the cry of the boy slave, a garden slave of about seventeen. He raised his arms to heaven in anger as the pigeon wheeled away, naked and angry and young he held out his arms. Then he turned and seized the girl in an access of rage, and beat her with his fist that was stained with pigeon's blood. And she lay down with her face hidden, passive and quivering. The woman who owned them watched. And as she watched, she saw another onlooker, a stranger, in a low, broad hat, and a cloak of grey homespun, a dark bearded man standing on the little cause-way of a rock that was the neck of her temple peninsula. By the blowing of his dark-grey cloak she saw him. And he saw her, on the rocks like a white-and-yellow narcissus, because of the flutter of her white linen tunic, below the yellow mantle of wool. And both of them watched the two slaves.

The boy suddenly left off beating the girl. He crouched over her, touching her, trying to make her speak. But she lay quite inert, face down on the smoothed rock. And he put his arms round her and lifted her, but she slipped back to earth like one dead, yet far too quickly for anything dead. The boy, desperate, caught her by the hips and hugged her to him, turning her over there. There she seemed inert, all her fight was in her shoulders. He twisted her over, intent and unconscious, and pushed his hands between her thighs, to push them apart. And in an instant he was covering her in the blind, frightened frenzy of a boy's first passion. Quick and frenzied his young body quivered naked on hers, blind, for a minute. Then it lay quite still, as if dead.

And then, in terror, he peeped up. He peeped round, and drew slowly to his feet, adjusting his loin-rag. He saw the stranger, and then he saw, on the rocks beyond, the lady of Isis, his mistress. And as he saw her, his whole body shrank and cowed, and with a strange cringing motion he scuttled lamely towards the door in the wall.

The girl sat up and looked after him. When she had seen him disappear, she too looked round. And she saw the stranger and the priestess. Then with a sullen movement she turned away, as if she had seen nothing, to the four dead pigeons and the knife, which lay there on the rock. And she

began to strip the small feathers, so that they rose on the wind
like dust.

The priestess turned away. Slaves! Let the overseer watch
them. She was not interested. She went slowly through the
pines again, back to the temple, which stood in the sun in a
small clearing at the centre of the tongue of land. It was a
small temple of wood, painted all pink and white and blue,
having at the front four wooden pillars rising like stems to the
swollen lotus-bud of Egypt at the top, supporting the roof and
open, spiky lotus-flowers of the outer frieze, which went
round under the eaves. Two low steps of stone led up to
the platform before the pillars, and the chamber behind the
pillars was open. There a low stone altar stood, with a few
embers in its hollow, and the dark stain of blood in its end
groove.

She knew her temple so well, for she had built it at her own
expense, and tended it for seven years. There it stood, pink
and white, like a flower in the little clearing, backed by
blackish evergreen oaks; and the shadow of afternoon was
already washing over its pillar bases.

She entered slowly, passing through to the dark inner
chamber, lighted by a perfumed oil-flame. And once more she
pushed shut the door, and once more she threw a few grains
of incense on a brazier before the goddess, and once more she
sat down before her goddess, in the almost-darkness, to muse,
to go away into the dreams of the goddess.

It was Isis; but not Isis, Mother of Horus. It was Isis
Bereaved, Isis in Search. The goddess, in painted marble, lifted
her face and strode, one thigh forward, through the frail fluting
of her robe, in the anguish of bereavement and of search. She
was looking for the fragments of the dead Osiris, dead and
scattered asunder, dead, torn apart, and thrown in fragments
over the wide world. And she must find his hands and his
feet, his heart, his thighs, his head, his belly, she must gather
him together and fold her arms round the re-assembled body
till it became warm again, and roused to life, and could
embrace her, and could fecundate her womb. And the strange
rapture and anguish of search went on through the years, as
she lifted her throat and her hollowed eyes looked inward, in
the tormented ecstasy of seeking, and the delicate navel of her
bud-like belly showed through the frail, girdled robe with the
eternal asking, asking, of her search. And through the years

she found him bit by bit, heart and head and limbs and body. And yet she had not found the last reality, the final clue to him, that alone could bring him really back to her. For she was Isis of the subtle lotus, the womb which waits submerged and in bud, waits for the touch of that other inward sun that streams its rays from the loins of the male Osiris.

This was the mystery the woman had served alone for seven years, since she was twenty, till now she was twenty-seven. Before, when she was young, she had lived in the world, in Rome, in Ephesus, in Egypt. For her father had been one of Anthony's captains and comrades, had fought with Anthony and had stood with him when Cæsar was murdered, and through to the days of shame. Then he had come again across to Asia, out of favour with Rome, and had been killed in the mountains beyond Lebanon. The widow, having no favour to hope for from Octavius, had retired to her small property on the coast under Lebanon, taking her daughter from the world, a girl of nineteen, beautiful but unmarried.

When she was young the girl had known Cæsar, and had shrunk from his eagle-like rapacity. The golden Anthony had sat with her many a half-hour, in the splendour of his great limbs and glowing manhood, and talked with her of the philosophies and the gods. For he was fascinated as a child by the gods, though he mocked at them, and forgot them in his own vanity. But he said to her:

"I have sacrificed two doves for you, to Venus, for I am afraid you make no offering to the sweet goddess. Beware you will offend her. Come, why is the flower of you so cool within? Does never a ray nor a glance find its way through? Ah, come, a maid should open to the sun, when the sun leans towards her to caress her."

And the big, bright eyes of Anthony laughed down on her, bathing her in his glow. And she felt the lovely glow of his male beauty and his amorousness bathe all her limbs and her body. But it was as he said: the very flower of her womb was cool, was almost cold, like a bud in shadow of frost, for all the flooding of his sunshine. So Anthony, respecting her father, who loved her, had left her.

And it had always been the same. She saw many men, young and old. And on the whole, she liked the old ones best, for they talked to her still and sincere, and did not expect her to open like a flower to the sun of their maleness. Once she asked a philosopher: "Are all women born to be given to men?" To which the old man answered slowly:

"Rare women wait for the re-born man. For the lotus, as you know, will not answer to all the bright heat of the sun. But she curves her dark, hidden head in the depths, and stirs not. Till, in the night, one of these rare, invisible suns that have been killed and shine no more, rises among the stars in unseen purple, and like the violet, sends its rare purple rays out into the night. To these the lotus stirs as to a caress, and rises upwards through the flood, and lifts up her bent head, and opens with an expansion such as no other flower knows, and spreads her sharp rays of bliss, and offers her soft, gold depths such as no other flower possesses, to the penetration of the flooding, violet-dark sun that has died and risen and makes no show. But for the golden brief day-suns of show such as Anthony, and for the hard winter suns of power, such as Cæsar, the lotus stirs not, nor will ever stir. Those will only tear open the bud. Ah, I tell you, wait for the re-born and wait for the bud to stir."

So she had waited. For all the men were soldiers or politicians in the Roman spell, assertive, manly, splendid apparently but of an inward meanness, an inadequacy. And Rome and Egypt alike had left her alone, unroused. And she was a woman to herself, she would not give herself for a surface glow, nor marry for reasons. She would wait for the lotus to stir.

And then, in Egypt, she had found Isis, in whom she spelled her mystery. She had brought Isis to the shores of Sidon, and lived with her in the mystery of search; whilst her mother, who loved affairs, controlled the small estate and the slaves with a free hand.

When the woman had roused from her muse and risen to perform the last brief ritual to Isis, she replenished the lamp and left the sanctuary, locking the door. In the outer world, the sun had already set, and twilight was chill among the humming trees, which hummed still, though the wind was abating.

A stranger in a dark, broad hat rose from the corner of the temple steps, holding his hat in the wind. He was dark-faced, with a black pointed beard. "Oh, madam, whose shelter may I implore?" he said to the woman, who stood in her yellow mantle on a step above him, beside a pink-and-white painted pillar. Her face was rather long and pale, her dusky blonde hair was held under a thin gold net. She looked down on the vagabond with indifference. It was the same she had seen watching the slaves.

"Why come you down from the road?" she asked.

"I saw the temple like a pale flower on the coast, and would rest among the trees of the precincts, if the lady of the goddess permits."

"It is Isis in Search," she said, answering his first question.

"The goddess is great," he replied.

She looked at him still with mistrust. There was a faint, remote smile in the dark eyes lifted to her, though the face was hollow with suffering. The vagabond divined her hesitation, and was mocking her.

"Stay here upon the steps," she said. "A slave will show you the shelter."

"The lady of Egypt is gracious."

She went down the rocky path of the humped peninsula in her gilded sandals. Beautiful were her ivory feet, beneath the white tunic, and above the saffron mantle her dusky-blonde head bent as with endless musings. A woman entangled in her own dream. The man smiled a little, half bitterly, and sat again on the step to wait, drawing his mantle round him, in the cold twilight.

At length a slave appeared, also in hodden grey.

"Seek ye the shelter of our lady?" he said insolently.

"Even so."

"Then come."

With the brusque insolence of a slave waiting on a vagabond, the young fellow led through the trees and down into a little gully in the rock, where, almost in darkness, was a small cave, with a litter of the tall heaths that grew on the waste places of the coast, under the stone-pines. The place was dark, but absolutely silent from the wind. There was still a faint odour of goats.

"Here sleep!" said the slave. "For the goats come no more on this half-island. And there is water!" He pointed to a little basin of rock where the maidenhair fern fringed a dripping mouthful of water.

Having scornfully bestowed his patronage, the slave departed. The man who had died climbed out to the tip of the peninsula, where the wave thrashed. It was rapidly getting dark, and the stars were coming out. The wind was abating for the night. Inland, the steep grooved up-slope was dark to the long wavering outline of the crest against the translucent sky. Only now and then a lantern flickered towards the villa.

The man who had died went back to the shelter. There he took bread from his leather pouch, dipped it in the water of the tiny spring, and slowly ate. Having eaten and washed his mouth, he looked once more at the bright stars in the pure windy sky, then settled the heath for his bed. Having laid his hat and his sandals aside, and put his pouch under his cheek for a pillow, he slept, for he was very tired. Yet during the night the cold woke him pinching wearily through his weariness. Outside was brilliantly starry, and still windy. He sat and hugged himself in a sort of coma, and towards dawn went to sleep again.

In the morning the coast was still chill in shadow, though the sun was up behind the hills, when the woman came down from the villa towards the goddess. The sea was fair and pale blue, lovely in newness, and at last the wind was still. Yet the waves broke white in the many rocks, and tore in the shingle of the little bay. The woman came slowly towards her dream. Yet she was aware of an interruption.

As she followed the little neck of rock on to her peninsula, and climbed the slope between the trees to the temple, a slave came down and stood, making his obeisance. There was a faint insolence in his humility. "Speak!" she said.

"Lady, the man is there, he still sleeps. Lady, may I speak?"

"Speak!" she said, repelled by the fellow.

"Lady, the man is an escaped malefactor."

The slave seemed to triumph in imparting the unpleasant news.

"By what sign?"

"Behold his hands and feet! Will the lady look on him?"

"Lead on!"

The slave led quickly over the mound of the hill down to the tiny ravine. There he stood aside, and the woman went into the crack towards the cave. Her heart beat a little. Above all, she must preserve her temple inviolate.

The vagabond was asleep with his cheek on his scrip, his mantle wrapped round him, but his bare, soiled feet curling side by side, to keep each other warm, and his hand lying clenched in sleep. And in the pale skin of his feet usually covered by sandal-straps, she saw the scars, and in the palm of the loose hand.

She had no interest in men, particularly in the servile class. Yet she looked at the sleeping face. It was worn, hollow, and rather ugly. But, a true priestess, she saw the other kind of beauty in it, the sheer stillness of the deeper life. There was even a sort of majesty in the dark brows, over the still, hollow cheeks. She saw that his black hair, left long, in con-trast to the Roman fashion, was touched with grey at the temples, and the black pointed beard had threads of grey. But that must be suffering or misfortune, for the man was young. His dusky skin had the silvery glisten of youth still.

There was a beauty of much suffering, and the strange calm candour of finer life in the whole delicate ugliness of the face. For the first time, she was touched on the quick at the sight of a man, as if the tip of a fine flame of living had touched her. It was the first time. Men had roused all kinds of feeling in her, but never had touched her with the flame-tip of life.

She went back under the rock to where the slave waited.

"Know!" she said. "This is no malefactor, but a free citizen of the east. Do not disturb him. But when he comes forth, bring him to me; tell him I would speak with him."

She spoke coldly, for she found slaves invariably repellent, a little repulsive. They were so embedded in the lesser life, and their appetites and their small consciousness were a little disgusting. So she wrapped her dream round her and went to the temple, where a slave girl brought winter roses and jasmine for the altar. But to-day, even in her ministrations, she was disturbed.

The sun rose over the hill, sparkling, the light fell triumphantly on the little pine-covered peninsula of the coast, and on the pink temple, in the pristine newness. The man who had died woke up, and put on his sandals. He put on his hat too, slung his scrip under his mantle, and went out, to see the morning in all its blue and its new gold. He glanced at the little yellow-and-white narcissus sparkling gaily in the rocks. And he saw the slave waiting for him like a menace.

"Master!" said the slave. "Our lady would speak with you at the house of Isis."

"It is well," said the wanderer.

He went slowly, staying to look at the pale blue sea like a flower in unruffled bloom, and the white fringes among the rocks, like white rock-flowers, the hollow slopes sheering up high from the shore, grey with olive trees and green with bright young wheat, and set with the white, small villa. All fair and pure in the January morning.

The sun fell on the corner of the temple, he sat down on the step in the sunshine, in the infinite patience of waiting. He had come back to life, but not the same life that he had left, the life of little people and the little day. Re-born, he was in the other life, the greater day of the human consciousness. And he was alone and apart from the little day, and out of contact with the daily people. Not yet had he accepted the irrevocable *noli me tangere* which separates the re-born from the vulgar. The separation was absolute, as yet here at the temple he felt peace, the hard, bright pagan peace with hostility of slaves beneath.

The woman came into the dark inner doorway of the temple from the shrine, and stood there, hesitating. She could see the dark figure of the man, sitting in that terrible stillness that was portentous to her, had something almost menacing in its patience.

She advanced across the outer chamber of the temple, and the man, becoming aware of her, stood up. She addressed him in Greek, but he said:

"Madam, my Greek is limited. Allow me to speak vulgar Syrian."

"Whence come you? Whither go you?" she asked, with a hurried preoccupation of a priestess.

"From the east beyond Damascus—and I go west as the road goes," he replied slowly.

She glanced at him with sudden anxiety and shyness.

"But why do you have the marks of a malefactor?" she asked abruptly.

"Did the Lady of Isis spy upon me in my sleep?" he asked, with a grey weariness.

"The slave warned me—your hands and feet——" she said. He looked at her. Then he said:

"Will the Lady of Isis allow me to bid her farewell, and go up to the road?"

The wind came in a sudden puff, lifting his mantle and his hat. He put up his hand to hold the brim, and she saw again the thin brown hand with its scar.

"See! The scar!" she said, pointing.

"Even so!" he said. "But farewell, and to Isis my homage and my thanks for sleep."

He was going. But she looked up at him with her wondering blue eyes.

"Will you not look at Isis?" she said, with sudden impulse. And something stirred in him, like pain.

"Where then?" he said.

"Come!"

He followed her into the inner shrine, into the almost-darkness. When his eyes got used to the faint glow of the lamp, he saw the goddess striding like a ship, eager in the swirl of her gown, and he made his obeisance.

"Great is Isis!" he said. "In her search she is greater than death. Wonderful is such walking in a woman, wonderful the goal. All men praise thee, Isis, thou greater than the mother unto man."

The woman of Isis heard, and threw incense on the brazier. Then she looked at the man.

"Is it well with thee here?" she asked him. "Has Isis brought thee home to herself?"

He looked at the priestess in wonder and trouble.

"I know not," he said.

But the woman was pondering that this was the lost Osiris. She felt it in the quick of her soul. And her agitation was intense.

He would not stay in the close, dark, perfumed shrine. He went out again to the morning, to the cold air. He felt something approaching to touch him, and all his flesh was still woven with pain and the wild commandment: *Noli me tangere*! Touch me not! Oh, don't touch me!

The woman followed into the open with timid eagerness. He was moving away.

"Oh, stranger, do not go! Oh, stay a while with Isis!"

He looked at her, at her face open like a flower, as if a sun had risen in her soul. And again his loins stirred.

"Would you detain me, girl of Isis?" he said.

"Stay! I am sure you are Osiris!" she said.

He laughed suddenly. "Not yet!" he said. Then he looked at her wistful face. "But I will sleep another night in the cave of the goats, if Isis wills it," he added.

She put her hands together with a priestess's childish happiness.

"Ah! Isis will be glad!" she said.

So he went down to the shore in great trouble, saying to himself: "Shall I give myself into this touch? Shall I give myself into this touch? Men have tortured me to death with their touch. Yet this girl of Isis is a tender flame of healing. I am a physician, yet I have no healing like the flame of this tender girl. The flame of this tender girl! Like the first pale crocus of the spring. How could I have been blind to the healing and the bliss in the crocus-like body of a tender woman! Ah, tenderness! More terrible and lovely than the death I died——"

He pried small shell-fish from the rocks, and ate them with relish and wonder for the simple taste of the sea. And inwardly he was tremulous, thinking: "Dare I come into touch? For this is farther than death. I have dared to let them lay hands on me and put me to death. But dare I come into this tender touch of life? Oh, this is harder——"

But the woman went into the shrine again, and sat rapt in pure muse, through the long hours, watching the swirling stride of the yearning goddess, and the navel of the bud-like belly, like a seal on the virgin urge of the search. And she gave herself to the woman-flow and to the urge of Isis in Search.

Towards sundown she went on the peninsula to look for him. And she found him gone towards the sun, as she had gone the day before, and sitting on the pine-needles at the foot of the tree, where she had stood when first she saw him. Now she approached tremulously and slowly, afraid lest he did not want her. She stood near him unseen, till suddenly he glanced up at her from under his broad hat, and saw the westering sun on her netted hair. He was startled, yet he expected her.

"Is that your home?" he said, pointing to the white, low villa on the slope of olives.

"It is my mother's house. She is a widow, and I am her only child."

"And are these all her slaves?"

"Except those that are mine."

Their eyes met for a moment.

"Will you too sit to see the sun go down?" he said.

He had not risen to speak to her. He had known too much pain. So she sat on the dry brown pine-needles, gathering her saffron mantle round her knees. A boat was coming in, out of the open glow into the shadow of the bay, and slaves were lifting small nets, their babble coming off the surface of the water.

"And this is home to you," he said.

"But I serve Isis in Search," she replied.

He looked at her. She was like a soft, musing cloud, somehow remote. His soul smote him with passion and compassion.

"Mayst thou find thy desire, maiden," he said, with sudden earnestness.

"And art thou not Osiris?" she asked.

He flushed suddenly.

"Yes, if thou wilt heal me!" he said. "For the death aloofness is still upon me, and I cannot escape it."

She looked at him for a moment in fear from the soft blue sun of her eyes. Then she lowered her head, and they sat in silence in the warmth and glow of the western sun: the man who had died, and the woman of the pure search.

The sun was curving down to the sea, in grand winter splendour. It fell on the twinkling, naked bodies of the slaves, with their ruddy broad hams and their small black heads, as they ran spreading the nets on the pebble beach. The all-tolerant Pan watched over them. All-tolerant Pan should be their god for ever.

The woman rose as the sun's rim dipped, saying:

"If you will stay, I shall send down victual and covering."

"The lady your mother, what will she say?"

The woman of Isis looked at him strangely, but with a tinge of misgiving.

"It is my own," she said.

"It is good," he said, smiling faintly and foreseeing difficulties.

He watched her go, with her absorbed, strange motion of the self-dedicate. Her dun head was a little bent, the white linen swung about her ivory ankles. And he saw the naked slaves stand to look at her, with a certain wonder, and even a certain mischief. But she passed intent through the door in the wall, on the bay.

The man who had died sat on at the foot of the tree overlooking the strand, for on the little shore everything happened. At the small stream which ran in round the corner of the property wall, women slaves were still washing linen, and now and again came the hollow chock! chock! chock! as they beat it against the smooth stones in the dark little hollow of the pool. There was a smell of olive refuse on the air; and sometimes still the faint rumble of the grindstone that was milling the olives, inside the garden, and the sound of the slave calling to the ass at the mill. Then through the doorway a woman stepped, a grey-haired woman in a mantle of whitish wool, and there followed her a bare-headed man in a toga, a Roman: probably her steward or overseer. They stood on the high shingle above the sea, and cast round a rapid glance. The broad-hammed, ruddy-bodied slaves bent absorbed and abject over the nets, picking them clean, the women washing linen thrust their palms with energy down on the wash, the old slave bent absorbed at the water's edge, washing the fish and the polyps of the catch. And the woman and the overseer saw it all in one glance. They also saw, seated at the foot of the tree on the rocks of the peninsula, the strange man silent and alone. And the man who had died saw that they spoke of him. Out of the little sacred world of the peninsula he looked on the common world, and saw it still hostile.

The sun was touching the sea, across the tiny bay stretched the shadow of the opposite humped headland. Over the shingle, now blue and cold in shadow, the elderly woman trod heavily, in shadow too, to look at the fish spread in the flat basket of the old man crouching at the water's edge: a naked old slave with fat hips and shoulders, on whose soft, fairish-orange body the last sun twinkled, then died. The old slave continued cleaning the fish absorbedly, not looking up: as if the lady were the shadow of twilight falling on him.

Then from the gateway stepped two slave-girls with flat baskets on their heads, and from one basket the terra-cotta wine-jar and the oil-jar poked up, leaning slightly. Over the massive shingle, under the wall, came the girls, and the woman of Isis in her saffron mantle stepped in twilight after them. Out at sea, the sun still shone. Here was shadow. The mother with grey head stood at the sea's edge and watched the daughter, all yellow and white, with dun blonde head, swinging unseeing and unheeding after the slave-girls, towards the neck of rock of the peninsula; the daughter, travelling in her absorbed other-world. And not moving from her place, the elderly mother watched that procession of three file up the rise of the headland, between the trees, and disappear, shut in by trees. No slave had lifted a head to look. The grey-haired woman still watched the trees where her daughter had disappeared. Then she glanced again at the foot of the tree, where the man who had died was still sitting, inconspicuous now, for the sun had left him; and only the far blade of the sea shone bright. It was evening. Patience! Let destiny move!

The mother plodded with a stamping stride up the shingle: not long and swinging and rapt, like the daughter, but short and determined. Then down the rocks opposite came two naked slaves trotting with huge bundles of dark green on their shoulders, so their broad, naked legs twinkled underneath like insects' legs, and their heads were hidden. They came trotting across the shingle, heedless and intent on their way, when suddenly the man, the Roman-looking overseer, addressed them, and they stopped dead. They stood invisible under their loads, as if they might disappear altogether, now they were arrested. Then a hand came out and pointed to the peninsula. Then the two green-heaped slaves trotted on, towards the temple precincts. The grey-haired woman joined the man, and slowly the two passed through the door again, from the shingle of the sea to the property of the villa. Then the old, fat-shouldered slave rose, pallid in the shadow, with his tray of fish from the sea, and the woman rose from the pool, dusky and alive, piling the wet linen in a heap on to the flat baskets, and the slaves who had cleaned the net gathered its whitish folds together. And the old slave with the fish-basket on his shoulder, and the women slaves with the heaped baskets of wet linen on their heads, and the two slaves with the folded net, and the slave with oars on his shoulders, and the boy with the folded sail on his arm, gathered in a naked group near the door, and the man who had died heard the low buzz of their chatter. Then as the wind wafted cold, they began to pass through the door.

It was the life of the little day, the life of little people. And the man who had died said to himself: "Unless we encompass it in the greater day, and set the little life in the circle of the greater life, all is disaster."

Even the tops of the hills were in shadow. Only the sky was still upwardly radiant. The sea was a vast milky shadow. The man who had died rose a little stiffly and turned into the grove.

There was no one at the temple. He went on to his lair in

the rock. There, the slave-men had carried out the old heath of the bedding, swept the rock floor, and were spreading with nice art the myrtle, then the rougher heath, then the soft, bushy heath-tips on top, for a bed. Over it all they put a well-tanned white ox-skin. The maids had laid folded woollen covers at the head of the cave, and the wine-jar, the oil-jar, a terra-cotta drinking-cup and a basket containing bread, salt, cheese, dried figs and eggs stood neatly arranged. There was also a little brazier of charcoal. The cave was suddenly full, and a dwelling-place.

The woman of Isis stood in the hollow by the tiny spring. Only one slave at a time could pass. The girl-slaves waited at the entrance to the narrow place. When the man who had died appeared, the woman sent the girls away. The men-slaves still arranged the bed, making the job as long as possible. But the woman of Isis dismissed them too. And the man who had died came to look at his house.

"Is it well?" the woman asked him.

"It is very well," the man replied. "But the lady, your mother, and he who is no doubt the steward, watched while the slaves brought the goods. Will they not oppose you?"

"I have my own portion! Can I not give of my own? Who is going to oppose me and the gods?" she said, with a certain soft fury, touched with exasperation. So that he knew that her mother would oppose her, and that the spirit of the little life would fight against the spirit of the greater. And he thought: 'Why did the woman of Isis relinquish her portion in the daily world? She should have kept her goods fiercely!'

"Will you eat and drink?" she said. "On the ashes are warm eggs. And I will go up to the meal at the villa. But in the second hour of the night I shall come down to the temple. O, then, will you come too to Isis?" She looked at him, and a queer glow dilated her eyes. This was her dream, and it was greater than herself. He could not bear to thwart her or hurt her in the least thing now. She was in the full glow of her woman's mystery.

"Shall I wait at the temple?" he said.

"O, wait at the second hour and I shall come." He heard the humming supplication in her voice and his fibres quivered.

"But the lady, your mother?" he said gently.

The woman looked at him, startled.

"She will not thwart me!" she said.

So he knew that the mother would thwart the daughter, for the daughter had left her goods in the hands of her mother, who would hold fast to this power.

But she went, and the man who had died lay reclining on his couch, and ate the eggs from the ashes, and dipped his bread in oil, and ate it, for his flesh was dry: and he mixed wine and water, and drank. And so he lay still, and the lamp made a small bud of light.

He was absorbed and enmeshed in new sensations. The woman of Isis was lovely to him, not so much in form as in the wonderful womanly glow of her. Suns beyond suns had dipped her in mysterious fire, the mysterious fire of a potent woman, and to touch her was like touching the sun. Best of all was her tender desire for him, like sunshine, so soft and still.

"She is like sunshine upon me," he said to himself, stretching his limbs. "I have never before stretched my limbs in such sunshine, as her desire for me. The greatest of all gods granted me this."

At the same time he was haunted by the fear of the outer world. "If they can, they will kill us," he said to himself. "But there is a law of the sun which protects us."

And again he said to himself: "I have risen naked and branded. But if I am naked enough for this contact, I have not died in vain. Before I was clogged."

He rose and went out. The night was chill and starry, and of a great wintry splendour. "There are destinies of splendour," he said to the night, "after all our doom of littleness and meanness and pain."

So he went up silently to the temple, and waited in darkness against the inner wall, looking out on a grey darkness, stars, and rims of trees. And he said again to himself: "There are destinies of splendour, and there is a greater power."

So at last he saw the light of her silk lanthorn swinging, coming intermittent between the trees, yet coming swiftly. She was alone, and near, the light softly swishing on her mantle-hem. And he trembled with fear and with joy, saying to himself: "I am almost more afraid of this touch than I was of death. For I am more nakedly exposed to it."

"I am here, Lady of Isis," he said softly out of the dark.

"Ah!" she cried, in fear also, yet in rapture. For she was given to her dream.

She unlocked the door of the shrine, and he followed after

her. Then she latched the door shut again. The air inside was
warm and close and perfumed. The man who had died stood
by the closed door and watched the woman. She had come
first to the goddess. And dim-lit, the goddess-statue stood
surging forward, a little fearsome like a great woman-presence
urging.

The priestess did not look at him. She took off her saffron
mantle and laid it on a low couch. In the dim light she was
bare-armed, in her girdled white tunic. But she was still hiding
herself away from him. He stood back in shadow and watched
her softly fan the brazier and fling on incense. Faint clouds of
sweet aroma arose on the air. She turned to the statue in the
ritual of approach, softly swaying forward with a slight lurch,
like a moored boat, tipping towards the goddess.

He watched the strange rapt woman, and he said to himself: "I must leave her alone in her rapture, her female
mysteries." So she tipped in her strange forward-swaying
rhythm before the goddess. Then she broke into a murmur
of Greek, which he could not understand. And, as she murmured, her swaying softly subsided, like a boat on a sea that
grows still. And as he watched her, he saw her soul in its
aloneness, and its female difference. He said to himself: "How
different she is from me, how strangely different! She is afraid
of me, and my male difference. She is getting herself naked
and clear of her fear. How sensitive and softly alive she is,
with a life so different from mine! How beautiful with a soft,
strange courage, of life, so different from my courage of death!
What a beautiful thing, like the heart of a rose, like the core
of a flame. She is making herself completely penetrable. Ah!
how terrible to fail her, or to trespass on her!"

She turned to him, her face glowing from the goddess.

"You are Osiris, aren't you?" she said naïvely.

"If you will," he said.

"Will you let Isis discover you? Will you not take off your
things?"

He looked at the woman, and lost his breath. And his
wounds, and especially the death-wound through his belly,
began to cry again.

"It has hurt so much!" he said. "You must forgive me if I
am still held back."

But he took off his cloak and his tunic and went naked
towards the idol, his breast panting with the sudden terror

of overwhelming pain, memory of overwhelming pain, and grief too bitter.

"They did me to death!" he said in excuse of himself, turning his face to her for a moment.

And she saw the ghost of the death in him as he stood there thin and stark before her, and suddenly she was terrified, and she felt robbed. She felt the shadow of the grey, grisly wing of death triumphant.

"Ah, Goddess," he said to the idol in the vernacular. "I would be so glad to live, if you would give me my clue again."

For her again he felt desperate, faced by the demand of life, and burdened still by his death.

"Let me anoint you!" the woman said to him softly. "Let me anoint the scars! Show me, and let me anoint them!"

He forgot his nakedness in this re-evoked old pain. He sat on the edge of the couch, and she poured a little ointment into the palm of his hand. And as she chafed his hand, it all came back, the nails, the holes, the cruelty, the unjust cruelty against him who had offered only kindness. The agony of injustice and cruelty came over him again, as in his death-hour. But she chafed the palm, murmuring: "What was torn becomes a new flesh, what was a wound is full of fresh life; this scar is the eye of the violet."

And he could not help smiling at her, in her naïve priestess's absorption. This was her dream, and he was only a dream-object to her. She would never know or understand what he was. Especially she would never know the death that was gone before in him. But what did it matter? She was different. She was woman: her life and her death were different from him. Only she was good to him.

When she chafed his feet with oil and tender, tender healing, he could not refrain from saying to her:

"Once a woman washed my feet with tears, and wiped them with her hair, and poured on precious ointment."

The woman of Isis looked up at him from her earnest work, interrupted again.

"Were they hurt then?" she said. "Your feet?"

"No, no! It was while they were whole."

"And did you love her?"

"Love had passed in her. She only wanted to serve," he replied. "She had been a prostitute."

"And did you let her serve you?" she asked.

"Yea."

"Did you let her serve you with the corpse of her love?"

"Ay!"

Suddenly it dawned on him: I asked them all to serve me with the corpse of their love. And in the end I offered them only the corpse of my love. This is my body—take and eat—my corpse——

A vivid shame went through him. 'After all,' he thought, 'I wanted them to love with dead bodies. If I had kissed Judas with live love, perhaps he would never have kissed me with death. Perhaps he loved me in the flesh, and I willed that he should love me bodilessly, with the corpse of love——'

There dawned on him the reality of the soft, warm love which is in touch, and which is full of delight. "And I told them, blessed are they that mourn," he said to himself. "Alas, if I mourned even this woman here, now I am in death, I should have to remain dead, and I want so much to live. Life has brought me to this woman with warm hands. And her touch is more to me now than all my words. For I want to live——"

"Go then to the goddess!" she said softly, gently pushing him towards Isis. And as he stood there dazed and naked as an unborn thing, he heard the woman murmuring to the goddess, murmuring, murmuring with a plaintive appeal. She was stooping now, looking at the scar in the soft flesh of the socket of his side, a scar deep and like an eye sore with endless weeping, just in the soft socket above the hip. It was here that his blood had left him, and his essential seed. The woman was trembling softly and murmuring in Greek. And he in the recurring dismay of having died, and in the anguished perplexity of having tried to force life, felt his wounds crying aloud, and the deep places of the body howling again: "I have been murdered, and I lent myself to murder. They murdered me, but I lent myself to murder——"

The woman, silent now, but quivering, laid oil in her hand and put her palm over the wound in his right side. He winced, and the wound absorbed his life again, as thousands of times before. And in the dark, wild pain and panic of his consciousness rang only one cry: "Oh, how can she take this death out of me? She can never know! She can never understand! She can never equal it! . . ."

In silence, she softly rhythmically chafed the scar with oil. Absorbed now in her priestess's task, softly, softly gathering power, while the vitals of the man howled in panic. But as she gradually gathered power, and passed in a girdle round him to the opposite scar, gradually warmth began to take the place of the cold terror, and he felt: 'I am going to be warm again, and I am going to be whole! I shall be warm like the morning. I shall be a man. It doesn't need understanding. It needs newness. She brings me newness——'

And he listened to the faint, ceaseless wail of distress of his wounds, sounding as if for ever under the horizons of his consciousness. But the wail was growing dim, more dim.

He thought of the woman toiling over him: 'She does not know! She does not realise the death in me. But she has another consciousness. She comes to me from the opposite end of the night.'

Having chafed all his lower body with oil, having worked with her slow intensity of a priestess, so that the sound of his wounds grew dimmer and dimmer, suddenly she put her breast against the wound in his left side, and her arms round him, folding over the wound in his right side, and she pressed him to her, in a power of living warmth, like the folds of a river. And the wailing died out altogether, and there was a stillness, and darkness in his soul, unbroken, dark stillness, wholeness.

Then slowly, slowly, in the perfect darkness of his inner man, he felt the stir of something coming. A dawn, a new sun. A new sun was coming up in him, in the perfect inner darkness of himself. He waited for it breathless, quivering with a fearful hope. . . . "Now I am not myself. I am something new . . ."

And as it rose, he felt, with a cold breath of disappointment, the girdle of the living woman slip down from him, the warmth and the glow slipped from him, leaving him stark. She crouched, spent, at the feet of the goddess, hiding her face.

Stooping, he laid his hand softly on her warm, bright shoulder, and the shock of desire went through him, shock after shock, so that he wondered if it were another sort of death: but full of magnificence.

Now all his consciousness was there in the crouching, hidden woman. He stooped beside her and caressed her softly, blindly, murmuring inarticulate things. And his death and his passion of sacrifice were all as nothing to him now, he knew only the crouching fullness of the woman there, the soft white rock of life. . . . "On this rock I built my life." The deep-folded, penetrable rock of the living woman! The woman, hiding her face. Himself bending over, powerful and new like dawn.

He crouched to her, and he felt the blaze of his manhood and his power rise up in his loins, magnificent.

"I am risen!"

Magnificent, blazing indomitable in the depths of his loins, his own sun dawned, and sent its fire running along his limbs, so that his face shone unconsciously.

He untied the string on the linen tunic and slipped the garment down, till he saw the white glow of her white-gold breasts. And he touched them, and he felt his life go molten. "Father!" he said, "why did you hide this from me?" And he touched her with the poignancy of wonder, and the marvellous piercing transcendence of desire. "Lo!" he said, "this is beyond prayer." It was the deep, interfolded warmth, warmth living and penetrable, the woman, the heart of the rose! My mansion is the intricate warm rose, my joy is this blossom!

She looked up at him suddenly, her face like a lifted light, wistful, tender, her eyes like many wet flowers. And he drew her to his breast with a passion of tenderness and consuming desire, and the last thought: 'My hour is upon me, I am taken unawares——'

So he knew her, and was one with her.

Afterwards, with a dim wonder, she touched the great scars in his sides with her finger-tips, and said:

"But they no longer hurt?"

"They are suns!" he said. "They shine from your torch. They are my atonement with you."

And when they left the temple, it was the coldness before dawn. As he closed the door, he looked again at the goddess, and he said: "Lo, Isis is a kindly goddess; and full of tenderness. Great gods are warm-hearted, and have tender goddesses."

The woman wrapped herself in her mantle and went home in silence, sightless, brooding like the lotus softly shutting again, with its gold core full of fresh life. She saw nothing, for her own petals were a sheath to her. Only she thought: 'I am full of Osiris. I am full of the risen Osiris! . . .'

But the man looked at the vivid stars before dawn, as they

rained down to the sea, and the dog-star green towards the sea's rim. And he thought: 'How plastic it is, how full of curves and folds like an invisible rose of dark-petalled openness that shows where the dew touches its darkness! How full it is, and great beyond all gods. How it leans around me, and I am part of it, the great rose of Space. I am like a grain of its perfume, and the woman is a grain of its beauty. Now the world is one flower of many petalled darknesses, and I am in its perfume as in a touch.'

So, in the absolute stillness and fullness of touch, he slept in his cave while the dawn came. And after the dawn, the wind rose and brought a storm, with cold rain. So he stayed in his cave in the peace and the delight of being in touch, delighting to hear the sea, and the rain on the earth, and to see one white-and-gold narcissus bowing wet, and still wet. And he said: "This is the great atonement, the being in touch. The grey sea and the rain, the wet narcissus and the woman I wait for, the invisible Isis and the unseen sun are all in touch, and at one."

He waited at the temple for the woman, and she came in the rain. But she said to him:

"Let me sit awhile with Isis. And come to me, will you come to me, in the second hour of night?"

So he went back to the cave and lay in stillness and in the joy of being in touch, waiting for the woman who would come with the night, and consummate again the contact. Then when night came the woman came, and came gladly, for her great yearning, too, was upon her, to be in touch, to be in touch with him, nearer.

So the days came, and the nights came, and days came again, and the contact was perfected and fulfilled. And he said: "I will ask her nothing, not even her name, for a name would set her apart."

And she said to herself: "He is Osiris. I wish to know no more."

Plum blossom blew from the trees, the time of the narcissus was past, anemones lit up the ground and were gone, the perfume of bean-field was in the air. All changed, the blossom of the universe changed its petals and swung round to look another way. The spring was fulfilled, a contact was established, the man and the woman were fulfilled of one another, and departure was in the air.

One day he met her under the trees, when the morning sun was hot, and the pines smelled sweet, and on the hills the last pear blossom was scattering. She came slowly towards him, and in her gentle lingering, her tender hanging back from him, he knew a change in her.

"Hast thou conceived?" he asked her.

"Why?" she said.

"Thou art like a tree whose green leaves follow the blossom, full of sap. And there is a withdrawing about thee."

"It is so," she said. "I am with young by thee. Is it good?"

"Yea!" he said. "How should it not be good? So the nightingale calls no more from the valley-bed. But where wilt thou bear the child, for I am naked of all but life?"

"We will stay here," she said.

"But the lady, your mother?"

A shadow crossed her brow. She did not answer.

"What when she knows?" he said.

"She begins to know."

"And would she hurt you?"

"Ah, not me! What I have is all my own. And I shall be big with Osiris. . . . But thou, do you watch her slaves."

She looked at him, and the peace of her maternity was troubled by anxiety.

"Let not your heart be troubled!" he said. "I have died the death once."

So he knew the time was come again for him to depart. He would go alone, with his destiny. Yet not alone, for the touch would be upon him, even as he left his touch on her. And invisible suns would go with him.

Yet he must go. For here on the bay the little life of jealousy and property was resuming sway again, as the suns of passionate fecundity relaxed their sway. In the name of property, the widow and her slaves would seek to be revenged on him for the bread he had eaten, and the living touch he had established, the woman he had delighted in. But he said: "Not twice! They shall not now profane the touch in me. My wits against theirs."

So he watched. And he knew they plotted. So he moved from the little cave and found another shelter, a tiny cove of sand by the sea, dry and secret under the rocks.

He said to the woman:

"I must go now soon. Trouble is coming to me from the

slaves. But I am a man, and the world is open. But what is
between us is good, and is established. Be at peace. And when
the nightingale calls again from your valley-bed, I shall come
again, sure as spring."

She said: "O, don't go! Stay with me on half the island,
and I will build a house for you and me under the pine trees
by the temple, where we can live apart."

Yet she knew that he would go. And even she wanted the
coolness of her own air around her, and the release from
anxiety.

"If I stay," he said, "they will betray me to the Romans and
to their justice. But I will never be betrayed again. So when I
am gone, live in peace with the growing child. And I shall
come again: all is good between us, near or apart. The suns
come back in their seasons: and I shall come again."

"Do not go yet," she said. "I have set a slave to watch at
the neck of the peninsula. Do not go yet, till the harm shows."

But as he lay in his little cove, on a calm, still night, he
heard the soft knock of oars, and the bump of a boat against
the rock. So he crept out to listen. And he heard the Roman
overseer say:

"Lead softly to the goat's den. And Lysippus shall throw
the net over the malefactor while he sleeps, and we will bring
him before justice, and the Lady of Isis shall know nothing of
it. . . ."

The man who had died caught a whiff of flesh from the
oiled and naked slaves as they crept up, then the faint perfume
of the Roman. He crept nearer to the sea. The slave who sat
in the boat sat motionless, holding the oars, for the sea was
quite still. And the man who had died knew him.

So out of the deep cleft of a rock he said, in a clear voice:
"Art thou not that slave who possessed the maiden under
the eyes of Isis? Art thou not the youth? Speak!"

The youth stood up in the boat in terror. His movement
sent the boat bumping against the rock. The slave sprang out
in wild fear, and fled up the rocks. The man who had died
quickly seized the boat and stepped in, and pushed off. The
oars were yet warm with the unpleasant warmth of the hands
of the slaves. But the man pulled slowly out, to get into the
current which set down the coast, and would carry him in
silence. The high coast was utterly dark against the starry
night. There was no glimmer from the peninsula: the priestess

came no more at night. The man who had died rowed slowly on, with the current, and laughed to himself: "I have sowed the seed of my life and my resurrection, and put my touch forever upon the choice woman of this day, and I carry her perfume in my flesh like essence of roses. She is dear to me in the middle of my being. But the gold and flowing serpent is coiling up again, to sleep at the root of my tree."

"So let the boat carry me. To-morrow is another day."